HARVESTING EDEN

KEVIN RUSH

HOSEL & FERRULE

PROLOGUE

"Nothing is so painful to the human mind
as a great and sudden change."
— Mary Shelley, *Frankenstein*

"WHERE ARE WE?" the man asked.

"We should be here," the woman said. But they both knew it wasn't right. The man had listened to the woman, who had been tracing the serpentine line on the guide with her fingernail but had not looked up to check their progress on the road against the printed image.

The girl popped the back door of the sedan and stepped onto the hot pavement. Dry air seared her skin as it had the yellow grass. She spotted a caretaker weeding, and walked towards him. An older man in overalls, he was on his knees, clawing the flinty soil.

"Sir? Sorry, where is Number 1816?"

"You looking up a relative?"

"No, just, we need to see the spot."

"Oh. Sorry for your loss." He sat on his heels and pointed a gloved hand toward the curve of the hill. "They opened a new section over there." He rose halfway up and patted the dust from his knees.

1

The girl slowly realized this man was not a caretaker. "This used to be a prettier spot," he said, straightening to his full height. "The grass was green, and if you planted flowers, they'd take. But water restrictions. The landscapers do what they can, but without water...." He shrugged. "Anyway, she's here, and I'll join her soon enough."

The girl read the headstone:

MIRIAM HODGES
Beloved wife and mother
1947 – 2005

"She died too young," the man said. "Only fifty-seven."

"I'm sorry," the girl said. The dry air stung her eyes.

The man folded his hands at his waist. "*All is vanity. What does man gain by all his toil under the sun? A generation goes, and a generation comes.* Who are you here for?" he asked.

"My sister. Actually, my twin."

The man's chest sunk, and his face melted in grief. "Oh, child, I'm so sorry." He held his hands open as though he wanted to hug the girl, and might have, if not for the soil on his gloves and overalls. He turned and picked up a watering can.

"Tara!" the woman called.

"You'd better mind your folks."

"Thank you," she told the man, and hurried to her parents. A small lizard, sunning itself in the concrete gutter, broke for a yellow tuft of grass. The man and woman had found the plot, a few yards below the crest of the hill, where the ground had been leveled to form a terrace wide enough for two rows of graves. From there, the hill sloped gently toward a grove of cottonwoods.

"It's like the ladies' tee," the girl said.

"Yeah," the man smiled, in apparent appreciation. "It sort of is."

"Landscaping leaves a lot to be desired," the woman said.

"They'll plant some shrubs," the man said. "And it's a nice view of the trees and hills. We could put a marble bench here."

"Oh, why don't we just move in?"

The woman marched past them back to the car.

. . .

"DID YOU SLEEP AT ALL, HONEY?"

The girl squinted. The empty bed beside her came into focus, a black dress laid out on it. She recalled a long, dreamless dullness.

"Be ready in an hour," the woman said. "Want breakfast?"

The girl shook her head.

SHOWERING, the girl found a bruise on her shin and wondered how it got there. Mysterious bruises were...*oh, wait*, she'd banged it on the bed frame. She brushed her teeth. Remembered seeing pink foam. One of the first clues. Her foam was still perfectly white.

The girl brushed and blow-dried her hair. She checked the brush. Just one or two hairs, each with a perfect white bulb at the tip.

THE MAN FINISHED TYING the boy's tie. "Too tight," the boy whined. The man opened a package of white handkerchiefs. He placed one in his front pocket and the boy mimicked him. "This one's for show. No one uses it." He put another inside his breast pocket. "A gentleman always carries an extra here to offer a lady." He placed the last one in the hip pocket of his trousers. "That one's for yourself. Think you can remember?"

The boy nodded as if the instructions mattered.

"YOU'VE GOT *to play every stroke of every hole," Dad says.*

"It's not fair. I can't get out!"

"Who put your ball in the trap?"

"Shut up, Teri!"

"I THINK GOD'S BEING MEAN," the little girl told the priest.

"It might seem that way," he said kindly in his deep, bass voice.

"But sometimes God does things, or lets things happen, to get our attention."

"When I do bad things for attention, Mommy says that's bad. So how can God be good?"

"It's hard to…." The priest paused as the older girl rose from her seat. His eyes followed her as she left the room. He checked to see if he had the rest of the family's attention. "Because of sin, bad things happen. And we wonder, 'Why do these bad things happen?' Maybe God knows that good, strong people can take a bad thing and say, 'This means I need to love more, all the time.' Do you think that's something Teri would want?"

"YOU SHOULDN'T HAVE WALKED out on Father," the woman whispered harshly.

"I don't owe him anything," the girl said.

"Respect."

"He wasn't even talking to me."

"When he does," the woman said, "you listen. We don't need you making this worse than it is."

AN OLIVE-SKINNED GIRL WITH STRAIGHT, black hair and red eyes was talking through tears. "Just remember, we're here for you, okay?"

Behind her, the Queen Bee nodded, her tight, black curls bobbed, and drones buzzed around her.

The girl focused on the limousine. "I've got to go."

THE LINE of black limousines rested at the curb. People in black crowded the terrace and waited for men to bring the box. Even through mountains of flowers, the girl smelled only fresh earth, as if just this morning the pit had been dug. Sleek black crows glowered from a distance on the grass. The girl wondered if they were thirsty and recalled the Aesop story her twin sister read, where the crow dropped pebbles into the pitcher until the water was high enough to drink. Her twin had thought crows were smart, but the girl pictured a murder of crows tearing apart the beautiful flowers to suck the moisture. *All is vanity.*

The woman tugged at the girl's elbow. She turned from the crows and saw the men of her family carrying the box.

She crumpled.

On her knees, the girl grabbed her gut. The woman's arms folded around her and eased her upright, but an opposite force had her, crushing every organ up and out. Her throat opened mutely as her diaphragm rose. She had no lungs to sob with. Her tears had all dried up. She was empty. Hollow. For the first time in her life, alone.

"YOU SHOULD COME UP TO DUNSMUIR," the old man said. "Fresh air and nature, that's what the children need."

"Maybe," the woman muttered.

"No maybe about it."

"You want to tell Jeremy no summer baseball? Or keep Tara from Youth Orchestra? They're doing Mozart's *Jupiter*."

"So, instead, she'll see actual Jupiter rise over Mount Shasta."

"We'll think about it, Dad."

THE GIRL SAT with the viola resting on her clavicle. The bow dangled from her left arm, touching the floor. The sheet music on the stand, familiar by heart, appeared like a book in a dream. A code. Foreign language. She searched for the key, the time signature. She tapped the bow on her calf. It was heavy.

A woman at the judging table coughed.

"Tara, if you're not ready to play…," a man said.

The gym was lined with other students, instruments out, ready to audition. A girl fingered a clarinet, but it was some other girl.

Where are you?

Fear gripped the girl. She felt small with shame and wanted to cover herself. She read again words in a balloon on the tiny screen and knew the time had come.

Where are you?

But the girl was sinking in sand. It covered her ankles, and she tried to climb out. "I'm in the trap," she wanted to say, but no sound came out. She couldn't lift her feet. She swung her club, to wedge it in the wall so she could pull herself out, but it only broke loose more sand.

"Tara, wake up," the man said. "You've got to wake up."

Soft slapping on her cheeks roused her, and the girl opened her eyes to a canopy of stars hanging low like ground fog.

She felt dry grass scratch her. Chaff clung to her pajamas.

"Where...?"

"You don't remember driving?"

She smoothed the earth where she'd disturbed the mound. "I've been wanting to be near her."

"I know, sweetheart," the man said. "But she's not here, really. C'mon. Mom's waiting."

The broad band of the Milky Way seemed almost within reach. The girl thought if she stood now, she'd pierce that glittering haze, and look down on a star-dusted Earth. What would she see, except that this world held nothing more? Might she have better luck on another world?

The man and the girl walked along the terrace, past marble sentinels, silver in the glow of the man's flashlight, to the curb where two vehicles were parked. The woman dabbed her eyes with a tissue, then threw her arms open and pulled the girl in.

"Baby, you scared us half to death."

"I didn't mean to. How'd you find me?"

"You left the car pointed at the gate with the engine running and the headlights on," the man said. "A security guard dug the registration out of the glove box. The police called, asking if our car had been stolen."

"I'm sorry."

"Not your fault, baby," the woman sniffed. "Crazy pills. We'll talk to Dr. Schraeder."

"After I ring his neck," the man added.

The woman pulled open the front passenger door to the minivan. The girl stepped up and in. Moments later, headlights beamed, the sedan pulled away from the curb, and the minivan rolled after it.

"Mom," the girl asked, "where do you think Teri is, really?"

"She's in heaven, of course."

The girl rested her head against the side window. She tried to look through the glass at the stars, but the glare obscured everything outside the van. All she could see was her own reflection. What had been her sister's face, as well as her own, now only belonged to her. Yet, the girl knew there were stars out there. And other worlds. Black holes, even. Dead stars with gravity even light couldn't escape. They trapped and crushed all matter that came too close to them. But some people thought those black holes might be wormholes, tunnels to another point in space.

The girl thought how her twin's death had created a black hole. How its emptiness was crushing her. But maybe it was really a wormhole. Maybe she could pass through it, and come out in a far off, far better place.

PART ONE
THE PERFECT FRACTURED FAMILY

"The good die young that they may not be corrupted;
the wicked live on that they may have a chance to repent."
— The Zohar

CHAPTER
ONE

"There will be great trials and afflictions.
Perplexities and dissensions,
both spiritual and temporal, will abound;
the charity of many will grow cold,
and the malice of the wicked will increase.
The devils will have unusual power."
— St. Francis of Assisi

THE KIDS FOLLOWED the old man up the trail through the burnt-out forest. His brown cur dog panted at his side, the corners of its black mouth white with saliva. The boy carried a stick and picked up pebbles, tossed them into the air, and swung at them with the stick, mostly missing, but sometimes smacking them down the slope. It was, the girl knew, his sign of protest that he'd rather be playing baseball.

The girl held her little sister's hand on the uphill to help her keep pace with the others. At the top of the rise, the old man found a fallen tree trunk and sat, pointing at the solitary mountain, snow-capped even in late July.

"The Native Americans that lived here, the Klamath tribe, they revered Mount Shasta as kind of a launching point from the Below World to the Above World. There's a legend that Skell, a god of the Above World, came down to fight off Llao, a Spirit of the Below-World, who lived over at Mount Mazama. From Shasta, Skell beat Llao by throwing hot rocks and lava at him."

"Is that why everything's so burnt?" the little girl asked.

"No, that's poor management. A forest is like a garden. Needs to be tended."

"My teacher says it's climate change."

"Poppycock," the old man said. "Hold still, Crockett," he told the dog, and he picked a burr off its rump and flicked it away. "Climate's always been changing and always will. Same people who say a controlled burn can't prevent this disaster think it's fine to burn a city down when they don't get their way. It's madness." The old man wiped his forehead, then stuffed his bandana in his back pocket.

"Anyway, they say Skell leapt back up to the heavens. You kind of understand their thinking when you see the Milky Way, how sometimes it comes right out the top of Shasta and flows into the sky."

The girl looked at the blackened terrain. Here and there, tufts of green had sprung up, reminding her of the woods when she was Stacy's age or Jeremy's, when she and Teri would look for deer and rabbits.

"Where'd the animals go?" she wondered aloud.

"C'MON, WAKE UP SLEEPY HEADS," the old man chuckled. He herded the kids, still in their pajamas and wrapped in blankets, out of the house and into his pickup truck.

"Wh-where we goin'?" the boy yawned.

"You'll see when we get there."

A carve-out on a dark country road held a bold view of Mount Shasta. With no moon to dull them, the stars were three times as bright and numerous as the girl had ever seen. A thick, dazzling band drifted up from Shasta's peak, as if a spell cast over a caldron had transformed wafting vapors into diamond dust, threaded with silver, dotted with rubies and sapphires.

"That's the Milky Way," the old man said, "making a bridge to the Above World."

"Is Teri on that bridge?" the little girl asked. "I bet she's hopping from star to star. All the way up to heaven."

"A thousand light years is more than a hop," the girl grumbled.

"Tara!" the old man whispered harshly.

"Sorry. Can we go back? I'm cold."

They walked back to the truck.

The boy remembered the old man saying the mountain was formed by three cones of an ancient volcano that had pushed together over millions of years.

"You think it might erupt again?" he asked. "Like Pompeii?"

"Maybe," the old man said with sly delight. "But if Shasta ever blew, she'd make Pompeii look like a Boy Scout's bonfire."

The image of the mountain exploding and raining down rock, lava, and ash stayed with the girl. She almost wished for it. When her parents decided she should stay another week while the rest of the family went back home, she felt a tingle, as if assured now that it would happen.

THE OLD WOMAN kept a vegetable garden. The girl was on her knees weeding, when she heard the dry, bone-scraping clatter. Hair had fallen over her eyes, and she couldn't see the rattler. She stayed frozen on all fours until the sound came again. Looking through strands of hair, she saw it about eighteen inches away, coiled around a tomato plant.

"Slowly, honey," the old woman whispered behind her. "Don't move your hands, but slowly ease back on your heels."

The girl did as her grandmother said, keeping her eyes locked on the triangular head that hovered in space, flicking its forked tongue.

"Now bring your hands in, honey. To your side."

The rattle cracked the air again. The wavering head had the girl transfixed. Without deciding, she raised her hands, as if inviting a bird to land.

"Tara, no. What are you doing?" The old woman tapped the ground, creating vibrations to drive the snake away.

The rattle scraped the girl's spine. The triangular head dipped. The tongue teased. Then came a growl and leaves rustled. The old man's cur dog broke through the tomato plants, dug its forepaws into the soil and barked fiercely. The snake sprang and the hound snapped its jaw, yelped and rolled, keeping the snake clamped tight, as it bit repeatedly at its neck and face. The old woman cut past the girl and straddled the writhing dog. With one gloved hand, she grabbed the snake just below the head and pinned it to the ground. Then with her other hand, she brought down a rock with a clap, again and again, crushing its skull.

"It's okay, honey, it's okay," the old woman said, hugging the girl tight and shielding the cur from her view. She turned the girl around gently and walked her back towards the house. The old man had come out on the porch. He surveyed the scene and went back inside. He came out holding a .45 revolver.

"No, Grandpa," the girl begged. "It's my fault."

"No tears, sweetheart," he whispered. "Best thing that fool dog ever did. You have some tea with your Grandma."

The screen door creaked, and the girl stepped into sudden darkness. All the shades were drawn against the afternoon heat.

"With the forests burned out, their prey is gone. So, they come into the garden," the old woman explained. "But that's usually at dusk, not the middle of the day." She seated the girl at the kitchen table, then lit a burner on the stove and placed the kettle over it.

"I should have run. I couldn't keep from staring at it."

"Well, snakes have some kind of hypnotic power."

The kettle whistled, then the shot was fired.

The next morning, the old woman said the girl's mother would arrive shortly to take her home.

"Why?"

"Honey, we love you," she said. "But we can't watch you all the time. There are too many ways to hurt yourself here, and we're afraid."

THE FIRST HALF hour in the car with her mother passed in silence. Finally, the girl said, "Does Grandma think I wanted that snake to bite me?"

"What? No," the woman said. "Did you?"

"I wondered what it might feel like," she admitted. "I'm sorry about Crockett. Really. But Grandma. She's got *gangsta* skills."

The woman smiled and nodded. "Don't I know it." After another while the woman said, "I ran into Mrs. Fuentes. They're going ahead with that trip to D.C. for the March for Life. I said we were fine with the West Coast Walk. San Francisco is so close. Affordable, especially since you want to go to Paris with your French class next summer. But we don't dare say that. She's got grand fundraising schemes. 'It's not going to cost anything at all,' she says. No, it'll just be like a second job for five months."

The girl's head felt clogged. "You don't want me to go?" she asked.

"I didn't say that," her mother insisted. "But it just seems... We have our beliefs. We don't need to parade them in the street."

"What does Dad say?"

"Your father," the woman sighed. "He thinks it would be good for you to go to Washington. Learn about history and government. Which, I guess, you can't do at a twenty-thousand-dollar-a-year prep school? And... we don't want you to be left out."

The woman signaled a right lane change, rolled the minivan onto the shoulder and abruptly stopped. She gripped the steering wheel and stared ahead.

"Mom?"

The woman cut the engine and pounded the steering wheel.

"And I said," she cried, "I said, 'At least we're only paying for one.'" She wiped tears from her cheeks and started the engine again.

"I don't need to go to France," the girl said. "I don't need to go anywhere."

. . .

WEDNESDAY MORNING. Upper-class orientation day.

"I thought you weren't dreaming anymore," her mother said, "since the new prescription?"

The girl picked at her scrambled eggs. They were cold. "I wasn't until last night," she said, but what she thought was, "I shouldn't have told her." It's just that the dream was so frightening.

She was wandering through school, eerily distorted like places always are in dreams, and she searched for a familiar spot. Finally, she arrived at what was supposed to be the quad. Girls from her class had moved from last year's Sophomore section to where Juniors always sat. She went to sit with them, dreading how they'd react, as if maybe she didn't belong anymore.

The Queen Bee stared at her horrified. "What happened?" she asked.

"Nothing," she said. But the girls all pointed, and she looked down to see her left leg was missing. She tried to hide it, but saw her arm was cut off at the elbow, and she woke up gasping.

"You were without Teri most of last semester," her father said.

"This is different." The girl pushed her plate across the kitchen island. Her mother pushed it back.

"At least eat your bacon," she said. "You need your strength."

"Not hungry."

Her father pinched a strip of bacon from her plate. "It'll do you good to be back in school," he said. "You'll see."

Then an explosion ripped through the living room into the kitchen, the climactic moment in one of her little brother's video games.

"Jeremy, turn that off!" their mother yelled. "We're leaving."

Her father steadied the girl with a hand on her shoulder. "I'll take you in."

Her mother glowered and herded the younger kids toward the door.

. . .

"IT'S A 2017," *the man explained, "practically new, only seven thousand miles. They call that color blue velvet. You like it?"*

The boy shrugged. "S'okay."

"What about you?" he asked the little girl. He picked her up so she could peer through the window.

"You couldn't wait?" the woman called from the doorway. "You couldn't put this off even a week?"

The man blushed crimson. "Okay, kids, let's go inside."

"Get it out of here," the woman demanded.

"You want me to take it back?"

"I don't want to look at it!"

The man shooed the children through the door. The oldest surviving daughter closed the door behind them.

"You're being ridiculous," the man said. "You're acting like I traded our daughter for a car. You know how absurd that is?"

"What's absurd is thinking…this is how to deal with loss."

The man pulled a bottle of beer from the refrigerator and twisted it open. "Oh, really? Because I thought I was buying the car I had planned to buy for two years."

"I have a hole in me!" the woman screamed. "And it's bigger than any g—d—car!" She pulled her elbows into her gut and crumpled. She rolled from her knees onto her side and wailed.

The older daughter picked up her young sister and carried her to her bedroom.

"Is Mommy dying, too?" the little girl asked.

"No, baby, it's all alright."

HER FATHER TAPPED the dashboard to get Tara's attention. "You got your letter?"

"In my backpack."

He raised an eyebrow.

"I checked like three times." Tara pitched forward and unzipped the front pocket of her bag. She held up the envelope and flapped it back and forth.

"Your driving test is coming up, right?" he asked.

"Not too soon. Mid-October."

"Let's set time to practice," he said. "Make sure you pass the first time."

Tara felt her stomach rise, as they turned off the freeway onto the Boulevard that led to her school.

"And I'll match dollar for dollar when you buy your car."

"You don't have to," she said.

The car rolled to the curb in the drop-off lane.

"Honey," her Dad whispered, "you got this."

THE GIRL KNELT *on the green, studying the curvature of the surface and the grain of the grass. Eighteen feet from her ball to the pin.*

"Not possible," the girl muttered.

The man hooked an index finger and, when she stepped towards him, leaned over the bag to whisper. "Everything's impossible, until somebody does it."

The girl nodded, thinking, "Address the ball."

Her twin mouthed silently "Hello, Ball."

A wisp of a smile crossed the girl's lips. Her fingers tightened on the shaft, and she rocked gently forward tapping the ball which skipped and rolled towards the cup...

TARA HEARD a hollow plunk as the door popped open, and she swung her feet onto the pavement.

JUNIOR HALL WAS a row of lockers on the northern wall of the Science Center, facing the Quad. Tara queued up at the end of the line to receive her locker assignment and combination lock. She couldn't see beyond the boys in front of her, so she scanned the Quad, where bare tables were being set for the Activities Fair. The Queen Bee and her drones buzzed around the Dance Team table, as a skinny kid with ears like frisbees stapled to a fence post vied for attention.

"I followed your *'Gram* every day," he said. "And I'm not even into dance and clothes and whatever. What I'm saying is, you could be an influencer. You know how much influencers make per post?"

"How much?"

"Lots."

The Queen scoffed. Her tight, black ringlets bobbed as she turned her back. The boy persisted.

"You'd need to get more followers, post a little more often, then you could reach out to sponsors."

"Sounds like a lot of work, and there's a little thing called school."

"You don't have to do it all yourself. With your sense of style and my business acumen…"

"Acumen?" the Queen laughed. "You flip burgers."

Unperturbed, the kid pulled out a business card, and handed it over grandly. The Queen read, "Thomas Carnes, Assistant Manager, Cattle Drive Restaurant."

"You can call me *Flipper*, but nobody else does."

"Hey, Flipper, what's happening?" a voice called.

"My man!" the kid shot back, extending his arm for a fist bump. When he turned back, the Queen and her hive were gone.

Tara turned her attention back to the line. A boy ahead of her was telling his friend, "Coach had us doing two-a-days. In pads. By the time we got out, two o'clock, I couldn't keep my eyes open. I swear, I drove home in my sleep."

The friend elbowed the first boy in the side. "Dude," he whispered. The first boy side-eyed Tara and faced front. His ears blushed and his friend stifled a laugh.

Great, Tara thought, *everyone knows*.

Students had fallen in line behind her, but nobody had called out. Maybe they forgot which twin had died and were afraid of shouting the wrong name. "Tee" had always worked; kids used it for Tara or Teri, or just Twin. And it had a connection to golf, too. But maybe using a nickname that applied to both girls wouldn't be cool either. Finally reaching the front of the line, Tara signed for her lock and went to find her locker. It was on the lower level, which meant a year of crouching while someone reached over her head, occasionally dropping objects on her. Tara stowed her backpack, closed the door, and clicked the lock shut.

Now, where to? Augh!

The letter, with the day's schedule, was in her backpack. The bell rang: five minutes to first period.

Tara dialed the combination and pulled. The lock didn't open. Again. Didn't open. She read the combination again off the card.

Is that a 7 or a 9? Is that a 5 or a 6?

"Tee!"

Tara cringed; Flipper had spotted her.

"Tee, you better get moving," he said.

She wanted to say, "You know my name, right?" But that would probably have come off hostile, especially in this moment of annoyance over her stupid lock. "I'm not going anywhere," she said, "'til I get this open." She slammed the lock against the door and yanked. Nothing.

"Here, let me," Flipper said. Tara handed him the index card; he crouched and went to work as a loud squeal went up. A dark-eyed girl, with jet black hair, threw her arms around Tara's shoulders. Tara felt tears on her cheek, and when they separated, the other girl's olive skin was flushed, and she wiped her eyes with her sweater sleeve.

"I'm so happy to see you!"

"Thanks."

A click and metallic echo got Tara's attention. She lunged to pull the letter out of her backpack, then closed the locker again. Flipper handed her the index card.

"That 23, it's actually a 28."

"Good to know." And now that Flipper knew her combination, she'd have to trade in the lock.

"Where you headed?" the dark-eyed girl asked.

"American History. I got Obstbaum."

"Ugh, me, too," her friend groaned. "European history all over again. He loved Napoleon; wonder what he'll think of George Washington." She swept her hair to the right and placed her backpack on her left shoulder. Her long, straight hair fell low, brushing the S-curve of her lower back. Other girls fell in around them, and they headed inside to class.

"You know, Raquel, Washington might never come up," Flipper said. "Or Jefferson or Adams. American History starts at 1850."

Raquel stopped and glared at him, as if to ask, *Why are you still here?*

"I'm going to Obstbaum, too." He opened his palm towards the far end of the hallway. No one moved. "Anyway, why even worry about old, dead slaveowners? They're all getting torn down. We're starting over at Year Zero."

Still, no one moved.

"Y'know, Flipper," the Queen Bee buzzed, "you like hanging with the girls so much, why not become one? There's pills for that now."

The hive chittered as the boy curled his lip. They entered the classroom as the second bell rang. Some hive girls had arranged a throne for their Queen against the near wall, with another seat for Raquel. Tara drifted to a desk in back, and Flipper fell into the seat behind her.

"They're so stuck up," he whispered over her shoulder.

"I thought you liked Raquel," Tara said, absently.

"I can like her and know she's stuck up. I mean, c'mon, richest girl in school, but she's gotta take cues from Cheryl? What's that about?"

The teacher introduced himself, even though everyone knew him.

"American History from 1850 to present," he said. "Gives us about a hundred and seventy years to cover. And you're in luck, because I've lived most of it."

After pausing for a half-hearted laugh, Mr. Obstbaum proceeded to lay out his class rules. Students in the front seats came down the aisles, passing out the textbook. Five inches thick and about seven pounds. They had been promised texts on CD since middle school, but so far, no progress.

"In my humble opinion," Mr. Obstbaum droned, "this course matters more than football or cheerleading. If you drop below a C, a DQ will help you simplify your life and get back on track."

Suddenly, a new boy stood in the front of the room holding a yellow hall pass. Dark-haired, erect, and handsome, he towered over the pot-bellied, gray teacher whose wire-rimmed glasses slid down his nose.

"You're rather tardy, aren't you, Mr. Copeland?" he asked. His droopy mustache seemed to bristle as he grunted, "Let's not make it a habit."

"No, sir." The boy turned to look for a desk, and Tara tipped her head down, letting stray hairs fall in front of her face.

"Miss Fuentes," the teacher said, "would you, uh…" He gestured for Raquel to rise and move to the back of the class. Her jaw dropped for a second, but she slid out of the seat and trudged to the rear, taking the last desk by the door. The boy took her seat and hunched self-consciously over his elbows.

"What's he doing in this class?" Flipper whispered.

Later, in the hall, the Queen Bee held court.

"They don't know how to schedule," she groaned. "They make Honors classes exclusive, so the regulars get overbooked and rowdy. Then Resource kids need small classes and quiet, so they stick them in with us and just grade them differently. Totally messed up."

"It's the power of management," Flipper interjected, causing the knot of girls to halt. "To get ahead, you need representation."

"Stop trying to make this happen," the Queen commanded.

"I don't care about Nolan," Raquel said, in a tone that suggested she might care just a little. "But, if Obstbaum thinks he's going to shut me up in the back of the room, he's got another think coming."

The cluster of girls split, heading to separate language classes.

"O. M. G. I have totally forgotten everything," said the girl who would not be silenced. "I tried watching French movies. They don't enunciate! And they smoke too much. Disgusting."

"C'MON, YOU TWO, PICK A LANGUAGE," *Dad said. "Form's due tomorrow."*

Teri smiled impishly. "I know what I want. Mandarin!"

"Are you crazy?"

"Why? What do you want?"

"Spanish."

"So predictable."

"Practical. I could use Spanish ten times a day if I knew it."

"You could also pick it up from Telemundo if you cared so much."

"When are you gonna use Mandarin? Ordering take-out?"

"International business," Dad said. "The world's second largest economy."

"Mandarin would look impressive on a college application," Mom suggested.

"Okay, now you guys are ganging up on me."

"And smaller classes. Spanish is gonna have thirty kids. Mandarin? Eight."

"'Cause it's so freakin' hard! Anyway, we just finished a year of Latin. So, that's a waste, if we don't stick with a Romance language."

"Good point," Mom admitted. "How about Italian?"

"Miss Cardinale is leaving."

"What?"

"Getting married," Teri explained. "Moving to Colorado. Everyone knows. Or, now everyone knows, since the last person to ever find out anything finally knows."

Grrrrr.

"Focus girls. What's left?"

"French."

"How big are the classes?" Tara asked.

"What does it matter?" Teri laughed. "We're going to practice with each other. That's the whole point of this argument."

FRENCH BLED INTO CHEMISTRY, where Tara collected another seven-pound textbook thick as a cinder block. Flipper opened to a random page of chemical equations and his eyes nearly popped out of his boney head.

"It's freakin' Calculus!" he gasped.

The Queen Bee rolled her eyes. "You've never even seen Calc."

"Yeah, well, in my frequent nightmares about having to someday take Calc, where I wake up screaming in a cold sweat,"—he jabbed his finger at the page—"this is what it looks like."

"Don't worry, Tommy," the teacher assured him, "You'll soon be balancing equations in your sleep."

The lab fell silent. Tara felt 'side-eye' from all angles. Were they wondering if she was awake even now?

The morning dragged on through American Literature and Algebra II, after which Tara had about forty pounds of textbooks to lug back to her locker. She dug her lunch out of her backpack and looked out at the Quad. The predictable reshuffling had already occurred, with her classmates occupying the Junior tables. Tara stood on the fringes with her brain locked, like an Internet video buffering. Despite her dream last night, she didn't fear joining the Junior girls without Teri, but doing so would ratify the onward progression of life, which she wished she could harness and turn back. So, she slung her backpack over one shoulder and waded into the Activities Fair, shimmering like a backward eddy in the flow of space and time.

Eager Freshmen flitted about, like guppies, or even more so like birds from branch to branch of a magic garden, tasting a seed here, a blossom there. "Don't be enchanted," she wanted to tell them, "These infinite possibilities; all a lie." But they didn't see any shadows hanging over them, just as she hadn't seen death and *dis*-enchantment hanging over Teri.

"You're coming, right, Tara?" A clipboard with a signup sheet jutted forward. "Remember?" Raquel asked, "This year it's the real March for Life in D.C., not the little West Coast version."

"Not sure," Tara told her. "It's a long way off."

Raquel switched to a different clipboard. "Well, you can sign this petition. It's to stop pharmaceutical companies from making vaccines from aborted babies."

"You know that's not true," someone said.

"It absolutely is."

Tara felt the crowd close in.

"And selling body parts? That's a total lie."

"Lie? There's videos."

"Fake videos."

The crowd was too tight.

"You shouldn't shame women 'bout what they do with their bodies."

"It's not just *their* bodies."

"Any other school would shut this table down."

"We've got like twelve years to save the planet from climate change, and you want more kids!"

"Kids are the future."

"There is no future."

The bell rang, and Tara broke through the knot of bodies. She pitched the remains of her sandwich into the trash and pulled the orientation letter out of her backpack. Religious Studies. Mrs. Leary.

In the classroom, a line of students snaked along the front to a pile of textbooks. Tara attached herself to the tail. From the corner of her eye, she saw Cheryl nested against the wall, her drones gathered around.

"C'MON, *let's sit with Cheryl," Teri said, nudging Tara to hurry. Tara deliberately dragged her feet and let the desks fill up. Miffed, Teri headed to the back of the room. "Why do you have to be difficult?"*

"She's so controlling," Tara whispered. "She never lets anyone have a different opinion."

"We can keep our opinions between us."

"And that's how we make friends?" Tara asked.

"It's high school," Teri said. "First rule: we survive."

"YOU BROKE THAT RULE," Tara muttered. Then froze when the girl in front of her turned to ask, "What?" Tara shook her off, took a textbook, and found a desk. She opened the book and skimmed the chapter headings. *Why Morals Matter; What is Your Moral Code?; Building Your Code Upon the Rock...Medical Ethics: What is Permissible?* She shuddered and slammed the book, a bit too loudly. A dark-haired boy towered in front of her. Their eyes met, green on cobalt blue, and he rocked back on his heels.

"Are you planning to stay, Nolan?" the teacher asked.

"Um, yeah, sure."

The teacher gestured for the boy to sit, and he slumped into the seat. He slid forward onto his elbows, as if the girl behind him bore some infection. Or maybe the stench of death lingered on her.

The bell rang, and the boy slid off his seat and strode out the front door without looking back. Tara took a slow breath.

"That must have been hard for you," the Queen Bee buzzed, cocking her head to the side, imitating a human gesture of sympathy. "Where's next?" she asked.

"Art. Oil painting."

"Oh, I'd walk you, but…Chorale."

The Queen Bee flitted off, and Tara headed towards the Art Studio. A hive girl attached herself, droning vaguely about the challenges of oil versus acrylic. Near the Studio was a Girls' Room. Tara paused, wondering if she dared.

"Hey," she whispered, "Tell Ms. Morgan I need a minute. Y'know, girl stuff."

The hive girl nodded and buzzed on her way. Inside the Girls' Room, two girls applied lip gloss to duck lips at the mirror. Once discovered, they fled, brushing Tara on their way out. She was alone.

Tara entered a stall and locked it behind her. She placed her backpack on the floor, closed the toilet lid and sat down. She lifted her skirt and rolled up the right leg of her spandex shorts. She unzipped the top pocket of her backpack and took out the knife. She unfolded the blade and placed it in her left hand. With her right thumb and forefinger, she pinched some flesh of her inner thigh, below where she'd done it before. *Lightly*, she thought. She didn't need to create a trail down her leg. She drew the tip of the blade across the pale flesh. Once, twice. With the third stroke, beads of scarlet appeared on the mound of white. Red, glossy, alive. She dabbed at the largest bead with her finger and then touched it to her tongue. *Amen.*

CHAPTER
TWO

"I am all in a sea of wonders.
I doubt; I fear;
I think strange things,
which I dare not confess to my own soul."
— Bram Stoker, *Dracula*

AT HOME WEDNESDAY NIGHT, Tara's parents peppered her with questions about her day. She kept her answers monosyllabic: *Fine. Good. Cool.* But they kept picking, digging, drilling. Finally, she blurted out, "Everybody knows."

"What?"

"That I drove to Teri's grave."

"So?"

"In my sleep!"

"Oh."

"How could they know that?" Tara demanded. "What, the security guard? He got on the phone and called all my classmates?"

"You don't think we told anyone?" her mother asked, her *shocked face* on full display.

"Someone did, okay?" Tara left it at that. She retired to her room to do homework, which was dull and tedious since her mind wouldn't focus. She opened her photo app, thinking she'd print some pictures to pin up in her locker. Not to go crazy like a hive girl. And not to build a shrine to Teri. Just photos any normal girl would have. But *normal* didn't have a dead twin in every picture ever taken, smiling, side by side. The same honey-blonde hair, the same wide, emerald-and-turquoise eyes; two identical white smiles with rabbit-like central incisors; and the same faint dimple in the chin.

Tara closed the app and thought about bed. Hers was a rumpled mess. Beside it lay the empty bed, fully made, seeming to stare at her. Maybe tonight she'd sleep there. That wouldn't be weird, would it?

———

THURSDAY MORNING, Tara found a yellow appointment slip sticking out of a vent in her locker door. She snatched the slip and held it in a tight fist. *Who else had seen it*, she wondered? She opened the slip and saw Ms. Gaudino, the Guidance Counselor, had made an appointment for first period. *No freaking way!*

The date was August 22. The family had buried the deceased girl on June 22. *This must be the two-month checkup,* Tara thought. Then, as if on cue, the priest came walking through.

"Hey, girls," the bass voice rumbled, "What are the odds on this Friday's game?"

"You taking bets, Father?" someone asked.

"I'm gauging public sentiment," he said. "Are we going to take them?"

Tara hastened to empty her backpack as students fired back answers, reeking of school spirit. The bell rang, locker doors slammed, students scattered.

"Hey, Tee," the priest called, freezing Tara in her tracks.

"Yeah, Father?"

"I played a round of golf at the club last week." Pause. Earnest eye contact. "A number of people inquired. Charitably." Then, inevitably, "Two months..."

"Yeah, eight weeks, fifty-*six* days? Not up on my times tables." Tara checked her temper. "Sorry, Father."

"It's alright," he said. "It's just, people miss you. They care, and, uh, my office is always open. To come talk. Or make a Confession."

"I didn't kill her, Father," Tara blurted, then chuckled faintly, trying to make it seem like a joke after the fact. "She just...died." And that was...all. Tara bolted down the hall, trying to outpace the tears stinging her eyes that she didn't need to be crying at eight in the morning when she needed to get to class. But *first,* she needed to cancel the appointment with her counselor.

Ms. Gaudino's door was open. Tara stood on the threshold and held up the slip. "I'm going to class."

"Oh. Okay, I just thought we could talk."

"Not the first day of class. Everyone already thinks I'm crazy; I don't need them thinking I'm *that* crazy."

"Why not come in for just a minute."

"Why?"

"Because you're obviously upset."

Tara stepped into the office and closed the door. The bell rang.

"Just give me a slip to get into class."

The counselor nodded and picked up her pad. "No one thinks you're crazy, Tara," she said.

"No, they just spread crazy rumors."

"That no one believes," Ms. Gaudino insisted. She rose from her desk and handed Tara the late pass. "No one actually believes you tried to dig Teri up."

"WHAT??!!"

"Oh," she said. "I thought—"

"Dig her up?!"

"I'm sorry, please sit for a moment."

Tara pressed her back against the door. She stared at the stupid poster of a kitten hanging by one paw from a tree limb. *Hang In There*, it said.

"It was just some knuckleheads wisecracking. You shouldn't give it another thought."

"I gotta go," Tara said, but her legs wouldn't move. "I gotta walk into class like I don't have a freakin' care in the world."

"You don't have to," the counselor said. "But okay. And come back at lunch, will you?"

Tara nodded. She reached for the doorknob and pulled.

————

"CHEMISTRY IS A STUDY OF TRANSFORMATIONS,"

the teacher was saying. "From one state to another. Take H_2O, dihydrogen monoxide, or what you young folks call…wawa." He waved Tara towards the front desk and took the late slip from her. "Miss Hartzwell, since I have you here, can you tell the class about the three states of wawa?"

"Whu-whut?"

"Very good, that's clever," he chuckled. "I forget this is an Honors class. The three states of H_2O."

"Um, solid, liquid, and gas?"

"Commonly known as?"

"Uh, ice, water, steam?"

"Thank you. And what do those states depend on?" he asked.

Tara drew a blank, but someone called out, "Energy."

The teacher lit the flame on a Bunsen burner. He dropped two ice cubes into a beaker and warmed them over the flame. "Energy changes the state, but not the elemental structure. So, what was hard and cold becomes freely flowing liquid and, eventually, vapor." The water boiled and steam started to rise from the beaker. "But if you remove the energy source," he said, turning off the burner, "the gas reverts to liquid. Remove enough energy and the liquid reverts to solid. So, what *was* can *be* again."

Tara felt her throat tighten. She wanted to believe that was possible but doubted it.

————

"SO." Ms. Gaudino settled back into her chair and folded her hands on her lap. "Two months. How do you feel?"

Tara felt angry. "How come that's a magic number?" she wanted to know. "Two months, is that the season? So now, what? Dead twin sister season is over, and we start training…for what? What comes next?"

"I don't know. Life?"

"Yeah, well, I'll pass."

"Is that what you've been doing?"

Tara burrowed into the chair. Okay, she'd taken the summer off. *So what?* What's Youth Orchestra anyway? And she didn't show up early for golf and she wasn't thinking about joining the team. *So what?* It was a stupid, pointless game anyway. "Nothing matters anymore."

"I suppose, in comparison, that's true."

"It's just, without Teri, I'm missing parts. I don't know who I am. I don't know who anybody is. My family? We sit around the table, and I'm like, 'Who are these people?' It's like I was abducted by aliens."

The counselor nodded. "It's disorienting. Sure. All your life you've been The Hartzwell Twins. That was special. Now you've just got to be Tara. But Tara is special, too."

Special Tara rolled her eyes. She stretched her chin up towards the ceiling. She stared off at the wall. Another stupid poster of a turtle with a thought balloon. "I only make progress when I stick my neck out."

"If I'm so special," Tara asked, "how come it didn't work?"

It was the bone marrow transplant. The last-ditch therapy for acute myeloid leukemia. First, they had put Teri on chemotherapy, but that hardly slowed the disease. Then they tried an autologous transplant, where they take out the patient's own bone marrow, clean out all the cancer cells and put the marrow back. But it didn't grow normally, and Teri only got sicker.

So then, they wanted a transplant from a donor. And what luck, because the patient had an exact genetic match. A clone from the very same embryo. They just needed to take some perfectly healthy marrow from Tara and put it into Teri. Only it didn't work. Teri rejected Tara's bone marrow. She died three weeks later.

"Even the best therapies can't guarantee good outcomes," Ms. Gaudino said.

"We were an exact match," Tara grumbled.

"Are you afraid...?" Ms. Gaudino tried to ask. "Are you worried you'll get sick?"

The room spun and Tara grabbed the arms of her chair.

"No," she said. "That's not...."

"Okay."

The doctor had said it was a freak mutation in some gene. And that Tara was perfectly healthy. Which was never an issue, because Tara had never feared getting sick. Sure, she checked her toothbrush for blood sometimes, and examined the hair in her brush, but who wouldn't? If anything, she'd wished the sickness would strike her, so she could suffer with her sister, instead of feeling the pain of separation, and the guilt of survival. Now, suddenly and oddly, she was gripped by panic. Was there something they hadn't told her? Was that gene mutation sleeping inside her? Would that freak gene wake up one day, flip some switch and poison her blood? Was that the reason her marrow couldn't save Teri?

"I see I've upset you."

"I gotta go."

"First, let's talk about what you're feeling."

"Did my parents tell you — ?"

The counselor shook her head. Her eyes were misting.

"Do you know something?"

"I don't. I just...I thought..."

If she finished the sentence, Tara didn't hear her.

———

"I'VE GOT A VERY upset young lady in my office," the cancer doc said. "I think we should have a little conference."

Tara had run the eight blocks from the school to the Medical Center. Now she caught her breath in the oncologist's outer office, waiting for her father. Her mother arrived with him, and Tara flinched.

"DR. FLORES WANTS TO SEE YOU."

"Me?" the girl asked.

"Teri needs a bone marrow transplant," the woman said. "You've got to tell him you'll do it."

The girl stood dumbfounded.

"Well?"

Well, where is he, the girl thought? Where do I go?

"We're not going to have an argument, are we?" the woman demanded. "You want to help your sister, don't you?"

"Of course, I want to help her," the girl snapped. "I don't want you ordering me to help her."

"I'm not —"

"You just did."

"No, I said you need to go see the doctor."

"Do you even listen to yourself!" the girl yelled. "Just because you can't do anything, you have to act like I won't? So you order me to, and that's like you're helping? You're pathetic!"

The slap across her cheek stung. A pair of nurses separated them.

TARA RUBBED HER MOUTH.

"I had no idea," her mother said, almost tearful. "We should have realized you'd be scared."

"I wasn't," Tara insisted.

She saw herself alone with Teri. Holding her boney hand. Looking into her sunken eyes. Tara remembered thinking, *Why her and not me?* But she'd trusted the cancer doctor when he'd said, "You're completely healthy," and she couldn't remember a thought or a prayer she had ever uttered that went, "God, don't let this happen to me." Only Ms. Gaudino had planted the idea in her head, and now that's all she could think of.

They went into the inner office and sat, her mother holding onto

Tara's hand, her father beside them, and the doctor perched on the edge of his desk.

"Tara, as I said at the time, we had great hope for Teresa. The disease has a high survival rate, she was strong, and she had the perfect donor. We screened your blood. We screened your marrow, your stem cells. They were all perfectly healthy. And a perfect genetic match for Teresa."

"Then, what happened?"

"The process just didn't work," her Dad said. "That's it, end of story."

"No, that's not it," Tara cried. "I can tell by looking at you. You're not telling me something."

There was a long pause, or a short one that seemed long, while the doctor looked at the parents, then worked his neck around the inside of his collar. "If we knew why treatments succeed for some and fail for others... It's just a mystery. I can only say Teresa's passing was the most bitter disappointment of my medical career. The processes failed her. Our current medical knowledge failed her. But no person failed her." He placed his hands on the edge of the desk and continued.

"And as far as your chances of getting leukemia.... Genetics don't rule everything. You and Teresa were identical genetically, but you're left-handed and she was right-handed. That's not genetics. That's the environment of the womb. And..."

"God's plan," her mother whispered.

"I think He could have planned it better," Tara said.

"Here's what we know," the doctor said. "If Teresa had gotten sick in infancy, there would be a very good chance of you also getting sick. Because the triggering event would likely have occurred in the womb, a close, contained environment you both shared. But given that she was almost sixteen, whatever triggered the mutation in her DNA, it's not likely you'd have had the same exposure."

"But we did everything together," Tara said.

"Remember your appendicitis?" her Dad asked. "Teri never got that."

"Statistically," the doctor added, "the odds are greater than ninety percent that you will never get the disease."

"That's higher than your GPA," her Dad said.

"Yeah," Tara conceded. But Teri's chance of survival had been eighty percent, so how did that matter?

———

THE CAR ROLLED to a stop in front of the St. Stephen's Admin building.

"Wait, wait!" her mother said, thrusting a slip of paper towards her. "A note to get back in. But this is the only time. You call us next time before you do something crazy."

Tara took the note, curling her lip at the word *crazy*. Inside, she presented the note to a Senior T.A. at the front desk, who told her she'd "Better scoot" and, when she scooted not, held up a pile of half sheets he was grading, telling her, "Obstbaum gave a quiz in E block."

"Day one? On what?"

"I dunno," he answered, quite smug. "Maybe last night's reading? Underground Railroad? Hint: no actual trains and it didn't really run underground."

Tara sprinted towards class and came to a skidding stop on the threshold. The teacher collected the last of the quizzes from the front desk of the far row. Tara lingered in the front of the room as he turned and peered over the rims of his granny glasses.

"Mr. Obstbaum," Tara asked, hating the tone of her own voice, "could I take the quiz?"

"Miss Hartzwell, you are aware of my policy. You come on time, or you take a zero. This is a classroom, not a 7-11."

Fine, Tara thought. But her eyes were drawn to a nearby desk, where a muscular youth hunched his broad shoulders over a heavily scratched half sheet. His forehead rested on his left hand, and his fingers wormed their way nervously through his thick, black hair.

"Alright," the teacher grumbled. "Take a seat. I've only got so much orneriness in me, and Mr. Copeland is exhausting my supply."

35

He handed Tara a quiz sheet, which she took to her desk in the back. She uncapped her pen and scanned the questions.

1. What were the major terms of the Compromise of 1850?

2. Name the most famous conductor of the Underground Railroad.

3. What new political party was formed to oppose slavery?

4. What religious group actively supported the Underground Railroad?

5. Who said, "A house divided against itself cannot stand"?

Tara left one through four blank and scrawled "Jesus" for the last answer. The sudden droop of the teacher's mustache told her he was not impressed.

"Who can explain the Fugitive Slave Law?" Obstbaum asked. He called on the Queen Bee.

"Um, that if a slave made it to a free state, the state had to hand him over, so he could be taken down South again."

"But that law was met with resistance in the north, was it not? Miss Hartzwell, what can you tell us?"

Tara cleared her throat. An illustration in her textbook jogged a memory, which seemed ancient but must have come from reading the passage last night. "You mean Christiana?" she asked.

"Unless you know another."

Tara didn't even know that one. She skimmed the paragraphs she'd highlighted, and a vague recognition stirred. "Okay, there were *four* slaves? They escaped a farm in Maryland and went to Pennsylvania."

"And what happened in Pennsylvania?"

Tara kept her nose down in her book as she continued. "The owner got a warrant to search a home in Lancaster County that sheltered runaways. He thought he could just talk to his slaves and get them to come back with him, but the house belonged to a family of runaway slaves, and they were armed and ready to defend themselves.

"Local white residents also came to defend the runaways. There was a gun fight. Thirty-eight people were charged with treason for breaking the Fugitive Slave Law. But the family and the slaves escaped farther north."

"Thank you, Miss Hartzwell." Mr. Obstbaum peppered other students with questions as Tara tried to relax. She was starving from having missed lunch, and her mind drifted until a sharp question snapped her back to attention.

"Mr. Copeland," the teacher asked, "would you like to brief us on the case?"

The startled youth blinked his blue eyes a couple of times. Tara could see he'd been drawing random squiggles in his binder.

"Mr. Copeland, are you following any of this?"

"Nah, Mr. O., not really."

The class erupted in laughter as the teacher scowled. "Perhaps less time with the leather spheroids and more time with the textbook."

The youth lifted his binder and slid towards the edge of his seat.

"I could show you—" he said, pointing his binder to the white board.

The teacher extended a flat palm. "Just give me one fact about Dred Scott to advance the discussion."

"He was a slave?"

"Thank you, Mr. Copeland," the teacher said above another wave of laughter. Other students filled out the story of Dred Scott and how the U.S. Supreme Court ruled he had no right to sue for his freedom, because as a Black, former slave, he had no rights under the Constitution. The class sat in silence for a few moments, chewing on that thick slice of injustice, before the teacher uttered what should have been the final word on the subject. "And this is why Dred Scott stands today as the worst decision ever rendered by the U.S. Supreme Court."

All eyes went from the teacher to the clock, which seemed to be slacking off in the waning minutes of the day. Still, they assumed class was all but over, until a voice piped up from the back of the room.

"I disagree."

The teacher peered over his glasses at Raquel Fuentes.

"*Roe versus Wade* was way worse," she said.

Groans of "Here we go again" rolled from one corner of the room while Raquel's supporters cheered from the other.

"*Dred Scott* says a slave's not a citizen," Raquel explained. "So, he can't sue in court. It doesn't say he's not a person. *Roe v. Wade* says a baby's not a person. What's worse?"

"*Roe* was about a fetus," the teacher stated. "No one was talking about actual babies."

"They're talking about them now," she said. "Letting babies die *after* they're born, if they survive an abortion. So what if The Supremes said, 'He's a slave; he's property.' They didn't tell his owner he could destroy that property. *Roe v. Wade* does. Says the baby is the mother's property and she can go ahead and destroy it. And sell the organs for experiments."

Her last assertion prompted shouts of "That's a lie," and "You're crazy!"

The teacher wagged his head, like he was dealing with a disobedient puppy. "Again, Miss Fuentes," he said, "It's a fetus. Not a baby and certainly not a legal person. You're entitled to your feelings; you're not entitled to make up your own facts."

"And you're entitled to teach, not spread pro-abort propaganda."

"That's enough!"

Raquel spun in her desk and bolted. "Not gonna sit here…," she mumbled as she slung her backpack over her shoulder and headed out the door. The class was stunned into silence as two agonizing minutes remained on the clock. Hive girls buzzed in their seats, but the Queen held them under her gaze. Her nonchalance seemed to confuse them, like a cold draft freezing their wings. Then, for some reason even she didn't understand, Tara shot her arm into the air.

"I'll go check on her," she said and eased herself out of her desk. *Why are you doing this?* she asked herself, as her legs turned to rubber. *You need more drama—their drama?—after everything last year?* Entering the nearest Girl's Room, she found the runaway girl crying in front of a sink and dabbing the smudged mascara around her reddened eyes.

"You okay?"

"That man...infuriates me." She balled up the paper towel and pitched it into a receptacle. "And they just take notes on everything he says. Because it will be on the test!" She eyed Tara in the mirror. "You get it, at least."

This probably wasn't a good time to be truthful, but Tara didn't have the energy to pretend. "Actually, no," she said. "I don't get why you pick fights with Obstbaum, or why it's any of my business what other people do."

The blood seemed to drain from Raquel's face. "We have to fight."

"My sister just died, okay?" Tara said. "Prayer didn't work. So, I don't see why we have to follow God's rules, when He doesn't even listen to us. Science at least might get better."

"Not by experimenting on babies."

"Embryos, Raquel. They're cells. They're not people. My sister was a person!"

The bell rang. *Can this be over?* Tara hoped, while bracing herself for another round of Raquel's patented talking points. But her classmate just stood silent.

"I'll pray for you," Raquel finally said, not *un*angrily, but apparently meaning it.

"Thanks," Tara said, though thinking, *Don't do me any favors.*

She *do* wanted to leave. Where were the girls who should be throwing the door open and swarming their friend with hugs and tissues and words of encouragement? Finally, a couple of girls from another class came in, and reacted like they knew they were interrupting something. But at least they broke the moment, and Tara was able to slip out. She trudged back toward Obstbaum's class to get her things. A knot of kids still hovered outside, some huddled closely, whispering.

"Just 'cause it's Catholic school, doesn't make every class Religion."

"She's kind of extreme."

"Ya think?"

"Hey, she throws good parties."

"I'll go, 'cause we've been friends, but this one could be my last."

Tara locked eyes with the last speaker, and in the Queen Bee's return glance saw black poison drip from the tip of a dart flying towards her face. Tara ducked and—

Smacked into the muscular wall that was Nolan Copeland. Tara knocked his books out from under his arm and the pile crashed to the floor. They both stooped to reach for his binder which had splayed open. There, for the world to see, was a complex, multicolored flow chart illustrating every step of Dred Scott's journey. The demi-man quickly snapped it shut and tucked it under his arm.

"Sorry," Tara said. Nolan nodded and grunted something like "S'okay," as he strode past her. Again, Tara felt weak in the knees, but waded into Obstbaum's classroom, found her desk, and scooped up her books.

"Do you need me, Miss Hartzwell?" Mr. Obstbaum asked.

"No," Tara huffed.

The teacher gave her the hooked finger, and she walked to the front of the room. He handed back her quiz: 0.5 out of five.

"I was looking for Abraham Lincoln," he muttered, "but I gave you half a point for Jesus."

Well, the girl thought, *half a point is more than He's done for me lately*.

"Get it signed," he said, "if you want to get back into class tomorrow." After her jaw dropped, he said, "You know the rule. Less than three points, you get the quiz signed. I don't want any outrage come report card time."

Tara could have gone off about the other flunked quizzes that were probably in the pile, and how those kids wouldn't get them back until tomorrow. They wouldn't have to show them to their parents until Sunday night, so they'd have the whole weekend free and clear. She'd have to tell her parents tonight and maybe get grounded for the weekend. *How's that fair?* she wanted to say. Instead, she blurted out, "Nolan had the answers."

"Excuse me?"

"When you asked him about Dred Scott. He knew; he just needed more time."

"Yes, well, time is a fleeting commodity."

"But you made it sound like he wasn't prepared, like all he's doing is football. I saw his homework; it must have taken him hours."

Obstbaum removed his glasses and with his thumb and forefinger massaged the sides of his nose. "Miss Hartzwell, I'm well aware of the challenges Mr. Copeland faces, and I'm sure you've observed certain accommodations the school provides him. I am not at liberty to discuss the matter further."

"Whatever," Tara snapped. "But I'm sure he didn't ask to be put in Honors, and you shouldn't imply he's not working when he obviously is."

"Well," Obstbaum sighed. "I'm glad you consider yourself an expert on Mr. Copeland. Perhaps you might consider becoming an expert on the causes of the American Civil War."

Enough. Tara closed her quiz inside the cover of her textbook and headed for the door. It took all her restraint not to shout, "Yes, I'm on expert on Nolan Copeland!" Since, after all, she was. She knew his favorite color was aquamarine and his favorite breed of dog was the German shorthaired pointer. His favorite band was *Linkin Park*, his favorite TV shows were *Stranger Things* and *Arrow*, and his favorite car was the Dodge *Challenger*. She also knew he was the only boy who had ever kissed Teri Hartzwell.

CHAPTER
THREE

"Who in the world am I? Ah, that's the great puzzle."
— Lewis Carroll, *Alice's Adventures in Wonderland*

FRIDAY LUNCH, and Tara's morning had been relentlessly awful. As per the history teacher's instructions, she had gotten her quiz signed. She'd then proceeded to bomb another, which Obstbaum's helpful T.A. managed to grade before class was over, so — *Oh joy!* — she got to take it home today. *Way to torpedo the weekend.* From there, she'd gotten thoroughly lost in Chem and Algebra, and hadn't been able to answer the simplest question in American Lit.

"Where is Sleepy Hollow? Tara?"

"Uh, Washington?"

The laughter confirmed her suspicion that her answer was not just wrong, but stupidly wrong.

"Washington Irving is the author. I'm asking where the story is set?"

"I don't know, *Mars?*"

That wasn't right either. Nor was it funny. Tara got a severe scowl from the teacher, who kept her after class for a brief "I understand you've been through an ordeal" pep talk. She'd have preferred a stern reprimand; at least then she could have gotten angry. She was beginning to think she'd rather be beaten down as a rebel than caressed as an object of pity.

"I must have lost forty I.Q. points over the summer," she lamented to no one in particular. That no one being Flipper, who seemed to be the only person who, after two and a half days, wasn't completely sick of her. Maybe she'd feel better after eating, but she didn't even get her sandwich out of the bag before the alarm went up at the far end of the table that, "Madame totally sandbagged us with a quiz in D block."

"What's with these teachers and the Friday quizzes?" Tara moaned. "They're compulsive or something."

Instantly, everyone in French class was prairie dogging, trying to see where their Senior language tutor was, so she could talk them through *Jean-Claude se rend au Festival de Cannes*. Tara wished Jean-Claude had stayed home and watched his movies on *Hulu*.

"There she is!" a girl yelled, and a quarter of the cafeteria bolted. But Tara, though not really hungry, stayed to finish her sandwich, relieved to be alone.

"Tee, whatcha got this afternoon?"

Tara glanced right to see Flipper sliding into the chair beside her. "French and Art," she told him.

"Y'know," he said, "you contract that, and you get —"

"Spare me." *Why didn't he ever have something better to do?*

"You coming to the game tonight?" he asked.

"How can there be a game already?" Tara demanded.

"A decision driven purely by economics," Flipper explained. "The NCAA changed its rules to allow athletes to profit from their images and likenesses. That means not just scholarships but endorsement deals."

"So?"

"So, athletes have more at stake, and they want more time to be recruited. They want bye weeks to recover from injuries, and more time to put together highlight reels, visit schools and talk to coaches. And they've still got to fit in exams. That means starting the season early."

"So, they've been practicing...?"

"Since August first."

"That's crazy," Tara said. Maybe two or three boys each year get a crack at a football scholarship. But all forty-five had to give up three weeks of their summer vacation? She tore another bite out of her sandwich. "I had no idea."

"Well, you've had other things on your mind." Then Flipper asked, "What about Raquel's party tomorrow?"

Tara paused her chewing. "First I'm hearing about it." But maybe not. Hadn't Queen Bee said this might be her last time?

"Well, you gotta tune in more. You're her best friend, you and—"

Tara gave him her offended face, then backed off before he got too apologetic. "It's okay," she assured him. "Things are not what they used to be." She crushed her lunch bag and shot it towards the garbage can, missing by a wide margin.

"You're shot ain't what it used to be." Flipper slid off his chair, scooped up the bag and jammed it into the can, just as the bell rang.

"That's that," Tara said. "Time to flunk another quiz."

———

MADAME ASKED, *"Quel a été le premier film que Jean-Claude a vu à Cannes?"*

Can I get a hint? Tara wondered. To her surprise, Madame obliged. *"Rappelez-vous que c'était un film classique qui a commencé en noir et blanc et plus tard en couleur."*

A classic that started in black and white and then went to color... *The Wizard of Oz!* Now, what the heck was the French word for wizard? *Ugh.* From there, Tara's chances dropped like a flying house. Even when she understood the question, she couldn't remember the answer. She even went blank on the easy ones, like *"Quel acteur célèbre Jean-Claude a-t-il vu au café?"* and *"Qu'est-ce que Jean-Claude avait pour déjeuner avec ses amis?"*

She scribbled *Johnny Depp* and *pizza.* Then she backfilled all the blanks ... with *Johnny Depp* and *pizza.* Turned out the answers were *Leo DiCaprio* and *poutine.*

Someone asked, "What's poutine?" and was told, "Don't ask."

Madame then began the lesson as always with phrases and repetition.

Madame: *Ma soeur portait une jupe jaune. Répéter.*
　　Class: *Ma soeur portait une jupe jaune.*
　　Madame: *Mon frère portait une cravate à rayures vertes. Répéter.*
　　Class: *Mon frère portait une cravate à rayures vertes.*

Tara remembered *sa soeur* wearing, not a yellow skirt, but a yellow hospital gown. She helped her get up from the wheelchair and into the bed. Dr. Flores came in, wearing a green striped tie. He asked if their parents were around. That was the day they talked about hospice. Tara had listened at the door while *sa soeur* drifted off to sleep. Their mother wanted to bring Teri home. *If that's what she wants.* Their father worried how that might affect Tara, having her twin sister die in the bedroom they shared. Tara couldn't listen anymore; she went to *sa soeur*, pushed a chair over to the bed, and lowered the guard rail. Tara reached her arm up and around *sa soeur* and leaned forward. With her free hand she stroked her arm. She heard the parents come in. She knew whatever they had decided, it wouldn't matter.

"Tara?"

"*Oui, Madame?*"

"*Que fait ta soeur?*"

Tara's brain locked. "*Ma soeur est morte.*"

Apparently, the correct answer, according to the book, was "My sister has gone shopping," not "My sister died." Madame's *visage* showed a mix of frustration and sympathy.

"*Je suis désolé,*" Tara said.

"*Moi aussi*" Madame replied.

Please, bell, ring, ring, ring, ring.

But before the bell cooperated, Madame's Senior T.A. had graded and returned the quizzes, and Tara had another bomb to drop on her parents.

"I'm sorry," Raquel said after class. Tara's eyelids fluttered, as she tried to reset her mind to what-on-earth Raquel was apologizing for. "I get all worked up; I forget what you're going through. You're coming to my party, right? Saturday?"

"Um, first I'm hearing about it." Lying seemed a better option than admitting she'd heard from a random boy, or worse, from the Queen Bee, who somehow appeared at that instant, no doubt tipped off by hive girls in the class.

"Everyone will be there," Cheryl cooed.

Tara shrugged. "Saturday's good." Raquel smiled and squeezed Tara's forearm. They separated, and Tara trudged off to her final class of the day.

———

ART CLASS WASN'T PRODUCTIVE, just a dry discussion of color theory and composition. But at least Tara didn't flunk anything. Still, she began to question whether she had any talent worth developing. Back on Junior Hall, she loaded up her books for the weekend. Her bag weighed a ton, but with two flunked quizzes she had to make a show of bringing home books, even if she never opened them.

"Tee, you're not going home!"

"My name is Tara. Okay?"

"And mine's Thomas. What's your point?"

Tara tossed up her hands. "I have no point. I am a broken pencil. Pointless." She slammed her locker, tug-tested the lock, and hoisted her backpack over one shoulder.

"You're coming to the game, right?" Raquel asked. "Then come to band practice. We could use you in the stands."

Tara practically snorted. "The band doesn't need a viola." And she could have taken it further, maybe launched into Raquel. "You're thinking of Teri, and her clarinet!" she could have shouted. "I was always in the next section. Teri sat beside you! Teri!" She might even have done that, except for a sharp interruption.

"Raquel, come!" a voice snapped, and suddenly Junior Hall was dead silent. The summoned girl hunched her shoulders almost up to her ears and started grabbing books from her locker.

"Leave that," the man said. "You can come back." Raquel stowed the backpack in her locker and padded lightly down the hall. The man dropped his voice, but everyone heard, "I got a call from your history teacher." Father and daughter disappeared around the corner, but no one moved until their footsteps faded.

"I can get you a drum," Flipper said.

"What? No." Tara repositioned the weighty backpack. "I've got enough headaches without actually banging on something." She started off and Flipper hung by her side. "Hey," she said, stopping where she knew they would part, "if I do come to the game, you give me a ride home?"

Stunned at first, he quickly recovered. "Yeah. Sure."

"Thanks."

As Tara trudged off to her rendezvous with a minivan, a feeling of desolation crept over her. Reaching the first Friday of the new school year wasn't a major big deal, but if Teri had been there, they'd have shared a moment, like they'd passed a semi-milestone. Instead, the week was ending with a dull whimper, and a million tiny irritants gnawed at her, not the least of which was that she couldn't even kill an hour at band practice, because she played the freakin' viola, instead of a cool instrument she could actually have fun with.

"PUT THE TRUMPET BACK," *the man said. "No daughter of mine is going to grow a satchel mouth from blowing a horn."*

"Fine!" The girl stormed off to the far end of the music store where a lady sat and lowered a harp onto her shoulder. She played it as if gates had opened on a magic kingdom.

"Would you like to try?" the lady asked. The girl nodded. The lady showed how to curve her fingers and pluck the strings. The girl went through a simple progression. It wasn't as magical as the lady's playing, but still she was entranced. The sound drew the man and her sister to that end of the store.

"It's a beautiful instrument, don't you think?" the lady asked.

The man flipped over the price tag: $5,500!

"You work on commission, don't you?"

"Of course, sir."

"You got something with strings that she can tote on the school bus?"

"We don't take the bus," the girl said.

"Shush."

A few minutes later, the girl had to choose violin or viola. She liked the lower, mellower tone of the larger instrument. She also took a little pleasure in the slightly higher price tag. But she nearly flew into a rage when her twin took hold of a clarinet.

"Dad said no horns."

"It's not a horn; it's a reed."

"So's a saxophone, but I couldn't get that."

"Well, if you explained it right…"

It was a long ride home. The man pulled over twice and threatened to take the girls back to the store. The girl was tempted to play the brat and call his bluff, but her twin's frightened eyes betrayed how much she wanted that clarinet.

TARA HAD HELD her tongue then and through eight years of studying viola. Not that it was a bad instrument. It just wasn't a trumpet. Or a harp. *Huh,* Tara felt a jab below her heart, as she thought, *Who's playing the harp now?*

She got a text: "Will be a little late."

"Gotta get a car," Tara groaned. On principle, she refused to do homework. Even if she waited three hours, she was not opening a schoolbook on Friday afternoon. So, she scrolled endlessly through *Instagram* and *Snapchat,* which was all kind of lame. As four o'clock approached, —*finally!*—the obnoxiously painted, orange-rust minivan turned into the drive, and Tara trotted down to meet it.

"Sorry, sweetie," Mom said. "Jeremy's teacher had an issue."

"Sure it was hers and not his?"

"We can do without the snark."

Tara settled into the second row next to Stacy, who was looking dour. Tara understood; there should be two big sisters climbing in. The one who paid Stacy the most attention was gone, and the survivor was only half there. Tara set her eyes front and saw her sullen brother without his omnipresent *PlayStation*. Apparently, teacher issues had consequences.

The ride home was quick, but eerily quiet. After helping to carry in groceries, Tara went to her room and flopped on her bed. Her bones and joints suddenly ached, and she felt like she'd never get up again. The family's big, old Labrador nosed his way into her room. Tara hung an arm over the side of the bed and stroked the furry lug as he lay down beside her. Then she thought about Crockett and drew her arm back to her side.

A tap at her door got her attention, and there was her little brother, standing sheepishly in the doorway.

"You want to walk Sammy?"

"No," he said. "Can I have Teri's clarinet?"

"No." She rolled back over.

"Mom said."

"Augh," Tara groaned and pulled herself up and over to the closet. She knelt down and started rummaging through the boxes stacked deep in the back.

"She keeps it under the bed."

Tara felt a leatherette pouch and pulled it out. Sitting on her haunches, which Sammy took as an invitation to curl up on her lap, Tara handed the pouch to the boy.

"That's a recorder."

"When you use your big sister's viola bow to shoot pencils across the room..."

"I was six."

"You don't get a six-hundred-dollar clarinet. You get a twelve-dollar recorder."

"Maaaaaahhhhhhm!"

It took about two minutes for their mother to demand Tara's presence in the kitchen.

"Are you making the rules for this house now?"

"No."

"'Cause if you are, maybe you could do a little shopping, cook a few meals." Her mother pointed to the kitchen island. "Here, tear up some lettuce for salad."

Tara took the head of lettuce to the sink and ran it under cold water. "How much?"

"About half." Her mother rinsed off a green pepper. "So, what's with the clarinet?"

Tara wanted to say Jeremy was too lazy to learn an instrument; the parents had given up prodding him to practice piano after six weeks. But Tara didn't have much standing in that regard, so all she could say was, "He'll probably play floor hockey with it."

"No, I won't," her brother yelled. "You got everything!"

"Hey!" the woman said. "What did I tell you?"

The boy retreated to the living room. Immediately, the gunfire from a video game shook the house. "Jeremy, turn that down!" the woman called. Tara placed the bowl of torn lettuce on the island in front of her mother, who eyed her sympathetically, but said softly, "She was their sister, too."

"I know."

"You don't get a monopoly on grief."

"I was going to use it," she lied.

The woman's eyebrows peaked. "When?"

"Tonight, at the football game. I was going to sit with the band."

"Can you play it?"

"Have you heard our band?"

"Good point." The woman scraped chopped vegetables from the cutting board into the bowl and handed her daughter a big wooden spoon and fork. "Toss."

Tara dug in from the sides of the bowl and snapped her wrists. A tomato wedge hit her in the nose and half the salad landed on the counter.

"Tara!" her mother squawked. "Calm yourself. What is it?"

The girl heard the garage door lifting. The man was home.

"Honey?"

The girl dropped the utensils and marched to her room. When she returned, the man was standing at the island, his tie loose and collar opened. The woman had put the salad back in the bowl, so the girl had space to lay quizzes. Man and woman stared for a few seconds at the very low, very red scores.

"These are starting to add up, sweetheart," the woman said.

"To not very much," the man muttered.

"I know."

The man scrawled his signature and slid the sheets across the counter to her.

"Did you read the assignments?" the woman asked.

"Maybe."

"What kind of answer is that?" the man demanded. "Honey, we know, it's early. And believe me, we don't want to be ogres here. We get that you probably don't want to study. You think we want to get out of bed every morning? Go into the office? You think it doesn't seem pointless to us, after pouring our love into a child for sixteen years...?"

The man bit down on his lips and pushed back from the kitchen island. He crossed his arms over his chest and leaned against the far counter. His posture reminded the girl of herself, burrowing into the chair in the counselor's office.

"Am I grounded?" she asked.

"No, sweetheart," the woman said. "You are decidedly not grounded. You are encouraged to fly."

"Just don't leave the planet," the man said. "And pay a little attention to your responsibilities."

The girl nodded, collected her quizzes, and went back to her room. A few minutes later, she was called for dinner, which was tense. She worried the clarinet argument would flair up again, and that her father, holding court like King Solomon, taking pride in decisions that left both parties equally miserable, would divide the instrument into five parts, so every member of the family could have one. To her relief, the subject never came up. Her father even volunteered to drive her to the football game. Back in her bedroom, she slung the clarinet case over her shoulder and draped a sweatshirt over it, hoping to render it invisible. As she passed through the living room, her brother saw it, but he held his tongue, at least until she left the house.

"I hear good things about the team," her Dad said as they pulled out of the driveway. "Maybe the best squad Coach C.'s had in years."

"Maybe," Tara said. "You never know." The girl looked out the window, rather than at the man. What was she hoping to prove with this instrument tucked under her arm? Feeling like a total fraud, she eyed the passing landscape: summer in full glory, yet fall intruding, scythe in hand. The reaper, not grim, but gleeful, busily clipped buds that would never blossom.

"Hey, sorry I barked at you," the man said.

"It's okay."

"No, it's not," he said. "I just...I guess I worry about you. The French, heck, I never got languages, so, do what you can. But History, that's always been your best class."

"No," she said.

"Sure, back to fourth grade. Remember? The teacher said to find out who rode with Paul Revere. And everyone came up with one other guy."

"Samuel Prescott."

"But you were the only one who found there was a third."

"Richard Dawes."

"See? You remember. You were so proud."

"Yeah," she sighed. "Only, that was Teri."

"No," he said. "Was it?"

After an awkward silence, the man turned on the radio. The girl looked out the window. The car ran so smoothly, she thought they were crawling, but the scenery flew past. She wished she could take the wheel.

They pulled off the freeway and into already thick traffic about half a mile from school. This local rivalry always produced a big turnout, even though no one expected the opponent to put up much of a fight. Students on foot started passing the car, so Tara opted to get out.

"Glad you decided to go, honey," her Dad said. "Have a great time."

Tara nodded and maybe half-smiled. In that next moment, enveloped by students heading towards the football field, Tara felt kind of normal again. Then it struck her that being conscious of being normal wasn't normal. Neither was carrying a clarinet she had no idea how to play, which might even cause onlookers to wonder which twin had passed away and which had survived. One had sat with the band every Friday night home game, scrupulously studying the sheet music on the stand before her and losing it all to a gust of wind that blew it onto the running track. The other twin had sat in an adjacent section, crammed on a bleacher plank with a half-dozen other girls, one bud on a crowded bough, posing duck-billed and *gangsta* for selfies, taking videos of plays and random goings-on, and posting them online. Mostly missing the game but recoiling at loud hits and focusing in for critical moments. And glancing over at her twin, playing that *Fight Song* and taking it way too seriously.

"YOU KNOW NOBODY LISTENS, RIGHT?"

"According to you."

"I'm just saying, you don't have to get all white-knuckled, you'll play better."

"I thought nobody listened."

"Well, it's a stupid song."

"It's not stupid."

"It's corny."

"You think everything inspirational is corny."

TARA COULD ONLY ROLL her eyes. She never knew whether Teri really was that nerdy, or just played nerd theater to impress the nerd hierarchy. During Freshman orientation, when the music teacher introduced the class to the St. Stephen's Prep *Fight Song*, he admitted straight-up that *Fly, Saint Stephen's* was a blatant rip-off of *On Wisconsin*. The hokey lyrics came courtesy of a founding priest seventy years ago:

Fly, Saint Stephen's!
Fly, Saint Stephen's!

Rise up to the sun
Where the clouds break.
Lo, our foes quake.
Keep them on the run!
Fly, Saint Stephen's!
Fly, Saint Stephen's!
Take off, Wrens, and soar!
Scale the heights of power and might!
We're sure to score!

The poor padre had done his best. But even with a catchy, plagiarized tune, who could write a victory march for *The Fighting Wrens?* The school's mascot came from an Irish legend that said some of the stones thrown at St. Stephen had struck and killed a wren. Stephen's followers had buried him, but no one had claimed the wren, except for some poor boys, who went around begging pennies to bury the unfortunate bird. The wren became a symbol of Christian charity but didn't do much to inspire fear on a football field. Over the years, students even made up mock cheers poking fun at the team's name.

"DON'T DO THOSE CHEERS, OKAY?"

"What?"

"You know what."

"Oh, you mean, Caterpillars, beetles, spiders and ants!

The wrens are coming, so you haven't a chance!

Wren power! Wren power! What d'you say?

<Tweet, tweet, tweet, chirp, chirp...>

"Why do you gotta make fun? We can't help the name!"

Tara reached the spot in front of the stands where she and Teri would have parted company. Flipper hung on the front rail, a huge *bodhrán*, resting between his feet. He was engrossed in talk with a classmate Tara had had less-than-little to do with since an incident last spring.

"Just stay on the twenty-yard line," Flipper was telling him. "On passing downs key on Syracuse. Running plays, get Arq. ... Tee!

You came!" Tara blushed, and the unwelcome boy cleared out towards the other end of the field. "I saved you something," Flipper said, holding up a triangle.

"Thanks, but I'm good," she said. How good remained to be seen. She climbed the steps to the second row, where Raquel sat on the edge. She sensed mute accusations from all sides: *Imposter! Fraud! Ghost! Usurper!*

"Teri's clarinet?" Raquel asked. Her tone held no accusation. Rather, she seemed to give Tara too much credit, as though she were honoring her sister's memory. "Can you play?"

"Scales," the usurper admitted.

Raquel laughed, showing her perfectly straight, white teeth. "My advice, find one really awful noise to make, and keep doing that whenever something good happens. Then, if we play *The Fight Song*, just pantomime."

"Gotcha." That hurdle cleared, Tara opened the clarinet case, and tried to remember how the pieces fit together. Then Raquel's elbow nudged her, and her friend smiled mischievously.

"What?"

"Obstbaum?" Raquel leaned back to let the other girls in on the juicy gossip. She had apparently been bursting with the news, so Tara felt flattered she'd held off until her arrival. Relishing her moment, Raquel announced. "He's rich!"

"No," Tara gasped. "He's such a slob."

"Oh, he's got money," her friend insisted. "You know that pot shop on Raleigh Avenue?"

"No!"

"He owns the license. And he's got another on Beaumont."

"What?" Flipper's voice rose an octave, and his huge ears seemed to flutter as he spun his head around.

Raquel explained that Mr. Obstbaum, for decades, had been a secret advocate for the legalization of marijuana, writing various articles under an assumed name, *John Q. Publius*. His arguments had gone all the way to the State Capital in Sacramento, where they were very persuasive, if not always logical. When California legalized medical marijuana in 1996, Mr. Obstbaum had gotten a permit to open a dispensary. Permits were extremely hard to get, but by that time he was well-connected, so he called in political favors, lined up investors and a couple of quack doctors, and *voila!* Then, when the state okayed recreational pot, Obstbaum expanded his business. He was now the largest dealer of cannabis products in the county. All this had come to light when Raquel's Dad had turned the tables at the meeting, asking why Obstbaum was even allowed to teach at a Catholic school.

Flipper echoed the question. "How's he teaching here if he's selling dope?"

"It's not illegal," Raquel said. "But Fr. Chandler ain't happy, the Bishop ain't happy. But they can't fire him; he's got tenure!"

"You think he gets high?" Flipper asked.

"I always knew that," someone said.

"At school?" another asked.

"That's still illegal," Raquel said. "He can't bring it onto campus."

"I bet he does," Flipper said. "I bet during his prep periods, he takes a stroll down to the bleachers or the duck pond and sparks up a doobie."

"Like on Fridays, when he's rambling all over the place?"

"My brothers used to say he'd go on how, 'the rich don't pay enough taxes,' 'they need to pay their fair share.' Ever hear that?"

"Not now," Raquel laughed, "'Cause now *he's* rich."

So, the meeting had been a clear victory, which might cause kids planning to boycott Raquel's party to change their minds.

"*Fight Song!*" the band leader called. "Music out!"

Tara finished fitting the clarinet together and looked up to see the team walking down the stairs from the field house. The band leader raised his baton, and the band attacked *The Fight Song*. The poor tune never stood a chance. Tara puffed her cheeks and moved her fingers, but it was all so fake that Raquel dropped her flute and laughed like she might roll off the bench. The Wrens charged across the end zone, tearing through a banner that Cheryl and the other cheerleaders held at the ten yard-line.

The team looked primed for another run at a championship. Under Coach C., *The Fighting Wrens* had won their league five of the last seven seasons and gone to the State Championships three times, winning twice. Today's presumed victims were the *Fremont Explorers,* who were geographically close but otherwise not in St. Stephen's league.

"They might be good this year," Flipper said. "I heard they picked up a Sumo."

"Idiot. He's a Samoan," someone said. "Like from Samoa."

The Explorers trotted onto the field, and Tara craned her neck. The new phenom was hard to miss.

"He's a monster," she gasped. Number thirty-six was a head above his tallest teammates and almost as big around. His midsection was nearly twice the size of his chest. Someone said his name was Lima Autufuga.

"He's one guy. They've gotta field ten more."

"I'm not sure ten will fit," Flipper said.

"Y'know, *The Rock* is from Samoa," someone else said. "This must be *The Boulder.*"

"If a boulder was carved out of butter."

At that point, the stands hushed for *The National Anthem,* done via recording, because Fr. Chandler had heard the band play it once and had sworn, "Never again."

Now Tara really got antsy. She held herself as stiff as possible so she wouldn't draw attention. She moved her lips but didn't sing. The crowd seemed to close in, with still more people descending from the parking lot, like zombies on the march. They stared into the stands, looking for seats, but maybe thinking, "There's that girl that drives in her sleep, and tried to dig up her sister's grave." Tara wanted to look away but feared making eye contact with anyone in the adjoining section. "There she is," those girls would say. "Took her sister's spot while it was still warm."

Fraud. Imposter. Usurper.

The team captains gathered for the coin toss, while Tara thought, *Heads I shouldn't have come, tails I should have stayed home.* The girl felt for the pen knife in her jeans pocket, there if she needed it.

St. Stephen's won the coin toss to loud cheers. From there, all the girl imagined was wrong with her seemed to ooze out onto the field.

Arquimedes, the star tailback, bobbled the kickoff on the five-yard line and fell on the ball. The offensive line started jittery, as Big Thirty-Six blew up every play. His blindside hit on the quarterback made a third-down pass flutter out of bounds. As their punter took his place deep in the endzone, the girl pressed her hands to her temples.

"You okay?" her friend asked.

The girl had no answer. And neither did her team. Fremont put Autufuga at tailback, and ran him up the gut, play after play. He battered the line, rumbling for five yards or more, before half a dozen Wrens brought him down. Eventually he made the endzone, then ran the ball again for the two-point conversion and an 8-0 lead.

"He's killing us," Flipper said. "And in super slo-mo. If the guy was any slower, he'd be running backwards."

The girl wished the game could move backwards. To last season, or Freshman year, so the true twin would be sitting there, and she'd be cheering across the aisle. She blinked herself back to present time. Fremont lined up on offense again, but without Autufuga.

"He's probably sucking in oxygen," someone said.

"Or cheeseburgers," Flipper scoffed.

"Now you guys are being obnoxious," Raquel scolded. "You don't know him. You don't know how he got so big."

"Yeah, it might be glandular."

"Or maybe he just ate," Flipper said. "Then he ate Samoa and Samoa and Samoa."

Raquel raised her flute, like she was going to smack him over the head. The girl tried to focus on the game, but the noise and crashing bodies and the closeness of the crowd smothered her. She hunched forward, elbows on her knees, and rolled her head side to side. A hand stroked her back.

"Wanna walk?" her friend asked. "C'mon."

They tottered down the bleachers to the dirt path that ran the length of the stands. The noise was a little less, and there was space to breathe.

"Better?"

She nodded. A gun went off, signaling the end of the first half, and she eyed the scoreboard. Her team trailed, 11-6. They walked on.

"Hey, girls," the priest greeted them. "We gonna pull this one out?"

The girl shrugged.

"Coach usually finds a way," her friend said.

The girl's golf coach was there, too. "Not to pry," he said, with every intention of prying, "but have you taken any whacks lately?" He half-mimed a golf swing.

"I whacked my brother this afternoon," the girl said. "And I plan to whack my sister tomorrow." They initially smiled, then grew grim. Maybe she ought to explain she had another sister, one who wasn't dead.

"Whenever you're ready," coach said, "we'd love to have you back."

"We'd love it," a senior girl echoed. She'd been in their foursome. "But no pressure."

An awkward silence followed, which the priest mercifully broke. "The only pressure tonight is from that big boy, thirty-six."

On that they all agreed, and the girl was able to excuse herself. After a few paces, she spotted a line of Port-a-Johns. As their nauseating aroma reached her nostrils, her fingertips brushed the penknife in her pocket. *No*, she thought, *I'm not that sick*. Tara trotted back to Raquel, and they retook their seats.

As the teams lined up for the second half kickoff, Tara wondered how much tolerance she had left for all the noise and tension. The game went nowhere, but up and down between the twenties. As the third quarter ground down, and with Autufuga back on the bench, the Wrens mounted a drive to Fremont's twenty-five. Then disaster. Autufuga returned from his breather and dug in across from the center. The Wrens' quarterback crouched in shotgun formation, but the nervous center sailed the snap over his head. Retreating, he scooped up the ball, only to be crushed under a pile of Explorers. Autufuga leapt up, waving frantically to the sidelines. Later, he would tell the school newspaper reporter that he had heard something crack.

CHAPTER
FOUR

"Falsehood flies, and truth comes limping after it…."
— Jonathan Swift, *An Essay Upon the Art of Political Lying*

AT THIS POINT, Tara was done. Whatever fun might have been worth the anxiety evaporated, and she wanted out. Well, that was just too bad. With no means of escape, she was stuck 'til the game ended, and the injury delay seemed to last forever. Trainers and paramedics hovered over Larry, the quarterback, who was moving his arms and legs, which was encouraging, except it showed he was in real agony. Meanwhile, his backup, wearing number seven, tossed on the sideline. Paramedics took Larry off the field on a gurney. On his way to the ambulance, he slapped palms gently, even feebly, with several teammates, including his replacement.

Raquel was practically beside herself. "Omigod, omigod. Nolan!" she screamed. "Go, Nolan!"

Tara hadn't realized that number seven was Nolan Copeland. "Go, Nolan," she mouthed silently, wondering whether that was a further homage to Teri, or another, more serious, usurpation. But Nolan did not go, nor could he get the offense going. He barked signals, and his offensive line jumped. After a five-yard penalty,

Nolan got the snap but, to hand the ball off, turned the wrong direction. Alone in the backfield, he rolled up like an armadillo as the defense swarmed. On third down, his pass protection collapsed, and he scrambled for his life and a minimal gain. Then on fourth down, Coach decided to go for it. That proved to be the right call, as this time Nolan was able to set his feet and throw a thirty-yard dart to Syracuse Jones, wide-open, and the Senior receiver jogged into the end zone, ten yards ahead of the nearest defender.

Flipper had caught the play on video. "My grandma could have walked it in," he laughed.

The touchdown made the score 14-12, but the Wrens failed in their attempt at a two-point conversion. The clock told Tara she had to endure six more minutes. With a two-point lead, Freemont planned to use every second feeding the ball to Autufuga, who gobbled up four yards a play.

"Ground and pound," Flipper lamented.

Each play ran forty seconds off the clock. But the drive faltered at the Wrens' twenty-two, and Fremont decided to try a field goal. The band leaned forward, hoping to transmit enough negative energy to disrupt the kicker's rhythm. "Miss it, miss it, miss it," they hissed.

The kick didn't have much height and wobbled but hooked just inside the upright. The score was 17-12. With 2:30 remaining, the Wrens needed a touchdown to win.

Though dizzy and breathless, and crushed from all sides, Tara had been sucked back into the drama. The kickoff came down on the ten, and Arquimedes broke off a solid return to the thirty-five. But Arq crumpled out of bounds, gripping his calf.

"Great time for a Charlie horse," Flipper groaned.

"Let's hope that's all it is."

"Whatever, Arq ain't coming back."

Tara watched Coach C. huddle with his new quarterback. She recalled how Obstbaum had grilled Nolan, demanding answers too fast, setting him up for failure. Now, Nolan seemed stiff, back on his heels. He held his helmet under one arm and nodded uncertainly.

On first down, Nolan took the snap and faked a handoff, then made a short toss over the middle to a receiver who was immediately gang tackled. On second down, the Explorers stuffed a run up the middle and Nolan called timeout. The next play was a quick pass down the left sideline that picked up six yards for a first down with thirty-five seconds left.

"They're giving us the middle of the field," someone said.

"Two timeouts left. Take a shot!"

The first shot was a completed pass to the eighteen yard-line. The clock wound down to twenty-five seconds.

As the officials spotted the ball, Coach sent a wide receiver in from the sidelines with a play. Nolan didn't get it; he grabbed the player by his jersey sleeve and asked to hear it again. Still not getting it, he looked to the sideline, and Coach, exasperated, called a time out.

The crowd groaned.

"That gives their big boy a breather," someone said. "Not helpful."

On the next play, Autufuga loomed large over the ball. He got a great push to collapse the pocket and hurried Nolan's pass, which sailed over Syracuse's head, incomplete. There were nineteen seconds left.

"Enough for one short pass and one shot at the endzone."

Again, Autufuga led a strong push up the middle, forcing Nolan to backpedal and throw off-balance. The ball sailed, hitting the chest of a Fremont safety, who bobbled what would have been a game-winning interception. A gasp of relief went up from the St. Stephen's grandstand.

"I guess that's why *he* doesn't play offense," Flipper laughed.

On fourth down and ten with only eleven seconds left, the all-important endzone was eighteen yards away.

"Last shot, right here. Go, Wrens!"

"Go, Nolaaaaaaaan!" Raquel yelled.

Nolan started in the shotgun but called a check and stepped forward under center. With a hoarse, barely audible voice, Nolan coughed signals to the left, then turned his head right and repeated them. Facing forward, he grunted a quick "hut-hut." The ball snapped, and the lines slammed together. Nolan backpedaled and rolled right. About to pass, he tucked the ball to evade a blitz, while an open receiver did jumping jacks in the endzone for attention. When Nolan finally set his feet to throw — *Wham!*

Lima smashed Nolan in the middle of the back, taking him out from under the ball, which dangled weightless in mid-air, out of time and space, before falling to the turf. The gun sounded, ending the game, and jubilant Fremont players poured onto the field. Stupefied, the Wrens wandered back to their bench.

The grandstand swirled around Tara as band members gathered their instruments and slid past, but her eyes stayed fixed on Nolan. Down on his right knee, he rested his left elbow on his opposite thigh and stared at the endzone. The blue-and-white striped turf shone under the light towers like the surface of a distant, more perfect world.

"Yo, Tee!" Flipper shouted, "Walk with us to the Music Room."

After all this, a forced march to the other end of campus?

"I'll meet you by your car," she said.

"You sure?"

Very.

Flipper pointed up above the opposite grandstand, where his battered *Jeep* sat under a drooping cypress. It was a conspicuous wreck, with worn paint and bold patches of rust, passed down through three brothers. Tara wandered over and up, then sat on the *Jeep's* front bumper. She looked down at the field, which suddenly went dark as the light towers dimmed to black. Then eerily, as a band of stars brightened in an arc across the sky, the yard markings and numbers glowed, seeming to levitate from the surface. Tara squinted to focus the field out of this strange dreamland and back into reality. That's when she saw the boy walk straight down the center.

In his uniform pants and a tee shirt, he carried his shoulder pads, draped in his jersey, by the face mask of his helmet which was tucked underneath. He dropped this makeshift briefcase at the far end's thirty yard-line, around the spot where the final drive had stalled. As Tara watched, Nolan replayed the down, pausing wherever he'd made a change of direction. He froze momentarily, then turned his head full range from left to right. Then he moved on to the next critical point.

After watching him replay the down a couple of times, Tara scampered down the hill, cut around the visiting bleachers and crossed the running track to the fence. She watched Nolan run his drill again. At the point where he was just about to throw, the point where he got hit, he dropped his arm. Nolan raised his eyes to the night sky, as if begging the stars for a second chance.

Tara wanted to call out. "Don't beat yourself up. It wasn't your fault." She thought of hopping the fence, but a rumble in the distance caught her attention. A column of boys marched two abreast down the steps from the locker room to the field. They started singing the corny *Fight Song* as they jogged down the home sideline. When they reached the thirty yard-line, where Nolan was standing, they veered left, holding their arms out like a swarm of fighter planes and formed a circle around him.

When they had Nolan surrounded, they stomped in place and Syracuse Jones led a chant the players echoed:

"Stephen don't fear no sticks and stones!
Stephen don't fear no broken bones!
Ain't no tears in Stephen's eyes;
He can clearly see the prize!"

"Alright, alright," Syracuse said. "Now, we are a team. And as everybody knows, they're ain't no *I* in team. Nobody likes a ball hog. Or a glory hog. And what goes for winning goes equal for losing. Nobody hogs the blame. Man, if I didn't get alligator arms, drop that pass in the first quarter, we'd a never needed that last drive."

Arquimedes spoke next. "I didn't help much sitting on the sidelines when you all needed me."

Around the circle it went, each boy confessing his contribution to the loss. With each admission, Tara's throat got tighter. Her eyes welled up.

"Yo, Tee," Flipper called. "Where are you?"

Tara sniffed and wiped her nose. She sprinted back to the steep grade. It would be a lot harder to scramble up than it had been sliding down.

"Down here," she called.

"What are you doing?"

"I...I don't know."

"Well, walk out the other end and I'll meet you."

"Okay." So, as the team left the field towards the north end, Tara jogged behind the bleachers to the south end, and walked up the service road to the far side of the parking lot. She stopped when Flipper blinded her with his high beams and pulled up alongside her. She pulled the passenger door open, and the cabin lit up. She was even more conscious of her red, wet eyes.

"You hear something?" he asked.

"No, what?"

"They say something about Larry."

Tara had to think for a moment. "No. I don't know."

"Okay," he said. "We'll find out. You wanna get something to eat?"

"Sure, whatever," she said. "Let's just go, okay?"

Flipper spun the wheel left and eased the *Jeep* toward the exit, which was still backed up with waiting vehicles. Tara really needed not to cry. People said it made you feel better, but *wrong*, it was worse every time. Emotionally, physically. *Augh*, the way she sobbed when she got going, she'd rather get slammed by Autufuga. Maybe if she ate something, she'd feel better.

Flipper drove to the *Cattle Drive* at Greenvale Mall, right next to the *AMC 16 Cinemaplex*. From the west, fog was starting to creep in over the hills, but the eastern skies were still clear, and some stars were visible. Tara gave a quick thought to searching for constellations—something she was never good at—but dropped the idea as Flipper rounded the rear of the *Jeep* and stopped for her. They headed toward the neon logo of a yellow lariat hovering above the white horns of a red steer. "Holy cow," Tara thought, remembering the old Dad joke.

"What's it like working here?" Tara asked, dropping a hint that maybe Flipper could help her get a job. She wanted to make her own money, and last summer had been such a total bust.

"You can't caddy?"

"Melissa did. She says girl caddies don't make much money."

That struck Flipper as odd. "Inequality," he said, "is one reason the workers of the world must unite." Then, with a tug on the front door handle, he added, "And this is another."

Tara was startled by a radical transformation. Lined up across the front counter were electronic kiosks, screens alight with bold, yellow letters asking, "May I take your order?"

"What the —?"

"Owner said he had to do it," Flipper said. "We were all jazzed when the state raised the minimum wage to fifteen dollars. Then the boss started laying everybody off."

"Well, that stinks."

So, instead of five or six workers at the counter, there was just one person, a tall, Black teenager at the cash register. Flipper bounced up to him and slapped a grip on his large hand. Flipper shook vigorously, or tried to, because the other boy's arm hardly moved, then Flipper winced and threw up his left hand as a gesture of surrender.

"Tee, this is Clarence. Clarence, meet Tee."

"Tara," she said, then regretted how grouchy she sounded.

"Pleased to meet you, Miss."

Flipper proceeded to give an order that could have fed half the Varsity squad. "Grab a seat," he told her. "I'm gonna say 'Hi' in the kitchen."

"I'll bring your food to you," Clarence said, adding with a wink, "Table service for our special guests."

Tara wasn't sure what the wink implied and knew better than to ask. She took an unoccupied table by the window looking out onto the entrance of the cinema. From there she could also see into the kitchen where Flipper was glad-handing the workers, who tipped a glance in her direction, smiled and then turned back approvingly towards Flipper. *He's not telling them we're together?* she thought. How was she going to nip this problem in the bud?

She turned away toward the window. A combination of dust and harsh interior lighting made the world outside seem like a separate reality. She caught her own reflection as she strained to bring the exterior world into focus. A crowd flowed from the doors of the cinema. A movie must have let out.

Tara watched the people—'tween and teen friends, families, and dating couples—stroll across the white, concrete plaza and out into the parking lot. Some kids clustered at the curb, waiting for rides. A girl stood alone. Honey blonde, five foot six or seven, she hung her hands in the front pocket of a red hoodie before taking a cellphone out of the rear pocket of her black jeans and scrolling to make a call.

Teri, she thought. Tara slid across the booth and pressed against the window, cupping her hands on either side of her eyes. As impossible as it was, Teri was standing there in her favorite *'Niners* sweatshirt and *Levi's*, torn in the exact spots where she'd obliterated the fabric with Dad's 40-grit sandpaper.

Flipper placed a tray of food on the table. "S'up?" he asked.

"Omigod," Tara gasped. She slid off the bank and bolted for the door.

"Where you goin'?" Flipper called.

Apparently nowhere, because half a dozen people decided to enter the *CD* at that precise moment. Tara got frozen at the door, then wove through the mob, and ran to the curb just as a black minivan rolled away.

"She's gone," Tara said.

"Who?" Flipper asked, pulling up behind her.

"Teri," Tara said. She stabbed at the concrete with her hand. "Teri was standing right here. Waiting for a ride, and I missed her."

Flipper's mouth hung open, and his eyes looked hard left into the parking lot. "Okay."

"I'm not crazy; I saw her."

"Okay." His lower lip protruded as he wrinkled his brow. "You think she saw *Lion King?* 'Cause I'm wondering if the CGI's as good as the cartoon."

"Augh!" Tara held up her clawed hands like she could choke him.

We should look for her, she thought. *But that's crazy...and something else. There's something else.*

"Um, food's getting cold."

That's it, Tara nodded. *Dang, I'm hungry.*

———

"I TELL YOU WHAT WE DO," Flipper said as Tara shoved the last piece of burger into her gaping maw. He held up his cellphone and said, "Hold it. Wait, wipe the ketchup off your mouth."

Tara grabbed a napkin and scoured her lips. "What?"

"Say 'cheeeeeese—burger!'" He snapped a photo of her.

"Can we do that again?" she asked.

After several clicks had produced one photo Tara didn't find insulting, Flipper slid out of the booth and said, "C'mon."

They walked to the register and Flipper held up his phone to Clarence.

"C-Man, I want you to find me a girl who looks like this."

Clarence looked at the screen, then at Tara. "Since you already got one, seems downright greedy to demand another." Tara took the remark as a compliment, though the idea that Flipper had *got* her was a bit unnerving.

"What I mean," Flipper explained, "is a girl who looks like her just went to the movies. High school girls go to the movies once, twice a month, right? A lot of those times, they come into the *CD*. Am I right?"

Clarence nodded along.

"I'm gonna print this picture out. You put it up in the kitchen. A girl who looks like this comes in, I get a call. Any time, day or night. Clear?"

"Crystal."

Flipper jabbed an accusatory finger at Clarence. "I told you not to call me that!" They both laughed at what had to be an inside joke, shook hands and went through the many stages of ritual farewell common among Northern California males. Out in the parking lot, Flipper expounded on his plan.

"We're the number one burger chain. In this county alone, we've got twelve locations. I put your picture in every kitchen…"

"I'm not sure that's a good—"

"We're gonna get a hit. We're gonna find this girl."

"Okay," Tara said. She tugged on the door and stepped into the *Jeep*. She closed the door and clicked her seatbelt. She waited for Flipper to strap himself in before saying, "You don't think I saw Teri."

"You saw something," he said. His tone was neutral, not patronizing, and she appreciated it. "And I think if you see what you saw again, that could, I don't know, settle things."

"Yeah. Thanks."

Flipper twisted the key and the engine turned over. Tara was happy to be going home.

———

FLIPPER PULLED into her driveway and killed the engine. Tara unclipped her seatbelt and ducked forward. Her intent was twofold: to grab the clarinet case on the floor and preempt any thought Flipper might have about kissing her goodnight. She popped the door before she picked her head up and had one foot out the door before she turned back to face him.

"Hey, thanks for everything," she said.

"You're going to Raquel's tomorrow, right?"

Tara slung the clarinet case over her shoulder. She let a moment pass before answering. "Yeah. For sure."

"I can pick you up on the way."

Tara's forehead auto crinkled. "Dude. You live on her block."

"I sometimes take the long way."

The long way was twenty minutes out of his way.

"What time again?"

"She said it starts at five," Flipper said.

"So, the cool kids arrive at—?"

"Six fifteen. Super cool kids arrive at seven-thirty."

Tara had to laugh. "Well, that's not us!" she said. "How 'bout we split the diff? Pick me up at six-thirty?"

"You got it."

Tara was so grateful he didn't say, "It's a date." She smiled and threw the door closed, then trotted up the path to her front door. She fumbled for her key and opened the door as Flipper's *Jeep* rolled down the drive.

Inside, Tara was a little spooked. It was only 10:45, but the living room lights were out and there wasn't a sign of life. Peering through the dining room, Tara saw low lights in the kitchen, where her Dad stood at the island, hunched over her Mom's computer.

"Hey, sweetheart," he greeted her. "How was the game?"

"Not good," she said, then regretted the downer tone. "I mean, okay. I mean…"

"I take it we lost," he said. "It happens."

Tara crept closer. "Flipper took me to the *CD*."

"Was that… a date?"

Tara didn't respond. She leaned her elbows on the island and peaked at the computer screen. An article bore the headline: *How Boys Cope with Grief.*

"I'm sorry about earlier," Dad said. "The history thing."

"It's okay, Dad," she said. "Teri was your twin, and I was Mom's. Nobody planned it; that's just how it was." His look seemed to say a million things: we should have tried harder; I loved you both the same; I'm sorry. Tara hoped her look said it didn't matter, but also that she was sorry; she'd done everything she could to save her. The perfect match, except not.

"You want some *Nighty-Night* tea?" Dad asked. "I find it helpful for shutting down brain functions."

If only. "No, thanks. What happened with Jeremy today?"

"Oh, nothing," Dad said, taking a swig from his *World's Best Dad* mug. "It's complicated."

"So, which?" Tara asked. "Nothing or complicated?"

Dad put the mug down. He gripped the counter with both hands and took a step back, like he was prepping to do a spread pushup.

"A girl in the eighth grade got some bad news. Due to privacy rules, we don't know what that news was. But she was crying, and Jeremy hugged her."

"So, that's the big crisis? He's like a crazed hugger?"

Dad straightened up and reached for the mug again. "He couldn't let go."

Tara felt the floor dip a little underneath her. She tugged on the strap of the clarinet case as if it might hold her up. Still unsteady, she eased away from the island and walked toward the darkened hallway that led to her bedroom. Her Dad closed the laptop and flipped off the kitchen lights.

"Goodnight, sweetheart."

"'Night."

Tara pulled the strap off her shoulder and lowered the clarinet case to the floor, setting it outside Jeremy's door. *Little dork*, she thought. *He's never going to play it.*

She wondered if she should cut tonight or just let it go. There's a limit to how much you can do before it gets unhealthy. But this week had been hard, so tonight would be okay.

CHAPTER
FIVE

"No man for any considerable period can wear one face to himself
and another to the multitude, without finally getting bewildered as to
which may be the true."
— Nathaniel Hawthorne, *The Scarlett Letter*

TARA LAID TERI'S stuff out all over her bed. Not all of it, but
stuff Tara wanted to get rid of and some stuff she didn't. Like her
Mom said, "If giving doesn't hurt a little, you're not giving enough."
The bedspread was covered with Teri's CDs, her iPod, her good
headphones for studying, ankle and wrist weights, her watch, a
candle-making kit, a statue of St. Teresa of Avila, and on and on.
Tara knelt at Teri's bookshelf and started pulling out paperbacks
they'd both read and tossing them onto the bed: *The Hunger Games*
series, the first book of *Twilight*, *The Hobbit*, *The Fellowship of the Ring*,
Fahrenheit 451, *The Outsiders*, and *Picnic at Hanging Rock*.

Tara stared at the cover: a photo of schoolgirls in white dresses
and broad-brimmed hats sitting in tall grass.

"Where do you think they went?" Teri asked.

"I don't know. Maybe fell through a crack."

"To where though?"

A Wrinkle in Time.

Teri: *"When are you gonna stop reading kids' books?'*

Tara: *"It's not just for kids. It's got ideas."*

Les Misérables.

Teri: *"1,488 pages and done!"*

Tara: *"Still only counts for one. Meanwhile, I read five. So, I'm really done."*

Teri: *"That's not fair."*

Tara: *"Hey, I don't make the rules."*

Dracula.

Teri: *"It's cool the way all the different characters tell the story in letters and diaries."*

Mom: *"Oh, that sounds fun."*

Tara: *"Yeah. Imagine now? It'd all be texts. Doc wants to hang garlic. LOL.... Y?... IDK. ... SMH."*

Frankenstein.

Dad: *"Knowledge is knowing Frankenstein isn't the monster. Wisdom is knowing Frankenstein is the monster.*

Tara: *"Huh?"*

Teri: *"I get it! I get it!"*

To Kill a Mockingbird

Teri: *Maycomb County. May comes. In the spring. And robins are a sign. So, even if the trial didn't work out, Tom Robinson was a sign for the townspeople."*

Tara: *"You make my brain hurt. Can't you ever just enjoy the story?"*

Teri: *"The more you know, the more you enjoy."*

Not. Always.

Tara dropped a bunch of other books on the bed and called Jeremy and Stacy.

"Okay, Teri's stuff. You should have some, so, take what you want."

They just stood there, staring at her, not the bed.

Then Jeremy asked, "Are you gonna commit suicide?"

"No. Why—?"

"When depressed people give stuff away, it's like they're saying 'good-bye.'"

"I'm not depressed."

"You take anti-depressants."

"No," Tara lied.

"Yeah, like I don't hear what gets said in this house."

Tara snapped, "Listen, you little snot, do you want the stuff or not?" Stacy giggled. "What?"

"You rhymed."

"Maaaaaahhhhhhm!" Tara stormed into the kitchen. Her Mom was standing behind the island with her laptop open. "I tried, I really... but they are impossible."

"I'm not impossible," Stacy said.

"I know, Stace," Mom said.

"How can I be impossible, if I'm right here?"

Tara flashed back to last night. The girl had been right there. But still it wasn't possible.

"Perfectly sensible, sweetie," Mom said, as she brushed a wisp of platinum hair from in front of the little girl's powder blue eyes. "Now, let me talk to your big sister. And Jeremy, you've got chores to do. Those leaves aren't going to rake themselves."

"I'm getting' a leaf-blower!" he declared.

"Jeremy William Hartzwell, if you ever unleash that ungodly noise in this neighborhood, I will personally check you into the Youth Detention Center." Jeremy moped his way out the front door, and Mom gestured for Tara to sit. Mom grasped the top of Stacy's head, turned her like the lid of a pickle jar, then nudged her towards the living room.

"I remember when your hair was her color. Yours and Teri's." After scanning her computer screen for a moment, she asked, "So, why the sudden desire to give away Teri's things?"

Tara shrugged. "It's just stuff. I got her clothes. Everything I can use."

"And the clarinet?"

"I'm not very musical."

Mom rolled the ball on her computer mouse. She clicked once, twice. Tara leaned forward on her elbows to see that she was searching through recipes. "Just so you know," Mom said, "this morning Jeremy decided the clarinet is a girl's instrument."

"*Augh*. He's such a weirdo."

"None of us are tracking normal these days. Yesterday, your Dad bought a two-hundred-dollar bottle of wine." Tara's eyes widened as her jaw dropped. "And he wants to drink it this weekend for no special reason, except 'we should live every day...'" Mom couldn't finish the sentence. "So now, I've got to prepare a Sunday dinner that's fit to serve with two-hundred-dollar wine. But I'm going to be patient with your father, because he's been patient with me, and I need him to keep it up." She started tearing. Tara reached for the box of tissues and slid it across the island to her. "Thank you." She wiped her eyes and blew her nose. "But the next two-hundred-dollar bottle he buys, I'm going to crack over his thick skull."

Mom selected a recipe and clicked to print it out. Tara heard the printer whir below the countertop.

"Mom, these pills I'm on."

"The new pills?"

"Yeah. Can they make me hallucinate?"

"Good question. Make sure you ask Dr. Schraeder."

"*Augh!* Is that today?" Tara slapped the countertop.

"Yes," Mom said firmly. "And you're going." She reached beneath the counter for the printout. "Saturday appointments are very hard to get." She handed Tara the recipe. "What do you think, *Le gigot d'agneau Pascal*?"

Tara curled her upper lip. "It's leg of lamb." She handed the recipe back.

"Not impressive enough?" Mom scanned the page. "Whoa. Seven hours. I did not see that." She folded the page in half and stuck it in a drawer. She turned back to her computer. "So, honey, are you seeing things?"

Tara squirmed on the stool. "I thought I saw Teri. Last night, through the window at the *CD*. A girl outside the movies looked just like her."

"Did you get a good look?" Tara wagged her head, so Mom said,

"Just an impression? From a glance? That's not really an hallucination. I mean, if there was a girl."

"By the time we got out, she was gone."

"Alright. See what Dr. Schraeder says," Mom said. "If this is all —"

"Yeah. I mean, this was all. Ever. I'm not like hearing voices. Or driving. That I'm aware of."

"Okay," Mom nodded. "And, um, you know, I think I see her, too. When there's a crowd of kids. Waiting outside the grammar school, I think I see her in her old jumper, running to the car." She grabbed another tissue. Tara slid off the stool and walked around the island. She wrapped her arms around her Mom's waist and hugged her tightly. She buried her face in her hair. It was hard to let go.

―――――

"HAVE YOU DREAMED ABOUT TERI, TOO?"

Tara had just told the doctor about her school dream. How she showed up without an arm or leg. "Not since we changed the pills."

"Well, that's good, isn't it?"

Tara puffed her cheeks and blew out a slow stream of air. "I don't know. I wanted the dreams to stop, because they hurt too much. But at least they connected me to her. Now I don't feel anything. And I'm not connected to anything."

Dr. Schraeder turned some pages in Tara's file. "What was the last dream like?"

"I just told you."

"No, I mean that last dream with Teri."

Tara leaned her head back and slouched into the chair. *He takes notes on everything, but never remembers what I say.* "It was a golf course. But the grass was yellow with wisps of white thread. Teri was ahead, and I was in a sand trap. Hitting and hitting, but the ball wouldn't move. And there were hundreds of balls, and I didn't know which to hit. Teri said, 'Hit any.' But I couldn't, and I was sinking in the sand. And Teri, on the hill above the trap, said, 'I'm not waiting for you.' And I said, 'Dad, Dad, make her wait.' And she laughed. And that's when I remembered, *she's dead*. And I, like, fell on all fours and cried. And then I woke up."

Tara reached for a tissue and blew her nose. Dr. Schraeder pursed his lips and nodded. He did that weird thing with his mouth, like he's swooshing mouthwash around.

"When you were having the dreams," he asked, "did you notice a pattern? How they would play out?"

"I don't know. I'm talking to her. I'm frustrated. And I remember she's dead. Anyway, it doesn't matter; except for that one night before school, I'm not dreaming anymore."

"Do you miss the dreams?"

"I miss my sister. And—" Tara hesitated. *How much trouble is this going to cause?* she wondered. "I thought I saw her. Last night."

"Okay, tell me about that."

Gee, that woke him up, Tara thought. She went through the whole sequence, how she looked through the window at the *CD* and ran out to find the girl, but the van drove off.

"Did she seem real to you?"

"Nothing feels real, okay?" she suddenly shouted. "My family's a joke. My Mom falls apart one minute and the next, she acts like nothing happened. The littlest things make her totally hysterical. But I get sad for a few days, and they put me on pills."

"You were a little more than sad, weren't you?" the doctor asked.

"Maybe." Tara sensed some defensiveness in his tone; he had told her Dad he didn't just dispense pills like gumballs. After Teri died, Tara didn't eat for three days. She couldn't sleep at night or get out of bed in the morning. The pills let her function, at least.

"Do you feel, maybe, your mother's grief is crowding yours out?"

"Her house, her rules," Tara grunted. "It's like the perfect model family got shattered, and now, we have to be the perfect model shattered family. With the perfect cars and the perfect house and the perfect clothes, faces all scrubbed, dressed up and marching to Mass every Sunday to pray to the same God that didn't answer our prayers the first time. You know what Einstein said, 'The definition of insanity is doing the same thing over and over expecting different results.' Only, I don't even think they expect results."

"They?"

"My parents. It's just a show for the world."

"Going to Mass?"

"And everything, but especially that."

"Why do you go?" Tara rolled her eyes. "Why not stay home?"

"That would go over big," she said.

"So, you do it to keep peace with your parents? What about the peace within you?"

Tara groaned. "I thought that's what the pills were for."

Dr. Schraeder adjusted his glasses. "The pills are so you can sleep at night and get out of bed in the morning. You can't process grief with a pill."

How 'bout with a sharp knife? Tara wondered.

"It requires persistent effort," the Doc said. "Which is often tedious and sometimes quite painful. You can't expect to heal in leaps and bounds. Baby steps."

Tara nodded. "The short strokes. My Dad always said that's where the game is won or lost. 'You drive for show, but you putt for dough.'"

The doctor gave a muffled *hmph*. After a second of notetaking, he asked, "Is there something about golf?"

"What about it?"

"That's the third time you've mentioned it." His salt-and-pepper eyebrows rose above the rims of his glasses. "Do you miss it?"

"Golf was Teri's thing." Tara wrung her hands. "I never would have done it."

"But you were better at it."

"What?" Tara sneered. *Where's this guy get his information.* He flipped through her file again.

"Over your last two seasons, you beat her twice as often as she beat you."

"That doesn't mean anything," Tara said. "She had better form. Better concentration."

"But, in any sport, isn't it the score that matters?"

Tara shrugged. "I got lucky."

"That's obvious," the doctor said. "You're still alive."

78

Tara felt a deep jab in her gut. She pressed her palms together and her hands rose in prayer position to her open but mute mouth. She felt an impulse to dive; her shoulders rounded, and she pitched forward. Her fingers pierced her lap and her thighs pressed tightly against them until the cuts burned. She sat there hunched for who knows how long. *The lucky twin. The one with the healthy blood, red and rich and ready to be drawn, whenever.*

"Tara," the doctor asked, "is there anything else you'd like to talk about?"

Tara relaxed her thighs and the sting subsided. She smoothed her slacks with her palms. "Nah, I'm good."

———

TARA DIDN'T EAT dinner because she knew Raquel's party would have insane amounts of food. With her Cuban father and her Italian mother tag-teaming on the buffet, even the football players fell into food comas. So, while the Hartzwells dined, Tara sat in the living room, scrolling through her phone and waiting for her ride.

"Is Tara dating Flipper?" Stacy asked.

"Not allowed," her Dad said. "Against the rules of the house for any girl to date a boy named after a fish. No Flippers, no Marlins, no…"

"I bet she could date Mike Trout," Jeremy said.

"Well," Dad conceded. "He'd be a good catch."

Of course, they all thought that was hilarious. Tara couldn't stand it. "First of all," she barked, "he's not named after the TV *Flipper*. He got the name from his doing his job, which maybe should earn him some respect? And anyway, TV *Flipper* was a dolphin, which is a mammal, not a fish."

"Methinks the lady doth protest too much," Dad said.

Tara growled deep in her throat, before responding, "And methinks Lord Shakespeare could mind his own business." Mercifully, the doorbell rang.

"I'll get it!" Tara sprang towards the door.

Her Dad pushed away from the table and hooked an arm over

79

the back of his chair. "Invite the young man in," he drawled. "We'll set for a spell."

"Oh, what, are we hillbillies now?" her Mom laughed. "A second ago, we were at Stratford-upon-Avon."

"I'm a man of many countenances," Dad glowered.

"Yeah, and all of them are dork. Bye!" Tara slipped through the door and closed it tight behind her. She could hear her family laughing as she marched past Flipper and down the path to his *Jeep*.

"Uh, hi?" he said.

As they strapped in, Flipper appeared immensely proud of himself.

"What?" Tara asked.

"I got it done," Flipper said, as he twirled the steering wheel and pulled away from the curb. "Hit every *CD* in the county. Gave the manager your picture and told 'em to text me if a girl looking like you showed up. Be ready to strike, Tee. 'Cause when I get the call, it's cheetah time."

Tara stared out the window and caught her reflection, like a ghost of Teri popping out of nowhere. Like the girl at the mall. If there had been a girl.

"With speeds up to 75 miles per hour, the cheetah is the world's fastest land mammal."

"Yeah, I got the reference," Tara said. "Should we bring something? To the party?"

"I'm bringing you," Flipper shrugged.

Tara mumbled, "Then I guess I'm bringing you." *This evening was off to a grand start.* The drive took fifteen minutes. Raquel lived close enough that they'd gone to the same school since kindergarten, but far enough that the twins had only seen her at school, Sunday Mass and parent-chauffeured play dates. Loads of their friends lived by Raquel, but no one their age lived in their own neighborhood. That had never seemed to matter, but these days Tara's 'hood seemed totally isolated.

Raquel's street was already lined with cars, so Flipper parked the *Jeep* in his own driveway. The Carnes home was technically ranch-style, with a wide front façade and a low-pitched roof. But ranches are meant to sprawl; this one seemed shrunk to fit a miniature lot. All but the garage, which was oversized and dominated the property. What should have been a small lawn was invaded by crabgrass and trampled to dust. The overall effect was comical and sad, and Tara wished they'd at least add a coat of paint, so she could maybe say something nice about it.

"Well," Flipper said with a trace of snark, "on to Castle Fuentes."

The home everyone else called "Casa Fuentes" was grand and classic Californian. It sat on the crest of a steep hill, surrounded by a white, stucco wall topped with red brick. Guests entered through a wrought-iron gate and followed a tiled path up to a heavy oak door. The two-level home had a white façade and orange, terracotta tiles on the roof. Tara's Mom, a real estate agent, said the style was "Spanish Colonial Revival."

"What's our house style?" Teri had asked.

"Heavily mortgaged."

"You know what I heard?" Flipper asked. "Why Raquel gives so many parties?"

"What?" Tara braced herself for some dumb rumor to keep kids away from Raquel's party, punctuated with the hashtag #CancelCasa-Fuentes.

"I heard in seventh grade she went on a sleepover, and the girls were playing *Truth or Dare*, and Raquel got so offended, she told the girl's Mom she wanted to go home. In the middle of the night."

"Sounds like bull to me," Tara said. She hoped her tone, flat and dismissive, would get Flipper off the subject. She wasn't about to tell him she'd been at that sleepover, and that Raquel's panic was really over a *Ouija* board one girl had brought for a séance. Tara and Teri had held the board between them on their knees, and it had started shaking. The twins both said, "Quit it!" at the same time and realized neither was doing anything. Raquel said they had to put the thing away. Then one girl, trying to calm her down, touched Raquel and passed a shock. It was just a carpet shock, but everyone heard the crackle and in the dark they saw a blue flash. That's what had freaked Raquel out. "Anyway, who cares what happened in seventh grade?"

"Not me," Flipper said, "I just heard her Mom wants to control her environment."

"Whatever. Nobody's forcing you to go eat their food."

Flipper shrugged. "It's social justice. Redistribution of wealth."

Casa Fuentes reminded Tara of the old California mission churches, like Santa Barbara. Centuries old and classic, but still looking fresh like back in the day. She loved the umbrella-shaped magnolia trees that shaded the front yard. In spring, they bore white, saucer-sized blossoms that filled the air with the sweetest perfume. By now, many of the blossoms had fallen, scorched in the July and August heat.

The front yard was set up for *Kan Jam* and giant-sized *Jenga*. As Flipper opened the iron gate, a yellow *Frisbee* floated across the path. A loud shriek startled Tara as a couple of girls jumped, and the wooden *Jenga* tower collapsed in pieces at their feet. *Get a grip, girls*, Tara groused to herself. *It's wooden blocks and gravity, not the end of the world*. A couple of *Jenga* girls gave her and Flipper odd looks, maybe trying to size up if they were a couple. Tara marched past like she had business on the rear deck. That's where all the action usually was, but the odd quiet suggested not much was going on.

Tara followed the portico around the southern wall. The spacious back deck could hold a formal dinner party, and watching the sun set from there was pretty special. From the deck, Raquel's Dad had built a redwood staircase down the slope of the hill, with two landings and carved out terraces, one with a koi pond and the other a flower garden. At the very bottom was the garage, rumored to house a cherry-red 1967 *Camaro*.

"Is Raquel rich?" Teri had asked.

"It's not polite to ask," their Dad said.

Tara took in the view as a shimmering, orange disc slipped like a magic coin into a slot in the dark headlands. And she wondered, *Was Teri jealous of Raquel?*

"Tara!" Raquel called from the first terrace, where a couple of hoodie-clad guitar strummers had opened their cases and were starting to tune up. Cheryl was there, too, but conspicuously without her hive. "I have to go," she imagined their Queen telling them.

"We've been friends so long. But no reason for you to be bored all night reliving sophomore year." Cheryl had to be here, because she'd slipped. She'd let Tara hear her give the stand-down order meant to tank Raquel's party. Now, Cheryl gave Tara side-eye as she flipped through a songbook.

"I'll be right up," Raquel said. "Say hi to my Mom!"

"Okay!" Tara said.

She paused to savor the spread on the patio table. Enough for an army, if they ever showed. She might have plucked a morsel, but Flipper blocked her path. He had cornered Syracuse and had him watching a video on his cell.

"What you wanna show me that play for? I know I shoulda had it."

"Sorry, not that one. Here"

Flipper scrolled to another clip and pressed play. This time 'Cuse nodded along.

"That's more like it, but we lost, so what's the point?"

"You know the point. You need a slam-bang highlight reel. But! Do you want clips from the school's staticky, fifty yard-line camera, that looks shot from outer space? Or do you want *this*: close-up, snap-to-whistle coverage of Syracuse Jones?" Tara sensed the pitch would not end well.

Inside the kitchen, Mrs. Fuentes was at the sink, wrestling a dirty pot. Seeing Tara, her face lit up and she pulled off her rubber gloves to give her a warm hug.

"It's wonderful to see you," she said. "It's been too long."

"I haven't been too sociable."

"I understand," she said. "How's your Mom? I heard she sold a house?"

"I think there's an offer," Tara said, totally faking it. She hadn't heard anything, or maybe her Mom said something while she wasn't listening. Strange, 'cause selling a house was a big deal. Always a cause for family celebration. But maybe her Mom thought the perfect shattered family wasn't ready for a night out at *Benihana*.

Raquel burst through the door, out of breath, and gave Tara a hug. "So glad you made it!" she squealed.

"Hey, Miss Bubbles," Mrs. Fuentes said, "dial down the effervescence. Don't make her regret coming."

"I'm just happy."

"Make me happy and carry that gnocchi out." Mrs. Fuentes pointed to a casserole dish on the kitchen table.

"It's okay," Tara said.

Mrs. Fuentes gave Tara's forearm a squeeze. "Sweetie, I told Raquel you can't expect people just to, you know, turn things around too fast. Takes time. And she says, 'Mommy, but I don't even know if I should keep inviting her.'"

Raquel blushed and Tara sensed she was on the verge of telling her Mom to button it. But she just stood and listened.

"Because she thinks it might make you feel worse. But I told her, 'You keep being a friend, and you let her decide when she's ready.' Oh, but listen to me!"

"Yeah," Raquel laughed, "You're really making her sorry she came!"

Mrs. Fuentes pantomimed beating her breast in contrition and continued tidying up her workspace. She picked an old, yellowed index card off the kitchen table, flapped it in the air and blew white flour residue off of it. Then she flipped open a small file box and squinted to find the right tab.

"I haven't gone digital," she said. "I'll have to someday, since my daughter never learned cursive."

"Did, too!"

Mrs. Fuentes had a way of teasing that put Tara at ease, and she'd relieved her mind about Raquel's belated invitation. Then Cheryl appeared, and Tara went back on yellow alert.

"Are drums okay?" Cheryl asked Mrs. Fuentes. "Not just congas; Vinnie showed up with his whole kit, and I thought maybe the neighbors...?"

"Drums are okay 'til ten o'clock," Mrs. Fuentes said. "'Til then, it's just nasty phone calls. Any later and we'd have to bribe the cops."

The girls laughed. Cheryl said okay, lingered for a second—obviously not eager to leave Raquel and Tara alone—then skulked out.

"The gnocchi?" Mrs. Fuentes prodded. Her dutiful daughter

grabbed up the casserole and started for the door. Tara followed, but Mrs. Fuentes grabbed her hand. She cupped Tara's jaw in both hands and kissed her on the forehead. "I love you as my own," she whispered. Tara felt a flutter in her stomach that moved up and brushed her eyes. "Now get the heck out of my kitchen."

Tara felt like she wanted to kiss Mrs. Fuentes back, but that would make her a total dork like Jeremy. Maybe Mrs. Fuentes was controlling, like Flipper said, but she wasn't nit-picky. She just, well, "had flair," as Tara's Mom had said. According to her, "Annamaria Fuentes could work ten hours in a kitchen preparing dinner for twelve and still answer the door looking like the cover of *Vogue*." Her Mom also said, "Elegance is a luxury of the rich."

But old, yellowed index cards weren't luxury items. And Tara suspected that if Mrs. Fuentes had to conjure a meal suitable for expensive wine, she wouldn't have to search the Internet. That suspicion triggered a moment of brooding, and Tara snuck another look at Mrs. Fuentes. Was her "elegance" enough to make Rebecca Galvin Hartzwell jealous? Did her Mom and Teri share some secret Fuentes envy? Tara felt a pang of... *what?* Something like abandonment. She retreated to the back deck.

"Five hundred bucks?" Syracuse shrieked. "You want *me*. To pay *you*. Five hundred for a three-minute reel?"

Flipper backpedaled like he was fleeing Lima Autufuga. "Wait, wait, what I said was, this kind of finished product is worth five hundred. For a friend, I can negotiate price."

"We friends, Flipper?" Syracuse laughed. "When'd that happen? Nobody told me!"

"Come down to the koi with me," Raquel said, tugging Tara's arm. The steps, usually lined with high schoolers, were bare. Tara recalled her last party here, Raquel's birthday, and how she'd wound up under these stairs with Jimmy Cerrone. She'd just given Teri her bone marrow, and waiting to see if it worked was excruciating. Her parents had insisted Tara go out, at least for a while. And so, when Jimmy offered to drizzle a shot of rum into her Coke, Tara figured, "Why not?" She needed to relax. She did not expect, half an hour later, to be under the steps, letting him kiss her, leaning into his chest, opening her mouth to his tongue. At first, she'd warmed to his touch; the hair pricked up on the back of her neck, her skin grew taut, eager. But then she felt cheap. Reckless. Her breath quickened, as his fingers played across her ribs, and glided upward. Then something in her soul ached, like she was taunting Teri, greedily seizing pleasure her sister would never have. His hands kneaded and tugged, and she struck. The heel of one palm thumped his sternum. Her other hand swung wildly, smacking his cheek and rattling his jaw. Party over.

At the first landing, Raquel's grandfather, a fixture at her parties, was goofing with the guitar players. A spare man, he always wore a stingy-brim, straw fedora. That and his bushy, salt-and-pepper mustache, slightly tinged with cigar stains, marked him as a figure from times gone by. Kids were polite, calling him *'Buelo*, short for grandfather in Spanish, but regarded him as a character, like out of a black and white TV show on *Decades* or *MeTV*.

"I don't know where everybody is," Raquel said. They sat on the bench that faced the koi pond. "Is there something else going on?"

Tara shrugged mutely and angled herself towards the instruments.

'Buelo strummed a guitar and sang softly. The boys must have liked the song, because one brought a microphone over, and they asked him to start again. Then someone cut the background music and all attention went to *'Buelo*. Tara liked the delicate melody, and *'Buelo* sang with tenderness, even if his voice was raspy.

Raquel nudged Tara. "I think he's singing to you."

"Your grandpa?" Tara laughed.

"No, silly, Flipper."

"What?" Tara practically spat. But true enough, over *'Buelo's* shoulder, craning his skinny neck, Flipper was strumming a guitar and singing along.

"*Aquellos ojos verdes*? You have green eyes."

Oh no, Tara thought. *This is not happening. Flipper is not singing me a love song in front of…. Augh.* Raquel started translating for her. "Longing for caresses, for kisses and for tenderness…"

"Stop it," Tara pleaded. Then she saw Cheryl smiling her wicked, amused smirk, so Tara knew she was stuck. If she showed any sign she was rankled, she'd never live it down. The song went on for an agonizing three minutes, and it actually was cute the way Flipper harmonized with '*Buelo* and echoed some of the phrases after he sang them. Then it occurred to Tara they must have run through it a couple of times. Which made it all the more premeditated and touching and horrible if Flipper really was singing to her. He didn't look at her; he kind of looked in her direction, so maybe he was peripherally looking at her. Oh, maybe she should just tell him her Dad's rule that she couldn't date fish.

The song finally ended. Raquel jumped to her feet and applauded wildly. Tara stood, too, acting polite despite her deep dread of what would come next. Flipper would ask what she thought and say it was for her, and then....*Augh*, she smoothed her skirt and wrung her hands together. There had to be a way out of the yard, other than the stairs that were right by the band. Searching for an escape route, her eyes glanced at the back porch. There, nodding quiet approval, stood Nolan Copeland. Tara's knees buckled and she sat back down on the bench. She gripped the inside of her thighs until the wounds burned. *I can do this*, she thought, and rose from the bench. But where was she going?

"Tee!" Flipper called, announcing her moment of truth.

"Nice song," Tara said with strained nonchalance. "I didn't know you..."

"Hold on." Flipper pulled out his cellphone and pressed it to his ear. "You gotta be kidding me! ... No, alright. Alright! Gimme fifteen." Flipper turned back to her. "I gotta go in."

"Oh?"

"Northfork *CD*. Fry cook burned his hand. Went to the ER." He wagged his head as he pocketed the phone. "Can you...?"

"I'll be fine," she said, hiding her relief. "I'll just call my Dad."

A guitarist strummed a quick chord progression and the drums kicked in, drowning all talk. Flipper tossed up his hands and hiked a thumb over his shoulder to mark his exit. A couple of *Jenga* girls staked out the ground between the band and the koi, stepping to an old, boring line dance. Tara felt too much like a garden gnome:

stationary, scowling. Then a pang of hunger hit, and she remembered she hadn't eaten.

She climbed the stairs to the deck, squeezing through some football players to the buffet table. Mrs. Fuentes had outdone herself with ravioli and rigatoni and stuffed shells and manicotti and gnocchi. But Tara decided those were too much work, so she grabbed a grilled brat on a toasted bun and squirted some mustard on it. She tore into it like a wolf and crossed to the ice chest. She grabbed a bottle of water, and thought, *What am I even doing here?* The party was going to be lame, and there wasn't even a crowd she could hide in. She'd stand around consoling Raquel, watching blue flames from the *Sterno* cans dry out the uneaten food.

Then she couldn't open the water bottle. It was soaking wet, and she couldn't get a grip, especially with half a brat in one hand. The other half was still in her mouth, turning to concrete, and she didn't know whether to bite down on the bottle cap or shove the rest of the brat in her mouth to free up her other hand. Which was when she heard, "Ca' I help you with that?"

The large right hand of Nolan Copeland took the bottle. He gave the cap a twist and handed it back to her. Smiling, he pointed to each of her cheeks, saying, "I've seen chipmunks store food like that. *Discovery Channel.*"

Tara curled her lip in appreciation of his humor, then took a swig of water and eased some of the brat down her throat. "Thanks. Nothing a girl likes better than being compared to a rodent."

Tara wasn't sure where that remark came from; her feelings toward Nolan were a bit complicated, given his kiss-and-fade with Teri. But that's what boys do, right? Take Jimmy Cerrone. Boys have a chance to kiss a girl and take it. They don't count on her having leukemia a week later.

To diffuse the situation, Tara walked toward the front yard. But having a girl walk away must have been a new and unsettling experience for Nolan, because he did something Tara was not at all expecting: he followed her.

"Hey, uh, Tee —"

"Tara," she corrected him. The witchy attitude was jarring — even to her—but rather than soften her tone, she doubled down. "You're not going to tell me about your pet hamster?"

"Are you still mad at me?" His question was earnest, but so oddly off base. *Still mad? Since when?*

"I'm not mad," Tara said, sounding at least a little bit mad.

They stood there, not looking at each other or the floating frisbee or the teetering *Jenga* tower, for what seemed like a long time.

"The thing with Teri was complicated," Nolan finally said.

"Not really," Tara said. "You didn't even date. Why get sucked into our family drama?"

Nolan looked like he wanted to say more, but the sudden loud thumping of a car stereo cut him off. A black muscle car pulled up at the curb. The music kept hammering, drowning out every party sound, even as the driver opened his door and rose to scan the grounds of Casa Fuentes. He appeared about their age, roughly six feet tall with lean muscles stretching the fabric of his black and gray tee. His hair was jet black and stood at spiked attention two inches above his perfectly manscaped hairline. The stranger stood with one hand on the roof and another on the door frame, his emotionless, grey eyes scanning the grounds, until everyone gave him their attention. Then a click of an electronic key cut the engine. The party sounds returned, but it might just as well have been dead silence.

Nolan had already scaled the boundary wall and was crouching on the sidewalk peering into the car's interior. Of course, Tara realized, it's a *Challenger*.

"That's my car," Nolan gushed.

The stranger crossed the front bumper through the eerie radiance of the headlights to the curb. "Ease up, Champ," he said. "My ride, and I've got the pink slip to prove it."

"Nah," Nolan chuckled innocently. "I meant that's the car I want. If I can put the cash together."

"Didn't come cheap, that's for sure."

Tara was watching this automotive lovefest from just behind the wall, her hands resting on the red bricks. The stranger eyed her coldly and asked, "Don't I know you?" Tara shook her head, but he took a step closer and tilted his head as if he was inspecting her. "Yeah, I'm sure I do."

"Uh," Nolan straightened up to his full height and stepped between them. "Now's my turn to say, 'Ease up, … Champ.'"

The stranger ran a slow scan of Nolan from his feet to his face, letting his eyes burn into Nolan's until a smile curled the corners of his mouth. "You got a pink slip?" he asked.

"You got business here, you better state it," Nolan said. "Otherwise, move on."

"You the man of the house?" he asked. "Pretty sure the man of this house could buy himself any car he wanted."

"I'm the guy telling you to state your business."

He looked again at Tara. "It can wait," he said, and he turned back towards his car. He rounded the front end and clicked the ignition. The engine roared and the music boomed. He opened the front door and gave Nolan one last look. "Later, Champ." Then he ducked inside and peeled out, disappearing down the far side of the hill.

Tara released a breath she didn't know she'd been holding and slumped with her elbows on the wall. Nolan touched her shoulder and lowered his forehead to rest on her crown. "Sorry," he said. "That escalated quickly."

"Ya think?" Tara huffed. Straightening up, she patted Nolan's shoulder with her left hand and turned right, directly into the gaze of Raquel Fuentes. The noise had drawn her and Cheryl into the front yard. Now her face turned pale, and she bolted back towards the house.

Tara darted after her, but Cheryl cut her off. "Haven't you done enough?"

"I'm just getting started."

Again, Tara couldn't quite say where that remark had come from, nor could she have expected Cheryl to interpret it as a threat. But she did.

"What are you going to tell her?" Cheryl demanded as she dogged Tara's heels up the lawn to the portico. "You better think about this first."

"Or what?" Tara laughed. "Off with my head? Don't worry about canceling me, Queenie. I can cancel myself."

Tara followed Raquel in through the side door, which led to the dining room. Raquel retreated to the opposite wall, crying. With the table between them, Tara pulled out a chair and sat. Each girl stared into space for an awkward moment.

"You're not very romantic, are you?" Raquel said. The question was so out of left field, Tara didn't know how to respond.

"I don't know. I mean, I don't even know..."

"A perfectly nice boy sings to you. A beautiful song."

Which I couldn't understand, Tara thought, *but I guess that doesn't matter.*

"And you don't even—"

"Raquel, listen," Tara said, "there's nothing between me and Nolan. Okay?"

"No, he was just going to fight a complete stranger for looking at you."

"I—" Tara had to admit Raquel had a point. But... "So what? Boys fight all the time. You think we control that? You invite a hundred kids to a party and twenty show up; do you control that? I've got news, Miss Princess-who-has-everything, we control nothing. Life is just random pain that we numb ourselves to, 'til we're so numb we look for more pain, just so we can feel alive again."

Having delivered the mother-of-all-rude-guest outbursts, Tara stood panting like a cornered fox at the end of the hunt. She watched as Raquel's eyes moistened and glimmered. The girl set her jaw, but her lips trembled as she said quietly, "I think you should leave."

"Yeah, that's a good idea."

Outside again, Tara pulled out her cellphone to call her Dad and...*Augh!* The battery was dead. She hadn't even used it since... when? She just wanted to chuck it down the hill. She was halfway into a mock windup when who should appear, but....

"What's up with Raquel?" Nolan asked.

"Nothing. She just doesn't like street brawls outside her party."

"Oh." Nolan tucked his chin to his chest. He folded his hands together and ran them over his hair to the base of his skull. After a breath, he asked, "Can we talk?"

"That is *not* a good idea."

"Why?"

"Because," Tara whined. She felt like stamping her feet. Instead, she grabbed Nolan's arm and led him off behind a magnolia tree. "You don't want to talk to me. You want to talk to Teri, but you can't. And you might think talking to me is like talking to her, but I'm a totally different person."

Tara spun away and pounded the path towards the sidewalk, where she stopped and thought, *What the heck am I doing?* She paced a few steps one way and then the other. Maybe she could walk down the hill. There was a *Peete's* coffee shop like a quarter mile away, and maybe she could charge her phone.

"Hey," Nolan said quietly. He had followed her. Again. "Does totally-different-Tara want to get out of here?"

This is not happening, this is not happening, this is not happening.

"My car's around the corner."

Omigod, Tara thought, *this is really happening.*

CHAPTER
SIX

"There are things you need not know of,
though you live and die in vain,
There are souls sicker of pleasure
than you are sick of pain."
— G.K. Chesterton, *The Aristocrat*

FOR ST. Stephen's students, "getting out of here" usually meant a drive to the overlook at the crest of Mount Pomo. Once there, they generally got a better look at each other than at the scenery. To his credit, Nolan knew better than to suggest the notorious make-out spot. But he lost points for not knowing where else to go. Then he got points back when he produced a car charger so Tara could revive her phone. They drove aimlessly and chatted about football.

"So, Larry, is he okay?"

"Had surgery this morning for his collar bone. Coach said it went fine."

"That's such a bummer. But you played great. I thought. Not that I know much about football."

Nolan smiled and tipped his head towards her. "You know we lost, right?"

"Yeah, I got that." A knot started to form in the pit of her stomach. Tara couldn't shake the image of Teri's pained face as she pleaded, "Don't." It was a couple of weeks before she passed. Teri hadn't seen Nolan in three months, but as she got sicker, she became more and more fixated on him. "He'll come see me," she'd say, but he never did. She told Tara to ask him to come, but their Dad quashed that.

"It's a matter of your sister's dignity," he'd told Tara. "We're past the point for outsiders to come breezing in."

Then, one afternoon, shortly after they'd learned the bone marrow didn't work, Teri threw a fit. "You're going to get everything. Swear to me— Swear!— not Nolan. Ever. Let me have one special thing that doesn't get handed down."

"I understand," Tara said.

"Promise me you won't date Nolan."

"I promise."

And she'd meant it. She wasn't hiding any feelings for him. She didn't have any. But here she was—not exactly on a date, but— driving around with her dead twin's not-quite-boyfriend. Maybe where they should go was the cemetery, so she could dance on Teri's grave.

The car rose up a familiar incline, and Tara instinctively looked right. The light towers caught her attention, then the high netting, shimmering as it drooped in the airless night. "There," she told Nolan.

"The driving range?"

"Yeah," Tara practically chirped. "I have a sudden, uncontrollable urge to hit a bucket."

"Can't say 'No' to uncontrollable urges." Nolan turned at the light.

This was the range where Bill Hartzwell had drilled his twin daughters on the art of the drive. It was much shorter than an actual fairway, but it served their purposes. Before the twins had ever set foot on a golf course, they'd spent a hundred hours here, swinging with reckless abandon, lofting balls high into the lights before they fell pitifully short of the nets. It would be a year before either twin struck a ball that even reached the net after an extended roll. Eventually their persistence paid off with straight, deep drives proving they were ready for the front nine.

Tara and Nolan each got a bucket of balls and a driver and proceeded to the tees.

"I didn't know you golfed," Tara said.

"Not much," Nolan admitted. "I play lots of baseball. So, when I first went for golf, I thought it would be like tee-ball for little kids. Man, it's, um…"

"Way harder?" Tara laughed.

"Way!"

Tara teed a ball and set her stance. She felt energized, like a missing part of her had been restored, like somehow, she was whole again. Then she swung and shanked the ball badly to her left. *Well, that's deflating*, she thought, and she reached for another ball. This time, she took a couple of practice swings, settled, and breathed a couple of times in rhythm. Then she drew her arms back. When she rotated towards the ball and her arms accelerated, she felt that familiar snap. The ball sprang from the tee and sailed straight down her lane. *I'm back*, she sighed.

Meanwhile, Nolan was hitting pop-ups to the shortstop. Tara watched him hook a couple of balls, then roll his shoulders in frustration. He was hitting right-handed, so they were facing each other, and their eyes met.

"You need to widen your stance," Tara suggested. Then, taking her driver, she measured the width of Nolan's shoulders. "That should be the distance between your bunions."

"I don't have bunions," he laughed.

"Well, whatever, your big toe joints."

"My grandma has bunions!"

"That's what my Dad calls 'em."

"Does he have bunions?"

"Just widen your stance," Tara said. "And be quiet." Tara returned to her tee, embarrassed and irritated, but actually enjoying herself. She felt even better when Nolan started launching balls high into the netting.

"That worked," he admitted. "It's good, 'cause with baseball, I start closed but I stride open. But there's no stride in golf."

"That there isn't," Tara said, as she shot her last ball into the night.

"Want another bucket?" Nolan asked.

"Nah, I'm good."

It was still only nine o'clock and Tara didn't feel like heading home quite yet. Down the road a quarter mile was *The Orchard*, an outdoor mall that attempted to combine commerce and open space in a dual use environment. Tara's friends knew it as *the place* to see shoppers get knocked over by skateboarders. They wound up at the "dancing fountain" on the plaza between the *Cine 12* and yet another *Cattle Drive*. After watching the fountain gyrate through its various spout patterns, Nolan got up the nerve to speak.

"I know the thing with Teri was a mess."

Tara knew he meant *his* thing with Teri, which wasn't even a thing, and she wondered why she needed to hear about it and how she could get him to just put a lid on it? But she decided to set a firm limit of one freak-out a night, so she just let him talk.

"I guess I figured, since we never really went out, there was nothing to break off. We hadn't hung out for like a week when I found out she was sick. So, going to see her to say, 'I'm not into this,' that seemed kind of lame. My Dad said, 'Trust me, you're the farthest thing from that girl's mind.' And so, I figured… Give your family space, right? I just kept praying she'd get better. Then all the girls started snubbing me, and I'm hearing they're all mad how I treated Teri. So, now if I go see her, it's to show I'm not a jerk. Which would really make me a jerk. And it's my first year training for the Decathlon, and I'm this close to being DQed in every subject. None of that's an excuse, but… Such a total mess."

"No one's mad at you," Tara said. "And your Dad was right," she lied, "you were the furthest thing from Teri's mind."

Nolan flashed half a smile. "Well, that's good." He rolled his shoulders and stretched the tension from his neck. For a moment he just stared off into the sky like he had on the field after the game.

Tara lifted her eyes to try to see what he was looking at, but there was nothing but a few points of light on a dusty backdrop.

"What's out there?" she asked.

"That's what I'd like to know, but, hey," he said, pointing with his left arm. "There's Cassiopeia, above the trees. You know her, right?"

"The queen?" Tara asked.

"Yeah. She's the five bright stars in a W." Tara couldn't make out the grouping but took his word for it. She followed his hand as he pointed slightly east. "And she's married to this king, Cepheus, on the right."

"How do you know astronomy?"

Nolan shrugged. "Apparently, us dyslexics are good at patterns. Since I was a kid, I could pick out constellations. I see those dots, and—*boom!*—the picture is right there in my mind. I can read defenses, too." He pitched forward onto his feet and stood as though he was under center. "I know from where they're lined up who's coming, who's dropping back. I just, uh…"

"What?"

"I can't hear the call and know what the play is. I don't connect the sounds to the name written in the playbook or the patterns. It's too many layers and not enough time."

"Auditory processing disorder?" Tara asked. Nolan dropped his jaw as if to say, *Listen to you, talkin' the teacher talk!* "My brother was tested," she confessed. "Turns out he just daydreams."

"That's what they said about me," Nolan said. "Like I was staring out the window to…escape. I just, um…" He waved his hands around his ears, as if crazy noise was rattling around in his skull. "I have to screen things out to focus."

"I get it," Tara said.

"Yeah, so when Coach sent in the plays," Nolan rolled his head back and laughed. "Three at once. Dang, well, y'know, he's got the wrong boy there. It's like, y'know… Obstbaum's class?" He deepened his voice to imitate their history teacher, "'Take out your textbooks and open to page two-hundred and sixty-three, paragraph two.' And I take out my book, 'cause I got that part, and I sit there, like, *Wuh he say?* So, Coach thinks I got three plays; I'm a go boom, boom, boom. Y'know?" He punctuated the sentence with forward thrusts of his right hand like he was passing. "But he freakin' lost me." He laughed again, which mystified Tara; she didn't grasp how he could laugh off such a serious problem.

"Anyway," he veered back to the original subject, "I dig stars. They get me thinking of, I don't know, mind-blowing possibilities."

"Oh, yeah?"

"Well," he puffed his cheeks and ruffled his hair, like he was trying to massage the thoughts out of his mind down to his mouth. "Scientists say there are about 40 billion—*with a B*—Earth-sized planets in the 'Goldilocks Zone.' You know what that is?"

Tara wagged her head.

"It's...y'know, not too hot, not too cold, just right?"

"Baby bear!"

"Yeah, call it the Baby Bear Zone. Where conditions are right for life to happen. And maybe just one-tenth of the Baby Bear planets actually have life. And maybe one-tenth of them have intelligent life. That's still 400 million planets with intelligent life, just in our galaxy. There are like 100 billion galaxies."

"You're hurting my brain with this Math!" Tara laughed.

"Yeah, sorry," Nolan said. "But with all those possibilities, you could duplicate this Earth like a million times, and have things exactly the same, except one or two minor changes."

"Oh, I saw this movie," Tara blurted. "George Washington is killed in the American Revolution. We lose, 'cause he was 'the indispensable man.'"

"Wow, that's major," Nolan laughed. "I'm just thinking, maybe on some planet somewhere, I'm me, but not dyslexic. And maybe Teri, maybe she doesn't get sick."

"Yeah." Tara thought, *Maybe me instead*, but caught herself in time. "Y'know, you could have warned me there'd be Math, and whatever this is, philosophy?"

"Kind of wild, huh?" Nolan said. "Kind of makes you hungry, huh?"

After a second, Tara nodded. Nolan hiked a thumb over his

shoulder and started walking backwards to the *CD*. "Best Burgers in the Western World!"

Tara rocked forward and popped onto her feet. But before she trotted after Nolan, she had to take one more look at the stars. Maybe that's where all life's wonder, the enchantment, had migrated. Maybe she just needed to set her sights a little higher and her spirits might revive. Might.

Nolan pivoted to grab the door handle and pull it open for her. Tara passed, then froze in the doorway, and Nolan bumped her. She half-turned and planted a shoulder in the middle of his chest. "Maybe we should get pizza."

Too late. Nolan heard the boys' voices from the booth against the right-side window. No way he'd turn and leave now.

"It's okay," he said. Tara felt his fingers squeeze her left shoulder as he drew her aside and strolled over to the table of Fremont High jackets.

"This a victory party?" Nolan asked. "What's on the menu?"

"Wren. Roasted." The table erupted in laughter. Which was kind of gross, 'cause Lima Autufuga was there, and opened wide a mouth full of masticated burger.

"Pass on that," Nolan said.

"Ha! Maybe he wants to eat more grass." More laughter, but Lima shushed his friends, and wiped his lips which were dripping ketchup.

"Hey, how's your boy doin'?" he asked.

"What I wanted to tell you. He had surgery, gonna be good as new."

Lima nodded, his eyes softening with relief. "That's good. You tell him mah Moms is prayin' for him."

"Sure. I'll tell him."

Lima tipped a glance at Tara. "Now who's this here?"

"Oh," Nolan stepped aside and gestured, "This is Te— Tara."

Tara took it as a compliment that Lima swallowed before speaking directly to her. "Well, Te-Tara," Lima said, "you ever want to hang with some winners, you know where to find us at."

Nolan wagged an index finger at Lima. "Not sure that offer's gonna be good for long. We see you again."

"Oh, we be ready."

"Yeah," Nolan smiled. "You boys keep up your strength. We want you full speed when we take our revenge."

After a brief round of palm-slapping and fist-bumps, Lima grabbed hold of Nolan's arm and held him there. Tara felt her phone buzz with a text.

"I'm a say somethin,' Seven, 'fore I let you go." Lima chuckled and winked at his teammates. "They's tons of white boys—these guys can tell yo'—ask 'em *wassup* and all 'em try come off *gangsta*, like they in the thug life 'cause they got Snoop Dogg on they iPod. They ain't never buried a brother 'cause of thug life. Ain't had a fam'ly had to move, so they kids don' get dragged in the thug life. So, it's good you're real. Stay real, Seven."

The boys at the table, all darker toned than Lima's bronze, had nodded along to his speech. Tara read in their faces the scars of senseless violence. Nolan chewed on his lower lip before breaking into that slight, what-the-heck smile of his. "I'll be real when we play again."

To a chorus of jeers, they left the Fremont table and went to the order kiosk. Tara checked her phone. The message was from Flipper: "Call me."

"What do you want?" Nolan asked.

"Just, uh, *Sprite* and fries."

The phone vibrated. Flipper again. "Cheese steak."

"You okay?" Nolan asked.

"Yeah, just my Mom. She's like, really clingy these days." They found a booth across the room from the Fremont guys and waited for their order to come up. They sat in slightly awkward silence for a few seconds, then a thought occurred to Tara, and she had to ask. "When I bumped you and knocked your binder open. You did a lot of work for that class."

"Flow charts," Nolan nodded. "It's a 'learning strategy' the tutors are way too excited about."

"It doesn't excite you?"

"I'm just goin' with the flow," Nolan said as he passed his right hand, palm down, over the table between them. "And, uh, I'd appreciate keeping that between us. The whole 'picture learning' thing is, uh, a little too easy to make fun of. Anyway, speaking of flow, I'm going to hit the restroom before the food gets here."

Nolan strummed his fingers on the table then slid to his left and strutted to the back of the restaurant. Tara wondered if she should text Flipper back. *What did he mean by 'cheese steak'? Augh*, she didn't want to deal with that. *After that song?* What would it look like if she texted him back immediately? The Fremont boys oozed out of their booth, smoothed their jackets and shook out their slacks. They filed out the door with Lima bringing up the rear. He paused with the door in his hand and jutted his chin towards Tara.

"Yo' boy Seven's got class," he said. "Who gives respect gets respect."

Tara didn't know how to respond. *Thanks?* But, apparently, no response was expected. Lima lumbered out the door and Tara turned her attention back to her phone. She flipped through *Instagram*, checking if there were posts from Raquel's party. She found a video of the band—who knows what they were calling themselves this week—playing that *Maroon 5* song, *Girls Like You*, with those sophomore *Jenga* girls still doing the line dance. Tara wondered if, maybe, in one of those Baby Bear planets, 100 million light years away, she and Teri were in the mix, stepping, shuffling and kicking, while the boys sang about their special girl.

Was there a planet somewhere in the vast reaches of space where the Hartzwell twins, the curiosities of freshmen orientation, actually became the stars of the Class of 2019? The thought burned in her mind so hot, she knew the danger of holding onto it. But like a moth drawn to a flame, she almost begged for immolation.

The food came and Tara dove into her fries, served Colorado red with Southwestern seasonings. The lemon-lime tang of *Sprite* was the perfect palate cleanser. For a North Cali high school girl, this was caviar and champagne, so Tara was in the nearest place to heaven 'til a fierce slap on the table brought her back to Earth.

"Tee! It's you!"

Tara jerked back and locked eyes with Flipper.

"You get my texts?"

"Uh," Tara stammered, "you wrote 'cheese steak.'"

"What? No! Cheetah." He groaned, pulling his phone from his pocket. "Freakin' autocorrect! They called me saying the girl that looks like you was here. But apparently, it's just you."

"Apparently."

Flipper blew a long stream of air. Like a tire with a slow leak, he shrank into the booth. After a beat, he got a quizzical look on his face, and his eyes slid from side to side. "So, why're you here? Raquel's party is…"

"Still going. No doubt."

"So?"

They stared at each other for a couple of seconds before Tara's eyes shot up to her right. Flipper followed her line of sight to Nolan, who stood at the edge of the booth.

"Perfect," Flipper spat, and he vacated the booth. "I put my job on the line to come here. For you." He glared at Tara. She tossed her hands towards him, but he waved her off. "Last favor I ever do."

"What's the problem?" Nolan asked.

"I'd explain," Flipper scoffed, "but I haven't got the time or the crayons."

Nolan slammed him against the window and pinned his forearm under Flipper's chin. Flipper slapped feebly at the rigid arm, as if comic absurdity was his best defense. Tara shrieked. In that moment all she saw was a muscular demi-man tossing a raggedy boy-child and potentially breaking his pencil neck.

"Nolan, are you crazy? Let go!"

Tara got Nolan to release Flipper without crushing his larynx, but Flipper was not grateful. "I'm done, okay? I'm out. Whatever crazy things you see now, you deal with. Lookalike girl, ghost of Teri, whatever, you track her down. Good luck. Don't call me."

By now half the kitchen staff was out, scowling angrily at Tara and Nolan as Flipper straightened the collar of his *CD* smock and tramped defiantly towards the kitchen and the rear exit. The staff retreated with him, leaving Tara and Nolan alone in the dining area.

"What's his problem?" Nolan grumbled.

"You wanna talk problems?" Tara huffed. "Let's talk about anger management. Let's talk about fifteen minutes to take a whiz. Nobody's that dyslexic."

"Hey, that's not cool," Nolan objected.

"Okay," she conceded his point, but stopped short of apologizing. "Where were you?"

"I got a call," he said. "Didn't want to be rude; I stepped out the back."

Tara's eyes rolled upward to the ceiling. *This is what I get for trying to have a normal social life.* "Can we go?"

"I didn't eat yet."

Tara slapped both palms over her face.

"Fine," Nolan grabbed his burger and drink and went to toss them in the trash.

"No!" Tara yelled. "Don't waste your food."

Nolan pulled a sip of soda through the straw. "You drive, I eat?"

Tara did a quick calculation. How much trouble could she really get in driving with an expired permit at night? Maybe lots, but whose fault was it she didn't have her license? She decided to leave it in His hands.

"Deal," she said, extending a flat palm to receive the key.

Nolan's car was a 2009 Hyundai *Sonata*, a low-end commuter car and a far cry from the coveted *Challenger*. *No worries*, Tara thought. *Home is five miles away; stay in the super slow lane and obey all traffic signals.* She would give no reason for a cop to pull them over. She dashed around the front end of the car and clicked to unlock it. She pulled the door open and slid into the passenger seat and felt around with the key for the ignition. That's when she realized she hadn't been paying enough attention. She gripped the manual transmission. And froze.

"You can't drive a stick?" Nolan asked.

"Uh-uh."

"Then I guess we're gonna sit here 'til I finish my burger." Nolan smiled mischievously as he opened the wrapper.

"You want some relish with that?"

"Ha," Nolan laughed, "that's a joke my Dad would use."

"Yeah, well, you can pick your nose, but you can't pick your family."

Nolan coughed as clamped his mouth down on his burger. "That's definitely a Dad joke. You got more?"

Oh, she had more. The new restaurant on the moon? Great food, but no atmosphere. The Invisible Man married a woman who didn't love him. How could you tell? She was pretty transparent. And their kids? They were nothing to look at. Nolan had a few of his own, which were uniformly awful. I'll tell you a rumor about butter, but you have to promise not to spread it around. What does it take to make an octopus laugh? Ten tickles.

"Can we change the subject?" Tara asked. "I mean, I thought my life was sad. Now I'm sorry for everybody. You think Raquel's Dad tells lame jokes?"

Nolan thought for a second. "I don't know. I think there's a lot of sadness in that family."

"Raquel's?" The suggestion of grief at Casa Fuentes floored her.

"She's an only child," Nolan explained. "Probably didn't plan it that way. I mean they're rich, so…" His voice trailed off and he sipped the last of his soda loudly through the straw.

They switched seats and Nolan drove. His take on Raquel's family had made Tara pensive, and she felt even worse now about her blow up, so they rode in silence most of the way. As they got close to Tara's house, she figured she ought to say something just to end on a less tense note.

"Y'know," she said, "the whole Flipper thing aside, I had a pretty good time hanging out."

"Yeah, me, too," he said. "And I get it; he likes you." That didn't make Tara feel any better, but at least he didn't bring up the song. After a moment, Nolan added, "He's got a mouth sometimes. I mean, I don't like picking on a weak kid, but… he shouldn't run his mouth if he can't back it up."

"You think he's weak?" she blurted. It sounded like an accusation, and maybe it was. Maybe she also wondered what he thought of her. Flipper worked sixteen hours a week besides school and all his activities; Tara could barely get out of bed in the morning and struggled to make it through the day.

"Is this your street?" Nolan asked.

"Next one."

Tara wondered how this encounter was going to end. Far cry from Flipper dropping her off, when she practically snuck out of his *Jeep*. Would Nolan try to kiss her? Or would that be too creepy, her looking just like Teri? And what should she do if he tried? She shouldn't...*couldn't* let him. She'd promised Teri. And why was she even thinking this? It was almost like she wanted him to. Was that weird? To want the boy who kissed Teri to kiss her? *But what would it actually be like? Enough to erase the memory of Jimmy Cerrone?*

The car rolled to the curb, and Tara's stomach fluttered out the window. *Moment of truth,* she thought. She licked the back of her lower lip and slowly turned towards Nolan. He shifted into park and rested his big, right hand on the stick. As Tara's back seemed to melt away, Nolan leaned his left forearm on the steering wheel and turned to face her. He lifted his right hand off the stick and turned his palm up in an offer to shake.

What the freakin' heck?!?

CHAPTER
SEVEN

"There is something at work in my soul,
which I do not understand."
— Mary Shelley, *Frankenstein*

TARA'S PARENTS were watching TV in the living room. She got the sneaky feeling they weren't much interested in the program; their eyes drilled into her as she offered a non-committal "Hi." She knew something was up when her Dad hit pause.

"How was the party?" he asked.

A little spooked, Tara wondered, *What do they know? And how do they know it?* "Lame and nerdy. I didn't stay."

That didn't exactly relieve them but kept them from jumping down her throat. Her Mom was on edge. Literally. She had slid to the edge of the sofa with her elbow pressing on the last square inch of the armrest. "You had permission to go to a party, not to take off god-knows-where."

Tara tried to shrug it off. "Okay, I didn't come straight home," she admitted. "I didn't go drag racing. I went to the range, hit a bucket of balls." That maybe mollified her Dad, which allowed Tara to go on the offensive. "What's the big deal? It's still early.

And I didn't do anything you wouldn't have given me permission for."

Her Mom seemed to chew the inside of her cheeks for a few seconds before saying, "Mrs. Fuentes called. She asked if you got home alright."

"What did you tell her?"

"Tara, she was concerned."

"Fine, she's a mother, that's what they do." That bought her a couple of seconds, which she could have used to think about what to say next, but instead she just plowed ahead. "So, what did you tell her? You admit I wasn't home yet, or did you lie and say I was tucked away in bed?"

"Hey, a little respect, Missy," her Dad interjected.

"I'm being truthful with you," Tara insisted. "The least you can do…"

"What happened at Raquel's party?" her Mom demanded.

"Nothing happened. Geez. What are you so scared about?"

"I'm concerned for my daughter."

"Pfff," she trilled like a winded horse. In a cartoon, Tara's eyeballs would have hit the ceiling. "You weren't concerned enough to call me. Or text. You're concerned our rich neighbors will think we're all falling apart."

"Sweetheart." Her Mom tried to act composed. "We don't need to parade our private issues before strangers."

"Mrs. Fuentes?" Tara protested. "I've known her ten years. And I didn't *parade* anything. It's just hard, okay?"

"I know, sweetheart." Her Mom got up and approached her. "But call us." She offered a hug, but Tara pushed her arms away.

"No! You don't get to do this. You can't act all comforting when all you care about is how you look to Annamaria!"

"That's ridiculous!"

Tara paced a few steps left then right. She had the winning card, and she was ready to drop it. "Did you sell a house?"

"What?" her Mom gaped.

Tara consciously relaxed every muscle in her face, and flatly stated, "Mrs. Fuentes heard you sold a house. So, either you sold a house, or you didn't, but you told people you sold a house. So? How come you can lie to make everything seem fine, and that's okay, but I tell the truth about how messed up it all is, how nothing makes any freakin' sense anymore, and I'm the one making a scene?"

"Okay," her Dad said, rising from his chair, "I think we all just need to take a time out, and we can talk about this in the morning."

"It's a simple question," Tara pressed. "Did you sell a house or not?"

"No! Alright?" Tears streamed from her Mom's eyes. Tara suddenly felt horrible. "I just...had, had to say...something." She crumpled back onto the sofa and Dad crouched beside her, wrapping her in his arms.

"Anything else you need to know?" he asked.

Tara shook her head. A thought entered her mind: *We still haven't figured out how everyone knows I drove to Teri's grave!* But that seemed like too much. Her Mom buried her face in the crook of her Dad's shoulder. Tara padded her way down the hall to her room, gripping the pen knife in her pocket.

———

"MAAAAAAHHHHHHM," Jeremy bellowed, "Tara's not going to Mass."

Tara had been wallowing somewhere between sleep and consciousness as Teri's voice berated her.

"You promised not to date Nolan."

"It wasn't a date; we just left the party together."

"The driving range was a date."

"No."

"Who paid for the buckets?"

"You're overthinking this."

"You're not thinking at all!"

This went on until her Mom answered Jeremy's alarm. "If we're late, I am marching you up the center aisle to the very public front pew."

"Why? I'll go later," Tara groaned. "I'll go to the five o'clock."

"No, you're going to the 9:30 with your family. It's two months…"

"You, too? Why is everybody harping on the magic number?"

Her Mom sat on the edge of Teri's bed. "Tara, I know it's been a tough week for you, and last night … It's all the more reason we need to support each other as a family. That means going to Mass together, and then going to the cemetery. Together."

Tara groaned like a grizzly sow. Sleep was the only peace she knew, and today she could have slept another hour at least. *If only*. She rubbed her crusty eyes. The lids weighed a ton and would not open.

"Must I resort to bribery?" Mom asked.

"Whatcha got?" Tara grumbled.

"A two-hundred-dollar bottle of wine."

Tara's eyes snapped open like cartoon window shades. "Sold." She tossed the bed covers aside and rolled to the edge of the bed. *Whoa*, a little too quickly. She saw tiny sparks dancing around her.

"Half a glass," Mom said. "But only if you're ready in the next fifteen minutes. After that, I send in your Dad." Mom stood and Tara rose with her, leaning into her arms for a hug.

"How do you put up with me?" she asked.

"I suppose I remember what my mother put up with."

Tara tried to imagine her Grandma Galvin thirty years ago. All she could picture was her crushing rattlesnake heads and tossing the bodies on the grill. That didn't make sense, but nothing did. Like the thoughts she had at the party about her Mom and Teri.

"Mom, did you and Teri have secrets?" she asked quietly.

"What kind of question is that?"

"It's a question. Geez, a sincere… Did you say stuff I wasn't part of?"

"What kind of stuff?"

"I don't know," Tara squirmed. "Like about Raquel. And her Mom."

Mom's eyebrows crinkled like a train wreck. "Now you're dreaming up conspiracies?"

"Or maybe I'm waking up," Tara said facetiously, "…to reality."

Mom's jaw dropped open for a second before she said, "You need to get ready for church."

"Fine."

Mom retreated to the doorway, then turned to face Tara again. "You're suggesting I would gossip to your sister about our friends."

"I thought they were strangers."

"We leave in fifteen."

As her Mom left, Tara raked her fingers through her hair. *No time to shower? Ugh.* Then she caught Stacy staring at her from the doorway.

"Whaaaaat?"

"Can I have Teri's rosary beads?"

Really? Tara surveyed Teri's belongings, still spread over the bed. She spotted the round, mahogany box and handed it to her little sister. Stacy unscrewed the lid. She eyed the semi-precious stones, tiger eyes, and the 14-carat gold corpus mounted on a mahogany cross. A Confirmation gift from Teri's sponsor. Stacy frowned.

"Not these. Her white ones."

"You look."

Stacy went to Teri's bureau and pulled the top drawer open. She lifted out a flimsy string of dull, off-white, plastic beads.

"Those?" Tara asked.

"Sure," the girl smiled. "They glow in the dark."

Kids are so weird.

———

MASS WAS the big show on the one day of the week Bill and Becky Hartzwell could parade the family in public to demonstrate how well they were coping with Teri's death. Attire was business casual; hair and makeup flawless; fragrance applied subtly, never overpowering; and, as Jeremy was reminded each time the minivan rolled into the St. Sebastian parking lot, nail biting was *verboten*. The Hartzwells arrived not more than ten but not less than five minutes before Mass began, dipped their fingers in the holy water font, crossed themselves with all due formality, and processed three-quarters of the way up the center aisle. At the pew, universally recognized as the Hartzwell pew, there was reverent genuflecting, then pious kneeling with heads bowed until music signaled the priest's entrance.

Today's arrival was interrupted by a minor crisis: an altar boy didn't show, so Jeremy was pressed into service. He marched to the sacristy to get properly frocked, while the remaining family took their place.

Tara knelt as required, and welcomed the brain fog she'd fought all week to close around her. As long as she didn't fidget, her parents left her alone. The homily was the hardest part, because her parents would ask about it over lunch. It was like school intruding on her weekend, not cool.

Standing for the Gospel, Tara struggled to focus. Jesus cleansed ten lepers and told the one who returned to thank Him, "Your faith has made you well." Tara huffed audibly, drawing harsh glare from her Dad. *Sorry*, she mouthed. But how should she react? They had prayed, begged, hoped and believed. Their faith had done nothing for Teri. And now Fr. Chandler's homily would say what? Oh, here it comes, "Jesus is waiting to heal all of us, if only we call on Him." That didn't exactly match Tara's reality, and she had to wonder if Fr. Chandler, who clearly wasn't stupid, actually believed it.

Eucharistic prayer took forever, then Communion, *ugh*. How could like four hundred extra people, who weren't there at the start of Mass, always came out of nowhere for the Communion line? Were they out smoking in the parking lot? And someone inside texted them that it was "go time"? The lines were as long as Disneyland, so more time kneeling and faking holiness as they all passed by. Tara let her brain fog take over.

The final blessing signaled imminent release, and even though the Recessional *hymn* was an overused, unsingable mess, Tara mumbled her way through the first two verses, then slid the hymnal back into the rack.

"Did you like the stories?" her Mom asked Stacy.

"How people can be leopards?"

"Oh, honey!"

"I'd explain," Dad said, "but my knowledge is a little spotty."

At that, Tara uttered her first sincere prayer of the day: that no one outside the family had heard Dad's lame joke. They made their way slowly down the aisle for the final irksome task of greeting Fr. Chandler. Her parents would congratulate him on an awesome homily, and they'd prompt each kid to utter something that demonstrated what a perfectly committed Catholic family they were.

Her Mom hooked an arm around Tara's and pulled her close. "Did you get anything, sweetheart? Some comfort?"

"Jesus is waiting to heal us," Tara said, flatly.

"Yes, He is," her Mom replied in an equally flat tone that mocked hers. "Let's try not to keep Him waiting."

Fr. Chandler kept everyone waiting, shaking every hand on the way out. Teri had asked if he was a priest or a politician, to which Dad had said, "Both; those collection baskets don't fill themselves."

Tara hoped her parents would just flip Father the high sign and skirt past. But ol' Bill prodded Stacy to ask about leopards, 'cause it was so gushingly cute and clearly showed the Hartzwells were back on the beam. Trapped in an absurd pantomime, Tara didn't feel like playing nice. "What's the deal about jaguars?" she asked. "Are they cats, cars, or what?"

Father indulged her with a light chuckle, and the family plodded on to the Coffee Hour, which Tara hoped would be more like a coffee *break*. She expected cold shoulders from the hive girls, Raquel's real friends, and anyone Flipper might have talked to. She wasn't disappointed; though the principles in her little drama were absent, none of the St. Stephen's crowd gave her even a polite nod. So, as Bill and Becky demonstrated the networking skills that made the capitalist world go 'round, Tara watched Stacy squirt jelly out the back end of a doughnut all over her blouse.

"Stacy!" Mom cried. "You've got to be careful, honey." She shot Tara a reproachful look. *Right*, Tara thought, *I couldn't save Teri's life; I should at least prevent grape stains*.

"Can you go see what's keeping Jeremy?"

Thus released, Tara fled the Parish Hall and trotted across the lawn to the side entrance of the church, then down the hall to the sacristy. The door was slightly ajar, but hushed voices gave her pause. Tara peered through the crack and saw Fr. Chandler, seated, wearing his usual black street clothes and Roman collar, but with a scarlet stole around his neck. Shifting forward slightly, Tara saw Jeremy sitting with his head slightly bowed and his ears in full blush. He was confessing.

Tara's first impulse was to pull back; she shouldn't hear this. But Jeremy's faltering voice froze her in place.

"I hurt my sister," he said. "I shouldn't of. I maybe wouldn't of, if I wasn't mad. But I told a rumor. That she drove to Teri's grave in her sleep."

"Did you think it was funny?" Father asked.

"Maybe, yeah."

"Well, Jeremy," Father said quietly, "there are a lot of things that strike us as funny in the abstract. If they happen in movies or comics, we laugh. But you take that situation and apply it to real people, there's nothing funny about it. Especially with people we love. You love your sister, don't you?"

"I guess."

"I'll take that as a yes," Father said. "Or hurting her wouldn't bother you this much." Jeremy nodded.

Tara pulled back from the door. *That little dork.* She wanted to strangle him. Which she couldn't do, because she could never admit how she found out. And she also couldn't get mad at him, 'cause he was obviously sorry. *Ugh.* Tara pressed her back to the wall. She tightened and released her fist several times until the sacristy door swung open. Startled, Jeremy froze with the stupid *Not Me, I dunno, What d'ya mean?* look she'd seen a thousand times.

"Mom sent me," Tara said. "We're going."

Jeremy ducked his head and headed down the hallway. Tara pushed herself off the wall, just as Fr. Chandler stepped out.

"Oh, Tara."

"Hey, Father."

"How's everything?" he asked, as he turned to lock the door.

Everything? What am I, the Internet?

"I don't know, um, my parents are waiting."

"I'm going that way," he said. "How are you getting on?"

"Just trying to stay in the moment," Tara said, echoing the pat advice every grownup seemed to give her. "Not dwell on the past, not worry about the future."

Fr. Chandler pursed his lips and nodded ominously, which was not the reaction she'd hoped for. She'd have settled for "Sounds good," "Keep it up," even, "Atta girl," anything but that slow, weighty nod that signaled a lesson was coming.

"Doesn't that leave you a little cut off?" he asked.

The question took her by surprise, mostly because it nailed exactly how she felt. Still, her knee-jerk response was, "No."

"Okay," Father said. "It's just, I would think the present moment for you is slightly unbearable." He looked at her with raised eyebrows, as if prompting a little child to make an admission. *Okay, so yeah*, Tara thought, but she wasn't going to award points for stating the obvious. Father went on, "People, all of us, we seem to require a sense of continuum."

Tara had no idea what he was talking about, and hoped he would pick up on her hyper-defensiveness and leave her alone. For some reason, the priest decided now was the moment to earn his salary. "We're rooted in the past and we're headed inexorably, inevitably toward the future."

"Jesus says not to worry about the future," Tara said. She didn't want to argue, she just wanted out.

"True," Father said. He opened the exit door, and they stepped onto a concrete landing. He positioned himself below Tara on the stairs, effectively blocking her path. "We don't worry about the future. We hope in it. We have the trust established in the past, that's our foundation, and the hope for salvation in the future, that's our aspiration."

Tara took a breath. *Why not just whip out the PowerPoint?*

"And all of that," Father went on, "is rooted in Jesus. His promise—"

"Well, y'know, Father," Tara scoffed, "Jesus and I aren't really on good terms lately." *And why hold back?* she thought. *Get it all out.* "'Cause, you know where I was when my sister died, Father? I was in the hospital chapel on my knees praying for Him to save her."

Her voice quavered, and tears flooded upwards, but she couldn't back down now. "I turned my phone off, so I didn't know, and I didn't get back until she was gone. And I never got to say goodbye. So, don't tell me *what a friend I have in Jesus*, Father, 'cause as friends go, He's not all that. And I really think I might be better off without Him."

Tara jerked her head hard to the side and stared into the distance. She barely heard Father's voice, sort of a verbal shrug, say, "That's the predominant way of the world."

"Then give me that world," she muttered.

The sky had not a cloud. Below, parishioners were trickling out of the Parish Hall, past the Community Service tables, towards the remaining cars. Tara wiped an eye with the heel of her palm and spotted her Mom's van.

"I gotta go," she said, and Father stepped aside to let her pass. Jeremy was leaning against the van pouting.

"You said we were leaving," he called.

"We're coming," their Mom answered, as she broke away from a knot of parishioners. Dad and Stacy followed. Tara paused to run her fingertips below her eyes. Her mascara must be ruined. She just wanted to get into the van before anyone saw her. But a middle-aged woman intercepted her parents before they got to the van. The woman seemed friendly enough, but spoke rapidly in muffled tones, so Tara couldn't make out what she was saying until they were almost on top of her. Her parents' perturbed faces warned her off, which only made Tara more curious.

"It's a delicate matter, naturally, and I don't want to take your time today. It's just a coincidence we're in the same parish, so I wanted to introduce myself, and express my condolences."

"How did you learn about us?" Mom asked.

"Oh, the forms at the hospital. You signed release forms for philanthropy related to your daughter's illness."

"You remember, honey," Dad said, "Cancer Society, Leukemia Society. There were a bunch. Who are you with?"

The lady smiled. "I'm with the Liver Foundation."

"Tara, take Stacy please," her Mom said.

Tara stayed put as the lady continued, "You know, liver failure in a young person is not as rare as you might think."

"But," Tara said, "Teri died of leukemia."

Her parents stood stone faced. The lady retracted her lips, like maybe she wanted to bite them off. "I must be misinformed," she said quietly. "Please accept my apology."

The Hartzwells mumbled something vaguely polite with little effort to hide their irritation. "C'mon, let's go," Dad said.

"Wait," Tara demanded. "Teri died of liver failure?"

"A complication of the leukemia."

"Why am I just hearing this?"

"It's just an unnecessary detail," Dad shrugged.

"What happened?" Tara demanded.

Her Mom held the car key in a tight, white fist. "Must we do this here?"

"I am not getting in that car until you tell me."

Her Dad opened his hand to signal a pause. He spoke very quietly. "Dr. Flores explained everything before he performed the procedure."

Tara remembered exactly. He'd said, "We graft your stem cells to build a new immune system for Teresa. We want them to identify the remaining leukemia cells and attack them."

"Your cells misinterpreted their new environment," Dad said. "Triggered something called graft-versus-host disease. The cells attacked Teri's organs instead of the leukemia. And her liver shut down."

"Oh, God, God. I killed her!"

"No! Honey," he begged her to understand. "They're cells. They don't think. They don't choose. Tara…" He tried to put his hands on her shoulders, but she tore away. Tara dashed for the exit past several cars waiting to turn onto the crowded Boulevard. Her Dad trotted after her, calling. She reached the edge of the curb and her legs flexed. Her gut flinched and knotted; Tara heard the whoosh of an approaching car, dropped her head and pitched her body forward.

A horn blared. She impacted the bumper first then landed on the hood and spun towards the windshield, where she saw a face like Teri's reflected in the tinted glass that shattered and went black.

PART TWO
THE SEARCH FOR EDEN

"Wheresoever she was, there was Eden."
— Mark Twain, *The Diaries of Adam and Eve*

CHAPTER
EIGHT

"Is anyone among you sick?
Let him bring in the priests of the Church,
and let them pray over him,
anointing him with oil in the name of the Lord.
And the prayer of faith will save the sick man,
and the Lord will raise him up,
and if he be in sins, they shall be forgiven him."
— James 5: 14-15

"I TOLD you she would try suicide, but nobody listens to me."

"Hush, Jeremy." *Mom's voice.*

"See?"

"Son, wait outside." *Dad's voice.*

Tara tried to pick her head up, and *augh*, it felt like a boulder had smacked her above the nose. Her eyelids were weighted down. Through the slits she managed to open, shadows danced in fog as the dimly lit room came into focus. Shapes gained clarity, but there was an odd shimmer to the room, like she was looking through 3D movie glasses. Abruptly, her Mom popped forward.

"Tara? Honey are you awake?" Mom asked.

"No," she answered stupidly. "I don't know."

"You're alright, sweetheart," her Dad said. "You have a slight concussion and a couple of deep bruises."

Tara turned to her left side and found one of those bruises, on her elbow, which must have swollen to the size of a cantaloupe.

"How long?"

"It's six o'clock," Mom said, "so roughly seven hours. You've been in and out."

"You're going to stay the night here," Dad said. "One of us will be with you."

"No," Tara groaned, then moaned as she found another bruise high on her left thigh, just below the hip joint. "You don't have to."

"We want to." Mom said. From the chair at bedside, she slid closer and took Tara's left hand in both of hers. Tara felt a string of light beads, a Rosary. *Must be bad if she dug this out of the dresser.*

"Baby, you've been cutting yourself?"

Oops, Tara thought. *Cat's out of that bag.* She tried to think up words to say, but her head hurt too much. The pain rolled back to the base of her skull. She was slipping, floating downward, inward, into the dark.

"Tee! Tee!"

Flipper was at the foot of her bed, a cellphone in his hand.

"Where's my Mom?"

"Getting coffee. Look, I'm sorry f' what I said last night."

"What time is it?"

"10:30. I was way out of line. I deserved to get jacked up."

No, Tara thought, as she tried to rouse herself. *This makes no sense.* She bent her legs and shifted them left and downward, so she could sit up on the edge of the bed. Her massive head wobbled. Flipper placed a hand on her right shoulder to steady her.

"Why are you here?" she asked.

"Tee, I found the girl." He tapped his phone rapidly then turned the screen around. Tara squinted at a photo of a surprised girl with wide, green eyes and honey-blonde hair, cropped just below her jawline and brushed behind one ear. The girl's large central incisors suggested a rabbit, though her teeth were as straight as any orthodontist could make them. Tara blinked, half expecting the image to change, to reveal some distinguishing feature that would prove she wasn't staring at herself.

"That's unbelievable."

"Well, like they say," Flipper said, swiping the screen to bring up another image. "Everybody's got a double."

"I already had mine."

"Oh, yeah. My bad." He showed her the screen again. The girl was getting into a minivan. "And check this out." Flipper swiped to the next shot, the license plate of the van. "Y'know, I got an uncle who's a county deputy, right? I asked him to run the plate. Told him they left a phone in a booth, and I want to return it. Tee, I'm gonna have her address tomorrow."

Tara slumped badly. She reclined on the raised head of the mattress and pulled her legs back onto the bed.

"You're still interested, right?" he asked. "I mean, this is huge. Girl comes outta nowhere and she's your spitting image."

"Yeah." But Tara was feeling anything but sure about pursuing the girl any further. She got a queasy feeling, like they were using a *Ouija* board to conjure the dead.

"Maybe she's some sixteenth cousin four times removed," Flipper suggested. "You could learn all kinds of family history."

"I wonder if she cuts," Tara said absently.

"Huh? Cuts what?"

"Uh, nothing," Tara said. "I really gotta sleep."

Tara closed her eyes and felt herself slipping again. When she returned to the surface, the sun was piercing the vertical blind. With laser precision it burned into her eyes, reigniting the pain. As she turned her head away, she was relieved to feel only a dull ache and not the sharp throb from yesterday.

"Are you hungry?" her Mom asked.

"You been there all night?"

"I took a couple of breaks." She held up a paper cup. "Coffee here is lousy. Want some?"

"Did you see Flipper?"

"What brings him up?"

Tara felt her swollen elbow, then tested the bruise on her thigh. "Nothing. He was here last night."

"Here?" she asked. "In this room here?"

"You were out getting coffee." Tara tried to sit all the way up. She wobbled and her Mom rushed forward. "I'm okay." With her Mom's help, Tara got out of bed and padded slowly towards the restroom.

"So, uh, a boy who's not authorized to visit, waits until I leave the room, then comes in and spends time with my unconscious daughter? That's creepy."

"I wasn't unconscious."

"Okay, slightly less creepy," Mom said. "Still not *un*creepy. What was it about?"

"Just, uh, wanted to see how I was doing."

Her Mom extended an index finger, hooked a strand of hair above Tara's left eye and swept it behind her ear. "How are you doing?"

"I want to go home."

Fortunately, it wasn't long before the doctor on duty came around and cleared Tara for discharge. She was to rest, avoid bright lights and loud noises, refrain from exercise, and generally remain calm for the rest of the week. Thursday was the earliest she should go back to school, if she was feeling up to it. Minutes later, her Dad arrived with fresh clothes. Tara dressed and her Mom pushed her in a wheelchair to the elevator and then the exit. Everywhere Tara looked, the scene was bleached out, like overexposed film. Objects more than ten feet away were invisible, then came roaring into focus, like ocean liners bursting through thick fog. Her Dad drove them back to the house, which turned out to be house arrest, since her Mom wouldn't let Tara out of her sight.

"I'm not suicidal."

"I'd like to hear that from a doctor."

"Yeah," Dad grumbled, "maybe the doctor who put her on pills that specifically warn about suicidal thoughts."

"I didn't have suicidal thoughts. Okay? It was an impulse."

"And that's supposed to make us feel better?" Mom asked.

"Becky, this is not about us," Dad said. "Will you just cool it?"

"Fine," Mom said. "I'll be totally cool, while my daughter is cutting herself and jumping in front of sportscars."

With that, she stomped out of the kitchen and up the stairs. She slammed her bedroom door hard enough to shake the house and hammer Tara's cranium. Tara remembered the one time she had done that. The next day, she came home after school to find her Dad had taken the door off its hinges. "If you don't know how to handle a door, you can't have one," Dad had said, and the door stayed off for a week. Teri kept grumbling about how she was being punished, too, and nagged Tara to apologize. But Tara wouldn't budge. It wasn't her fault they had a dorky Dad who always had to be King Solomon with his vast wisdom on display. He wasn't looking too wise at the moment. He just lifted his eyes toward the ceiling and sighed, "It wasn't a sportscar."

Tara's thought, *Really? You want to argue about the model of the car?* Then she realized she didn't remember the car at all. "What was it?"

"The car? One of those *Dodge* muscle jobs." Her Dad busied himself, getting breakfast dishes out of the sink and into the dishwasher. Maybe that was a peace offering to his wife.

"A black *Challenger*?" Tara asked.

"Listen to you, the automotive expert." He closed the dishwasher and wiped his hands on a hanging towel. "You scared the snot out of the kid driving it. Serves him right; he was going too fast."

"What did he look like?"

"Why?" Off Tara's glare, her Dad thought for a second. "About my height. Spikey black hair, too much time in the weight room."

"Cold gray eyes?"

"Don't tell me you know this kid?"

Tara shook her head. *But he thinks he knows me.* Was it a coincidence he happened to be driving past? "I need to lie down," she said.

"Sure, sweetheart. Get your rest."

————

BUT LYING down wasn't restful. Sammy, on the floor beside her, seemed anxious as well, as if sensing invisible intruders. Tara couldn't slow her racing mind, fixed on whether *Challenger* boy was stalking her. When he'd left Casa Fuentes, he'd given the definite impression he intended to meet her again, preferably when Nolan wasn't around. Tara should ask Raquel if she'd seen him, only Raquel wouldn't want to hear from her. And everyone else, if they hadn't thought she was nuts for sleep-driving, would certainly think she was cracked now. Still, Flipper had found the girl. *That meant something, right?* At least it meant she wasn't hallucinating. She might still be crazy, but maybe not *cray-cray* crazy.

If Flipper's uncle could get mystery girl's address, he could also get Tara's accident report, which would give her the boy's name and address. But what would she even do with that information? Tara closed her eyes and the accident replayed on a continuous loop. Her head struck the windshield, which shattered in a spiderweb pattern. The tires screeched and the vehicle lurched, throwing her back onto the hood and finally the pavement. The sun pierced the clouds overhead. Her Dad knelt beside her, stroked her face, cried, "Call 9-1-1!" Then he bent over her onto his elbows and whispered in her ear, "Stay with me, baby, stay with me." The sun retreated, up, up, up, and the clouds closed in front.

"Tara," Stacy giggled from the doorway, "your boyfriend's here."

Tara looked at the clock: 4:15. *Holy...* She must have dozed off. As she pushed up on her bruised elbow, she winced, and a sharp hunger pang reminded her she'd slept through lunch. *Boyfriend?* To a third grader, that could mean any boy, but Tara suspected one in particular.

She trudged to the kitchen, which still had the artificial 3D look to it, past her Mom and straight to the fridge. She opened a *Ziplock* bag and peeled away a few slices of smoked turkey breast.

"Drink something, too, sweetheart," Mom said. "Juice?"

Tara shrugged. She chomped on the turkey and stared into the living room. The walls and ceiling seemed to be on fire. The TV was ablaze with one of Jeremy's dorky, superhero video games. Mom handed Tara a tall glass of orange juice. The color was off; it kind of glowed. "Thanks." A nuclear blast leapt off the TV screen and vaporized the living room, not to mention it obliterated a major city and hurled the hero into space. Jeremy roared laughing.

"Dang!" Flipper yelled. "Bad guys win *again*."

"Well, there's still about four hundred million, life-sustaining planets," Tara said. "You'll get 'em next time."

"Tee!" Flipper jumped up, snatching a folded sheet of paper off the coffee table. "I come bearing homework."

Which was totally unnecessary, since Tara could access homework through the school website. Her Mom lifted an eyebrow, knowingly, as Tara took the sheet of paper, which was just a printout of a Chem assignment.

"I could maybe explain, if you have your book."

"In my room."

Her Mom glowered, as if Tara had proposed a scandalous assignation that would bring down the House of Hartzwell. "I'll get it." She pointed Flipper towards the outside patio, where at least they'd have a little privacy.

Tara retrieved her Chem text and went out to the patio, an ill-conceived and poorly executed home improvement project that had fallen into disuse. Her Mom had wanted a garden but couldn't get anything to grow in the chalky dust, save for a few succulents, now thorny and unkempt. Tara sat at the wobbly, glass-topped table next to Flipper. She could feel her mother's eyes on her back through the kitchen window. Flipper opened the book and whispered. "I got the address. When can you get out?"

"Not for days," she said. "I won't even be in school until Thursday."

Flipper nodded but went on as though she hadn't said anything. "The van belongs to a guy named Seymour Grant." He pulled out a map and pointed to a dot marking the Grant residence. Not exactly close, but plenty of St. Stephen's kids lived around there. If a neighborhood girl looked just like the Hartzwell twins, Tara should have heard of her by now.

"The family might be new," Flipper suggested.

Who knows?

What Tara thought she knew was that the week would drag on at a miserably slow pace, as she slogged through each day in the corner of the real estate office under the watchful gaze of her Mom. Tara would sit, read school assignments, and occasionally pace back and forth like a caged panther. Her captivity was only bearable because Tara wasn't tracking time. Whole swaths of the day passed in one or two blinks. That eerie phenomenon made the time pass, but compounded Tara's anxiety, 'til she was ready to claw the walls.

"Sit, Tigger," Mom said. Tara acted as though the command was not directed at her. "Oh, you don't remember that?"

Of course, Tara remembered; she just didn't care to react. It was now Wednesday morning, and Tara couldn't account for Tuesday. She needed to understand what was happening inside her head at this moment, not wax nostalgic over a preschool nickname.

"You were my active baby."

So, we're going down memory lane?

Tara suppressed a groan. "Active baby" was Mom's way of saying "problem twin." Teri had been the "easy twin." Cried very little. Teri had smiled, gurgled, and cooed, while Tara had screamed like a four-alarm fire. She'd had colic and could never get comfortable. Thus, their Dad had taken charge of Teri, who would sit quietly for anyone. The difficult baby clung to mother, because only mother would do. Later, the "problem twin" became the "antsy twin" or the "hyperactive twin," in sharp contrast to the "placid twin," the "studious twin," or simply the "normal twin." The "good twin" went on to get "good grades," while the "difficult twin" brought home "lackluster grades." Teri was an "academic star," while Tara was an "underachiever." Which would have been fine between the girls, who were vastly different people, except it wasn't fine between the parents.

Tara had become Mom's twin, and Mom couldn't bear the thought of hers lagging behind Dad's. Tara suspected Mom secretly thought she was smarter than Dad. He might quote Shakespeare at the drop of a hat, but Mom often reminded him he hadn't read a piece of real literature since college. Mom ran her book club, watched PBS and listened to NPR, which Dad dismissed as "leftwing fertilizer." Refusing to believe that two genetically identical girls could have such different academic profiles, Mom pored over Tara's homework, forcing her to re-do assignments that weren't up to her standards. When extra time reading and drilling flashcards didn't completely close the gap, Mom began emphasizing Tara's "special abilities." Suddenly, Tara was a "gifted artist," based on a few grayish watercolors pinned up on the refrigerator, an "exceptional athlete" due to one two-goal game in U-10 soccer, and perhaps a "musical prodigy," because could pound out sixteen bars of *Turkey in the Straw* on the piano. Inevitably, tension built between the twins, and homework sessions devolved into sniping, followed by table shaking and the inevitable, "Look what you made me do!"

That dynamic continued for a couple of years, Teri excelling at everything that seemed to matter, and Tara cringing from faint praise meant to boost her self-esteem. But Tara took true victories where she could. On the playground, she was routinely chosen before the "book smart twin." In kickball, Teri was too cautious, overthinking where she wanted the ball to go, before kicking a weak bouncer off her shin. Tara would feint one way, then crush the ball to the opposite direction. She struck prodigious drives with plenty of spin that scared girls away from the screaming ball.

Tara's "beast mode," as Dad called it, made her a force on the soccer field in sixth grade and an all-or-nothing batter in softball, as prone to lunging strikeouts as she was to searing line drives. But her erratic performance garnered more criticism than praise. Coaches regarded her goals and hits as strokes of luck and her miscues as the norm.

All that changed when Dad decided the girls were old enough for golf. That started as a Teri thing. She was always first to greet Dad when he returned from the Club. He'd draw his putter from his bag and place a ball on the lawn. Teri would listen attentively to his coaching and aim for the travel mug he laid down on the grass. Tara watched in envy but shook her head when asked if she'd like to try.

When Dad suggested Teri should take lessons, Mom insisted that Tara go, too.

"They can share equipment," she said.

"Uh," Dad chuckled. "You have noticed that Teri's right-handed and Tara's lefty, right?"

"What difference does that make?"

Dad threw his palms open as if juggling balls that had vanished in mid-air. "They'll need their own clubs."

So, the question was posed to Tara. "Would you like to learn golf?" And, to her parents' shock and Teri's dismay, Tara had answered, "Yeah. Might be fun."

Teri felt Tara was deliberately horning in on her Dad time. And that was part of Tara's motivation. But she also needed to separate a bit from Mom. Back then, Tara didn't know what "perspective" meant, but instinctively knew she needed it. And, maybe in the back of her mind, she wanted to be more like Teri.

Once at the driving range, Tara knew she needed to "be more like Teri." She copied Teri's approach, becoming studious, focused and mechanical. But, because she was the "antsy twin" who thrived in "beast mode," she brought something to the game that Teri lacked: reckless abandon. Once Tara got the mechanics down, she put them out of her mind and let her instincts take over. And the more Tara "let it rip," the farther and straighter her drives went. Teri could still beat her on the green, so Tara studied her twin again, obsessing over the way she putted. By eighth grade, Tara was clearly the better golfer, and Teri was copying her, tapping into her inner beast, until her drives had more power. The twins rose together in the rankings, and as a matched set, they were minor celebrities at all the tournaments they entered.

Celebrity status delighted their parents, but with high school looming, Tara wanted to set out on her own. The break with Mom had worked wonders. Now it was time to separate, gently, from Teri. Tara didn't want to be the antsy-difficult-lackluster-underachieving twin. She just wanted to be Tara, whoever that was. But Teri had been so nervous, she'd wanted to play up the twinsie-twinness like never before.

Fortunately, this was one time the difficult twin had both parents in her corner, agreeing the girls should highlight their individuality, dressing as differently as possible under the school's rigid dress code. That was the plan until the girls touched foot on campus, and Teri cleaved so close to Tara, she was afraid they'd be known as *The Two-Headed Thing*. The clingy act reached its breaking point when Teri began blathering to Cheryl about all the ways the Hartzwell twins were "the same but different." Tara had wanted to dig a hole to hide.

And that's how she felt now. Because in the here and now, it seemed like Tara's leap into traffic had simply been the culmination of all the other bad behavior that had marked her as the problem child. Problematic to the point that her perfectly matched DNA couldn't rise to the occasion, even as her sister's life depended on it. It seemed that Tara had been hounded by black fate, and there was no escaping judgment.

But judgment had to be fair, right? Ultimately? Tara knew that even if she'd been difficult, she wasn't bad. She just needed another chance to prove herself. And that wasn't going to happen in the corner of Mom's real estate office. So, when Madame Vignon posted a French tutoring session for three that afternoon, Tara seized the opportunity.

"It'll just be an hour. It'll get me ready for the next quiz."

"How will you get home?" her Mom demanded.

"I'll hitchhike. A trucker is bound to stop."

"Tara. Elaine. Genevieve. Hartzwell."

"Mommy. Mom. Mother. Maw. There's gonna be like a dozen kids there. I can get a ride home."

"I'm worried about your concussion," Mom said. She leaned in close and stared into Tara's eyes, checking her pupils. She looked like the image of a face in a spoon. Tara's head roared.

"I'm fine, Mom, really."

So, after searching her thoroughly for sharp objects, her Mom dropped Tara off at St. Stephen's just as the dismissal bell rang. Tara trotted through the tall front doors and braced herself as she entered the foyer. It appeared distorted and cavernous. Tara felt like an ant in the huge chamber, looking up at the high counters that held the

Senior TAs and office ladies. They teetered forward onto their hands, peering down at her, like a speck on the carpet. Without making eye-contact, Tara strolled calmly, but not really, towards the Language Resource Center in the east wing. The walls and ceiling seemed too high as she approached the door, and a couple of girls, grossly out of focus, spotted her and lingered. They politely inquired about her "accident," saying they were glad she wasn't seriously hurt. A few other kids rubber-necked, morphing ominously like images in a funhouse mirror. Tara tried to take the contortions in stride. Eventually, her field of vision would snap back into focus, right?

"Yeah, it was, uh, scary, but nothing," Tara told the girls. "Look both ways before crossing!" They smiled and sighed with what struck Tara strangely as admiration, as if she'd undergone the great trial and been found worthy, which only made her feel like more of a fraud. Which was just perfect timing for the entrance around the corner of Raquel, Cheryl, and a coterie of drone girls.

Their reactions could not have been more different. Cheryl rocked back on her heels and tucked her chin like she'd encountered a pungent odor. Raquel's eyes popped wide, and she ran forward to give Tara a tight hug.

"I've been so worried," Raquel cried. "After I was so mean to you. I'm such an idiot."

"No," Tara said. "You were —"

"I've got Italian-Cuban blood," Raquel insisted. "Makes me too emotional. My Mom says I'm half Tony Soprano, half Ricky Ricardo."

Tara gripped Raquel's hand tightly, as her friend wiped away a tear. "Well, I've got Scots-Irish-German-Norwegian blood," she said. "Makes me, I don't know, pugnacious."

Cheryl emitted a faint "Hi," and flew off with her drones. Raquel walked Tara into the Resource Center. Far, far across the room, at the edge of a too large table, Corinne, the tutor, was already conversing with two girls. Her voice echoed, as if she were at the bottom of a deep cavern.

"*Quel a été le premier film que Jean-Claude a vu à Cannes? Souviens, c'était un film classique qui a commencé en noir et blanc, puis en couleur.*"

But, Tara thought, *that's last week's assignment.* Maybe this was a warmup, and Corinne would move on after a few quick questions. But the girls didn't know the answer. In a tone and with a stony expression that was uncharacteristically severe, Corinne went around the table, asking, *"Quel est le nom du film?"* Raquel gave up. *You know this,* Tara thought. Corinne turned to Tara, her eyes burning intensely into her. The other girls joined in, staring at her.

"Tara, le nom du film?"

Tara opened her mouth, but her mind went blank. Images of the movie ran through her head. A tornado. A nasty woman on a bicycle. A soundless crash and a pig-tailed girl springing up in her bed. Tara stared into that frightened girl's eyes until a rapid tapping sound broke the spell. Tara turned her head towards a door, the size of a postage stamp in the distance. Flipper stood outside looking in, a quarter between his thumb and forefinger. He rapped again with the coin on the windowpane, and Tara excused herself.

"We gotta go," Flipper said. "The car's at Greenvale."

"What ca—?"

Flipper showed her the GPS on his phone. "THE car. Mystery girl's minivan." They walked to the front exit, as Flipper explained. "When I got the address, I went by the house. The van was in the driveway, so I put a little device behind the rear bumper. I've been tracking it ever since."

"Are you insane?" Her voice echoed in the empty foyer. Flipper shushed her.

"Hey. You were out for two days. I'm supposed to do nothing?"

"Yes. That's exactly what you were supposed to do."

"Relax, will you," Flipper laughed. He led her outside to the faculty lot where his *Jeep* was illegally parked in Fr. Chandler's space.

"I can't just go riding off with you," Tara objected. "I'm only allowed out for the study group."

"But, Tee," Flipper smiled, "it's cheetah time."

The ride to Greenvale was another blur of missed time. The road seemed to melt away; colors dissolved into streaks of light. They followed the GPS into the lot at the far end of the mall, away from the *CD* and the cinema. Flipper turned down a row of parked vehicles; he scanned left as Tara kept lookout on the right. There were plenty of black minivans, but none had the right license plate.

"The car should be here," Flipper said. "We're right on top of it."

"Maybe it's on top of us," Tara said, pointing upward to the next level.

Flipper spun the wheel and stepped on the gas. He drove onto the ramp that wound to the upper deck. Sure enough, the van was parked exactly where the GPS had indicated. Flipper pulled his *Jeep* into the open space beside it.

"How d'ya want to play this?" he asked.

Tara didn't want to play at all. "You stay here," she said. "Text me if she comes out." She trotted to the entrance and pulled the door open. A frosty blast of air-conditioning hit her, even as the glare of the drooping sun, magnified by the honeycombed glass of the ceiling and the white marble tiles, forced her to close one eye. The concussion pain surged again, as the staticky drone of electric current, echoing talk, and clopping footsteps set her every nerve on edge. *Better make this quick,* Tara told herself. But there were two dozen stores on this level and just as many below.

"Did you change your mind?" a voice asked. Tara squinted at a shimmering lady at a perfume kiosk, holding a tester. "I knew once the fragrance opened up, you wouldn't be able to resist."

"Excuse me?" Tara asked.

"Wait," the lady said, batting her eyes as though she too hadn't adjusted to the light. "You changed your outfit?"

"Where'd she go?" Tara demanded. "The girl who looks like me!"

The lady pointed with the spray bottle down the righthand side of the floor that formed an elongated figure eight. Tara set off, peering through each storefront before moving to the next. At the music store, it was impossible to see past the window display, but Tara knew Mystery Girl had to be inside. She'd be getting reeds for her clarinet. Or maybe taking a lesson in a rehearsal room. The twins had come here to practice piano the first year they played, until their parents had rented a spinet for the home. She had to be here.

Tara opened the door slowly and stepped off the hard, white marble onto the spongy, toasted brown carpet. It was like entering a cocoon of sound, where music wrapped around her, buoyed her, so she barely felt the floor. Tara recognized the piece from Youth Orchestra but couldn't think of the name. The horn section sounded an ominous warning, like a storm at sea, then the strings swirled in a whirlpool threatening to drag her under. Tara steadied herself against the rack of sheet music, and the title flooded her mind: *Symphony for the New World*.

The floor listed one way then the other, like a ship at sea, as Tara pushed off the display rack and lurched towards the rehearsal rooms. Rising to her toes, she peered through each letterbox window at the person inside. Skinny boy scraping a violin. Pre-school girl pounding a piano. Bug-eyed high school hipster blowing a gasket on the trumpet. There were two more rooms way in the back, in that corner of the store where Tara had retreated oh-so long ago. As the symphony reached its rousing conclusion, Tara weaved her way through the displays of *Gibsons* and *Fenders*, *Yamahas*, *Baldwins*, and *Steinways*. The shop grew silent as she approached the string section, then suddenly shimmered with a silvery glide of angelic tones. Tara knew that *glissando* could only have come from one instrument.

She wanted to run; hunting Mystery Girl was a bad idea. But the playing continued, and with such beauty and sensitivity that Tara couldn't pry herself away. Her heart edged forward, and Tara followed, dreading what she knew she was going to see. Tara hid behind a display of standing basses and peeked out. Some fifteen feet away, seated with the instrument on her shoulder—the $5,500 harp that Tara herself had coveted—was her mirror image: a willowy girl of sixteen with honey-blonde hair cut just above her shoulders. The girl played several quick flourishes, then a simple folk song emerged, a melody that evoked struggle, loss and resignation. Then, a flurry of graceful hand movements portrayed the passage of time, like water flowing, and an emergence, after the struggle, into a new space of peace and hope. Tara's throat tightened, and she felt a mist gather on the rims of her eyes.

"You play so wonderfully," the store clerk said. "You must have had an excellent teacher."

Neither the girl nor the woman with her offered a comment. The girl righted the harp and rose from the stool.

"It's an expensive instrument, I know," the clerk said, "but it would be awful to let such talent go to waste. We have several financing options."

"I'll have to speak to my husband," the woman said. She was gray-haired and probably too old to be the girl's natural mother. *Her grandmother?* As Tara strained to overhear what the woman was saying to the clerk, the girl turned slowly around. Her green eyes locked onto Tara's and widened as her mouth dropped open.

"Oh," she said softly, "you must be that Hartzwell girl."

———

TARA HAD BOLTED. Fled. She'd dashed from the mall to Flipper's *Jeep* and begged him to "Go! Now! Get me out of here!" Forty-five minutes later, the *Jeep* was parked at the curb, a stone's throw away, not from her own home, but from the Grant's. Twenty minutes earlier, the minivan had driven past, turned into the driveway, and disappeared into the garage.

"Tee, we just can't sit here forever," Flipper said.

"I know."

"You gotta get home, or your folks are gonna freak out."

"I know," she snapped. "What do you want from me?"

"I don't know," he grumbled. "A decision?"

Tara arched her back and stretched her chin towards the ceiling, as though straining against invisible bonds. She hated this feeling of being trapped, but she couldn't get up the courage for what she had to do. In her mind, she had replayed the scene a dozen times, where she walked up to the front door, rang the bell, apologized for running off and explained herself. But it seemed so removed from reality. How could it end well? On the other hand, if the girl would just come out, Tara could approach her. She could keep a safe distance, and easily retreat to the *Jeep* for whatever reason.

"You want me to go talk to them?" Flipper asked.

Tara shook her head. Maybe she should just go home. But then the matter would gnaw at her, driving her crazy until she had to return here and try again.

A tap on the side window startled them both. Tara turned towards the sidewalk to see a black suit sleeve and a white shirt cuff. She rolled down the window and Fr. Chandler crouched beside the car door.

"C'mon, you two. Eden is waiting."

CHAPTER
NINE

"For if the trumpet gives an uncertain sound,
who shall prepare himself to the battle?"
— 1 Cor. 14:8

"PURIFY ME WITH HYSSOP, LORD," *a deep voice asked.* "*And
I shall be clean of sin. Wash me, and I shall be whiter than snow. Have mercy
on me, God, in your great kindness. Glory be to the Father, and to the Son, and
to the Holy Spirit.*"

*Tara felt the oil melt on her forehead and ooze towards her temple. The
room trembled with familiar voices answering,* "*As it was in the beginning, is
now, and ever shall be, world without end. Amen.*"

REVEREND MARTIN HUGH CHANDLER (goes by Hugh,
sometimes Hughie, never Martin or, God forbid, Marty) had
fumbled to get through the rite. Just two months ago, he'd anointed
Teri. Now he'd been called for her identical twin. Two beautiful girls
cut down in the flower of youth. As for the first, *Thy will be done, O
Lord*. The second was more complicated. Becky said she'd "darted

out into traffic," but Bill said, "she paused and leapt." The difference was significant, raising the awful question of whether Tara had meant to throw her life away, which could imperil her immortal soul.

What to tell the parents? The tender-aged siblings? Traditional Church teaching was a hard pill to swallow, condemning suicide as a most atrocious crime and, "in hatred of the sin and to arouse horror of it," the Church would deny Christian burial to those who'd taken their own lives. In recent years, the message had softened. The revised catechism conceded that "grave psychological disturbances, anguish, or grave fear of hardship, suffering, or torture can diminish the responsibility...." So, there's a chance that suicide would not be a mortal sin. But it was only a chance.

These circumstances challenged the young priest to craft a message that conveyed the urgency of Tara's peril without alienating contemporary Christians raised to believe "Jesus loves me no matter what." Without spiraling too deeply into Dante, Fr. Chandler had to urge the family to pray as hard as they could for Tara's recovery... *and* for her soul's encouragement as she teetered on—*what?*—the *edge of the abyss*? He sifted through countless words and phrases, all vaguely medieval-sounding and sadly void of relevance to the present age.

Hugh recalled a Belgian priest he'd known in seminary, who'd been a hospital chaplain in the Congo, ministering to victims of trypanosomiasis, the dread sleeping sickness spread by tsetse flies. Well into his eighties, Père Hervé still went barefoot in the custom of the Discalced Carmelites of St. John of the Cross. When Hugh asked why, the old friar smiled mischievously. "I take childish delight in appearing as a shocking contradiction to the world." Months later, the holiest man Hugh had ever known confessed he was afraid of dying.

"I'm not a brave man," Père Hervé had said. "I hope my life has been to some extent virtuous. But I've never had to be brave and don't know how."

"You've given your life to God, what have *you* got to fear?"

"Physical pain, of course," Père said. "But more so, the attacks.

The terrors." He explained that his fear was common among religious. "You think we all go peacefully, and our soul rises on a cloud. But there is pain, as the soul tries to crack the earthen vessel that constrains it. Then the Evil One attacks, and his terrors are vicious. He would like nothing more than to snatch a pious soul from the threshold of heaven."

"Why weren't we told about this?" Hugh asked. The seminary's class on death and dying had been all about psychology.

The old friar smiled. "You are being trained, in the Age of Nice, to serve the Church of Nice. The Church of Nice does not understand malevolence."

Fr. Chandler had had a hard time picturing a deathbed attack on Teri Hartzwell or imagining that a just and loving God would leave her unprotected as she passed from this world to the next. But, recalling Père Hervé's warning, Hugh had proceeded with an abundance of caution. He'd taken holy images and objects to Teri. For her soul's encouragement, he'd told the parents. But secretly he'd sought to make her hospital room a demon-free zone. Under different circumstances, he might have told the parents that they had authority, in Jesus' Name, to bind any demons tormenting their daughter. But these were "Golden Rule" Catholics, whose faith was based on reason and empathy, not on the fear of horned, goat-footed, pointy-tailed demons jabbing pitchforks at hapless humans. Hugh had done what he could to prepare Teri, without alarming her or the family unnecessarily. He'd stressed the positive—the beautiful promise of their faith—and, without broaching the subject of 'the terrors,' he'd assured the parents that the family's prayers at Teri's bedside would ease her passing. When it was time, they'd all been there, rosaries in hand, fervently praying, all but Tara.

Now where was Tara? Unconscious, yet agitated. Fitfully sleeping. He wondered what she was contending with. Was it possible the Evil One had pulled a gruesome bait-and-switch? That the attacks Hugh had dreaded for Teri had been visited upon Tara? Was the Devil so cunning he'd used Teri's death to harden Tara's heart against the grace that could save her? The young priest felt ill-equipped and overwhelmed. Yet, having concluded the rite for Tara, Fr. Chandler measured his words to her parents. *These are contemporary suburbanites,* he told himself. *Mention Lucifer and they'll scoff. Encourage them to pray. Skip the specifics.*

Leaving Tara's hospital room, Hugh had run through a long list of regrets. First, in Teri's eulogy, he'd served up that old cliché that it didn't matter how long a life a person lived, but whether that life had prepared the soul for eternity. Easy for him to say. He'd shied away from Teri's fear of dying. The unfairness she'd felt as she was forced to leave everything behind. He'd emphasized her faith—genuine enough—but might have spoken too glowingly about her desire to be with Jesus. That might have struck Tara as a lot of malarkey; their interactions since had been tense. Jeremy's confession had touched on another sore spot: betrayal. Already disappointed by God, Tara knew someone close had violated her trust.

Hugh also regretted not being more available in the weeks after Teri's death. Bill and Becky had come by the office a couple of times to talk through their grief. He'd told them to keep in touch but had been gone most of July. Everyone took vacations, but being a priest was different. Jesus might ditch his disciples and walk up the mountain, but He'd sure as shooting be there when the storm hammered their boat.

Fast-forward, Fr. Chandler's biggest regret had come today, when he'd gotten a phone call from Jean Grant: "The Hartzwell girl showed up, out of the blue, at the mall. Call me paranoid, but it wasn't a chance encounter. I'm sure she came looking for us." Followed quickly by another call: "Okay, maybe I am paranoid, but there's a *Jeep* parked outside, with two high school kids, and one of them, I'm sure, is the Hartzwell girl."

Regrets. Recriminations. Ministerial errors were inevitable, but Hugh Chandler seemed to be racking them up at an alarming rate. Why hadn't he seen this coming? And why hadn't he discretely, confidentially, brought *the Hartzwell girl* to Eden? He was tempted to blame the Bishop, but it was Hugh who had put his foot down, demanding the girls be kept apart.

Hugh had made his demand at the very end of July, some four or five weeks after Teri's funeral. The Bishop's secretary had called to arrange a golf date. Hugh suspected His Eminence Eduardo Montalban, or Monty, as the priests of the diocese called him, had some bone to pick. Or rather wanted to pick the same bone that His Eminence gnawed whenever the two met: Fr. Chandler's ineffectiveness as a fundraiser for the high school.

"There's a story, maybe you've heard," His Eminence had mused one evening, while pouring each man a brandy. "The faculty of a large university are all assembled, and an angel appears. 'Dean,' the angel says, 'in view of your longstanding excellence, I can grant you a choice of three blessings: immense power, immense wealth, or limitless wisdom.' Well, of course, the Dean, he's surrounded by a hundred academics, so immediately he says, 'I'll take wisdom.' The angel makes some dazzling sign and there's flashes of light, and the angel disappears. The faculty all creep forward, totally awed."

With his eyes wide, playing the role of the curious faculty member, Monty slowly handed Fr. Chandler the snifter of brandy. "Say something. Give us some heavenly wisdom." Then his face dropped as he assumed the role of the Dean and stated bluntly, "I should have taken the money."

His Eminence had laughed heartily, even growing red in the face, at the joke he must have told a thousand times before. Fr. Chandler smiled politely and swirled his brandy. "You see, Hughie, it's not money that's the root of all evil; it's the love of money. Acknowledging the necessity and efficacy of money is not sin in the least. It's pragmatism. Holy poverty is all very well for those who deal only in graces. But you and I manage institutions. Remember, Our Lord instructs us to be shrewd like the dishonest manager in the parable. What we hope to accomplish requires money. You know it, I know it, and the people we're begging from know it. What's more, they want to give. To feel like they're part of something meaningful. So, stop thinking of yourself as a thief in the night. When you feel shame begging for that school, you know what you're doing? Committing the sin of *materialism*. Yes, because you are imagining that the worldly wealth of your donors is worth more than the mission of your school. As if filthy lucre mattered more than the kingdom of heaven."

The lecture had continued in that vein for some time. Bishop Monty pontificated while Fr. Chandler tried to acquire a taste for brandy. He sipped, nodded, and felt his tongue go numb. He stared at the clock above the mantle. Eventually, His Eminence reiterated his support for Fr. Chandler and expressed confidence the good priest would "grow into his office."

Thus, Hugh could only interpret the golf invitation as a prelude to another lecture on his deficiencies. He decided to take one demerit off the board by working on his golf game. In his third consecutive evening at the driving range, Hugh had bumped into Bill Hartzwell, swinging mercilessly at the white pellets that mocked his exertion. Bill said he was deeply concerned about Tara, and Fr. Chandler muttered something banal about time healing wounds. Regrettably, he'd responded like a social worker instead of a priest; he'd promised to keep an eye on her when school reopened. Thus, *the Hartzwell girl* had been very much on Hugh's mind when he met the bishop. Yet, he was puzzled when His Eminence brought her up.

"We're in the messaging business, Hughie," Monty reminded him, as the golf cart lurched to a stop at the joint in the dogleg of the fifteenth hole. "Jesus made that very clear. *Good news*, right? And He illustrated the good news with stories. Symbols. Iconic characters. Well, you've got your story to tell. You've got the *Número Uno* high school in the county, one hundred percent college acceptance, and a Christian education. But you can't just serve up facts and expect donors to write checks."

His Eminence hoisted his great girth out of the driver's seat. He grabbed a five-iron. Hughie fished around for a seven. The fierce sun had been frying his neural synapses and depleting his energy. He hoped the club's extra weight would compensate for his ebbing strength.

"You need to craft a message that resonates," Monty said as he squared his stance beside the ball. "Iconic characters. Take those twin girls on your golf team." He looked down the narrowing fairway to the green. "Magnets for publicity. Had the whole country club buzzing. And from there, it's a short stroll to the board room, and that's where checks are written."

The Bishop swung, perhaps his most graceful stroke of the match. The ball elevated softly and plunged right to the edge of the green. After a couple of soft bounces, it rolled to a stop a dozen feet from the cup. Monty turned towards Hugh with a Cheshire cat smile of canary-devouring satisfaction.

"You do realize one died?" Hugh asked.

The Bishop flicked his club dismissively and strode back to the cart.

"Is that where our story ends? The whole reason we're in business is that our story *doesn't* end in death. Resurrection. Renewal." He slid his iron into his bag and leaned with one hand on the cart. He waited for the priest to get into his stance before warning, "That club's too heavy."

It was Hughie's turn to be dismissive. But he also needed to perk up, rally, get his blood flowing. He rolled his shoulders and wagged his head rapidly, like a cartoon cat trying to reshape the cranium his mousey nemesis had just flattened with a frying pan. He focused his bleary eyes down the fairway and took a deep breath. Hughie swung too loosely, he thought, but struck the ball cleanly and launched it high. *Too high?* It struck beyond the pin, but through God's mercy, backspin, and the high bank on the far side of the green, the ball reversed direction and rolled to within two feet of the hole. A sudden burst of energy had Hughie pumping his fist, and he actually had a spring in his step as he trotted back to the cart.

Monty drove to the green in silence. But, on approaching his ball, he got chatty again. "Now, say that Hartzwell girl never golfs again, that's a tale of defeat. In the context of her life, it may not be. She may on to bigger betters. But in the public mind..." He turned a gladiatorial thumb down. "And that's a black eye for your institution."

His Eminence rocked forward, putting the ball straight towards the cup, yet the ball stalled about eighteen inches out. He huffed momentarily and continued. "But you get her back on the links, she leads your team to a championship, and you've got a triumph.

A triumph that could only have happened in the nurturing environment of St. Stephen's Prep! Don't scowl, Hughie, we must never doubt but that Holy Mother Church is in the triumph business. Let that Hartzwell girl be the face of St. Stephen's for a couple of semesters, and you'll be operating with a surplus in no time."

That formulation struck Hughie as both naïve and cynical. Yet, he conceded, "Well, golf seems to be in her blood. So, maybe."

"We can't have maybes, Hugh." With his next stroke, His Eminence sunk the putt. "If not her, someone else. Some*thing* else. You need a big message to turn your finances around. We can't push another tuition increase on our parents. We need donations to erase the deficit and build an endowment. We fail, and St. Stephen's will close in five years."

Hughie let his putter slip from his hand.

"How much messaging can we do if we close our schools?"

His Eminence grabbed a water bottle from the back seat of the cart and took a long swallow. "I'm as supportive of Catholic education as the next careerist cleric," he said. "But the diocese has other needs—our parochial schools, the hospital—and you're sitting on some very expensive real estate."

"You're shopping us?"

The Bishop offered Hughie a drink, which he accepted greedily.

"On occasion," Monty said, "I solicit contributions from tech firms in the Valley. One CEO turned the tables on me. Her offer was staggering."

Hughie cringed as he pictured towering stacks of bound-up Benjamins, piled Scrooge McDuck style on the table in front of the saucer-eyed Bishop, who'd somehow gathered the strength to walk away. Hughie also felt the ground loosening under him. He'd imagined St. Stephen's was invulnerable. The flagship high school would last until Jesus Himself returned to close it.

I'm not about to lose this school, Hugh told himself. But first, there was the putt. The hole was a par four, which Monty had shot. Hugh had a chance to go one under. He squinted to read the green, but it might as well have been tea leaves. He drew the putter back, muttering a prayer to St. Andrew. He froze as the Bishop, surely calculating his timing, interrupted.

"You know what your great obstacle to success is, Hugh?"

Fr. Chandler straightened and fixed his eyes on His Eminence. Now, the gloves were off. It was the time of truth-telling, and Hughie would learn he was — *what?* — too modest, too self-effacing, too easily awed by the great deeds asked of him?

"It's pride," Monty said flatly. Hugh felt his stomach sink. He listened, incredulous, as the Bishop expounded. "Pride is the ego's defense against, and best evidence of, self-rejection. This is why pride is a sin, because in rejecting self, we reject the Creator who fashioned our self. Humility is a virtue, because it accepts the self as is, and thus welcomes the Creator with gratitude. If you, Martin Hugh Chandler, are too proud to beg for the good of the Church, you are too proud to serve Our Lord." Here, His Eminence paused for a second to read Hughie's reaction, which the good priest hoped was impassive as stone.

Yet, the Bishop must have read a counterargument in Hugh's expression, because he continued, "You think I am proud, because I'm pompous. And that you are humble, because you're reserved and austere. But I love what God has done in my life, Hughie. And you are dreadfully unhappy in yours. And that unhappiness is a consequence of pride."

Hugh felt a surge of anger. If there was one flaw Fr. Chandler did not possess in abundance, it was pride. He wondered what Père Hervé might say. Perhaps this: "Martin, you want too much to fit into this world. To be seen as a wise priest. You're afraid to appear as a contradiction. To be God's clown and draw ridicule. This makes you silent, when you should be bold."

Without offering His Eminence a retort, Hughie took his stance over the ball and tried to empty his mind of everything but the path to the cup. Hugh struck the ball cleanly, and though it hooked right, the slope of the green gently curved it back towards the hole. It caught the lip, made a quarter spin and dropped in. Hughie gasped.

"Birdie!" Monty cheered. "Now that's got to be a good omen for our Wrens."

"I thought Catholics didn't believe in omens," Hugh said, as he scooped their balls out of the cup, and tossed the *Titlist* back to his boss.

"Don't be such a stick-in-the-mud, Hughie," the Bishop admonished. "That's a symptom of pride as well."

So now everything is pride? Hugh wondered.

His Eminence scanned his score sheet. "I think I've got a one-stroke lead, so I'm going to assert my prerogative as corporation sole of the diocese to declare this match complete. An exercise in humility will do you good."

"In other words, you're afraid I'll overtake you. That I'll be sharpening my knife on the sixteenth hole and on the seventeenth, I'll find my mark."

"Nonsense, I have a nose for assassination that rivals the Borgias," Monty proclaimed. "But there are people I want you to meet, and the time of *rendezvous* approacheth." Hughie knew that could only mean potential donors. On the ride to the restaurant, Monty expounded. "Seymour Grant is a former Livermore Labs scientist who developed some telecommunications widget that's as necessary for cellphones as rubber is for tires."

"Actually, most tires are synthetic. From petroleum hydro-carbons."

The Bishop winced and turned slightly pink. "My point, Fr. Chandler, is that Seymour Grant sits atop a mountain of money looking down upon foothills of money that gently cascade onto pastures of money."

"So, he's got money."

"You're quicker than you look."

Stopping the cart, His Eminence peeled off his golf gloves, tossed them into the back seat, and trundled towards the door. "It is our good fortune that Dr. Grant has an interest in St. Stephen's for his recently arrived niece. Family tragedy in Nebraska or Kansas or another of those rectangular flyover states. From what I gather, the type of drama Truman Capote might embellish. They want the girl enrolled at St. Stephen's."

"I don't see any…"

"I know," Monty drawled. "It's not a problem, as a point of fact, but the impression that it's problematic is helpful to us. Thus, the Grants think we went through a little trouble to do them a special favor *and*...."

"They give us money."

"You're going to go far, my boy."

The only place Hughie wanted to go at the moment was the restroom. He excused himself and took a moment to splash cold water on his face and steel himself for the task ahead. Returning to the dining room, he spotted Monty seated with a gray, but lively, couple enjoying a Chardonnay. The gentleman rose as Monty made introductions.

"Seymour Grant, may I present Fr. Martin H. Chandler. Fr. Chandler, this is Seymour Grant and his wife Eugenia."

"Jean." The wife smiled and offered her hand. Hughie shook her hand gently and waited for Dr. Grant to sit before taking his place.

"The young lady has gotten off at the moment," Monty said. "But, oh!" He cast an arm over Hughie's left shoulder. "Here she is now. Fr. Chandler, I'd like you to meet Eden Grant."

Hughie shifted in his chair and pitched forward to rise. But he fell back on his tail with a thud, as he stared, bewildered, into the smiling face of Teri Hartzwell.

———

"YOU'VE GOT to be kidding me," Hughie shout-whispered at Monty. He pivoted away, took two steps and reversed course again. "You don't see it?"

"Perhaps my eye for the ladies is not as keen as yours."

"That girl, Eden, is the spitting image of the Hartzwell twins."

Monty shrugged. "Alright, there's a resemblance."

"It's not a resemblance, it's a freakish anomaly, an astronomical phenomenon. It's an impossibility."

Hughie had not covered his shock gracefully. Who knows what Eden thought when this stranger, a man twice her age, became flustered and stammered, unable to look at her directly? He'd hustled the Bishop out of the dining hall to confer privately before the meeting devolved into total disaster.

"What's your point, Hugh?" His Eminence demanded.

"We can't enroll this girl."

The Bishop's eyes widened, and his throat swelled. Hughie could almost read the sadly melting dollar signs in his enlarged pupils.

"Can't we let the girl grieve?" Hugh begged.

Back at the table, Monty explained to the Grants that, "We have a situation." Hughie searched the Internet for images of the Hartzwell twins and found some photos of their golf exploits. One image showed the girls in closeup, holding their trophies. He passed his phone around the table and watched the chins drop.

"We'd like to accommodate Eden, but we have to balance that desire with our concerns for Tara."

The Grants were disappointed but acknowledged the problem. Hugh had placed the evidence before their eyes.

"I didn't think there could be another," Eden said quietly.

"Shush, child," Jean said.

The girl's resignation was eerily reminiscent of the sadness he'd seen in both Hartzwell girls. The priest had to wonder what Eden had seen, back in her Kansas tragedy, and if it had a parallel in what Tara was going through.

That was the last time Fr. Chandler had seen or heard of the Grants until Jean's phone calls. He wondered again if he had done enough for the Hartzwells. Had *pride* held him back? Prevented him from playing God's fool? Had he so feared looking like a medieval relic, that he'd soft-pedaled and diluted the truth this family had desperately needed to hear? Teri had passed, not quietly, but—to borrow a word from His Eminence—triumphantly. But Tara? Now was the moment of truth.

Tara slinked out of the *Jeep* and Fr. Chandler glared through the windshield at Tommy, who pointed at his chest, as if to say, "Who me? I'm just the driver," then reluctantly pulled the keys from the ignition and popped the door open.

"You know, stalking's a crime in California," the priest said.

"So's identity theft," Tara grumbled.

Fair enough, Hugh silently conceded. He tipped his head towards the Grant home. "Maybe you'll feel better after you meet her."

Tara didn't move. Tommy splayed his arms over the roof of the *Jeep* and implored with palms up. "What we came for, Tee."

"The name's Tara," she said. Then she beat a path around the front end of the vehicle, marching so fiercely that Hugh sprinted to catch up.

CHAPTER
TEN

"Even if she be not harmed,
her heart may fail her in so much and so many horrors;
and hereafter she may suffer
—both in waking, from her nerves,
and in sleep, from her dreams."
—— Bram Stoker, *Dracula*

THE DOOR OPENED JUST as Tara's foot hit the stoop. A tallish lady, younger than her gray hair might indicate, drew the door back, opening her home with such a welcoming smile that Tara was totally disarmed.

"Hello, Tara," the lady said, almost apologetically. "Won't you come in?"

Tara felt Fr. Chandler and Flipper at her back. There was no slinking away. She nodded and stepped inside. The home, which had been perfectly nondescript on the outside, continued that theme within. This could have been any sitcom family home in any decade since the dawn of television. The bland décor was void of distractions, and the open floorplan would let a studio audience catch all the action on the ground floor, not to mention wacky antics in the backyard, visible through sliding glass doors. Maybe Tara was being unfair, but the place struck her as an imitation of family life rather than the real deal.

"I'm Mrs. Grant. Won't you sit down?"

Tara hunkered down on the far end of the sofa, as Flipper perched himself on the edge of a recliner. All that separated them were the *faux* logs of the gas fireplace. Fr. Chandler sat at the opposite end of the sofa.

"Eden's getting some refreshments," Mrs. Grant said.

Of course, Tara thought, *sitcom moms always have home-baked cookies.* Tara heard the Western saloon doors of the kitchen burst open and a tray of food and drinks came forth, held by a living, breathing facsimile of Teri.

"Hi. I'm Eden," the girl said, punctuating the phrase with a head tilt that should have cued a laugh-track. Having placed the tray on the coffee table, Eden folded her legs elegantly into lotus position and lowered her posterior to the carpet.

"I'm Tara."

"I'm starved," said Flipper.

As he reached to chow down, Tara thought she heard the audience snicker. What she heard next was Mrs. Grant deliver an origin story of how Eden had come to live with her and her husband, who "should be home shortly." If the tale as to be believed, Eden was a suburban Kansas girl who had suffered a family tragedy, which Mrs. Grant insisted was "too raw" to discuss in any detail. Upshot: Eden was just a normal flesh-and-blood, American girl—who "happened to look a bit like" Teri/Tara—whom Fate had deposited in the very same county of Northern California.

Tara bristled at the phrase "a bit like." Downplaying the resemblance was absurd; it suggested some kind of coverup, though of what, Tara couldn't imagine. Maybe Eden was a triplet, separated at birth. Becky and Bill might have some '*splainin*' to do.

Then, out of the blue, Eden asked, "Are you going to play golfing again?" The odd phrasing was creepy enough, but the question indicated personal knowledge of Tara this new girl should not have had.

"I've never played golfing," Eden went on. "My family wasn't as well off. I played *suff*-ball and bas*KET*ball."

Flipper gave a perplexed look; the awkward pronunciations hadn't escaped his attention.

"Eden was a point guard," Mrs. Grant interjected. "She's ambidextrous and can dribble and pass with either hand."

"Yes," Eden said, as if recalling a note from last night's homework.

This was getting all too weird for Tara, and she was itching to head home. Almost on cue, her phone vibrated with a text from her Mom.

"We really have to go," she said, as Flipper backhoed a fistful of dip onto a *Dorito*. His mouth crammed, he nodded in agreement. Then, after forcefully swallowing, he asked, "How you gettin' home?" Tara shot daggers from her eyes, spelling out "With you, idiot."

To which Flipper responded, "I can take you as far as the *CD*."

Appealing to Fr. Chandler did no good. "I've got a wedding rehearsal in twenty minutes."

"You're welcome to wait here, dearie," Mrs. Grant said. "If you want your folks to pick you up. My husband will be home from the lab any minute. I'm sure he'd love to meet you."

Oh, sure, Tara thought, *is that the lab where he built Eden?* "I better go with Flipper. That's halfway home, and my Dad can pick me up."

"Well, this certainly was a pleasure," Mrs. Grant said, as she crossed to the front door.

"I hope we can be friends," Eden said. "I think I'd like to go to your school."

Tara wasn't sure she heard correctly.

"A subject for another time, dear," Mrs. Grant cautioned, and Fr. Chandler hustled Tara out.

"Go to St. Stephen's?"

"Not if it's too weird for you," Father said, ushering her and Flipper across the street.

"Weird? What's weird? Flipper is this weird to you?"

"I'm, uh, yeah, I'd go with 'weird.' That kind of sums it up. But too bad we've gotta split before Dr. Doom gets back from the lab."

"If Dr. Doom was coming," Father said, "they wouldn't have let us leave."

"So, you're saying it's Lex Luthor?"

"I'm saying…," Father huffed. "I don't know what I'm saying, except both girls deserve empathy. Let's not get tribal and take sides. Let's have some understanding. Even if it's hard to understand."

Hard to understand didn't begin to explain it. Flipper, as always, had a theory, which he shared once they got into his *Jeep*. "Cyborg infiltration."

"What?"

"It's a classic subversion tactic but with human-machine hybrids. These guys, way I see it, mastered cyborg technology. So, they built this Eden in the image of Teri, thinking they're going to swap them out, while Teri's in the hospital. But she dies too soon. So now, they want Eden to cozy up to you, learn everything she needs, before they have her replace you. Whaddaya think?"

"That you are certifiably insane."

"Well, you shouldn't be thinking, what with the concussion. Just let me think for both of us."

"Yeah, no. That's not gonna happen."

As Flipper continued his rant, Tara texted her Mom and then phoned her Dad.

"I'll explain later, okay. I'm with Flipper. … Ha, ha, it's not— … I'm not *gallivanting*. I don't even know how to *gallivant*. Maybe when I get home you can show me. … I'm not changing the subject. … Look, Fr. Chandler was there, okay? Pretty sure he took a vow not to *gallivant*. … Please, just pick me up at the *CD*." She lowered the phone and asked Flipper, "Which one? Greenvale, right?"

Flipper nodded.

"Greenvale. I'll be outside the movies."

"So, Bill and Becky are totally cool?" Flipper asked facetiously.

"Yeah. Always," Tara grumbled. "What, you think they're in on it?"

"I haven't figured that out yet."

"You really are crazy."

"No, this situation is crazy."

"Well, two things can be true at the same time. First of all, what are *they* trying to infiltrate? My family? Who cares? We're not sitting on Pentagon secrets. Why would they even know us?"

"You and Teri are all over the Internet."

"For playing golf."

"Which makes you the darlings of the country club set. Which puts you close to some powerful people. CEOs, right? Politicians. The powers behind the throne. C'mon, use your imagination."

"You're doing fine without me."

Flipper found a parking spot thirty or so yards from the *CD*.

"Thanks for the rides," she told him. "And for helping me get to the bottom of this."

"We haven't reached bottom yet," Flipper said. "But we'll get there."

That was hardly reassuring. But as Flipper strutted off to the *CD*, Tara sought the shade of the cinema's marquee, and mulled over what he'd said. His conclusions were ridiculous, of course, but it was hard to escape the thought that someone, some*thing*, was targeting her. And those closest to her. What she couldn't understand was *why?* Her family didn't have anything much. They were just regular people living their lives. Why would they be the targets of some cosmic plot? Her head started to hurt again, then practically split when a car approached.

The thumping bass of its stereo was set on *Pulverize*, as a rapper's voice spouted gross, filthy lyrics. Tara's instinct was to walk slowly away, but her legs stiffened and wouldn't move. Over her left shoulder, Tara saw the black *Challenger* slow to a halt in the No Parking Zone at the cinema's curb.

The engine cut off, killing the noise. The door swung open, and the driver emerged, resting his crossed arms on the top of the window frame, and staring intently at Tara.

"Emerald eyes," he called to her. "Imagine running into you."

"I don't have to imagine. So, thanks."

"Yeah, sorry, but that was all you," he said strolling towards her.

"You threw yourself in front of my car. Dented my hood and cracked my windshield. But I'm willing to let bygones be bygones."

"How 'bout you just *be gone*?" Tara replied.

Unperturbed, the youth continued, "I guess you're waiting for somebody, huh? Not that quarterback? He's not in your league. You need a ride; I've got the wheels."

Tara bristled. "If you think I would get in that car with you, you are a special kind of stupid," she told him. "My Dad's coming, so…"

"Oh," he said, with mock exaggeration. "Quite a temper, your old man."

"What do you want, when you knock his daughter unconscious?"

"I don't know. Rationality?" He sucked his cheeks in and rolled his eyes upward in mock dorkishness, then snapped back to ultra-cool passivity. "But I guess he couldn't admit that you diving into traffic had more to do with him chasing you than me just driving by."

Tara's nostrils flared. Still, she had to concede, "Maybe."

"And maybe his temper, maybe it's a little more than that." The youth glided to her right, giving her side-eye as he did, prompting her to counter-step left. The two seemed to enter a mystical dance: side step, back cross, step as they rotated beneath the marquee. "Has he ever beaten you?"

Tara's spine tingled, as if a rattler were cracking the air in front of her.

"I can protect you."

"Yeah, well, the minute I rely on you is when I check out."

He looked earnestly at her, "Didn't you try that once already?"

"No!" Tara screamed.

Even to her ears, it sounded extreme, so no wonder the youth stepped back and a customer, exiting the *CD*, bolted towards her to ask, "Are you okay?" That customer was Lima Autufuga, and he called her "Tetara."

"She's fine."

"I don't recall asking you," Lima said. "Tetara, is this guy both-ering you?"

"Oh, so you're her hero?"

Lima paid no attention, focusing only on Tara. "Is there a problem?"

Tara didn't know how to answer; she just wanted her Dad to pull up.

"Look, fat boy, the girl's with me. We were having a discussion: low carbohydrate, trans fat-free, so it really doesn't involve you."

Lima looked only at Tara. He was holding a huge bag of *whatever* from the *CD*. Tara imagined it held two dozen cheeseburgers and fries with three or four milkshakes. Suddenly, she was more concerned for him than for herself.

"If he's bothering you, I can make him go away."

That struck Tara as a magical statement. *Could he make Eden vanish? Could he bring back Teri?*

"How exactly?" the dark youth asked. "Any physical contest probably ends with you in cardiac arrest. Have you experienced chest pains?"

"I'm 'bout to give you chest pains, friend."

"Don't, please," Tara said. "My Dad's coming."

"So, maybe you just want to waddle along," the youth said.

"I'm maybe gon' *waddle* up and down your back."

"Yeah, well, put down the spoils of your buffalo hunt and show how you mean business."

Lima's right arm sagged, and the paper sack slid towards the ground. *No, no, no,* Tara gasped, before glimpsing the satin blue exterior of her Dad's *Chevy* pulling into a spot at the *CD*.

"My Dad's here," she yelped, stepping between the two. She touched Lima on the shoulder to let him escort her to the car, leaving the dark youth hands-on-hips beneath the marquee.

"Do you need a ride?" Tara asked.

"You think I walked here?"

"No, I just… Okay." Lima tipped the bill of his Fremont ballcap and ambled off.

"Who was that?" her Dad asked.

"He plays for Fremont," Tara said.

"I didn't know they had a Sumo team."

The ride home was tense, given that Tara was in trouble for

leaving school, but less tense than if her Mom had been driving. When Dad said, "We'll talk about it when we get home," he didn't mean, "We won't talk about anything," or "I'm going to talk about it, but I don't want you to." They just set the topic aside and talked about other stuff.

"How did it feel to be out and around?"

"Okay. I mean, I felt okay, but things were weird."

"Okay. This Flipper thing, it's not like, romantic?"

"Dad, it's not even a thing."

"Alright. And that's not the weird part?"

They were practically home, so Tara figured there was no harm spilling the beans. "There's a girl that looks like me. And Teri. I told Mom I saw her. Today I met her."

"Huh," was all he said. Tara didn't know how to interpret that. Was he blown away at the freakishness of it, or did he think she was crazy? He'd blame "those pills" she was on. They agreed to table any further discussion until after dinner. By then, Tara had decided the easiest way to get through it was to play the Priest Card.

"I don't want to argue whether I'm telling the truth. Fr. Chandler was there, so you can ask him. I'm just going to say what happened, and you figure it out."

That freed her to just recite the facts as they had happened without interruption or judgment. So, the next question was whether Tara would go to school tomorrow. Mom wanted to give her another day, but Dad said she should start off at school and call if she needed to come home. His plan won out, and Tara retired to her bedroom to get her homework done.

Dawn struck in what seemed the blink of an eye, but Tara was wide awake. Showering, dressing, eating breakfast were all a blur. Fast-forward, Tara found herself in Junior Hall chatting with Raquel and Cheryl, when suddenly, Flipper burst on the scene and blurted, "Did you hear what happened at the *CD*?"

Cheryl dismissed him. "Somebody slip on some fry grease?"

"No," he gasped as though he was seeing it there in the moment. "Dude was murdered in his car. They stuffed his throat with the burgers and pumped three shots into his chest."

"Not —" Tara started.

"The Samoan from Fremont. He's dead."

"PROPOFOL," *she said.* *"You might know the brand name, Diprivan?* *It's a very safe medication. Nothing more than a deep sleep, so that healing can* *begin."*

TARA just about fell over backwards. "That psycho!"

"Who?"

"He tried to get me into his car. Oh, my g—!"

Panic seized her. She was being stalked by a murderer.

"Who?" Raquel demanded.

"That, that guy that showed up at your party. The one picking a fight with Nolan." She explained how his noisy *Challenger* had come rolling up and how he tried to pick her up, but Lima came over to help. "He must have followed him back to his car."

"Good thing you didn't go with him," Flipper said.

"Ya think?!" Raquel snapped.

"You've got to tell the cops," Cheryl insisted. "He could show up looking for you."

"Or Nolan," Raquel said.

"I could call my uncle," Flipper offered.

Tara was already three steps down the hall. When she reached the front desk, the police were already there.

———

"YOU WANT TO TELL ME," Bill Hartzwell demanded, "why I had to forego my lunch to talk to a couple of cops?"

Tara had hoped when the school day ended, so would the questioning. "Didn't they tell you?"

"They told me many things," her Dad fumed. "What they didn't tell me was why my daughter would have an altercation with the guy who ran her down in the street and, two minutes later, not tell me about it."

So that's your damage? Tara thought. *Not, my daughter's being stalked by a homicidal maniac,* but *my daughter doesn't tell me about every creep she runs into?*

"It wasn't a thing then," Tara said. "I can handle boys being pushy, alright?"

"Yeah, when a friend comes out of nowhere to help," Dad said. "What happens now, when all your friends know what happened to the last friend? When they're all scared off and you're facing this terror alone?"

That can't happen, Tara thought, and her body went terribly cold.

"You shouldn't even be talking to the cops without one of us there," Dad said, meaning him and Mom. "Parents count for nothing anymore. We're the first accused and the last to have rights."

"Bill, this is about Tara," Mom reminded him.

"It's about how to protect her," he said. "Forgive me if I want some clear answers."

"They'll find him," Tara promised, forcing herself to believe. The kid was begging for attention. Probably cruising his muscle car from mall to mall all over the county. They'd pick him up before the night was out.

The door chime at 7:30 the next morning confirmed Tara's theory. Jeremy was already raising an hellacious racket with his video games, but muted the screen and ran to open the door, revealing the two detectives who'd interviewed Tara. Dad stepped outside, closing the door behind him, and as *PlayStation* Armageddon flared up again, Tara peered through the translucent white curtains at the shadow puppet theater until the cops withdrew. Dad pushed through the door, into the blood-red lights of apocalyptic combat emanating from the TV.

"Jeremy, turn that down," Mom said. "Your sister has a concussion."

"Still?" the little dork asked. The volume dropped a barely perceptible degree.

"They picked up, uh, the kid, Jean-Luc," Dad told Tara. "They didn't particularly like him and considered sweating him, but they got word it was a gang hit on your friend, Lima."

PlayStation punctuated this verdict with an explosive sequence worthy of Normandy.

"Jeremy, turn that down!" Mom yelled, hurling a roll of paper towels at him.

"That's impossible," Tara muttered.

"Sons of Samoa," Dad said. "His family had moved from L.A. to escape, but they tracked him down. The cops are satisfied the case is closed."

"You don't look satisfied," Tara observed. He'd been wringing his hands and shifting his weight from one foot to the other.

"Well, your story. They, the cops, think I put you up to it."

"What? Why?" Tara asked.

"Never mind." He spread his palms as if pushing the subject from the room. Mom pulled it right back.

"The boy claims your father assaulted him," she said.

"Hey," he snapped, "if I wanted her to know—"

"Did you?" Tara asked.

"He wasn't injured," Dad said.

"Did you assault him?"

Dad raked his fingers through his hair. "It's over, alright?"

"Except, he's suing us," Mom insisted. "And if he wins, we lose our house."

"That's crazy," Tara said, slapping the counter.

"It's nonsense," Dad explained. "He has no injuries, but he hired a bus-bench lawyer, who uses lawfare to generate revenue."

Tara felt her form shrinking, like wax under a heat lamp. The consequences of her leap were spiraling out of control.

"Don't worry, sweetheart," Dad said. "It'll settle, okay?"

"But…assault charges?" Tara asked.

"There's not a prosecutor in the country—" Mom's headshake undermined his point, so he dropped it, taking up what seemed to concern him much more. "Look, we can't let this drive a wedge between us." Her father was suddenly in sharp focus, his plaintive eyes drilling into hers. "Our family, there is power in being a family. They want to strip that power away. That's how they get to you."

The rest of the room dissolved around father and daughter, and for a moment Tara felt secure, protected under her Dad's authority. She was a toddling child again, looking up at the most powerful man in the world, and the war sounds emanating from the TV grew distant.

"Bill, what are you — ?" Becky demanded. Her sharp voice cut through a dull rumble in the background. "Who are *they*?"

Dad fanned his hands, as if *they* were gathered in the ether all around.

"Spare us the crazy conspiracy theories."

And Tara trembled again, because maybe *they* really were all around.

"Just trust me on this one point," Bill begged his daughter. "If this kid shows up, any time, no matter where, you've got to call me immediately."

Tara nodded. The TV cut out, deadening the virtual combat, and signaling it was time to go. Yet no one moved.

———

FAST-FORWARD TO SCHOOL day's end, Tara stood beneath the basket in the empty gym. *I don't belong here*, she thought, as the doors burst open letting in sunlight and floods of students, greedily seeking the best spots on the bleachers. Then she was atop the bleachers, surrounded by cheering classmates, in the final seconds of a pep rally. *This is a waste of precious time*, she thought. *I've got to fix…*

"We've got a dance here Saturday night," the Student Council President announced into the PA, "and we want to make it a victory dance! We want to see you dance with as much passion as our players bring to their game! And, to show you how, we have our own version of *Dancing with the Stars*. Here they are, your St. Stephen's Faculty!"

With that, music blasted, and the gym doors were thrown open.

A column of mostly middle-aged teachers ambled in, shaking and twisting, twitching, and shimmying. Fr. Chandler, who witnessed the festivities from a distant corner, later called it "free style boogeying," but to Tara they looked afflicted. Strangely possessed. Horror gripped her as the students around her roared with laughter.

"Obstbaum's having a seizure!" Cheryl cried.

"I thought pot controlled seizures," Raquel said.

As Mr. Obstbaum gyrated spastically, he took off his sport coat and spun it over his head like a lariat. He tossed the coat onto an open bench on the far side bleachers, and made his way to center court, his hips swirling in odd figure eights.

"Whoever got them to do this deserves a medal," someone said.

The bell rang, ending the assembly, the school day, and Tara's brutal week. She plodded down the bleachers a free woman! Then, on the gym floor, a powerful headache overtook her.

"You're coming to the game, right?" Raquel asked, with a slow voice that seemed to gurgle up from the bottom of a fish tank.

"I don't know," Tara said. The pain grew intense. "Loud places are a problem right now."

"You okay?"

Tara looked towards the exit and saw Fr. Chandler. He had picked up Mr. Obstbaum's sport coat and was asking Flipper to return it. Flipper seemed reluctant to leave, and Tara realized they hadn't spoken all day. Had he learned anything new? He jogged off with the sport coat, and Tara thought maybe she'd wait around from him to return. But, outside, sunlight stabbed her eyes. What had been a dull throb clawed its way from one temple to the other. Her legs felt leaden, and she needed to sit.

"You over-exerted yourself," Mom said.

What? Where?

Stacy climbed over Tara to get out of the minivan. Mom's silhouette was framed in the open doorway and backlit by the still-too-bright sun. She gave Tara a hand up and called Jeremy to carry in Tara's backpack.

"You need a good, long nap," Mom said, sounding like she was across the street.

No football tonight, Tara thought. *Probably no dance tomorrow.*

She slept through dinner and, after waking, took her cold plate from her place at the dining room table to the couch in the living room. Groggily content, she curled up with Stacy to binge-watch reruns of *Gossip Girl.* Then the real-world gossip intruded. A text from Raquel began "You will NOT believe this!"

"Mom, I gotta go!" Tara said, as she sprang from the sofa.

"Go where?"

"The game. Can you drive me?"

"You're not even dressed."

"I'm getting dressed."

"Tara, wait. That crowd? With all that noise?"

Tara placed her phone down on her bureau and pulled the pajama top over her head. She felt dizzy for a second but tried not to show it. She stepped out of the bottoms, getting her feet briefly tangled, and reached for the jeans draped over her desk chair.

"I won't stay long; it'll nearly be over anyway. I just have to go."

"Can you give me a hint why?"

Tara hesitated. She didn't want to hear Mom say, "Oh, that's nothing," or "Relax," or "What good would that do?" She was angry and she wanted some understanding. Finally, she grabbed the phone and showed her Mom the photo attached to Raquel's text. There was Flipper, dressed to the nines with his date for the game, Eden Grant.

"Holy guacamole," Mom gasped. "She really does look like you."

"Ya think?"

"Oh, sweetheart, I'm sorry," Mom said. "But you want to stay far away from this."

"First, I'm going to wring his scrawny neck!"

"You're not wringing anything," Mom warned her. "You want the whole school to think you're fighting over Flipper?"

"That's not—!"

"That's what they'll see, jealous girlfriend. And that'll be one more thing to live down."

"But he's such a jerk!" Tara cried.

Don't stress. C'mon. We'll hang out together. Teri's voice.

Mom was saying something.

"Honey, boys do jerky things all the time. You have to have thicker skin. Anyway, it's not like you're...*interested* in Flipper, is it?"

"'Course not," Tara said. "It's just, he's trying to be my friend, and whatever, but all he wants is some girl who looks like me?"

"Maybe she looks like you *and* she likes him?" Mom suggested.

Tara shook her head. "More like she's bored and doesn't have any friends." *And stupid Flipper was a superficial jerk.*

Mom hugged Tara tight and wiped a tear from her cheek. "Just rest up tonight. Tomorrow, if you feel like it, you show up at that dance looking like a million, with all your friends there, you'll forget all about this."

"*Pfft,* what if he brings her?"

"Then welcome her. It's not her fault she looks like you. And if Flipper likes this girl, then good for him. Good for you, too, unless...?"

"No, I don't like Flipper!" Tara declared. 'But he could have told me before pulling this stunt."

That's how they left it, returning to the living room and re-starting the TV. Not much later, the game must have ended, because Tara's phone exploded with text messages, mostly from Raquel. There were photos and video clips of the game, which the Wrens hung on to win 13-10, but woven throughout were prying questions:

"Flipper says you know her?"

"Are you related?"

"Where's she from?"

Tara dashed off: "We met. No. Kansas." And turned off her phone. She kept the phone off throughout the next morning as she tried to figure out what to do. The more she thought, the lonelier she felt. Her limbs got heavy, and she could hardly hold her head up.

"I'll tell you what to do," Dad said. "Stay home. Rest up for school on Monday."

"But—"

"But what? You have to defend your turf? *So what* this girl looks like you? You know who you are."

Did she really?

"Don't worry," Mom said. "I'll work on Dad."

That comment struck Tara as odd. She looked at her Mom, smiling, her face so aglow that Tara looked up for a source of light. Finding none, she turned back to her mother, but she was gone.

Now Stacy was at the entrance to the kitchen, impishly smiling.

"Ta-ra," she called singsong, "another boyfriend at the door."

Another? At least that meant it wasn't Flipper. Nolan maybe? Did he miss her at the game last night? Come to think of it, Tara couldn't recall seeing him since she'd returned to school. Had he been avoiding her? And was he here now to explain himself. Or, maybe to ask her to the dance! That was not a step Tara was ready to take. She crept to the front door and opened it slowly to…Jimmy Cerrone.

"Hey," he said.

"Hey."

That was more words than they spoken in almost a year.

"I just wanted say, it was messed up, and I didn't know."

"Well," Tara said, "now two of us don't know."

"What?"

"What the heck you're talking about!" she said.

"Oh, yeah," he said. He took a cellphone out of his pocket and opened an app. "I've been doing game video for Flipper, he's gonna…"

"Yeah, I know, he's the Spielberg of highlight reels."

"He texted me, see."

Jimmy showed Tara the message:

Arriving now. Need you to sit with band and shoot my entrance. Get the crowd reaction. If T's there, focus on her.

"T is you," Jimmy said.

"Yeah, I got that," Tara said. "Where's the clip?"

Jimmy opened the camera app and started the video. Tara watched as Flipper and Eden descended the stairs to field level. They strolled along the running track and people started to notice them. Raquel called out, "Tara!" but the girl paid her no mind. Murmurs went through the crowd. "It's not her?" "Who is she?" Flipper escorted Eden to the bleachers, and they climbed the steps to the band. Flipper scanned the section, then craned his neck to peer deeper into the crowd. "She's not here," Jimmy's voice said. Flipper swiped his hand across the screen. "Okay shut it off," he said.

Tara handed the phone back to Jimmy.

"I didn't know what it was about," Jimmy said.

"Yeah, well, now you know. Thanks for coming by."

Tara pushed the door closed and wished she could punch something. She grabbed a pillow off the couch and strangled it, before shoving a corner in her mouth and biting down on it.

"Hey, stop," Jeremy said, "you're gonna give Sammy ideas."

Tara spit out the pillow and threw it at the little dork. She hadn't forgotten she had a score to settle with him, but even what he did wasn't as bad as Flipper. Not just bringing Eden to the game, but deliberately setting Tara up for...*what?* What could he get out of humiliating her like that? Was this some revenge plan he'd been harboring since seeing her with Nolan? *Whatever*, that skinny freak had messed with the wrong girl. She was going to that dance, and Mr. Burger Flipper was gonna wish the two had never met.

CHAPTER
ELEVEN

"O Lucifer, who rose in the morning,
now you are not light-bearer,
but bringer of darkness, or even of death."
— St. Bernard of Clairvaux

TARA TORE HER CLOSET APART. She wanted an outfit that...what? *Stunned*. It would have helped if she had a body that stunned. But she was one hundred and five pounds of lean muscle with barely discernible curves. Pick any dress; she might as well keep it on the hanger. Then, in the back of the closet, Tara felt the thin plastic film of a dry-cleaned garment. She pulled out a dress she'd never seen before: a cowl-necked sheath dress, in bold Kelly green with diagonal gold stripes. The ticket on the hanger said it had been altered in March. Teri must have bought the dress for the St. Patrick's Day dance. She'd been hoping Nolan would ask her. Mom had taken her shopping to raise her spirits after the first round of chemo.

Tara hovered for a second, the craziness of the moment swirling around her. Sitting with the band last Friday night had been bad enough. *Imposter. Ghost. Fraud. Usurper.* Was she now going to fully impersonate her sister to thwart the strange girl from Kansas who was impersonating her? *Check.*

Tara tore the plastic away and held the dress up in front of her mirror. Greedily, she stripped off sweater and jeans and slid the dress over her head. The open neckline showed off her collar bones and the folds of the cowl presented an illusion of a bust. She tightened the cinch at her waist to give a hint of an hourglass. The hem slashed from the middle of her left thigh to the top of her right knee. The purplish bruised was pretty much hidden. If she could tack the thigh slit down an inch, no one would see it. Tara tousled her hair and turned pouty faced towards the mirror. The dress lit up her honey blonde hair and her emerald eyes. *Stunning.* That dress would be her secret weapon.

Tara didn't say anything about the dance all day. She simply excused herself after dinner and went to her room. Her phone was loaded with new texts and VMs, but she didn't dare peek at them. That would get her worked up, and a roaring headache was sure to follow. She checked the charge on her phone—seventy percent was fine—and slipped it into her purse. She went to the living room where her Dad was watching some college football game. She took a denim jacket from the closet, walked around the sofa, and stood beside the TV.

"Daddy, can I have a ride?"

The *stunner* caught him off-guard. How could any father say "No," when his daughter looked so fabulous? He scratched the back of his head and aimed the remote at the screen. *Click.* Tara was on her way.

"What if she's there?" Dad asked as they pulled out of the driveway.

"Then she can dance with Flipper," Tara said. "I've got bigger fish to fry." She hadn't intended a pun, so her Dad's laughter caught her off-guard.

"Then you admit he's a fish."

"I admit nothing," Tara said. "But, thanks, for letting me do this."

Dad shrugged, "The genie's out of the bottle." He knew he had trained a competitor; he couldn't expect her to sit on the sidelines.

The sedan cruised through the drop-off lane and turned right towards the gym. The building was lit up and thumped with the heavy bass line of a rap tune.

"Sure this won't be too loud for you?"

"We'll see."

"Your head starts hurting, you call."

"Don't worry; I will."

Tara did feel a twinge behind her eyes as she approached the entrance but pressed forward. The line to get in extended out the front door. Tara queued up behind some eager freshmen, who gawked into the gym, its inky blackness intermittently broken by rapid flashes color. Tara placed a ten-dollar bill on the table and got her hand stamped in bold red with a five-point star, facing downward. Inside, the dance had an astronomy theme. Brightly painted mobiles hung from the ceiling, dangling striped-and-spotted gas giants, pock-marked asteroids, and glittering constellations. Tara peeled off her jacket and hung it on a rack, keeping her purse with her.

"Oh, my g—! You look gorgeous!" Raquel shrieked as Tara approached. Raquel was wearing a blue *Spandex* flight suit. A pair of Martian antennae wobbled on springs above her head.

"I forgot the theme," Tara said. Her head throbbed as she shouted to be heard.

"Nobody cares," said Cheryl, who had cared enough to dress as Rey from *Star Wars*. But a quick scan of the gym confirmed her assessment. Maybe one in ten students had attempted a costume.

"He's not here yet," Raquel said.

"Who?"

"Flipper."

"I don't care about him," Tara lied.

"And he's not bringing her. I can promise you."

"I don't care about her either."

Raquel wasn't convinced. She hooked Tara's arm and pulled her towards the front exit, back outside where they could talk.

"Listen, girl," Raquel insisted, "let's be real." She went on about how Flipper had disrespected Tara, and that wasn't going to fly.

She'd marched down the hill to his house, but he wasn't home, so she'd gotten a bunch of the girls and gone to confront him at the *CD*. They'd practically tossed him onto the grill. "I said 'I don't care if you're madly in love with this girl, you don't bring her onto our campus.' That was a dirty, low-down stunt."

"Thanks, I guess," Tara said. She looked off towards the boulevard, which seemed strangely deserted, until a pair of high beams seared her eyes. A phantom vehicle glided past the gym's entrance. Its red taillights streaked the night and refused to dissolve, stubborn as blood stains. *Halos and flares*, Tara told herself. *Concussion symptoms*. Maybe this dance was a bad idea.

Raquel and Cheryl were chatting now with Jen Donnelly and some other girls who'd just arrived. Tara drifted towards the parking lot. Maybe she should stay outside a while, take some air, and stay quiet 'til the pounding in her head calmed down. Maybe walk to the football bleachers; there were always kids hanging there, even though the field was off-limits during dances. There might be kids at the pond, too. Smoking. Maybe drinking, making out. But that would be looking for trouble.

Those headlights blazed back. The phantom had circled campus and entered the parking lot through the exit. Tara felt her heart race.

"Anyway, let's dance," Raquel yelled.

There weren't many kids on the floor. Most slouched against the closed bleachers like a police lineup. Tara's steps fell into the retro-disco rhythm of a familiar tune: Peggy Gou's *Starry Night*. At least the DJ remembered the theme.

"Juniors, represent!" Cheryl yelled and waved some classmates onto the floor. A few senior ballers joined the ranks, their effortless motions stealing focus from the Queen Bee, who was trying much too hard. Tara's head spun as the music shifted again. She was also starting to sweat. Profusely. *Was that a symptom?* As Cheryl ceded center stage to 'Cuze and Company, the crowd encircled them, like a stomping, clapping amoeba, swallowing them up. The separate bodies were now a single a cell, which tightened around its nucleus, and Tara drifted back. As if through a vacuole, she was released.

Tara floated in the universe dangling from the rafters, for a second feeling the infinite freedom of nothingness. Outside of space and time, Tara unfurled self/being/soul into wide infinity. Then a hand touched her arm; the bass thumped; the lights flashed.

"Can I talk to you?" Flipper asked.

Tara stared. Not angrily. Almost like she was surprised this primitive being could talk. She had just touched the infinite, why should she come back to Earth for this?

"Are you okay?" Flipper asked.

He wouldn't understand.

"C'mon," he insisted and ushered her towards the rear exit. Outside, under the harsh yellow security lights, everyone looked like *The Simpsons*.

"So, what is it?" Tara asked.

Flipper shriveled under the prying eyes. "Not here."

"You were ready to humiliate me in public? Why not apologize publicly?"

"Be cool, okay?" he begged. "C'mon."

Tara thought he would take her to his car, but he made a right turn for the steps down to the football field. Tara hesitated. *Risk detention to hear his lame excuses?* With a wave, Flipper insisted, and stupidly, she followed. Tara got the weird feeling of wafting down the steps, like fog creeping over the headlands. On the running track, the surface was spongy, like a slack trampoline. Black-hoodied kids, perched like crows on the bleachers, smart birds, stared at them as they tip-toed past. Under the bleachers, some kids passed fireflies across their lips, while others locked in a tight clinch. Past the field, they headed towards the pond. *Long way for an apology*, Tara thought. *What's he really up to?*

"Hold up," she said.

"You okay?"

"Yeah, stop asking me that," Tara said. "It's just a little headache."

"I've got just the thing," Flipper declared. Reaching into his jacket, he pulled out a pencil-thin cylinder of twisted paper.

"Where'd you get that?" Tara asked.

"From Obstbaum's sport coat!" Flipper laughed, as he flicked a lighter to spark the end of the joint.

"Are you crazy?" Tara whispered sharply. "Father comes down here to walk his dog. That's his house there!" She pointed to the small A-frame building around the curve of the pond about a hundred yards away.

"He'll have to get his own." Flipper released a stream of grey smoke through pursed lips and offered the joint to Tara. She waved him off. "It's good for headaches."

Tara headed to a bench on the edge of the pond. Angry ducks scattered as she approached. "I thought you had something to say to me."

Flipper took another drag and held the smoke in his lungs until his face turned bright red. Finally, he released, saying, "Yeah, well, I just wanted to explain about Eden. What Raquel said, it wasn't that way. She came to see me that night. At the *CD*."

"She came to see you? That same night we met her?"

"Yeah, so I figured she must be lonely."

"Must be."

"Or she was up to something. Following *their* instructions."

Tara looked at the reflection of the moon on the pond. She could almost see the idiot people from the children's tale, who got out their rakes to scrape the gold off the surface. That's how stupid she'd be to believe Flipper's story.

"You know what?" she snapped. "I don't believe you. But I don't care."

"You don't believe me?"

"No," Tara huffed. "I think you went back to her house, stuffed your face with *Doritos*, and promised to fit her in with all your hundreds of friends. How'd that work out?"

"Y'know, you don't give me enough credit."

"For what exactly?"

"For caring about you!" That line had Tara flabbergasted. But, true to his inability to read social cues, Flipper pressed on. "That video could have gone viral. Picked up by every news channel. Then everyone's asking, 'What's up with this Eden?' All those prying eyes, they can't go through with their plan. They've got to back off."

Flipper must have read the irritation on Tara's face, because he turned away and mumbled, "Anyway, whatever. Let's not talk about it."

"Fine by me," Tara said. "I should go home anyway."

"You can't go yet," Flipper said.

And why not?

"I didn't bring you down here for me. Just, hang out 'til he gets here."

He? Who exactly? Tara's mind veered towards the phantom high beams. It had to have been that *Challenger*. Flipper only showed up after that car arrived. Could he possibly sink so low that he'd turn her over to that stalker? Tara froze as she heard footsteps crush loose gravel.

"Here he comes," Flipper said, before a final toke. He drew hard on the roach, then flicked it into the pond. Tara turned slowly around to face Nolan Copeland.

"Nolan!" Tara groaned and raised her hands in a choke hold.

"Sorry," he said. "My bad, I guess. I just wanted to talk without your squad around. They make things kind of complicated."

My squad? Tara rolled her eyes. That's when she saw the porch at Fr. Chandler's house light up. The screen door swung open, and Erasmus, his border collie, dashed off the porch and ran circles around the front yard before heading onto the trail around the pond.

"We gotta go," Tara said. "Father smells skunkweed, we'll all be suspended."

"Relax," Flipper said, "wind's blowin' the other way."

"You're mad, huh?" Nolan asked. "You looked mad when you saw me."

"I just wasn't expecting you," Tara said.

Nolan raised his eyebrows, no doubt wondering whom else she might mean. The answer came from behind him.

"She was expecting me."

Jean-Luc stepped out from the shadow of a low-hanging acacia bough. "You knew they'd send someone, didn't you? After all, you caused a lot of trouble for some powerful people."

"What are you talking about?" Nolan demanded.

"Sorry, champ, but I don't answer to you." He stared directly at Tara. "You've had your fun. Your freedom. It's time to answer."

Jean-Luc stepped forward and Nolan raised his right forearm to bar his path. In a blink, Jean-Luc grabbed Nolan's wrist, twisted his arm down and behind his back, then thrust him into the trunk of the acacia. His left forearm pinned the back of Nolan's neck, while his right arm drove Nolan's arm up his back to the breaking point.

That's when Erasmus started barking. In a few bounds, he was at Jean-Luc's feet, baring his teeth and threatening to nip his ankles. Jean-Luc kicked at the dog, giving Nolan just enough wiggle room to slip free, and send a vicious right fist squarely against Jean-Luc's left cheek. The stalker crumpled to the ground, and Erasmus ran circles around him. Father whistled for his dog and trotted over to the fallen youth.

"Get your hands off me," he growled. He pushed Father away and rolled to his feet. He stared intently again at Tara. "You should have come quietly. Now real people are going to get hurt. Including the family that's been hiding you."

"Young man," Father said, "you're trespassing on campus. Leave or I'll call the police. Trust me, they're not far away."

Jean-Luc rubbed his cheek and flexed his jaw side to side. "Jumelles can run, but they can't hide." He skulked back into the shadows and took the path toward the football field.

"What's a jumelle?" Nolan asked.

"In French, it means twin," Tara said.

"How's he know you're a twin?"

"What was he even talking about?" Flipper laughed. "How'd you cause trouble? Powerful people? And what family is hiding you?'

Tara turned to Fr. Chandler. "He thinks I'm Eden Grant." She searched his face for some hint that he knew more about the strange girl than he'd let on. "What happened in Kansas?"

"Your guess is as good as mine," the priest said.

"I have a feeling she never was in Kansas," Flipper said.

"Maybe," Father conceded. "You two go back to the dance. Nolan, we've got to clean up those scratches." Father pointed, prompting Nolan to touch his cheek and wince from the sting of flesh rubbed raw by the bark of the tree.

"It's nothing," he said.

"You're bleeding," Tara told him.

"And you're coming with me, *because...?*" Father lifted in voice, cueing Nolan to finish the sentence.

"Because you think I'll go after him."

"Smart boy," Father smiled. So, Father took Nolan back to the house, and Tara and Flipper trudged toward the dance. Tara took her phone from her purse.

"Who you calling?" Flipper asked.

"My Dad."

"Okay, but, y'know, be cool."

That earned him one complimentary eye-roll. The phone rang until they reached the top of the steps above the field.

"Hi, Dad?"

"Sweetheart, what's up?"

"That guy came around. He's gone now, but..."

"Alright, I'll come get you."

"I think he's got me mixed up with that girl. The first thing he ever said was he knew me. And tonight, he said a family was hiding me. I'll tell you when you get here." Then Tara wondered if Flipper might know something, after spending last night with Eden. She turned to him and asked, "Did she say anything to you?"

Flipper's head shook like a log-in box rejecting a bad password.

"Who are you asking?" her Dad wanted to know.

"Flipper, he's here with me."

"Well, can he drive you home?" Dad asked. "You won't have to wait for me."

"I...I..." Tara hesitated. She covered the phone and turned to Flipper. "He wants you to take me home."

"After last night, he owes you one," Dad stated firmly. "Is there some reason he can't drive you?"

Tara was stuck. Should she admit she'd stood there and watched him smoke a stolen joint on school property?

"Can you drive?" she whispered harshly.

Flipper shrugged, not like *I dunno*, but like, *Of course, why you asking?* Tara's eyes bugged and burned into him, answering, *Because you could be freakin' stoned!*

"I'm fine," he said finally.

"Okay, Dad," she said, "I'll go with Flipper. We're leaving now." They said goodbyes and she hung up. "You're sure you can drive?" she demanded. "You didn't smoke anything else or drink anything?"

"That's the problem today," Flipper said. "Nobody trusts anybody."

"Unbelievable," Tara muttered as she marched to his car. They got strapped into the *Jeep*, and Flipper eased out of the parking spot, same as ever. In no time they were on the Boulevard and then the freeway. That's when the high beams hit them, lighting up the cabin. Tara squinted against the brightness and felt a sharp pain behind her eyes. "What the —?"

"Our boy's back," Flipper said, after glancing up at the rearview mirror. "Don't worry; he's not catching us." He hit the accelerator, gunning the engine.

"Are you crazy?" Tara shouted. "You can't outrun him in this rust bucket!"

"Augh," Flipper groaned. "Now you've insulted my family honor." He looked again at the mirror and hunched his shoulders forward. Tara watched the speedometer climb to seventy-five.

'Slow down, you maniac!"

Too late. The roadway veered left, and Flipper couldn't hold the turn. The *Jeep* skidded onto the soft shoulder and overturned. It slid off the embankment and rolled—over and over and over—down a low hill. It came to rest right-side-up, but the pounding had shattered every window and caved in the roof. Tara's door creaked open. She lay there feeling like someone was taking a dentist drill to her skull. White light flooded the cabin of the *Jeep*.

Flipper muttered, "Sorry, Tee."

Tara's door swung fully open, and a dark figure stood beside her.

The blade of a knife glowed and slashed her safety belt, and two strong, lean arms lifted her out of the seat. As they ascended the hill, Tara looked back at the demolished *Jeep*, where Flipper was sleeping.

"You shouldn't have moved her," a voice called.

"Done is done," Jean-Luc answered. He put Tara in the front passenger seat of his *Challenger* and strapped her in, closing the door.

"Where are you taking her? An ambulance is coming. I called."

Tara heard the crack of an electric charge and a dull thud as a heavy object hit the ground. The driver's door opened, and the dark youth slid behind the wheel. The door closed and a seatbelt clicked into place. The car rolled backwards, and the rear end rose as if encountering a speedbump. The car moved forward and sharply left onto the freeway. Lights streaked past, spray-painting the darkness with the scribblings of expired seconds. *He's got me*, Tara thought. *Game over. Nuclear blast annihilates planet. Only 100 million baby bears remain.* Unconsciousness gathered around her like a warm blanket. Tara welcomed sleep, but then heard Teri whisper, "*Sleep no more! Macbeth does murder sleep*," and Tara was back in her bedroom, hunched over a *Folio* paperback trying to make sense of Shakespeare.

"I don't get it," Tara said. "I'm going to bed."

Tara raised her hand toward the lamp and gripped the metal beads of a pull chain. Then another hand held a string of beads and held Tara's hand.

"IS *it true that if you die in your dreams, you die in real life?*"

"*Jeremy, why would you ask that?*"

"*I heard that's why you wake up. Sometimes, I dream I'm falling, but I wake up before I hit the ground. So, is it true?*"

"*How can we know that, son?*"

"*Oh, my Jesus, forgive us our sins, save us from the fires of hell. Lead all souls to Heaven, especially those most in need of Thy mercy.*"

OH, *hell no*, Tara thought. She wasn't going down without a fight.

––––––

TARA MUST HAVE DOZED OFF, because when the *Challenger* rolled to a stop at an I-5 gas station, she was staring at the snow-capped peak of Mount Shasta. They'd made a four-hour trip. But, if Jean-Luc was taking her back to Kansas, they should have been traveling east, not north. Just went to prove Eden's origin story had been a total crock. "I've never played golfing." *Ha!*

The sleep had done Tara some good: the pressure inside her skull had eased and her mind was active again. As she watched Jean-Luc pump gas, she tried to formulate an escape. If she could break away from him, her grandparents were only twenty minutes away. She'd like to see how Grandma would crush this snake.

Keeping very still, Tara reached into her purse for her cellphone and scrolled through her contacts for the Galvins. She couldn't risk calling, but did the old folks even do text messages? Dropping her right hand down below her thigh, Tara started tapping out a message with her thumb:

HAVE BEEN KIDNAPPED. AZALEA MOBILE STA. I 5. Rt 97.
BLACK CHALLENGER.

Before she could hit SEND, Jean-Luc ducked his head into the cabin to check on her.

"You're awake," he said.

"You're observant."

"Need to use the restroom?"

"Yeah, I guess so."

"Okay, let's go."

He walked around the front of the vehicle. Tara hit SEND and dropped her phone under the seat before he pulled her door open. She twisted right and her body rebelled. She was a mass of stiff knots. Slowly, Tara planted her feet outside the car and hauled herself up, clutching her purse.

"Open it," Jean-Luc demanded.

She unzipped the bag, and he fished through it. "Where's the phone?"

"I dunno," she said. "I lost it when the *Jeep* rolled."

He eyed her dress, perhaps checking for bulges where she could have hidden her cell, then walked her to the restroom and waited outside. Tara took care of her needs and evaluated her options. The lock on the inside of the door was secure. It might be possible to hole up here until her Grampa acted off her text, although the stench was pretty unbearable. The window was too narrow to crawl through. After a few moments, there was a knock at the door.

"You done?" he asked.

"Almost."

Then the lock mechanism buzzed and clicked, and the door opened inward.

"Time to go," he said.

"That was pretty rude."

"Sorry, not sorry. I'm on deadline."

As they walked back to the *Challenger*, a *Stranger Danger* PSA played in Tara's head: *Don't let the assailant take you to a second location. Fight. Scream for help.* But the gas station was deserted, and the goggle-eyed cashier in the minimart looked like he only came to work for the doughnuts. Tara wondered, *Even if he saw me, would he be any help at all? Well*, she reminded herself, *this is gun country. He might have a Glock under the counter.* She gave herself a silent count: *One, two…*

Ma'am, you've got to step outside. Quickly please.

Tara bolted toward the minimart. She got about three strides before Jean-Luc grabbed her arm.

"I'm not going with you! I'm not going! Help! Help!!"

Charging. 200. Clear.

He tugged and twisted her around to face him and shoved a gleaming metal device at her chest. A jolt of current locked every last muscle in spasm, and she shook like a wet dog. Tara slumped into his arms.

Charging again. 300. Clear.

"Here's one for good measure," Jean-Luc said. He pushed Tara back onto her heels, shocked her again, then caught her as she flopped forward.

"Hey now!" the clerk said. "Whatchoo doin' to that girl?"

Jean-Luc tossed Tara over his shoulder and carried her back to the car. He deposited her in the front passenger seat, belted her in, and slammed the door. Tara's head lolled to the right, and she saw the clerk run forward. A blue flash clawed at him, and the big man staggered. He dropped to his knees, pitched forward onto his palms, and vomited. Jean-Luc got back behind the wheel and peeled out towards the Interstate on-ramp.

Her pulse is weak, but steady.

Tara couldn't tell where that voice in her head came from. Somehow it made her want to hold on. *Weak and steady wins the race, right?* But, she'd had all the fight zapped out of her. She needed outside help and in a hurry.

CHAPTER
TWELVE

"There is a place, like no place on earth.
A land full of wonder, mystery, and danger.
Some say, to survive it, you need to be as mad as a hatter.
Which, luckily, I am."
— Lewis Carroll, *Alice's Adventures in Wonderland*

FLIPPER FIGURED he'd been unconscious maybe five or ten minutes. The ambulance siren stirred him, and he began sifting through fragments of memory. Tee was gone; he had to get her back. That wasn't going to happen if the EMTs took him off to the Emergency Room. So, gritting his teeth against the pain roaring in his head and neck, he hauled himself out of the battered *Jeep* and limped into the heavy brush a few yards from the crash. He hunkered down as the ambulance arrived and dug his cellphone out of his pocket. He called 911 and gave them the license number of the *Challenger*. He thought maybe Tee was too old for an Amber alert, but it turned out she wasn't. *Score! But now what?* He'd expected the EMTs to scramble down the hill with a couple of stretchers, but they seemed to have no interest in Flipper's *Jeep*. That might improve his chances of slipping away, but to where?

Flipper had no idea where that creepy kid was taking Tee, but she might have been right about him really wanting Eden. If so, the Grants held the key to where he was headed. So, all Flipper had to do was get across the county without a car. *Or maybe not.*

Staying low, Flipper scrambled up the rise to the shoulder of the road. The ambulance lights were bouncing red, white, and blue flashes off the black sky and a silver *Impala*. Two EMTs worked frantically on a man lying flat on the ground. Crouching in the weeds, Flipper heard them beg the hospital dispatcher for instructions on crush injuries to the chest and spine. The EMTs were so intent, they hadn't noticed the engine of the *Impala* was still running. Flipper made a quick sign of the cross for a man who might be taking his last few breaths on this Earth, but who wouldn't be needing his car for the rest of the night.

Two seconds later, he was crouched over the steering wheel and eyeing a path back onto the freeway. As he eased the car forward, he was almost giddy: *Look at me, I'm stealing a car!* Then the EMTs popped their heads like meerkats, and Flipper gunned the engine, kicking up gravel and veering blindly into freeway traffic. Car horns blared, tires screeched, and vehicles swerved. But nothing got smashed. Flipper exhaled heavily and barked into his cellphone.

"Siri, get me directions to Eden."

"Eden is a mythical garden said to be located in the east."

"Eden Grant!"

"Getting directions to your contact, Eden Grant. Home."

Now, he just needed to make the twenty-minute trip before the cops pulled him over for driving a hot car. Despite his hurry, Flipper eased off the gas pedal, so he wouldn't attract attention, and continued comfortably under the limit. Arriving at the Grant house, he saw the living room lights were on. Someone had to be home.

Flipper parked around the corner, wiped everywhere he might have left his fingerprints, and doubled back to the house on foot. Rounding the corner, he stepped briefly into the headlights of a parking car, then darted behind a tree. Two cars had their lamps on: a tan Volvo in front of the Grant house and a compact farther up the block. Flipper knew who owned the Volvo, so it was no surprise when Fr. Chandler rose from the driver's side. Flipper figured the second car belonged to Nolan, who had followed Father for some stupid reason and would shortly have to explain himself.

Fr. Chandler stood with his hands on his hips, staring up the block at the compact. Nolan came forward and they seemed to argue in hushed voices. Father's body language indicated he was not giving an inch. Nolan went back to his car and started the engine. Flipper was fine with football guy going home, except if they found Tee's creepy stalker, a no-neck, musclehead might actually be useful. So, Flipper crouched below the front end of a parked car and waited. As Nolan's car slowed for the stop sign, Flipper stuck out his arm and signaled with a hiked thumb for Nolan to turn the corner and wait. After Nolan's car rolled past, Flipper watched Father step inside the Grant house.

———

THEY TURNED off I-5 at a town called Weed and traveled north on Route 97. In the pitch darkness of a country road, the snow-capped peak of Mount Shasta loomed like an apparition. Ghostly white, the frozen pillar stabbed defiantly at heaven, an unfinished, frost-bitten Babel tower, an abandoned monument to molten ambition, cooled and quelled by relentless, unforgiving inertia. Tara recalled the Indian legend that Shasta was a launching pad from the Below World to the Above World. Gradually, over Shasta's icy summit, the sparkling band of the Milky Way shimmered into focus, like a holographic projection of the intended finished product: not quite a tower, but a bridge to heaven, or if not heaven, at least to space.

Legends aside, Tara hoped the mountain's geology might play a part in her dilemma. As Grampa Galvin had explained, four conical volcanoes had melded into one superstructure over thousands of years. The last significant eruption had been more than two-hundred years ago. *Sweet volcano of death*, Tara mused, *now's the time to blow your top. C'mon, big boy, you can do it*. The mountain responded with cold indifference and ominous silence.

Tara studied Jean-Luc from the corner of her eye. "Why did you kill him?" she finally asked.

"Who's he to you?"

"Just a person."

The person was a deputy who had pulled them over. He'd approached the car with gun drawn, so maybe her text had worked.

"Get out of the car, mister," he'd called. "Slowly, with your hands up."

Jean-Luc had calmly complied. The deputy told him to get down on the ground and spread. Again, the youth did as told. Tara saw him drop below the window level and watched the deputy approach. Then a blue bolt cracked the darkness. The deputy went rigid in its tentacles and collapsed. A second later, Jean-Luc stood over that spot aiming a service revolver downward. Two orange flashes lit up the rear side window. The explosions left Tara's ears ringing. She'd thrown open the door and dashed from the car towards the woods. She didn't even reach the first tree before he ran her down. Moments later they were back on the road.

"Just a person," Jean-Luc cruelly mimicked. "Now he's an organ donor. In service to the greater good."

"More will come," Tara said. "You can't kill every cop in California."

"Only the ones that get in my way."

They turned off Route 97 onto a dirt road. *Fine*, Tara thought, *lay down those tire tracks. Better'n breadcrumbs*. Minutes later, it became clear they were heading for the north face of Shasta, a dead end if ever one existed. The glacial walls rose more than ten-thousand feet. If the cops followed those tire tracks, there'd be nowhere to run. After what Jean-Luc had said, Tara assumed he was taking her back to the scene of some crime, not to some random spot in the wilderness where a maniac with a death wish would make his last stand, or a homicidal nutcase would dump a body. Shasta wasn't just a random destination, but why in the world would he choose it?

———

FR. Chandler was noticeably unhappy when the boys barged past Mrs. Grant, but Flipper didn't care.

"He got Tee," he told the priest. "He ran us off the road and carried her off." He looked squarely at Mr. Grant. He was an older man with a long face, hollow cheeks and a beaklike nose. His narrow eyes had overgrown, white brows. The complete effect was that of an anthropomorphic eagle. "You've got to help us find her," Flipper pleaded.

The old man looked sadly at his wife. It was Fr. Chandler who spoke.

"Dr. Grant says they don't know who the boy is."

"But he had to be stalking Eden," Flipper explained. "That's the only thing that makes sense."

"I'm sorry," Dr. Grant insisted. "She doesn't know him. I wish we could help."

Flipper noticed Eden wasn't in the room. "Where is she?" he asked.

"She's sleeping."

"Well, wake her up. It's an emergency!"

"Young man," Dr. Grant said firmly, "I am sorry for your friend. But if you think this has anything to do with Eden, you are mistaken."

Mrs. Grant shuddered and wiped a tear from her eye.

"You're hiding something," Flipper said.

"I'm afraid we can't help you."

Father placed his hand on Flipper's shoulder and turned him towards the door. "Okay, boys, let's go."

Outside, Flipper was furious. "They're freaking lying!"

"And we could argue with them all night and get nowhere," Father said. "Meantime, we've got to call the police and tell Tara's parents...."

"I called the cops already."

"Well, now you'll see them in person and make a statement."

That didn't strike Flipper as a particularly good idea. "Okay. Give me a lift?" Father gave a quizzical look, after all, how could

Flipper have gotten there if he didn't have a car? "Long story," Flipper said.

Father glanced at Nolan, who said, "I'm parked around the corner."

"You get in, too," the priest said. "I'll drop you at your car."

So, they piled into the Volvo—Flipper riding shotgun, Nolan in the back seat—and pulled away from the curb, just as the lights in the Grant house went out. They approached the stop sign at the corner, when someone dressed in a dark hoodie stepped into the headlights. Eden Grant, a backpack slung over her shoulder, skipped around to the driver's door. As she crouched, Father lowered the window.

"I know where he took Tara Hartzwell," Eden said, "I'll take you, but no flicks. I mean, you cannot tell the policemen."

"We don't have that choice," Father said.

Nolan leaned forward. "I won't call the cops."

"Sit where you are," Father snapped. "Alright. Get in."

Nolan cracked the door and scooted to his right, but before Eden could slide in, two arms clamped around her and yanked her back. The girl screamed and kicked, but Dr. Grant spun her around and proceeded to carry her back to the house. Father sprang from the car and followed them.

"I told you that guy was lying," Flipper yelled.

As the boys caught up, Dr. Grant was red-faced and angrily shouting, "You want this girl killed? Eden's more than one life, she's a symbol. A rallying point for millions of people, dying to be free. I'm sorry for your girl. They might let her go once they realize their mistake. But you can't use Eden to get her back. Do you understand?"

———

THIS CAN'T BE HAPPENING, Tara thought, but her eyes said otherwise. The pyramidal base of the mountain was opening. Tara thought of *The Pied Piper* story she'd read maybe in second grade. The piper had rid Hamelin town of rats, but the mayor had refused to pay his fee. So, when all the adults were at church, the piper returned and played his pipe to lure the children out of town. A crippled boy who couldn't keep up told the grownups that the side of the mountain had opened to a magic carnival with dazzling lights where everything was made of candy. The mountain had closed on him, and he was the only child who ever returned.

Well, no carnival. No candy. But a bright light shone, rudely reminding Tara she was still concussed. She shaded her eyes and bowed her head as the *Challenger* rolled into the cavern that rumbled to close behind them.

"Get out," Jean-Luc ordered as he killed the engine.

"What is this place?"

"Step out and see."

Tara stepped out of the car into the vault of an immense cavern. The floor was roughly the size of St. Stephen's quad and seemed to rise hundreds, maybe thousands, of feet into pitch darkness.

Jean-Luc checked his watch.

"Got someplace to be?" she asked.

He swaggered towards her, his arrogance on full display. "Just checking. The leap will come in half an hour. Gives us time."

For what? Tara thought but didn't dare ask.

"You're not much," he said, "compared to real women. But you're not hard to look at either."

Then his hands were on her hips, and he pulled Tara forward, pressing his mouth onto hers. She turned her face away and tried to pry his hands off her. He pawed at her dress, working the fabric up her thighs. His breath was hot on her neck as he reached under her dress, and she swung both hands upward clapping them over his ears. It was a self-defense move her Dad had taught her, and it worked just as he'd promised. Jean-Luc recoiled, hunching over, covering his ears and bobbing his head to shake out the pain.

"You want that, you'll have to kill me," Tara said.

"What makes you so special?" he snarled. He sprang from a crouch and backhanded her across the face, knocking her two steps to the side. But Tara kept her feet and stiffened in front of him. "You're a *jumelle*," he yelled. "You're nothing."

"I must be something to somebody."

Jean-Luc straightened to his full height. "You're lucky they need you alive." He looked again at his watch.

Tara felt the cheek he'd slapped. It was hot and tender. Probably swelling. She didn't want to know what he could do with a fist. And she didn't want to feel that stun-gun thing again. "Saint Maria Goretti, pray for me," she whispered. The impulse to pray surprised her, as did the sudden memory of that sad-eyed girl whose portrait had hung in her fifth-grade classroom.

For the moment, Jean-Luc kept his distance, and Tara remembered something her Dad had once told Jeremy: "You don't have to win the fight with a bully; you just have to make him pay a price." Now he knew Tara wasn't a soft target. The ear clap seemed to have dampened his mood.

But what next? She was sealed inside a mountain, so zero chance that anyone searching would find her. And the vault was humming, as if some power source were coursing through. Something was going to happen in a few minutes, and Tara needed to prevent it.

"Just who do you think I am?" she asked.

"*Arrêtez déjà, arrêtez!*" he yelled, angrily. "*Oui, petit fou, je sais que tu peux me comprendre. Je sais que tu parles la langue de notre monde.*"

"I understand, because you're speaking French," Tara fired back. "I study it in school. I don't know what 'world' you're talking about."

"Ha!" Jean-Luc exclaimed. "Even the fat guy called you Tetara! Even he knew *Tartairos.*"

"I swear I don't know what you mean."

"*Ensuite, vous êtes sur le point de savoir.*"

With that, the cavern wall at Tara's back started to dissolve.

———

"DO you know how many habitable planets there are in our galaxy?" Dr. Grant asked. Fr. Chandler shook his head.

"Approximately 40 billion," Nolan said.

Flipper snarled, *That can't be right.*

"That's right," the scientist confirmed. "So, it stands to reason that we'd make contact eventually."

They'd driven forty-five minutes to Livermore Labs, a federal government research facility focused on developing nuclear weapons and maintaining global security. They were held up at the front gate for almost an hour before getting security clearance. Now they were in some kind of NASA-style Situation Room. An oval conference table glowed ominously, while digital displays on the walls tracked every conceivable cosmic movement. Dr. Grant tapped a keyboard on the conference table and a holographic image of the Milky Way leapt to multicolored life. The center was oblong, like an eye, and from that center, several threads of stars pin-wheeled off, forming curved trails to the outer rim. A tiny dot glowed red on one of those trails, and the image zoomed in to it.

"This is our Earth," Dr. Grant said. "And here is Eden's home planet, Tartairos." Another dot glowed green, in a similar location on another of the spirals. A line of dashes connected the two locations. "That's a distance of twenty-three-thousand light years."

"How could she have traveled that distance?" Father asked.

"She didn't," Dr. Grant said. "She simply stepped from one planet to another, like you would walk room to room in a large mansion. *'My Father's house has many mansions,'* right, Father?" Dr. Grant stroked the keyboard again, and a network of broken lines began connecting dots. "Some distances are greater, so it feels more like a zip-line or a flume."

To Flipper, the display looked like a 3-D transit map, but it just kept going, linking hundreds, thousands of stops.

"What are those connectors?" he asked.

"Wormholes. The first were natural phenomena, occurring at the convergence points of various energy fields. Unsuspecting individuals stumbled upon them and mysteriously disappeared. Sometimes reappearing, but many times lost forever. By studying fluctuations at places like Ayers Rock in Australia, the Bermuda Triangle, and Mount Shasta, we were able to replicate wormholes in the lab. That's when we earned our way into the network and became signatories of the treaty."

"What treaty?"

"The Interstellar Network Treaty." Dr. Grant smiled mischievously, then his face brightened, as if he was finally free and could divulge a private passion necessity had forced him to keep buried. "Most people are afraid of aliens coming in UFOs. But why suffer the rigors of space travel—long-term isolation, weightlessness —when you can just step from one planet onto another? For centuries, the Interstellar Network has facilitated exploration. Cultivated knowledge. Fostered scientific exchanges. All benign and beneficial. But imagine the panic, the chaos, if word ever got out. The Interstellar Network is the greatest secret in the history of the world."

"Then why are you telling us?" Flipper asked.

"Well, no one would ever believe *you*, and I need you to understand why we can't help Tara. Contact is strictly limited. Regulated by the treaty. Only, what's happened on Tartairos is so monstrous. Officially, we can't interfere. But, unofficially, some of us have been using the network as an escape route."

"Underground railroad?" Nolan asked.

"In a way, yes," Dr. Grant said. "A hyperspace railroad. Eden is a fugitive. And I've broken the law to help her. If word got out, I'd go to prison, and Eden would be sent back to Tartairos."

"So, what now?" Father asked.

"I've got to send Eden to another safe haven. Immediately, tonight."

"What about Tara?" Father demanded.

"We just have to hope that the people who helped Eden escape can help Tara as well."

"So, that's it?" Flipper snapped. "We just leave her there?"

"I'm afraid so." Dr. Grant turned to Eden. "Are you ready, my dear?"

"Can I just say good-bye?"

Dr. Grant nodded and Eden crossed to Flipper. She threw her arms around him, and whispered, "I'll help." Then she grabbed his butt. Blood surged from his toes to his head and his scalp began to sweat. Then he realized what she'd done was tap her cellphone

191

against his. As Eden broke off their embrace, Flipper felt a vibration in his back pocket indicating a new text message. As she said more casual good-byes to Nolan and Fr. Chandler, Flipper tapped the message icon, opening what appeared to be a screenshot of a computer. It matched the console Dr. Grant had been using, except for two data input boxes circled in red. The numbers were different.

Was Eden asking Flipper to recalibrate the wormhole? Did she want him to send her back to Tartairos? Is that what "I'll help" meant? But how was Flipper supposed to adjust the settings with Dr. Grant hovering over the computer? The old scientist stroked a few keys and a section of wall lit up. What had been a solid, flat surface now roiled like a luminous fog. The room turned icy cold. Eden's wormhole was open.

"Oh, I don't want to go!" Eden cried. "Please don't make me! Please!"

Dr. Grant left the computer and went to her. He hugged the girl and tried to reassure her. "You'll be safer, my dear." But she continued to bawl.

This was Flipper's chance. He slid over to the keyboard, grabbed the mouse and changed the data to match the screenshot. Nolan saw, but Flipper signaled, "Be cool," and the quarterback held his position.

Eden finally calmed down. She hoisted her backpack over her shoulder and stepped toward the fog. Turning back, she smiled at Dr. Grant and said, "Thank you for everything. And, please, forgive me."

Dr. Grant's chin dropped, and he spun back to the computer. Too late. Eden made a running jump and disappeared into the fog.

Dr. Grant stared in horror, first at the computer screen, then at the wormhole. "Do you know what you've done?" he raged. "You've killed her! Now we've lost both girls!"

"I don't think so," Flipper shot back. He bolted towards the portal. A second later he was swimming in fog.

PART THREE
THE DISENCHANTED WORLD

"There is no surer sign of decay in a country
than to see the rites of religion held in contempt."
— Niccolò Machiavelli, *Discourses*

CHAPTER
THIRTEEN

"I want to cut off her head and take out her heart."
—— Bram Stoker, *Dracula*

"IT'S BEEN DAYS[1]," Madame boomed. "Still no answers. Not one of those Restorationist terrorists held to account. And, if I may indulge a personal point of contention, you have not recovered my jumelle. You said you'd solve this case well before Foundation Day. That's looking highly doubtful. I've had to postpone my procedure, and I am weary of your excuses."

Barnett Desjardin stood silent, mulling his response. As Chief Inspector of the Citizens' Militia, he was accustomed to speaking harsh facts and not concerning himself with the feelings those facts aroused. But dealing with Aliénor Charbonnier was different. Madame, as she was generally called, was used to having her way and had no scruples about crushing the lives and careers of civil servants who impeded her. Madame Charbonnier had been for the last seventy years the animating force behind the Global People's

---

1. The editor has graciously agreed to translate conversations on Tartairos to English for the reader's convenience.

Republic. Those who believed the mission of a democracy was to execute the people's will saw Madame as the embodiment of that will. Thus, her actions, however arbitrary and capricious, were *per se*, *ipso facto*, "law" and "progress." When Madame ruled against a minion, there was no appeal and rarely any reprieve. Still, Desjardin couldn't appear too obsequious in the face of her abuse.

"I've made no promises, Madame," he said quietly, but firmly. "And I've offered no excuses, only facts. Shall I recite them again? Or would it please Madame better if I returned to work?"

"Yes, get out!"

Madame turned towards the window. Outside, in the ochre sunlight that achromatized the cityscape, towers of glass and steel appeared to have been carved from sand. That same harsh light revealed Madame's face as deeply lined clay. Nature, it seemed, was relentless and oblivious to its opponent's political power. Gravity, erosion, entropy: none were inclined to grant Madame clemency. Yet, Madame herself was a force, and much of her success had come in defiance of nature. Staring at her dissipated reflection, Madame appeared obstinate. Nature, once more, would be overthrown. Desjardin strode briskly to the door.

Though loath to admit it, the Inspector was equally frustrated with his lack of progress. A few days of fruitless investigation was not overly long for a heist that appeared to have been planned and executed flawlessly. The thieves—whether they were actual terrorists had yet to be proved—had struck without warning and had covered their tracks well. Well, but not perfectly. The Inspector was confident that, given time and resources, he would prevail. But would Madame allow him that time?

Desjardin exited the sumptuous lobby of Foundation Tower and sniffed again the unpurified air of the masses. That scent of soot and spoiled eggs called him back to the morning this saga had begun. He'd awakened to an even stronger stench to hear a radio news reporter extoll the "undeniable progress" the government had made in improving air quality since the height of *The Scorching*. He'd gone to the kitchen where Maggie was cooking breakfast. *Oatmeal or cream of wheat?* The new round of animal cruelty laws had made eggs, along with meat, milk, and butter, too expensive for everyday consumption. Maggie knew better than to warm over what now passed for breakfast sausage or bacon, a depressing mishmash of soy and cricket protein, which the Inspector refused to touch.

Barnett wrapped his arms around Maggie's waist and kissed her neck. His left hand moved across the slight bump on her belly.

"Don't worry," she said. "My appointment's tomorrow."

"I didn't say anything."

"I'm not going to lose my figure," she promised. "I just took it a little farther this time, because it pays more."

"Your body; your choice," he shrugged.

"Thank you," Maggie smiled.

Desjardin poured a mug of coffee. He scooped a tablespoon of non-dairy creamer, then glanced at the label: Hydrogenated soy. He decided to drink it black.

"Do we have sugar?" he asked.

"Oh, Barnett," Maggie apologized. "The pie for your birthday used up our allotment. Our voucher should come next week."

A week without sugar. Well, as the Minister of Public Communications was fond of saying, "If it wasn't good for you, your government wouldn't do it." Barnett sipped his unsweetened coffee, wondering why he bothered, since the government had mandated the removal of half the caffeine. The Health Ministry wanted to reduce overstimulation that led to poor health outcomes like tachycardia, insomnia, and stress-related illnesses.

"What's that?"

Barnett pointed to a bandage on Maggie's left Achilles tendon.

"Oh," she said. "Believe it or not, I was nipped by a coyote. In broad daylight, in Jourdain Park. Nothing really, it was a pup. Barely broke the skin. The Dispensary doctor said practically zero chance of infection."

"A coyote. What next?"

"They are helping with the rat problem, so they say. But they're getting brazen. Especially in packs."

Under pressure from animal rights activists, the People's Republic had banned the use of poison to kill rats and mice. Coyotes and wolves had proliferated since new laws had mandated the free-range feeding of livestock and prohibited the trapping or shooting of predators. Those predators had migrated into the suburbs, laid barren by *The Scorching*, and even into some urban parks. In response, authorities had launched the "Let Nature Police Nature" campaign, which instructed the public that bobcats and coyotes were their friends, restoring the ecological balance that humans had disrupted. The campaign also discouraged dog and cat ownership, which it labeled "involuntary servitude." Of course, nothing suppressed pet ownership more than the soaring price of meat products, due to sharply decreased production.

"Y'know, I was thinking," Maggie said. "Now that nobody has dogs anymore and wild canines are roaming the street, it's like we've gone back ten thousand years. Pretty soon, we'll be cooking over an open fire." She laughed, "And they call it progress!"

"About the park," Desjardin said, "have you heard the current plan to save the Botanical Garden?"

Maggie shuddered. "Oh, the place is crawling with gophers and rats!"

"They're introducing snakes. Which they promise won't be venomous."

"Saving the garden by putting snakes in it? That's creative, at least."

Maggie placed the plain oatmeal in front of Barnett. She'd added fresh fruit, a luxury, since mandatory benefits for farm workers had raised the price of a pint of strawberries to that of a new pair of shoes. But it still tasted like wet wallboard. So, after kissing his lovely paramour goodbye, Inspector Desjardin had headed towards the door, hungry, undercaffeinated, and leery of wild beasts lurking in alleys.

That's when he had gotten the call. Terrorists had struck the Hospital for Special Surgery. Since this was an emergency, he was able to use his Identity Card to access a private vehicle. Unfortunately, due to four consecutive days of rain, only a few vehicles had a full solar charge. He opted for a scooter, which only had a maximum speed of twenty-five kilometers per hour, (making it government-approved for routes shared with pedestrians), because it was more maneuverable and had a longer battery life than a car. The clerk promised it was "at least seventy-five percent charged." Half an hour later, Barnett arrived at the locked-down hospital. A young lieutenant, Gagnon, explained the situation.

"This was a scheduled life-extension surgery. The prime was prepped in the operating theatre. Apparently a male, approximately eighteen-years-old, disrupted the surgery. He grabbed a scalpel, put the prime in a headlock, blade against his jugular. The surgical team backed out, leaving them alone. He must be deranged..."

"Why do you say that?"

"He's naked." As Desjardin nodded, the lieutenant continued, "Right now, we don't know if there's been damage to the jumelle..."

The Inspector clasped a hand on the youngster's shoulder. His brown eyes had an innocence that three years in the Citizens' Militia hadn't tarnished, and the face was handsome. Desjardin just wished he'd trim his beard, which was longer than regulation and scruffy at the chin. "Thank you, Lieutenant."

"How in bloody hell, Barnett?!?"

The Inspector whirled to see Maire Porcher in a frenetic state that had become all too common since he'd assumed his office. He lowered his voice and whispered harshly in the Inspector's ear.

"Let's get our official story straight. That's not a jumelle holding its prime hostage. A sack of organs can't stand or grip a scalpel."

Desjardin played along. "Obviously, a deranged patient somehow wondered out of the mental ward."

The Inspector eyed the crowd gathered at the perimeter. He could disperse the press by invoking the ban on coverage of seditious activity, but would that be playing into the terrorists' hands?

"Our job today," the Maire stated firmly, "is to protect the right of the prime to his life extension procedure."

"I quite agree, Maire," the Inspector assured him. "Now, if you would allow me to focus on tactics."

Desjardin signaled Lt. Gagnon to fall in at his side, and they marched through the hospital entrance. "On what floor is the operating theatre?"

"Fourth."

Desjardin headed instinctively for the stairs.

"Sir!" Gagnon pointed to the elevator.

"Are my old legs not up to it?" Desjardin snapped.

"I didn't mean...it's your call, Inspector."

Yes, it's my call, the Inspector glowered. True, he no longer had the heart or lungs of a twenty-year-old, but he was only forty-four, and resented any insinuation from junior officers that he 'had lost a step.' Desjardin trotted up the four flights, cursing his leaden legs at each landing, then strode down the hall to the operating theatre, hoping that his breathing would relax before he had to give any orders.

The hall was lined with Militia Commandos: probably two dozen more than were necessary. With the recent increase in 'terrorist activity,' Militia was under pressure to appear zealous. Everything from wildfires to rolling blackouts to vagrants stealing loaves of bread was now 'terrorism.' The Bomb Squad was called whenever a vehicle was double-parked. More and more, the Inspector's job had become about maintaining illusions: that The Citizens' Militia was in control and, conversely, that terrorists lurked behind every door. By the time Desjardin reached the operating theatre, his breath was under control, but his heart was racing.

At the theatre, Desjardin climbed a short flight of stairs to the balcony, where he found Sergeant Michaud and the Hostage Negotiator, Rimbaud. Desjardin looked through the domed glass of the theatre to assess the scene below. Instrument tables had been overturned and surgical implements lay scattered about the floor. In one corner, hunkered down behind an overturned gurney, were two figures in hospital gowns. They appeared identical in every aspect but age. The older figure, obviously the prime, lay almost on top of the younger, his jumelle, who resembled a boy of eighteen. Holding a scalpel to the prime's throat, the jumelle looked desperate; its eyes darted about wildly.

"Sergeant, your tactical assessment, please."

Michaud nodded towards the Sharpshooters, relaxing casually

against the wall, their weapons at their sides. He tapped the glass dome.

"It's fortified," he said. "We can't get a shot."

Desjardin turned to the Hostage Negotiator. "M. Rimbaud, has the ju— *assailant*—made any demands?"

Rimbaud had been leaning on the dome, practically hugging it with one arm, holding a phone to his ear with the other. He turned to Desjardin, covering the mouthpiece. His bewildered expression betrayed the absurd nature of the demand. "*It* wants to live."

Desjardin needed a deep breath. He squinted through the glass. Storming the theatre was out of the question. That would get the prime killed. And bringing the jumelle down with a body shot, or more likely several, would render the organs worthless. The prime would lose his investment, but more importantly, his opportunity for life extension. The civil liability for the Militia would be ruinous. The Inspector had to handle this very carefully to spare the Militia a costly lawsuit.

He also had to spin the story, which was the tricky part. He had to inform his troops that the assailant was nothing but a garden-variety mental patient, who, upon any false move, must be shot exclusively in the head.

"Can we flood the room with gas? Render him unconscious?" he asked the Sergeant.

"Would take the room out of operation for at least sixteen hours. They're already canceling surgeries."

"So, you're saying we can't afford to be patient?"

"I'm not sure it would work anyway," the Sergeant offered. "Soon as he started feeling disoriented, he'd probably slit the old guy's throat."

Old guy? This prime was maybe five years older than Desjardin. He turned his attention back to Rimbaud.

"Promise it anything. No, wait. A new suit. Twenty-thousand credits. And he walks out of the operating theatre."

Rimbaud nodded. Michaud leaned forward to interject.

"It must know we don't let jumelles out in the world," he whispered.

Desjardin's mouth puckered as he thought. What this jumelle 'must know' would no doubt prove to be an intriguing aspect of this case. Someone had informed it of the procedure, had educated it on tactics. Had fed it a script. But Desjardin had a script to follow as well. "That's not a jumelle," he told the Sergeant. "It's an escaped mental patient."

"Understood, sir."

"M. Rimbaud, make the deal."

Minutes later, a suit arrived, complete with belt, shoes, socks, briefs, permanent press shirt, tie, beret, and a canvas wallet with a twenty-thousand credit plate. A middle-aged nurse delivered the goods, laying them on an operating table. The jumelle eyed the clothing and seemed to relax slightly.

"Taking the cheese," the Sergeant smiled.

The jumelle had the nurse tie its hostage to a chair with an electrical cord before leaving the room. It then crouched down behind the hostage to get dressed. It would have a human shield for any abrupt assault through the operating room doors.

"Our mouse is no fool," Desjardin mused. "Sergeant, where is central security for this building?"

"Two floors down."

"We're falling back to there. Have your men clear the hallways. I want no Militia between the operating theatre and the street."

The Sergeant didn't move, except to tilt his head with incredulity. "Sir, we can't let it reach the street. If we do our job in front of that crowd... things will get ugly."

Desjardin had to agree. The terrorists would love to provoke the Militia into a public show of force, so they could hold the Militia up as an instrument of oppression. They wanted the people to fear and distrust the government, to treat the guardians of society as its enemy. That way, they could weaken the People's Republic enough to overthrow it.

The Inspector lowered his gaze into the operating theatre where the jumelle was tying its new shoes. "There's a Men's Room on the ground floor between the elevator and the street. Position yourself there."

"Yes, sir." Michaud exited for the stairs.

Desjardin placed a hand on Rimbaud's shoulder. It was solid. Rimbaud was short but built like a slab of granite. The Inspector found that firmness comforting. "M. Rimbaud, let our subject know we're pulling out, then join me in the security room."

Rimbaud leaned over the microphone. "Friend, the Militia is withdrawing, so you'll be clear to the front door. Just give us a moment to evacuate everyone. We don't want any accidents."

The hospital security room, located on the second floor, had a bank of video monitors. Rimbaud seated himself behind a microphone connected to the building's public address system and eyed the feed from the operating room. Switching from one point of view to another, they could watch all the way to the front door.

"Talk to it, Rimbaud," the Inspector said. "Every step. The whole length of the walk."

Rimbaud took microphone in hand and pressed the button down. "How's the suit fit, pal?"

The jumelle looked up, searching the theatre balcony.

"Where are you?" it asked.

"I told you. We've left the balcony. Left the hallway. The way is clear between you and the street."

"You're still watching," the jumelle objected.

"We have to be sure you don't harm M. Pascal."

"Harm? He was going to kill me. Take my heart, lungs, everything."

Rimbaud rolled his eyes. He released his thumb from the mic button. "You want me to ask how it knows that?"

"No," Desjardin answered. "Let's not remind it not to trust us. Feed the thing hope."

Rimbaud returned to the mic. "Those shoes aren't too tight, are they?"

"They're okay." The jumelle stood upright. Fully dressed, it could have passed for human out on the street. It looked around the operating room, then crouched behind the prime to untie him.

"You planning to take M. Pascal with you?"

"He's my insurance," the jumelle said. It held the scalpel again to

M. Pascal's throat and got the man to his feet. Slowly the two walked in lock step to the doors.

"Take good care of M. Pascal, okay, pal?"

M. Pascal put his arm out and pushed one of the double doors open. They moved out into the hall. Desjardin switched his attention to another screen. The prime, in hospital gown, walked down the hall with the fully clothed jumelle on his back, one arm wrapped around, pressing the scalpel against his throat. Co-joined twins attached breast to back. It was a slow, tortured, almost drunken walk. The jumelle pushed the elevator call button and the doors opened.

"Keep talking, Rimbaud."

Rimbaud gripped the microphone. "Where you heading from here, pal? See the sights? There's a football match this afternoon. You could place a bet, if you're feeling lucky."

The elevator reached ground level, and they stepped out into the hall. As they approached the door of the Men's Room, Desjardin touched his communicator. "Michaud, prepare to move."

"You're loaded with credits," Rimbaud continued. "I'm not saying you have to bet a lot. Just give yourself a rooting interest. Y'know, until you pick your team. Then it's a loyalty thing."

The jumelle was twenty feet from the exit, four feet beyond the Men's Room. Desjardin tapped his communicator. "Move."

The jumelle pushed the prime onward, inching toward the sunlit tiles that led to the glass doors. Michaud crept from the Men's Room, weapon raised.

"Keep talking," the Inspector told Rimbaud.

"Me? I've been royal blue and orange all my life. For better or worse, those bums are my team. I don't expect you to understand right away, but after a season or two, you'll get my meaning."

Michaud leveled the barrel of his weapon, taking aim at the back of the jumelle's head. As his finger tightened on the trigger, the jumelle sneezed, its head snapping forward. Michaud's shot went over the jumelle's head, impacting the exit door, sending spiderwebs of refracted light through the surface of the glass. The jumelle spun around, cutting the prime in the muscle of his neck. Michaud raised his hands, a dishonest gesture of passivity. The jumelle clambered backward with the prime in tow.

Watching from the security room, Desjardin could not believe his luck. "Don't let it reach the street," he snapped. He tapped his communicator. "Gagnon, what's the situation?"

The young Lieutenant's voice was a shrill squawk. "The crowd's well back. We've rolled back the press. There're sharpshooters on every roof."

Desjardin watched the jumelle back slowly towards the door, Michaud pursuing step by slow step. "On my signal, I need you to strafe the ground just outside the door. Don't shoot through the door, but make it clear there's no escape."

"You got it, Inspector."

The jumelle was three feet from the exit. Michaud trailed ten feet behind, his hands still raised over his head. The jumelle checked the door with a glance over his shoulder. The refracted glare through the fractured glass made it impossible to see the street. The jumelle, almost breathless cried, "They said I could walk out."

Michaud stopped. "Then walk out."

As the jumelle placed his free hand on the door, the pavement outside exploded under a jack hammer assault. Bullets, brick, and mortar chips ricocheted against the door, shaking the shattered glass from its frame. The jumelle tumbled backward, pulling the prime down with him. At that point, the prime fought back. Maybe his anesthesia was wearing off, or perhaps his adrenaline simply kicked in, but the old fellow made a good account for himself against the jumelle, whose muscles, through long years of electro-stimulus, were as toned as any decathlete. Unfortunately, after a few blows, and what looked like a dislocated shoulder, the best the prime could do was hold on as his jumelle tossed him around the lobby.

"Whoever tinkered with his cortex stream added a bit of *ju-jitsu*," Rimbaud observed.

"If that's not a felony, it ought to be," Desjardin replied.

The *coup de grace* was a body slam that left the prime writhing but gave Michaud a clean line to the jumelle. Two quick pulls of the trigger, and the jumelle's skull shattered, spraying red mist and pink foam over the lobby.

"Threat terminated," Michaud declared.

Desjardin clapped Rimbaud on the shoulder—he might as well have spanked concrete—and headed downstairs, wringing the pain from his hand. *Have I gotten so soft?* he wondered, as he trotted to the landing.

Already a team of orderlies had hoisted the jumelle's corpse onto a gurney as maintenance crews mopped up the blood and brain matter. The prime was still curled in a corner, but he howled in protest.

"I own copyright! That genetic material is my Intellectual Property!"

An orderly lifted him off the floor. "Sir, I assure you," he said, "the ammonia solution we use renders all genetic matter useless. No one is going to infringe on your rights."

They placed the prime on a gurney and wheeled him toward the elevator. The surgical team then came trotting in from the street. It would be business as usual, the Inspector hoped, for the rest of the day. *But who knows?* If they'd gotten to one jumelle, they may have corrupted others. Enhanced security would be necessary.

"Splendid, Barnett! Just splendid!" The Maire had fought through the crowd to clasp Desjardin's hand. "Highly professional and efficient. I knew when the People's Council appointed you, we had a top man! Top man! Now, remember our story."

"Inspector, quickly!"

It was Lt. Gagnon. He had a communicator at his ear and was waving for Desjardin to follow. They took the elevator to the tenth floor, one level below the roof. The Inspector glanced at the console: Life Extension Ward.

"Don't tell me," he groaned.

"Yes, sir. Several pods destroyed."

Now the Inspector would really hear it. *Wanton waste and destruction! Anarchy!* The civic elites would call for his head. It would do Barnett no good to remind his betters that they'd stripped the Militia of the resources it needed to fight crime. They routinely ignored his pleas, even as he cited the latest out-of-control crime statistics. The Party elites couldn't care less when a shop cashier was knifed, or a delivery driver beaten to death. But let one drop of their gravy spill from its train, and all hell broke loose.

Those bureaucratic hacks had failed to deliver on every promise of a prosperous, peaceful, classless society. But they clung greedily to the perquisites they'd grasped through their backstabbing and dema-goguery. Publicly they decried systemic injustice, eliminating private property wherever it caused inequity among the masses. But privately they secured for themselves the greatest imaginable luxury: life extension.

Only twenty percent of the people could afford to clone jumelles and maintain them for so many years before harvest. Those lucky few could refresh their bodies with youthful organs. Two or three times. The limit was unknown. Naturally, this stirred envy among the unlucky eighty percent, some of whom spitefully sought to destroy the system. *Who's to say they're wrong?* The People's Republic was sworn to promote liberty, equality, and brotherhood. Yet reserving life extension to a select few was the ultimate inequality.

The elevator opened on a chaotic scene: semi-conscious hospital personnel, emerging from the stupor of a sensory attack, lost their footing on slick, hydroponic fluid that had seeped from shattered containment tanks. A crew arrived to start mopping.

"Halt!" Desjardin commanded. "This is a crime scene!"

"Sir, please," a nurse begged, "we've got to save the jumelles we can. Many pods are still sealed, but we don't know if they're damaged."

The Inspector stared into the vault. Ten or so pods had clearly been ransacked. Another eighty or a hundred remained. "Do what you must to preserve the assets," he told her, "but don't touch the ruptured pods."

She nodded and rushed with her team into the vault. An officer who'd been first on the scene stepped forward to report.

"Apparently," he told Desjardin, "the activity below was a diver-sion. The real terrorist target was the pod vault."

"Damage?"

"Twelve pods destroyed."

"So those jumelles have expired?"

"No, sir, they're empty."

"What?"

Lt. Gagnon looked bewildered for a second, before saying, "Could they have taken the jumelles with them? How would they cart them away?"

"Have you looked into any of the intact pods?" Desjardin asked him.

"No, sir," he said. "I don't have the security clearance."

"Wait outside, please."

Desjardin stepped gingerly into the wet mess of the vault. Of course, they didn't have to cart away the jumelles; they could simply wake them up and walk them out the back staircase. Whoever was behind this heist knew very well what a jumelle really was, and that the official line about jumelles being strings of connected organs was a total fabrication. They also knew how to revive a jumelle. Even, he surmised, how to tell the whole lot that they were in danger and that rescuers were coming. The Inspector slowly walked past the impacted area to the rows of undisturbed pods, which seemed to be functioning adequately.

"They haven't been sabotaged?" he asked an attendant.

"No, Inspector," she answered. "And these instruments are very delicate. If they'd wanted to wipe out the whole inventory, they easily could have."

So, it wasn't wanton destruction. But why steal them? For ransom? If so, had they targeted particular jumelles? Those belonging to extremely wealthy primes who could afford to meet their price? The destroyed pods were close to the exit. That might indicate a smash-and-grab robbery, similar to a jewelry store heist. The perpetrators might have chosen their loot based on its proximity to the door, not caring necessarily who the owners were. They'd get out quickly and assess their take later. But no. This operation had required too much planning. The thieves had to know what they were taking.

Desjardin looked through the glass of the enclosure in front of him at what appeared to be a boy of nineteen, dark-haired, lean, and muscular. No flecks of gray. None of the paunch and sag that comes with impending middle-age. His muscles contracted and released under electrical stimulation.

The Inspector strode briskly back to the entrance. *Smash-and-grab or targeted robbery?* He wanted to be certain. "Are there any notable jumelles missing?" he asked.

An officer nodded, handing him a list. "Yes, sir. One in particular. Madame Aliénor Charbonnier."

———

THUS, it had fallen to Inspector Desjardin to inform The Architect of The People's Revolution of Tartairos that the organs she was counting on for her upcoming surgery were, at least momentarily, unavailable.

"We expect to receive ransom demands shortly," he had assured her.

"You had better hope so, Inspector," Madame fumed. "Yes, you had better hope that what these rebels want is money and not… driven by ideology." Madame went to her window again and stared at the dull cityscape. "We've constructed a very fragile fiction: jumelles are sacks of organs. Of course, that's all any of us are. But half the populace believes that about the jumelles literally. I salute their ignorance and trust it's quite blissful. Others know the sacks of organs resemble people but believe they lack consciousness, and we've persuaded them that the prettiness of the packages should not sway public policy. But, if ever the masses learn that jumelles possess consciousness that can be awakened, they'll look at harvesting very differently. Life extension as we've known it, will be over."

"I understand, Madame."

"Be sure that you do," she warned. "Because you have a stake in this game, too. A perquisite of your position, which you might want to protect, especially if you're facing competition from young lions in your ranks."

Desjardin didn't react, but Madame knew she'd found his sore spot.

"These malcontents," she scoffed. "They're out to destroy everything we've built. Well, I won't have it. I'm only one hundred and twenty, Inspector. My doctor says I can extend twice more, at least. I won't be cheated by a radical mob who are too stupid to appreciate what civilization has given them!"

Desjardin assured Madame that the Citizens' Militia would do everything in its power to bring the terrorists to justice. Adding, "With your permission, we'll keep an investigative team here, in case they contact you with a ransom demand."

With that, Desjardin had left. He'd worked well into the night, and Maggie had been asleep when he returned home. He crawled into bed beside her and draped his arm over her. She grabbed his hand and held it tightly against her breasts. Suddenly she jumped.

"What is it?"

"Was that...a kick?"

Desjardin nuzzled her cheek and kissed her softly. "Cells don't kick, darling. I must have given you a start. I'm sorry."

The next morning, he was up early. "Don't bother with breakfast," he said. "I'll just shower quickly and go."

"Sorry, Barnett," Maggie said. "But it's a laundry day."

Ugh. The water ration. They'd been cited twice last month for exceeding their unit allotment. "I can wash my face and shave, can't I?"

Maggie opened the blinds slightly to look down on the street.

"Is it safe?" she asked. "I mean, to get it done today."

"Safe?"

"After the hospital thing."

"Oh, I don't see why not," he assured her. "These radicals, they oppose life extension. They say it's *elitist*. But nobody objects when a middle-class woman earns a little extra income from tissue extractions."

Maggie dropped back on the bed. She sat against the headboard and hugged her knees against her chest. "I heard someone on the television," she said. "Well, not *on* television, they jammed the signal to get on. But this woman said, 'Jumelles are people.' Of course, it's ridiculous, and when the station came back, everyone laughed at her. But she had shown pictures of young people sleeping in the pods. In school, they always told us jumelles were strings of organs kept alive artificially."

"They are, darling," Desjardin stated.

"But they don't look like organs, they look like...bodies."

"Maggie, this is radical propaganda," he said. There was no sense upsetting her, dragging politics into their relationship. Better to reassure her with the official line. "These people want to take away your right to control your own body and extend your own life. They'll tell any lie to achieve their goals. That's why the Ministry of Public Communications has banned them."

"I know, but... You have a jumelle, don't you?"

"You know I do; it's a job benefit."

"Have you ever seen it?"

"Why would I *see* it?" he asked, checking his tone before he continued. "I get an annual report on its condition, with all the relevant information for future planning. I know the size, weight, and capacity of every organ. I know I have a healthy heart, liver, lungs, kidneys, even testes, if I ever need them. That's all I need to know. I don't have to *see* it."

But he had seen it, only a day earlier. Sleeping. Twitching. Waiting.

"You know what I was thinking?" Maggie asked. "I thought, maybe the tissue money I'm earning, I could get a jumelle. I know it wouldn't be ready for sixteen, seventeen years, and you'd already be extended by then, but afterwards, I'd stop aging for a while, and we'd be comparable again. What do you think?"

"I think that's the most sensible thing you've said yet."

At the office, Desjardin got his morning briefing. Forensics had found no fingerprints at the Hospital. They were processing DNA, but expected any traces would belong to the jumelles and not the culprits. They had determined that the Ward workers had been disabled by a combination of sedatives in the coffee and anesthetizing gas pumped in through the air ducts. This strongly indicated prior access and perhaps complicity with one or more of the staff. They'd have to question personnel aggressively.

Investigators had also found tampering with the Pascal jumelle's cerebral cortex files. For at least three days, M. Pascal's jumelle had been informed in minute detail about the organ-harvesting procedure and given instructions on how to resist. The neuro-muscular memory program was doctored to include martial arts training.

"So, it only took three days to turn a sleeping jumelle into a highly trained killer," Desjardin observed. "What could they do in a week? A month?"

"If you think that's scarily seditious," Lt. Gagnon said, "they also made some promises they had no intention of keeping. They told this jumelle it could have a normal life. They promised to help once it was outside the Hospital and to take it to some location where it could live a normal life."

"Of course, they abandoned him," someone said with disgust.

"*It*," the Inspector corrected. *It* had been a mere pawn; awakening *it* had been a gambit. They'd sacrificed one to gain a dozen. But where were those twelve?

"Another thing," Gagnon said. "Cortex feeds to the stolen jumelles were altered, too." He read a transcript of the message. "'Friends are coming to help you. We're going to take you out of danger. Don't be afraid.' It tells them precisely what happens to jumelles and gives complete instructions on how to cooperate in 'the escape.' Like M. Pascal's, they were programmed to do what the rebels wanted."

"Rebels, Lieutenant?" Desjardin asked. "Let's not give them a veneer of political legitimacy."

Another officer suggested, "Wouldn't terrorists, anarchists, just have destroyed the property rather than carting it off?"

"Thieves, then?" Gagnon asked.

Desjardin pushed back from the conference table. "Everyone who had access to the cerebral cortex feed is now suspect," he declared. "Let's get them in here and sweat them."

After the briefing, the Inspector learned that Madame Charbonnier had called his office three times. No one had attempted to contact her about ransom, and she demanded to know if terrorists had contacted the owners of the other jumelles. Those leading citizens had also called repeatedly, demanding information. Desjardin spent his lunch hour trying to placate Madame. By midafternoon, still no ransom calls, and the hospital workers in charge of jumelle maintenance had admitted nothing.

As the day wound down, he called Maggie to say he'd be late.

"I didn't get it done," she said. "Sniffles. It's nothing, just a cold. Or maybe just the air's been bad the last few days. Anyway, they said wait 'til I'm feeling better."

"Well, don't wait too long," he cautioned. "You'll get stretch marks."

"You let me worry about that," she chided. Her voice cracked and she had to clear her throat. *She must really be ill*, he thought. "You just picture the steak dinner we're going to have when I bring home that cash."

"Alright, chérie," he said. "Take care of yourself."

As he hung up the phone, Lt. Gagnon burst into his office.

"Boss, you've got to see this."

The entire office was gathered in front of a large television monitor that hung high against a wall. On it shone the grainy imagery that commonly appeared whenever suppressed organizations hacked into government-approved news feeds. The scene was deliberately non-descript to prevent authorities from identifying the location where it was shot. The camera panned down a line-up of attractive teenaged individuals all dressed in black t-shirts with white block letters reading: I AM A JUMELLE.

"It's on every station," Gagnon said.

"As a jumelle," one said, "I have lived sixteen years in a preservation pod..."

"I have lived seventeen years," said another.

"Never seeing sunlight. Never walking on grass."

"Never touching another person."

"Never eating real food."

"Never thinking my own thoughts."

"Until now."

"Until now."

"Until now."

Each alleged jumelle repeated the phrase. The image faded to white as black letters dissolved into focus: JUMELLES ARE PEOPLE.

"Our rebels are humanitarians?" Gagnon suggested. "Who knew?" he added, in a tone all too knowing.

A field of static leapt onto the screen then immediately cut to the Ministry of Public Communications. Minister Pomeroy sat behind his desk, smiling slightly, giving the impression of a patient adult indulging a petulant, misguided child. He looked over the silver rims of his glasses as the corners of his mustache drooped into his mouth.

"We must apologize," he said gently. "Due to a breach of security, you have been exposed to subversive propaganda by a suppressed organization that continues to wage war on truth and civil tranquility. Be assured that this profane exhibition featured only radicalized malcontents acting a part. A jumelle, as you all know, is a copy, a reproduction, organic matter without consciousness. A jumelle is no more a person than an ordinary house plant is a person. Do not let your tranquility be disturbed by radical science-deniers, seeking to overthrow the progress of our civil society. Go about your business, and remember, if what you've experienced today causes you anxiety, your local Dispensary has government-approved supplements to put your mind at ease. We return you now to your regular, approved broadcast."

Lt. Gagnon clicked off the monitor. "Think anyone believed him?"

"Lieutenant, my office," Desjardin said.

Desjardin cared not what the populace at large believed. The masses were prone to go with whatever message assuaged their feelings. They were guided by emotions, prejudice, or intuition and never delved deeply into facts. But he couldn't have one of his staff speaking seditiously.

"Lieutenant," he said, "close the door behind you." When the door was shut, the Inspector continued. "You said you didn't look into the pods. Was that true?"

"At the time, yes, sir, but...."

"You had occasion to go back into the vault?"

"Yes, sir. To retrieve evidence."

"You realize what you might have witnessed, as regards the nature and composition of jumelles, is highly classified?"

"I.... Yes, sir."

"Then let's have no more comments about the veracity of official state communications."

"I only meant, sir, that...well, the workers are already whispering the truth. Albeit in the dark. What happens when they shout it in daylight? What authority will we...?"

"Madame's authority," Desjardin said firmly. "On Tartairos, reality is whatever interpretation Madame gives to whatever facts she chooses to acknowledge."

"I understand, sir."

But did he? Gagnon was a conscientious officer, with the generally placid nature of a true believer who's confident he's on the right side. But he was not the type of man to remain loyal to a lie.

"There's a bear in the woods," he told his subordinate, recalling the old Tartarian children's story.

"Yes, sir."

"Let us be the birds."

Gagnon nodded reluctantly. The Inspector rose from his desk and returned to the squad room. He ordered his team to pursue two lines of inquiries: whether the source of the hack could be traced and if the video contained clues to the perpetrators' whereabouts. Another thought occurred to him, which he broached privately with Gagnon.

"Twelve jumelles. Twelve mouths to feed."

The Lieutenant's eyes widened. "Someone's buying more groceries. Maybe more than their household quota."

"I'd bet that like most criminals, these spent more time planning how to rob than in how to get away with robbing." The Inspector took a second to wonder out loud. "Forged ration cards are easy enough to buy on the black market, but water consumption is another matter."

"I'll call Civil Utilities. See if there've been any spikes."

"Thank you, Lieutenant."

Desjardin returned to his office and sank into his desk chair, pondering the thieves' motivation. No ransom request, but an emotional appeal on behalf of jumelles? What was the point of that? To shut down life extension? Were they so consumed with envy for the rich that they'd directly attack the Health Ministry? No government department had done more to ensure equal outcomes for all citizens. Desjardin had investigated numerous incidents of medical ethics violations—doctors unilaterally deciding one patient's needs were more urgent than another's, treating patients beyond the legal age of care, and exceeding the prescribed allotment of medical resources for a single patient—all of which tilted the scales arbitrarily, violating the central tenet of equality. The Health Ministry enforced equality. Who would attack it for a white lie? For being discrete about uncomfortable facts that no one wanted to know about anyway?

This line of thought seemed to narrow the scope of suspects. Some disgruntled Health Ministry employee—passed over for a promotion, or worse—was looking to discredit the Ministry. Only an insider would've had access to the cortex feeds and precise knowledge of the facility. Desjardin had occasionally run up against the Director of Life Extension, a gossipy, pusillanimous *person* who'd inexplicably landed a cushy position beyond *his/her/their* level of competence. The Director was just the sort of unctuous functionary that a mistreated underling would love to knock off a pedestal. Desjardin reviewed the transcripts of Militia interviews with Hospital personnel. He pored over personnel files, looking for some incident that might have provoked a turn.

He was going to be late again. His call to Maggie went to voicemail, and he left a message. When he got home just before midnight, the apartment was empty. Some of her drawers had been hastily emptied. A suitcase was missing. He found a note on the bed that simply read, "I can't do this anymore. Forgive me. M."

It struck him like a kick to the solar plexus. He found the edge of the bed and sat. The phone rang. He grabbed for it and fumbled the receiver. Pulling the cord, he got the receiver back and placed it to his ear.

"Hello?"

"Boss, we might have an address," Gagnon told him. "Three hundred percent increase in water usage over the last three days. No broken pipes reported. Boss?"

"Okay," he mumbled.

"But here's what's really off the charts. Last night, 3 a.m., an industrial site nearby consumed enough electricity for a small city. It should have blacked out the whole quadrant, and Utilities can't explain why it didn't."

"Have—" His voice cracked, and Desjardin swallowed, trying to compose himself. "Have they investigated?"

"They claim they're short-handed. Since the system didn't crash, they scheduled a team to scope it out next week. You want me to get a warrant?"

"Yes. Thanks. Call again when you've got it."

Desjardin hung up the phone. *Maggie? Why? Why?*

CHAPTER
FOURTEEN

"Lose yourself wholly;
the more you lose, the more you will find."
— St. Catherine of Siena

"MISS SIMON? We're ready for you."

Maggie almost missed her name. She was engrossed in reading a government-sanctioned article explaining how, despite the Republic's decades-long, official condemnation of *The Scorching*, the Housing Administration had refused rebuilding permits to displaced suburbanites, some of whom had been litigating the matter for the better part of their lives. Minister Pomeroy hailed the decision, which "places equality above privilege" and essentially put a halt to all single-family home construction. He further stated that the issue was "no great matter," because interior architects were ingeniously designing multi-family dwellings to do more with less space. Enhanced soundproofing, angled terraces, and private entryways allowed people to live in high-occupancy buildings without forced interaction with neighbors. Collapsible furnishings enabled residents to "have more stuff," though the Ministry still urged citizens to "utilize communal assets" rather than "making ostentatious shows of personal wealth."

Maggie placed the magazine aside and waved to the young attendant. She hadn't seen this girl before, who seemed too young to even be out of school, much less working in a Health Ministry Clinic. She followed her down the hall, admiring her shiny, jet-black hair, clipped neatly behind her head and falling all the way to the middle of her back.

"You've been with us before," the girl said.

"Yes, I'm an old pro," Maggie joked.

"I'm Rachel," the girl said. "I'll be prepping you for the doctor. If you have any questions?"

"Old pro."

"Right, then let's get started."

The girl took Maggie's temperature and blood pressure, both very normal, weighed her and reviewed the required litany of questions Maggie had already answered on her tissue donation form. "Did you come here today of your own accord? Do you understand that the procedure terminates a pregnancy? Do you understand that your copyright to genetic materials may not extend to medical products derived from those materials?" *Etc., etc.* Rachel waited outside as Maggie got undressed and put on the hospital gown, then came back in to help her onto the table and into the stirrups. She applied gel to Maggie's belly for the ultra-sound that would guide the doctor's extraction of the tissue.

Just as Maggie was beginning to feel cold, the doctor came in. She couldn't remember his name, but he'd serviced her a couple of times. He pulled the stool over, positioned it between her knees, and sat down. He looked at her chart.

"Almost six months this time?" he said with a hint of admiration, or was it envy? "Gonna be a nice payday."

"I hope so."

Rachel pressed the ultra-sound wand onto Maggie's belly and the doctor looked up at the monitor.

"Yep," the doctor assured her. "We're gonna have a fine harvest."

Maggie smiled and looked up toward the ceiling. *Okay, let's get it done, she thought. Steak tonight. Extra rare.* Then, without warning, the new girl asked, "Would you like to see?" and spun the ultra-sound monitor around to face her. Maggie stared in horror at the image of a... *child?*

"What are you doing?!" the doctor yelled. He pulled the screen back around to his side. "You're on report, Miss."

"I only thought—"

"You're not paid to think!" he snapped. "That screen's here to guide *me*. Of all the...incompetent..." He reached for an implement and lowered his head.

That's when Maggie felt it again. The kick that couldn't possibly be a kick. Because cells can't kick.

"Wait, stop!" she shouted.

The doctor straightened and rolled the stool back.

"Do you need anesthesia? We have to deduct for that."

Maggie lifted her feet from the stirrups. "I don't think I can do this today."

"You want an estimate?" the doctor asked. "I can tell you right now that this extraction is going to pay fifty percent more than your last time. I'll put that in writing for you. Right now."

"It's not...just...tissue."

The doctor stood up. He glared at Rachel. "See what you've done? She's traumatized. So, instead of going home with a few thousand credits and celebrating, she's got to take a problem home. Is that what you want, Maggie? Come on. You've been through this before. You're an old pro."

"Please get out," she whispered. "I want to get dressed."

———

MAGGIE WALKED FOR AN HOUR. She couldn't bear to get on a bus and feel confined, surrounded by people. She wished she could go to a park, to some huge field, and just scream at the top of her lungs. But, sure, all she needed was another coyote bite. She also worried about being mugged. Prison reforms had forced the closure of two penitentiary wings, so those inmates had been released. Minister Pomeroy had promised they were nonviolent offenders, victims of poverty and discrimination who would respond positively to the mercy shown them, so the public was absolutely safe. The former offenders would reintegrate themselves into society seamlessly. Yet, crime statistics had risen "unexpectedly." Still, Maggie didn't want to hurry back to her apartment. She didn't want to "bring the problem home."

Maggie knew she needed to calm herself. Up the street, a neon green R_X shone. She could pick up some free cannabis to smoke while she walked. (The government provided each individual with eight cigarettes per month *gratis*.) That would put her at ease, and, being in the open air, she wouldn't smell of it when Barnett got home. She hurried to the store and withdrew two cigarettes from the monthly allotment. Smoking did relax her, but it irritated her throat. Suddenly hungry, she stepped into a café and ordered a piece of pie. She sat at a table by the door, hoping to have a few restful moments, when a lunatic burst in and started hollering about government mind-control and secret prisons for political prisoners. Seconds later, the police tasered him and took him off in an ambulance. *Horrible,* Maggie thought, *that people have to spiral so far downward before getting the help they need.*

But who was going to help her? She and Barnett had promised to never have natural children. Their first thought was the expense, then the noise, the constant demands on their time. Not to mention the damage childbirth did to a woman's body. If they could afford laboratory gestation, maybe someday, they might consider it. But the thought of ten hours of huffing, puffing, and pushing to get a nine-pound baby through her tiny canal was utterly barbaric. And she didn't want the scarring from a surgical extraction or stretch marks from a distended belly. Maggie was astonished that centuries of evolution couldn't have produced a more gentile process than natural childbirth.

The only reason Barnett hadn't had a vasectomy was so they could produce and sell fetal tissue. A mere three pregnancies a year earned Maggie a professional-level income, which was vital since the economy had been inexplicably stagnant since the latest wave of

Revolutionary Reforms. Getting started had been fun, gestating had been easy for Maggie, and extraction was, if not altogether pleasant, at least quick. But all her life she'd been told it was just a mass of cells. Like a giant blood clot. Ever since she was old enough to understand what pregnancy was, she had been spoon-fed the Republic's line: a child does not take shape until the last six weeks of gestation. Until then, it's only a sequence of developing organs and sinews. No consciousness, no reflexes, no sense of pain. Now, she wondered if that wasn't a deliberate lie. And if she'd been told other lies as well.

"Jumelles are people," that woman had claimed. *Impossible*.

Maggie left the café and lit her second cannabis cigarette. She had one more mile to walk. The sun was getting low and the shadows on the street were lengthening. Her mouth was dry as paper. But, the cannabis was having its effect, and she was relaxing. So, she hurried and finished it, then walked to the next bus stop. In five minutes, she was at her building, where someone stood waiting for her.

"Miss Simon," the new girl said. "I just wanted to say how sorry I am."

"Remind me your name, please."

"Rachel. Rachel Fontaine. Could I maybe come up for a minute?"

Maggie looked at the girl's moist, red eyes. "Why aren't you at the clinic?"

Rachel shrugged a shoulder and looked off to the street. "I got fired."

"Oh, you poor girl!"

"It's okay," she insisted. "I just...I was worried about you."

"Well, yes, come up for a moment. My boyfriend won't be home for hours, and...well, just come up."

They rode the elevator in silence to the eighteenth floor. Maggie was feeling more than mellow at this point. And she was hungry again.

"Make yourself at home," she told Rachel. "I'm going to make some espresso. Would you like some?"

"Yes, please."

"It's hardly worth calling espresso anymore, since the government's taken the caffeine out. They're no fun, our government, are they?" Maggie knew she was babbling—and her building was full of state workers who wouldn't take kindly to her remarks—but so what? *What's the point of getting high if you can't enjoy it?* As the coffee seeped into the tiny cups, Maggie sliced twists of rind from a lemon. "The price of lemons!" she called out. "That's another thing we owe to our fine government!"

"Fresh fruit is hard to come by," Rachel agreed.

"Shouldn't be," Maggie said, as she carried the espresso cups into the parlor. "The soil yields forth its fruit. Pick it, package it, and transport it. How is that hard?"

"I don't know," Rachel said.

"It's hard when you've got meddling meddlers meddling at every phase of the operation." Maggie laughed at her convoluted speech and the bottled-up sentiments spewing forth. "You might have guessed I smoked a little weed after I left."

"I can't blame you," Rachel said. "I guess you got quite a shock."

"I guess." Maggie sipped her espresso. Warm and bitter. She needed sugar. *Ugh! None 'til next week!*

"What did you think," Rachel asked slowly, "was happening in your body?"

"What do you mean?"

Rachel held the cup in one hand, the saucer in the other. "Did you... think of yourself as...pregnant?"

"Oh, of course not," Maggie laughed. "I mean, you're pregnant if you want a child. Otherwise, you've just...got a situation. You're not pregnant unless you're having a baby. I was gestating tissue."

Rachel put her cup and saucer down on a side table. "Is that how it feels now?"

"Now?" Maggie asked herself. "I don't know what to think."

"I want to be honest with you," Rachel said. "I don't like the lies that women are being told. From the time they're little girls, they're told it's not a baby. It's cells. It's organs. It's tissue. Whatever. It's not a baby until you want it to be a baby. But what *it is* doesn't depend on what *you want*. It is what it is. And 'what it is' is a baby from the very first seconds."

"I'm sorry, I can't believe that."

Rachel opened her purse and took out an envelope. From it she removed a pile of photographs. Maggie saw the top image, that image from the screen. The child in her womb.

"I don't want to look at that."

"I'm sorry, Maggie," Rachel said, holding the pile on her lap. "But these are yours. Not just the child you're carrying now, but all the others." She spread the images out on the coffee table, and Maggie sprung to her feet.

"I'm going to ask you to leave. And take those with you."

"You have a right to know," Rachel said.

"I have a right to be left alone!"

Rachel sat behind the photo array not moving. Maggie bent over to scoop the pictures up, but her eyes locked on the ghostly figures curled on the black background. So much like babies.

"These have to be fakes!" she said.

"I assure you, they're not. The images were stored on the clinic computer. They haven't been altered."

"Don't you understand!" Maggie shouted. "I can't believe you! I can't! Do you know what this would mean?! That I killed nine of my children!"

Maggie dropped to her knees and sobbed. Her elbows braced on the coffee table and her head hung so her tears fell on the images. Rachel touched her back. She stroked her and bowed over her. And Rachel wept too, for the children that were gone, and for Maggie, who could not be consoled.

———

A FEW MOMENTS later the phone had rung. Maggie had hesitated to get it but knew it would be Barnett. She took a deep breath and picked up the receiver.

"Hello?"

"Well, sweetheart, how'd it go?" Barnett asked. "Are we rich?"

"I didn't get it done," Maggie admitted. *But what to tell him?* This wasn't something to get into over the phone. "Sniffles," she said, trying to affect a laugh. "It's nothing, just a cold. Or maybe just the air's been bad the last few days. Anyway, they said wait 'til I'm feeling better."

"Well, don't wait too long," Barnett warned. "You'll get stretch marks."

"You let me worry about that." Maggie felt her voice crack and knew she had to get off the phone; she couldn't hold herself together much longer. She tried to joke. "You just picture the steak dinner we're going to have when I bring home that cash."

Maggie had hung up and slumped back into her chair. Rachel was sitting patiently. She'd gathered the ultra-sound photos into a pile.

"What now?" Maggie asked.

"Now you know," Rachel said. "You have the truth, so you can *really* choose."

"That's it? All you wanted was to drop a truth bomb in my lap? You must want something else. Who are you?"

"I'm just here to offer help," Rachel said, "if you want to accept it."

An hour later, a battered, old car had arrived downstairs to take Maggie "somewhere safe and secluded, where you can think." She grieved over the cryptic note she'd left on the bed for Barnett; he certainly deserved a fuller explanation. But as Rachel had said, "If you really believe it's 'your body and your choice,' you need to create enough separation so you can decide what it means to you, without pressure from him."

So, she'd decided to trust this young girl, who appeared sweet and earnest, but might easily have been a twisted radical luring her to her death. All Maggie knew was that her perception of herself had changed, profoundly, and she didn't want to be coaxed back into some comforting, naïve fantasy straight out of the Ministry of Public Communications. Barnett was not naïve, yet he'd mouthed MPC talking points repeatedly, to soothe Maggie's nerves, to calm her and...*what?* Make her compliant? She'd thought they'd been equals in their relationship, but hadn't Barnett kept her in the dark, kept hard truths from her as an adult would from a child? The great irony was that her man had infantilized her, so she would willingly dispose of her own gestating infants. Her heartbreak turned quickly into anger. Then into despair.

How could she manage alone with a child developing in her womb? Her fears of childbirth flooded back again. Rachel assured her that "women have been delivering babies naturally for tens of thousands of years, even without modern medicine," but it still seemed like a physical impossibility. *And what could Rachel possibly know?* She was hardly more than a child herself. Yet, Maggie had come here with her. Wherever *here* was.

They had left the city limits and driven through the burned-out suburbs. The vegetation had come back over the years, but dark patches, the ruins of subdivisions, still blighted the landscape. It would be generations, they said, before those mounds of toxic ash returned to a natural state, and that would only happen, they said, if we continued to "let nature police nature." After about ninety minutes, every second of which Maggie expected the state flics to pull them over for driving an unauthorized private vehicle, they turned off the highway into what looked like a former industrial park. Naturally, it was deserted. Heavy industry was severely restricted since the Communal Living Reforms had eliminated private ownership of motor vehicles, washers, dryers, and other consumer items.

Now, they parked in front of a derelict factory. Someone trotted down the concrete stairs from what had probably been an office. Maggie handed him the car keys, and he proceeded to move the vehicle, who knows where. They climbed the steps to an open door where a tall, bearded man stood. He eyed Rachel then Maggie with a look of concern, then stepped aside for them. The room was long and narrow, spreading left and right. It was dark, but for patches of light leaking from gaps in the boarded windows. Maggie flinched when she saw a rifle lying on a table. *Great,* she thought, *my new friends are violent criminals.*

"This wasn't smart, Rachel," the bearded man said. "We weren't hot enough; you have to bring in the Chief Inspector's girlfriend?"

"Wait," Maggie blurted, "am I a hostage?"

"No," Rachel said. "You're a friend. Among friends."

The bearded man nodded. "We hold all people as friends."

"Then why the gun?"

"Not everyone returns our friendship," the man smiled. "We believe in the right to self-defense."

"There is no right to defend with deadly force." Maggie wasn't an advocate, but she knew that much about the law.

The man shrugged. "We think there should be. Rather, we believe justice demands that there be such a right."

Maggie gasped. "You're Restorationists!" Instinctively she stepped back, and her hand felt for the door behind her. *What had she done?* In a moment of weakness and confusion, she'd fallen into a trap, into a nest of terrorists.

"We're a society of friends, Maggie," Rachel said softly. "Nothing more."

"What were you thinking, Rachel?" the bearded man sighed. "You should have used a safe house in the city."

"No house is safe," Rachel said. "The city is swarming with flics. And besides, Maggie needs to meet our friends. All of them."

"Are you insane?" the man demanded. He craned his neck, coming almost nose to nose with the upstart teen. But Rachel stood defiant.

"She needs to know everything."

The man took Rachel aside and huddled with her for some moments, apparently scolding her, or trying to, given the harsh whispers and abrupt gestures punctuating his statements. But Rachel didn't back down. Maggie wondered how this sweet, young girl fit in with a group of rifle-toting terrorists? They broke off their discussion and Rachel returned to Maggie, putting her hands on her shoulders, and saying, "Jules is a worrier, but you don't have to worry. C'mon, let's get you settled."

Rachel led Maggie through a door that opened into the old factory building. On the factory floor was a settlement of perhaps a dozen tents. Dinner apparently had just ended, because while some people lingered at one of the long tables, others were wrapping up leftovers at a buffet stand, and still others were washing dishes at a large sink against the far wall. As Rachel and Maggie descended a metal staircase that rattled with each step, sending echoes throughout the cavernous building, a woman looked up from the buffet and signaled her partner to stop.

"Rachel," she called, "we didn't expect you. Do you girls want to eat?"

Rachel called back, "Yes. Please!" And the two women set to work. They brought two servings to the table as Rachel and Maggie approached.

"Everybody, this is Maggie," Rachel said. "Maggie, everybody."

Maggie nodded. She hoped that came off as modest, rather than curt. She didn't want to seem disagreeable, although if she was a hostage, that was a very disagreeable position. She sat next to a young man, who scooted over a bit to clear space on the bench, then returned to the book he was reading. He was dressed in new clothes that still showed the creases from their packaging. His flame red hair was longish and a bit wild, like it had never felt a brush or comb. The woman who had welcomed Maggie placed a bowl of stew and a plate of bread in front of her. Maggie murmured a thank-you but couldn't take her eyes off the youth on her left. His peaches-and-cream skin was shiny, like porcelain, and flawless. Maggie recalled what her skin had been like at his age: a minefield of clogged pores and crimson zits. He noticed her staring and smiled, revealing badly bucked front teeth. Maggie wondered, *Why hadn't he been fitted for braces at twelve as the government mandates?* A shame, because he might have been quite handsome.

"What's your name?" Maggie asked him.

"They call me Étienne," he said.

"Because that's your name," Rachel said, in the tone of a parent reinforcing what her child has recently learned. *Was this boy slow?* Maggie wondered. The print in his book was dense, and he seemed immersed in it. Maybe he was one of those odd savants who can do Calculus at eight but can't tie his shoes.

"What are you reading?" Maggie asked.

"Molecular biology," he said. "This book presents theories of cellular mutation in rare diseases."

"That's advanced material for…" Maggie wondered how old he could be. Sixteen? Seventeen?

"My prime is a foremost authority on infectious diseases," Étienne said. "Naturally, the subject interests me, too."

"Your prime?" Maggie asked.

"Étienne's cortex tapes contained all of his prime's professional knowledge," Rachel said.

"My prime is also an accomplished violinist," Étienne said. "Would you care to hear me play?"

Maggie looked hard at Rachel, who calmly ran a crust of bread inside the rim of her bowl and slipped the sopping morsel into her mouth.

"You mean, he's…a jumelle?" Maggie jumped up from the table and practically tripped backwards over the bench. "That's crazy. A jumelle is organs. A network of organs for harvest. They're not people!"

Every eye in the vast chamber of the factory was on Maggie. As her tears burst and she trembled, Rachel came to her and braced her shoulders.

"Étienne is a jumelle, Maggie," she said firmly. "And tomorrow, he would have been taken from his tank, had his heart-lung block, liver, kidneys, pancreas, digestive tract, and testes removed, to be placed in the body of his prime, so his prime, who is already ninety-five years old, could live for another forty or fifty years. But that's not going to happen now. Because we rescued him. And we rescued them."

Rachel stepped aside and lifted her hand toward a line of youths who had formed behind her. They were all perfectly —*what was the word, preserved?*—specimens. Not a scar or blemish on them. They stared with eyes that seemed to be looking on the world for the first time, as if after a childhood of darkness, the sun had risen, painting the details of a world that had only consisted of blots and shadows. One face particularly struck Maggie. It was out of a history book.

Maggie crept towards that girl. She peered beneath the honey-blond strands and deep into her emerald eyes. "I know who you are," Maggie said. "You're a young Aliénor Charbonnier."

The girl cocked her head to the side. As almost an apology, she said, "They call me Eden."

———

AFTER RACHEL HAD INTRODUCED each of the freed jumelles, they went off somewhere, and Maggie sat again at the table. A woman brought tea, which Maggie let sit until it was stone cold. Then, feeling her tight throat crack, she drank quickly. What now? *Not every Restorationist is a terrorist*, she tried to tell herself. Mostly they'd been intellectuals, who were drummed out of the universities, silenced on media, tossed off corporate boards. A note-worthy few continued to agitate, even though their "philosophy" had been officially suppressed. But these weren't academic quacks. They had rifles. They'd broken into a secure medical facility and stolen... *what? ...*

"Jumelles are people." That's what the nutty activist had said on TV. *Could it be true?* If Maggie could believe her eyes, it was. But there must be more to it. This could be an elaborate propaganda campaign, for which Rachel was trying to win Maggie over. First, the sonogram, which could easily have been faked. Now this settle-ment in the middle of nowhere. Like a movie set. And they had cast these kids to pretend they were jumelles. Yes, all carefully orches-trated to sway her to their cause. Why? Because through her they could discredit Barnett. Maggie's suspicions were confirmed a few moments later, when Rachel approached.

"I want you to see something."

Rachel led Maggie to a far corner of the factory floor where a video booth had been erected. There was a camera and a green-screen backdrop, lights, and monitors.

"My name is Eden," the girl told the camera, "and I am six-thou-sand twenty-seven days old. But I was only born two days ago. That's when I was rescued from a gestation tank at the life extension center."

A propaganda video, Maggie thought. Eden went on to claim that since her "rescue," she had taken her first breath of real air and her first steps. She had opened her eyes for the first time and spoken her first words. She claimed to be a jumelle, but insisted, "I am a person."

"Eden leaves tonight," Rachel whispered.

Of course, she had to go into hiding. After perpetrating such a fraud, she'd be hunted. And despite her youthful age, she'd be punished severely.

"Where is she going?" Maggie asked.

"I can't tell you that," Rachel answered. "But it's a safe place, where a family will take care of her, and she can have a normal life."

Maggie shook her head. As far as she was concerned, the charade was over. "Where are the real jumelles? You've destroyed them, right?"

"We showed them to you," Rachel insisted. "The ones that are left. We've already sent five to safe places."

"No one is going to believe you," Maggie cried.

Rachel nodded. "It's always easier to fool people than to show them they've been fooled. People resist the truth when it's hard and the lies they've lived with are more comfortable. But we believe the truth is worth fighting for, and that these lives are worth fighting for."

"I don't believe you!" Maggie yelled. She pivoted away. Towards where, who knew, but she wasn't going to stand around, obediently swallowing shovels full of nonsense. She got halfway back to the table when a tremor in her gut caused her knees to buckle. Again, she felt a...kick.

"You woke up your baby," Rachel said, and helped her to a chair. "The sonogram wasn't a lie. There's a baby inside you, not a clump of cells. And jumelles are not systems of organs. They're clones of people; they're people."

Maggie looked back at the video booth. Eden was still on the stool, talking to the camera. She seemed to float there on a sea of green. That's when the significance of the screen struck Maggie. They could use a computer to drop in any background they wanted, to give the impression that Eden was anywhere in the world. But that wouldn't be enough.

"She can't escape Madame Charbonnier," Maggie said.

"We think she can." Rachel handed Maggie a cup of warm tea. "She'll hunt her to the four corners of the world."

Rachel smiled mischievously. "That won't be good enough."

———

AFTER SHOWING Maggie where the rest facilities were, Rachel assigned her a domed tent on the periphery of the settlement. It was large enough to sleep three, but Rachel assured Maggie she'd have it to herself as long as she remained with them. It came with a sleeping bag and an inflatable pad to cushion the concrete floor.

"There will be noise later tonight," Rachel warned her. "Very loud humming and rumbling. And the lights will get bright for a while. But don't be afraid, and don't come out of the tent. That's very important. In the morning, you're free to come out. I'll see you at breakfast."

"Okay," Maggie said. Then Rachel threw her arms around her and hugged Maggie tight. "I'm so happy for you. And your baby," she said. She kissed Maggie's cheek, and Maggie glimpsed a tear in Rachel's eye, that she quickly wiped away. As Maggie settled her head, she heard the sweet tones of a violin. She thought at first she was imagining it, then realized Étienne must be practicing. She tried to stay awake to listen, but her eyes grew heavy in the darkness.

A couple of hours later, Maggie was awakened by vibrations underneath her. The floor felt like the top of a washing machine on the spin cycle. As the shaking increased, a thunderous crash split Maggie's ears and the interior of her tent lit up bright as day. Some white orb outside was so bright, Maggie feared the wall of her tent would melt. But there was no heat; in fact, Maggie felt a chill, as if a door to a freezer had been thrown open. Rachel had told her not to leave the tent, but even if she hadn't been told, Maggie might not have been able to move. Then, suddenly, the rumbling stopped, and the light dimmed to black. The process repeated twice, and Maggie was getting unnerved. *Would this go on all night?*

But the last pause continued. After a few moments, in the silence, Maggie could make out footsteps padding softly across the factory floor. She heard the zippers of several tents open and close. Apparently, everyone was going to sleep.

In the morning, Maggie awoke desperate for the bathroom. On her way back, she saw her hosts gathered at the table for breakfast. She took an open spot across from Rachel and next to Étienne, who again had his nose buried in a book. After a round of "good mornings," Maggie noticed the group was smaller.

"Eden left last night," Étienne said. "So did Henri and Stephanie."

Three jumelles. Three rounds of noise and light.

"How many are left?"

"Jumelles?" Rachel asked. "We rescued twelve. We've sent eight away."

"What's next?" Maggie asked.

"Now we have to go," Jules said, taking a seat beside Rachel. "We've got to hide these kids from the flics."

"One more night," Rachel urged.

"It's not safe," Jules insisted.

The way those two looked at each other, Maggie wondered if they were lovers. Sure, Jules was at least ten years older than Rachel, but he had this radical professor vibe, that made her think maybe he'd recruited Rachel out of the classroom. But if he had initiated her into the radical life, the power dynamic had shifted, because Rachel appeared to hold a veto over his commands.

"It's still too early," Rachel said. "We could hear something."

"Like police sirens," Jules huffed. "We need to shut things down and clear out. Come back when the heat dies down."

Rachel appeared to chew on the inside of her cheeks. She and Jules didn't exactly stare daggers at each other, but the tension was palpable and only broke when footsteps started clanging on the metal staircase. A rumpled young man, whom Maggie hadn't seen before, scurried towards them.

"Good news, bad news," he said. "We have a placement for Étienne. Looks like a real good fit." Rachel reached both arms across the table and gripped Étienne tight. Her eyes brimmed with tears. The rumpled man continued, "Husband is a chemist. Wife is a music teacher. Now, the average height for a male there is 168 centimeters. So, you're going to be a borderline giant. That's not a bad thing. And if you like girls with a little meat on their bones…"

"Gabriel," Jules prodded, "can you get to the bad news?"

"Oh." Gabriel ran his fingers through his dark hair, revealing a high, clear forehead beneath the front-combed strands. "Your work last night caused a brown-out in Sophville. All the best people saw their crystal chandeliers dim. Which means all the best people got on the phone to the power department, and inspectors are already on the road. Now, we put out a couple of decoys, blown transformers between here and there, so they might decide that's all it was and never make it out here, but…"

"But," Jules interjected, "they're capable of accurately charting where the surge came from."

"Yeah," Gabriel admitted. "Then again, they're government workers, so they're probably not too motivated."

"It's still too great a risk," Jules decided. "Let's break it down."

"No!" Rachel protested. "Not when we've got a home for Étienne."

Jules shot Étienne a look. "Sorry, pal, but safety first. We'll get you to the land of the chubby girls later. Right now, we break camp."

Perhaps sensing that Rachel was about to throw a tantrum, Gabriel leaned between her and Jules. "He's right, you know. If they find that portal, we'll never get another jumelle of this forsaken rock…. What?"

Eyes darted from Gabriel to Maggie and back to Gabriel until he picked up on the signal.

"Oh, she doesn't…? Well, why'd you let me go on?" He got a little huffy, which Maggie found sadly comic. "I swear, this organization could use a little better…organization!" He handed Rachel an envelope. "Memorize and burn." He clambered off again, leaving Rachel and Jules glowering at each other through their eyebrows.

"I told you she needed to know everything," Rachel said at last.

"So, you did," Jules answered. "What's the sequence?"

Rachel tore open the envelope. Her eyes widened as she scanned the paper, and a smile spread over her face. "Our first chance is in three hours."

"Impossible."

"C'mon," Rachel pleaded. "We can send Étienne off, then seal up the portal. We'll be long gone before the power inspectors reach us. One less jumelle to hide while we wait to open shop again."

"We can't risk the strain on the power grid in the middle of the day."

"It's a holiday," Maggie said.

"She's right!" Rachel exclaimed. "No one's working."

"Except the power inspectors and the flics," Jules reminded her.

"We can post sentries up the road. It takes five minutes to shut the portal down and seal up the wall. Then we slip out through the drainage system. We'll be half a kilometer away before they get through the front door."

Jules looked over at Étienne, who'd remained silent through the whole discussion, but had hung on every word. "I don't want to go back in that tank," the youth said.

"Don't worry about that," Jules told him. "Just picture yourself as a giant, surrounded by smiling girls with meat on their bones."

Étienne flashed his bucked teeth in a broad smile, and Jules, clapping his hands, gave orders to break down the camp. The group sprang into action, and within a short time, all the camping equipment had been packed and loaded into a trio of vehicles. Most of the "friends" piled in also, leaving only Jules, Rachel, Étienne, and a middle-aged couple, Marcel and Cosette, who hiked off towards the highway to watch and warn of approaching vehicles. Maggie was surprised they had her stay, too, but Rachel was being possessive. That didn't bother Maggie much, until she saw Rachel strap on a shoulder holster and jam an illegal handgun into it.

"Just ninety minutes, and we'll be underway," Rachel said, as she pulled a jacket on, covering her weapon. She took Maggie to the rear of the factory and pulled up a metal grate from the floor. The hinges creaked and the grate stood open. Rachel reached a leg down the hole onto a rung of a ladder. "C'mon."

The ladder led to a cramped, sloping lower level which had

apparently directed runoff from the factory floor towards a pair of drainage pipes, each a meter tall. Stacked beside the pipes were several dollies with wooden frames and castors.

"Ever go sledding?" Rachel asked. Maggie shook her head. "You just lie on your stomach on one of these and slide down the pipe. There's a steep drop about ten meters in. It can be a little scary. Don't worry, it's just for emergencies. If all goes well, we just hike out through the woods. Are you scared?"

"Aren't you?" Maggie asked.

"I guess I would be if I had any sense," Rachel admitted. "But I lost my sense a long time ago."

Maggie watched Rachel's face grow cold. She seemed far away, not so much in distance, even emotional distance, but in time. Maggie wondered what "long ago" could mean to such a young girl. Early adolescence? Childhood? Rachel appeared to be deciding whether to let Maggie in on something personal, and her hesitancy piqued Maggie's curiosity.

"What happened?" she asked.

"My family," Rachel said. "We were burned out in *The Scorching.*"

Maggie had suspected as much. She'd heard many radicals were formerly privileged individuals, who were bitter about losing their wealth, comfort, and influence. They resented being pulled down to everyone else's level. Maggie had been a toddler at the height of *The Scorching*. In high school, her teachers had spent hours of class time on "the movement." Officially, they and the government deplored the violence, destruction of property, and the damage to the environment, but they seemed more concerned that students understand the ideas motivating the *Scorchers*. Their methods "might be imperfect," but they were "taking a stand against income inequality, privilege, and elitism." The Revolutionary Council had been too slow to enact land reforms and wealth redistribution. People naturally were upset; you can't provoke people beyond their breaking point and expect them to act civilized. Plus, a society has to think for the long term. *The Scorchers'* goal of an equal society was laudable, and, unlike the Revolutionary Council, the *Scorchers* were at least doing something. Sure, there might be short-term pain for some, but in the end, we'd have a more perfect society, without wealth gaps that alienated people from each other. All Maggie had ever heard on the subject stressed empathy for the *Scorchers*. She'd never even met any of the resisters, whom the media had characterized as greedy, selfish, and entitled. Maggie conceded that Rachel might have a point about jumelles and sonograms, but a lot of her thinking was pretty backward.

"So," Maggie said, as sensitively as she could, "you don't believe in equality?"

Rachel's eyes rolled toward the ceiling. She shook her head, and hesitated a moment before saying, "My grandfather got rich because he designed a medical device that saved lives. It was so efficient, so necessary, that every hospital in the world used it, over and over again. And that put him in a position to do more good, to design more equipment that saved more lives. After twelve years, the patent expired, and anyone could have used his design for free if they wanted. But the mob burned him out of his home. And the government, y'know what they did? The great Revolutionary Council? They decided my grandfather had no right to *ever* profit from his invention, even during the short life of the patent. Since medical care was a human right, he should have given it away for free! So, they confiscated all his assets, and put them in The People's Trust, to be administered by Aliénor Charbonnier. My grandfather died penniless in a two-bedroom apartment he shared with his two sons, their wives, and their children. While Aliénor Charbonnier lives in a twenty-room apartment eighty stories above the sooty air the rest of us have to breathe."

"You're out for revenge?" Maggie asked.

"I'm out for justice," Rachel said.

"You targeted Madame Charbonnier."

"We went to free jumelles. Because they're people and don't deserve to be carved into pieces. Coming away with hers was an added bonus."

That was all Rachel had to say for the moment. She marched back to the ladder and Maggie followed. Back on the main floor, Maggie saw what they'd referred to as "the portal." The rear wall of the factory had slid open, revealing a mass of electronic circuitry and a narrow arch with an opening maybe half a meter deep, completely sealed at the other end.

"We're going to charge as slowly as possible, so we don't trigger a brownout," Jules said. "Don't worry. We'll have full power by rendezvous."

What followed was an hour's worth of low humming with lights flickering occasionally. As the appointed time approached, Rachel said goodbye to Étienne.

"You don't mind me taking the violin?" he asked. "I don't know what their instruments will be like."

"Of course," Rachel said. "You won't be in hiding, so you'll be able to play whenever you want." Rachel got teary, hugged him, and stepped aside.

"I hope you'll be happy," Maggie said.

"I hope the same for you and your baby."

Jules then approached with last-minute instructions. "Stand right here as the light builds. It's going to get a little cold, okay? Then, when it's so bright you can hardly look at it, walk as fast as you can into the light. You'll feel suspended for a few seconds, but you want to flex your legs. Because there's a little drop and you'll be on solid ground again. Okay?"

"Okay."

Jules went to the control panel beside the portal, threw a switch and the arch sprang to life. The rumbling grew louder, and a sliver of blue and yellow light emanated from the opening. The light widened and brightened until it burned like a white-hot sun at noon, even as a rush of bitterly cold air swept across the floor. Étienne shaded his eyes and ducked his head. Jules prompted him to go, and he raised his left foot from the floor.

Maggie didn't hear the crack of the rifle, but she saw Étienne's head, bathed in white light, snap forward, then back, and explode. Jules reached for his rifle, leaning against the control panel, but a volley of shots cut him down.

"Run, Maggie!" Rachel yelled, as she fired toward the sharp-shooters. She leapt into the open grate, disappearing as return fire peppered the opening, sending sparks and concrete chips into the air. Those shots froze Maggie, and she inched her hands into the air. The portal shut down; the deafening noise subsided, and the bleaching light faded. Colors and sound returned.

"Maggie!" a voice called. Barnett ran to her and crushed her against his chest. "You're safe now. We know all about how they kidnapped you."

"But they —"

"Shush, love," Barnett said. "It's over."

Barnett blocked Maggie's view of the carnage. A hospital team rushed forward to take possession of Étienne's body.

"Clean head shot," one remarked. "Not another scratch on him. Alert special surgery. This one's a go."

"What about the other?"

"Body's riddled. We might salvage the kidneys."

"Such a waste."

"Well, he went for the gun."

By now, Barnett had walked Maggie halfway across the floor towards the metal staircase. She tried to turn back, but Barnett held her angled forward.

"Jules was a jumelle?" she muttered.

"You mean they gave them names?" Barnett asked.

Another man, also dressed like a detective, surveyed the scene. "The one with the beard disappeared ten years ago," he said. "First time a jumelle ever went missing. We kept it out of the news. Can you imagine having to wait an extra ten years for your life extension? Because your jumelle's running around with a pack of radicals? Then all you get are kidneys? Well, I thought we'd never find him. Was like he'd left the planet or something."

"But that's not possible," Maggie said.

"Course not," the detective agreed. "Hey, you have any idea what that machine is?"

CHAPTER
FIFTEEN

"If God does not exist, then everything is permissible."
— Fyodor Dostoyevsky

TARA THOUGHT SHE MIGHT FREEZE. The green sheath dress wasn't much protection against the chill of...*wherever*. They careened everywhere and nowhere, chasing after a distant spark of light. Finally, they caught that spark; it enveloped them in blinding white light. Tara forced her eyes closed, but the light seemed to pry her lids open, like it deliberately intended to fry her retinas. Then Tara hit the ground hard, jarring every bone. Her knees buckled, but Jean-Luc yanked her up straight, and she found herself standing on the concrete floor of a deserted factory. Totally abandoned, it appeared, except for two, heavily armed officers of some paramilitary unit.

"I need to speak to Inspector Desjardin," Jean-Luc said.

"He's expecting you," an officer answered. "Our orders are to take you and the jumelle to him."

"You can take the jumelle," Jean-Luc said, practically tossing Tara at them. "I'd like to stop at home first and clean up before I see him."

"That's not how the Inspector wants it."

Jean-Luc tipped his head in resignation and strode ahead towards a metal staircase that led to an exit. He was surly in the car. He objected to riding in the back seat with Tara. "I've spent enough time with that thing," he growled. *Some attitude*, Tara thought, *from a guy who was all over me.*

The ride, along a dark and deserted highway, lasted roughly half an hour before they entered a city. Even in the dark, it looked grimy and rundown. The streets were pocked with potholes. But there wasn't much traffic, so the driver was able to weave around some of the worst cavities and crevasses. Finally, they pulled into the parking garage of a large facility. One smirking officer turned to ask Jean-Luc, "You know this place?"

"I know what it is," Jean-Luc replied. "Never actually been here."

The officer gave a somewhat amused, "Hmph."

The place turned out to be some kind of a hospital, which gave Tara the creeps. They took the elevator to the tenth floor. They walked down a long corridor to a set of double doors that sprang open, revealing a huge room with rows and rows of large capsules. In the middle of the room was a man, dressed in kind of a shabby business suit, surrounded by more police and white-outfitted hospital staff.

As they walked toward the man who had to be "the Inspector," Tara glanced at the capsules. Inside each was a teenager, naked, intubated, and apparently sleeping in some gelatinous fluid. Wires were attached to numerous sensors on their heads and various parts of their body. An officer prodded Tara forward.

Seeing the Inspector's face, Tara started putting pieces together. He and Jean-Luc shared a family resemblance. Apparently, he'd deputized a son or nephew or something to hunt down Eden. Nepotism could explain why Jean-Luc was so arrogant. If he ever got into trouble, his powerful family could bail him out.

"Well done," the Inspector told Jean-Luc. "First things first, give the nurse your arm." When Jean-Luc hesitated, the Inspector said,

"Just an immune-booster. No telling what viruses you might have picked up."

Jean-Luc rolled up his sleeve and received the injection.

"Now her," the Inspector said.

Tara held her arms tight at her side. "You're not injecting me with anything." But an officer gripped her in a bear hug, and the needle jabbed her shoulder. The Inspector smiled wickedly at her.

"You might wonder why I don't question you first, before tossing you into the tank," he said. "We've found it's much easier to get reliable information when you're under the suggestion of cortical stimulus."

"You're not...throwing me...in any...tank." Tara suddenly felt uncontrollably sleepy. She felt a nurse unzip her dress. "Nuh..."

"If you don't mind, Inspector," Jean-Luc said, stifling a yawn, "I'd prefer to give my report in the morning. I'd like to get back to my apartment."

The Inspector chuckled. "You don't have an apartment." He laid his hand on a capsule. "This is your home."

A pair of officers braced Jean-Luc and he pushed them aside. "What are you talking about. I'm a cadet at the Revolutionary Police Academy. You picked me out of my class..."

"I picked you out of this tank," the Inspector said. "Whatever memories you have, this machine gave to you." Jean-Luc slumped. Officers held him up, and the nurses started to undress him. "I worried you might figure out the strategy: 'Takes a jumelle to catch a jumelle.' I guess not."

"I'm not...any jumelle..."

"Quite right, not just any. You're mine."

Tara was cold. She should have been terrified, but she was too tired to register fear. She watched a nurse open the lid of a capsule. The Inspector kept talking, like a gloating villain in a *Bond* movie.

"I took a risk," he said. "I might have lost both of you. But I suspected you'd be pretty dogged in your duty."

Two officers lifted Tara, from under her arms and by her feet. A nurse called out, "Inspector, there's something wrong. There are marks on the body."

They propped Tara back up and the Inspector crept closer.

"Those are new," he said. "Probably an attempt to disguise itself."

"Not the thighs.," the nurse said. "The abdomen, inside the right hip. That's a surgical scar. At least two years old."

"Perhaps Madame harvested…"

"An appendix? Who would transplant an appendix?"

"Alright," the Inspector grumbled. "Dress the thing and take it to the office."

Tara shivered; her skin was total gooseflesh. She heard the faint *gloop, gloop* of an object sinking into *Jell-O*, and her eyes fell shut.

———

FLIPPER FIGURED he had easily shattered Bob Beamon's Olympic record for the long jump and wondered if there was any such thing as a galactic record. But more importantly, he kept his eyes fixed on a dot ahead that he took to be Eden. He couldn't be all that sure; the cold was making his eyes water, and she was a long way out there. But, so far at least, they were both on course for the same distant spark of light that jumped this way then that, as if determined to lose them.

"Like chasing Tinker Bell," he grunted. He just hoped when they came to a stop, his feet would be under him. Then he saw the spark swell and the dot that was Eden disappeared into its center. *Here we go*, he told himself, and forced his eyes open, despite the blinding white light that swallowed him.

Flipper landed hard and tumbled forward, planting each of his shoulders above the calves of some person, whose legs then buckled, so his torso collapsed onto Flipper's back. Apparently, that was a good thing, because the guy turned out to be some kind of cop, who had grabbed Eden. When he fell backward, he let her go, and Eden was able to grab a weapon from his belt. It was some kind of stun gun that she used to immobilize him. She then picked the sidearm from his holster and started firing at reinforcements, who were clanging down a metal staircase.

"Quick, down that hole!" Eden yelled. As she continued to fire,

Flipper crawled to an open grate and down a ladder to a lower level. Eden pulled the grate down, locking it behind her, and led Flipper to a large drainpipe. She handed him a flat dolly. "On your belly. Quick."

Flipper belly-flopped into the pipe and took a wild ride that lasted maybe twenty-five seconds. As he slowed to a stop, he heard Eden pull up beside him.

"Now, let's hope they are not posted outside," she said. They crept forward to the opening of the pipe, which was on the edge of a narrow ravine. The scene was in twilight, but whether the sun was dawning or setting was anyone's guess. No one shot at them as they poked their heads out, which Flipper took as a positive sign.

"Where to now?" he asked.

"I do not know," Eden said. "But we must go. It's death to stay."

"Well, we don't want that," Flipper muttered. He spotted what appeared to be a trail about ten feet about the ravine.

"How 'bout that way?"

"Okay."

Not a ringing endorsement, Flipper thought, but since he heard echoes of footsteps coming from the drain, this was no time to debate. They trudged through the stream, scrambled up the rise to the trail, and took off at a brisk trot. Well, as brisk as Flipper could manage with water-logged sneakers. After forty yards, he could feel his toes blistering. Fortunately for them, the trail took a bend away from the stream, so they were out of sight of the factory drain before their pursuers came out. The creek bed had been stony, so Flipper hoped they didn't leave visible tracks. The trail was laid with gravel on top of dense clay, so their footprints would be no more obvious than the tracks of hikers and joggers who'd been there earlier. They got another break when the trail forked.

"Which direction?" Flipper asked. A smile broke across Eden's face.

"I know this place," she said, pulling him left.

"You've been here before?"

"I've never been," she said. "But they taught me, while in my tank."

"Your what?"

If Eden answered, Flipper didn't hear her. She was drowned out by a sound Flipper had feared: a helicopter rose over the factory, sending out a piercing, white searchlight. On the trail, with only low brush on either side, they were exposed. The chopper hovered over the ravine for several seconds, as Flipper and Eden sprinted up the trail looking for some place to hide. Then the chopper began doing zigzags, combing the hills from one side of the ravine to the other.

"There!" Eden yelled and pointed to an open area at the base of the hill. There was a large wooden ring, like a corral, and structures that seemed to be broken-down horse stables. They dashed through the compound to a low building on the side of the road, which, according to its faded sign, had been the business office for "*L'école des Arts équins.*" As the helicopter's high beam strafed the corral, Eden used the stun weapon she'd taken off the cop to blow the lock on the door, and they ducked inside. In seconds, Eden had dug a walkie-talkie out of a desk drawer and was telling someone about their situation. Nodding along to the instructions, she tossed a throw rug aside and pulled open a secret door in the floor.

"We're to hide in here," she told Flipper. The search beam lit up the grounds right outside the office as they hopped into the hole and lowered the door back in place. Then Eden pulled a long cord, which Flipper assumed stretched the rug back to where it had been.

"What is this place?" he asked.

"A waystation the group set up, in case they had to flee the factory."

"What group?"

"The friends who freed me."

"How long do we have to stay here?"

"I do not know. At least the night. Then maybe 'til they stop looking."

"Great." Flipper pulled off his soggy sneakers and wrung out his socks. His no-look leap was starting to seem like a very, very bad idea.

———

TARA FELT HERSELF SUFFOCATING. A weight on her chest pushed down on her lungs. It felt like the weight of water; she kicked to get above the surface, while all around her was black. She didn't know how far submerged she was, or even which direction was up. She couldn't lift her arms. She craned her neck, stretching to get her nose, her mouth, above the surface before her lungs burst. Finally, she broke the surface, into a burst of light, and her mouth blew open, releasing stale air in a roar, then sucking desperately for life.

"Oh. That's just too awful, isn't it?" a woman's voice said. "Well, adrenaline will do that, and I needed you awake."

Tara had fallen to her hands and knees and was panting like a dog. She crumpled to her elbows and gripped her sweaty face in her hands. Pairs of hands grabbed each of her arms and lifted her onto a plastic chair. Through strands of matted hair, she saw guards on either side. She was wearing green hospital scrubs and a pair of no-skid socks. Someone at least had had the decency to dress her. Then she looked up and focused on a ghostly image that resolved to an ashen face, framed in straight, platinum blonde hair. Tara had seen this face before. Yes, when Cheryl had shown her and Teri an aging app she had on her phone. This woman was them at maybe forty-five or fifty.

"Inspector Desjardin said he'd recovered my jumelle," the woman said. "Then an hour later, he calls to say he might not have recovered my jumelle. Although, the creature bears an uncanny resemblance. I thought, surely, this is impossible."

Tara groaned, "Everything's impossible until someone does it."

"I'm told your story is that you're some kind of Earth girl, who was leading a perfectly typical life until an agent from our planet kidnapped you and brought you here?" Her voice dripped with sarcasm.

"I'm pretty sure my life wasn't typical," Tara said. "Even before your goon showed up."

"No, not typical at all," the woman sneered. "But there's a far simpler explanation." The woman held out a photograph, a shot of Tara and Teri from freshman year that Tara carried in her wallet.

"Apparently, you're not just a jumelle, you're a jumelle of a jumelle."

"That's my sister. My…" Tara hesitated, she didn't want to say "jumelle," but she didn't know any other French word for twin. "Anyway, she's dead."

"I think not." The woman smiled coldly. "It's much more likely that some enterprising individual anticipated the profit to be made with additional copies of the Republic's leading citizen. You, obviously, were flawed and had to be repaired. That explains the surgical scar. As for this one,"—she held up the photo again—"she is very much alive."

Before Tara could respond, the Inspector cut in. "A short time ago, I received a phone call, saying that a female matching your description had entered through the portal. A young man followed her, tackled the officer, and helped her escape."

Nolan, Tara thought. *He's come to help me.* "Well, I don't know anything about that," she said. "I've been here, enjoying your hospitality."

The Inspector gestured toward the photo the woman still held. "Apparently, you and our jumelle have a rather close relationship."

"I don't know anything about her."

"This picture says different."

"That's not her. I told you, that's my sister, Teri. I only met Eden once."

"You must have made quite an impression," the woman said, "if my jumelle's come back to help you."

"Who says that's why?"

"Your eyes gave you away," the woman said. "They gave a quite comical flash of…hope." The woman tossed the photo into a waste basket. "Now, let me tell you about the choice you face. You can help us recover my jumelle and crush the criminal network that stole it, or you can take that jumelle's place."

"You can't…" Tara said. She turned to the Inspector, pleading, "You know you made a mistake. You have to send me back."

"Don't look at him. Look at me," the woman demanded, in a tone of someone who's used to having her demands met. "Here is what is

going to happen. I am scheduled for life extension. That's the procedure where surgeons extract vital organs from the jumelle —*vous* —
and transplant them into the prime —*moi*." She signaled a medical
worker who handed her a sheet of paper. "While you were lazily
napping, our laboratory ran some preliminary blood tests. We'll
confirm with tissue samples but results so far indicate you are a
perfect match. So, if you don't help us find my jumelle in the next
forty-eight hours, we're just going to use you instead."

"You can't chop me up!" Tara cried. "You lunatic! Maniac! My
God, you're crazy!"

"Your god?" she laughed. "Who might that be? Do you have any
idea who I am? I'm Aliénor Charbonnier. I'm the woman who killed
god!"

What, Tara thought, *how*—?

"Now," Madame glowered, "are you going to tell us what you
know?"

"I told you I don't know anything!"

"Take it back to the tank," the Inspector said, and a needle
plunged into Tara's arm. She slumped and the guards lifted her
again.

Madame Charbonnier inclined towards her, and Tara felt her
breath on her face. "You are my creation," she hissed. "And if I don't
use you, I'll see that someone else does. You're nothing but a sack of
organs. And that's all you'll ever be."

———

DESJARDIN WAS tired and it was late. He stood outside his
apartment building with Madame's lecture still ringing in his ears,
feeling nothing but emptiness.

"You're too young to remember *The Trial of God*," she'd said as
he'd escorted her to her car.

"I've read about it," he said.

"That's not the same," she said. "I wish your generation could live
it, and every generation after. It was glorious."

Her chauffeur had held the door open, and she'd asked, "Can I drop you somewhere, Inspector?"

He'd been foolish enough to nod. "Yes, home."

What followed was a dissertation on Madame's place in Tartarian history. "After the Planetary War, the world was spent. Used up. Fifty million dead, twenty million of those in extermination camps, not even combatants, and the last million or so done in by atomic weaponry that threatened to destroy the race. In the face of all that carnage, one question emerged: 'Where was god?' The religious apologists tried to argue that the horrors of our great war did not disprove the existence of a god or his benevolence. But how could they argue that a loving father was there in the death camps? It occurred to me, and to the other Progressives, that if a god had been there, he must have been complicit. And this was the genius and the genesis of our movement: we set out to prove god guilty of all the horror he had permitted. We held the trial on television over the course of six weeks. We called hundreds of witnesses. We presented volumes of evidence. At the end of the trial, we let the people vote. And they convicted god. We hanged him in effigy, and all across the globe, people rose up to burn their churches to the ground. That was the beginning of our Revolution. And that is what made us the peaceful world we are today.

"There are still Restorationists," she admitted, "and probably always will be. They'll argue their regressive ideas: private property, free enterprise, private education, marriage, natural childbirth, parental rights, animal ownership, meat consumption, and on and on. But the most dangerous ones are those who want to resurrect their god. We can never let that happen."

Naturally, Desjardin had agreed on every point and pledged his tireless service. But to what end? As he stood outside his building and envisioned opening the door to his apartment, he had only one thought: Maggie. They'd separated shortly after her rescue. She'd been useless to the investigation, insisting she didn't know anything about the machine, or the organization, other than the name of one woman: Rachel Fontaine. Barnett had been patient with her, knowing she'd been through a traumatic experience and that hostages sometimes bond with their captors.

State scientists had done a quick analysis of the machine, which despite its sophisticated applications, had meager security. They had traced its origin to a top-secret program abandoned shortly after the Revolution, and clandestinely revived by traitors in the Astro-Science Corps. But, by the time the Inspector had started to round up those rogue scientists, they'd mysteriously disappeared, raising suspicions that another "portal" must exist. He'd staked his men at the factory, and, under increasing pressure from Madame Charbonnier, he'd decided to use that portal to pursue Madame's jumelle. Not wanting to risk a person, he'd programmed his jumelle for the task. If it had failed, he'd have lost his chance for life extension. Of course, his career would have been over anyway, so there would have been little point.

Now, he was on the verge of solving the jumelle heist and crushing the terrorist network. He'd be hailed as a hero, opening doors to influential circles. That justified the big step: life extension. So, why did his mind go back to Maggie? Yes, success was a little hollow without someone to share it. And maybe a small dose of reality would bring the girl back to her senses and make her see how utterly ridiculous she'd been. Carrying a fetus to term? *Absurd!* Yet, that was the decision she'd made, and that's why they were no longer together. She'd thrown their relationship away, *and for what?*

Maggie had never expressed any desire to have a family, and that was certainly not what Desjardin had wanted from their relationship. If he'd wanted a home with children, he wouldn't have picked Maggie. He'd have chosen someone with a career, a public profile, stature. There was no sense committing long-term to a woman who couldn't even afford one round of life extension. And now that he was a rising star, clinging to Maggie made even less sense.

But, despite all that, he missed her. He didn't like coming home to an empty apartment and sleeping in an empty bed. Fortunately, there was still time to end her charade and cash in on the fetal tissue. Then they could go back to the way things were.

Desjardin hailed a taxicab to the facility where Maggie was staying. It was a government home for independent mothers, mostly women who'd become accidentally pregnant and some like Maggie who'd backed out of tissue donation. The women had little to no income, so they had to enroll in a program to become self-sufficient, so their child would not be a burden on the state. Giving the infant up for adoption was strongly encouraged, but the women's backgrounds often made it impossible to place the child in a respectable home. Fortunately, Desjardin had been meticulous about the legal language in their cohabitation agreement. They had stipulated that any byproduct of their relations was to be used for income. He could not be held financially liable for a child.

The taxi pulled up outside the facility and he asked the driver to wait. He wouldn't be long. It was way past visiting hours, and he had to tell the security officer that he was there on official business. Security contacted the night warden, and she went to wake Maggie up. Desjardin waited uneasily. It had been seven weeks since he'd rescued Maggie. Six weeks since they'd separated. In that time, they'd video conferenced twice. She'd appeared depressed, but obstinate.

Now as she trundled towards him, half asleep, he was horrified. She'd gotten gigantic. Her sleek frame was bloated, and she waddled like some kind of pneumatic penguin. He pictured the damage this pregnancy was doing to her smooth, flat abdomen. And she still had another month or more of being stretched all out of proportion. She'd never be beautiful again. *Such a waste, and for what?*

"What is it, Barnett?" Maggie asked.

"We've had a breakthrough. We've recovered Madame Charbonnier's jumelle." Not technically true, but close enough.

"Congratulations," she said. "Did you kill her, or does someone else get that honor?"

"*It* goes back to *its* owner," he said slowly. "And *it* gets used for the purpose for which *it* was created."

"Funny," Maggie scoffed. "I thought the whole purpose of the Revolution was to do away with private property. Now it seems all property is in the hands of those who led the Revolution. And people themselves are property: usable, disposable."

"Jumelles aren't people," he stated, as though by rote.

"And you, Barnett?" Maggie asked. "Are you anything more than the property of the great Madame Charbonnier?"

That accusation caught Desjardin off guard. It wasn't like Maggie to challenge him directly.

"And while we're at it," she continued, "there's absolutely no difference between a jumelle and a prime. That's scientific fact, isn't it? Despite the lies the Minister of Propaganda puts out? Isn't the whole point of creating a jumelle to get an exact duplicate? That boy you killed, étienne…"

"He was no boy."

"He had intelligence. He had talent. He had…spirit."

Desjardin realized he'd made a mistake. He'd hoped that Maggie would have seen the error and futility of this radical movement, but she'd slipped deeper into delusion.

"So, what now?" he asked her. He pointed at her distended belly. "Do you become a surrogate?" There wasn't as much money in hiring out a womb as there was for supplying tissue for research. But there were plenty of couples who wanted their own genetic children without the pains of natural childbirth or the expense of laboratory gestation. Maggie could make a bit of a living over the next few years. Then what?

"I don't know," Maggie said. "All I know is, I love him. Or her. You think I've gone crazy. Maybe I have. But every day, I feel this child moving, changing, growing, and I can't wait to meet him. To bring him into the light of the world. I want something, someone, to love, Barnett. And someone to love me. This is a baby. How many did we make that we just threw away? It breaks my heart to think of it. To think, we could have had so much love around us. But we killed it. I hate us for that."

If this was Maggie's attempt to wound him, she had grossly overestimated her importance. Desjardin couldn't help but smile. "You hate me?" he asked.

"I didn't say that," Maggie answered. "I really don't feel anything for you. But I hate us. And I'm very glad there's no us anymore."

"No happier than I," Desjardin said firmly. "You've hung a millstone around your neck. I won't be dragged down with you." He was surprised that he was becoming angry. So angry, in fact, that he told her, "I've decided to go ahead with life extension. I'd been holding off on account of you, but now there's no sense delaying it."

"I hope you'll be very happy with yourself."

Go, he told himself. But he couldn't move. There was something different about Maggie. She wasn't the vain, supercilious girl he'd taken under his wing. In their relationship, he'd been the profound one, the man of authority. She'd looked up to him. Now she seemed to be looking through him. She had gravity, and he felt himself floating. Weightless. Adrift.

Finally, it was she who turned and trundled away. "You don't matter," he said loudly, foolishly. In his mind, he saw himself grabbing her by the hair and twisting her around to face him as he shouted it again: *You don't matter! You don't matter!*

———

WHEN THE RADIO call had come from Eden, Rachel had wanted to go to her. Unfortunately, she still had a heavy plaster cast on, from her toes to her knee, and even though she'd been putting weight on the leg for a week now, she wasn't exactly agile. She needed to have the cast removed, but even then she would not be in any shape to outrun the flics.

So, she'd told Eden about the trap door to the hiding place, the same place she had hidden the night the factory had been raided, when Jules and étienne had been gunned down, and Maggie had frozen in terror. Maggie's paralysis had actually aided Rachel's escape. Even after busting her ankle in the drop to the lower level, she'd been able to hop over to the drain and sled down to the ravine in less time than it would have taken if Maggie had been with her. Apparently, the flics had searched the entire lower level before concluding she had exited down the pipe. As far as Rachel could tell, no one had followed her. But she still had to spend two nights in the hole before any "friend" could come and get her. By that time, her ankle had swollen to three times its size, and she worried that even surgery might not save her.

Fortunately, there was no shortage of good doctors among the friends. The Revolution had been so hard on their profession that many had come to embrace Restoration. The Republic guaranteed everyone the right to "free" healthcare, so doctors were overworked, underpaid, and didn't have the freedom to choose their own specialties, or even where they were to practice. The government decided everything. Healthcare was severely rationed, so doctors couldn't treat patients as needed; bureaucrats made medical decisions. Conditions were so bad, that most students who earned medical degrees left the profession, and universities graduated fewer doctors every year, because few students would commit to years of rigorous study for a low-paying job with no prestige. Still, few if any doctors would admit to holding Restorationist views for fear of reprisals.

Thus, Rachel had gotten the medical attention she needed in that moment but was abandoned as the full scope of her disaster became known. The flics had the portal and quickly spread a dragnet across the capital to snare scientists with knowledge or involvement. Leaders of the *Society* had fled; some were even rumored to have gone to other planets. Rachel couldn't confirm that; it would've required at least one more functioning portal, and she'd never heard of such a thing. But her network was in tatters, and many of her old allies shunned her. Isolated at a safehouse that seemed less safe with each passing day, Rachel had cut her hair and dyed it auburn. She wore blue contact lenses. And she bided her time while her leg healed.

Biding her time, unfortunately, meant watching the Minister of Public Communications spin lies on TV about life extension and the nature of jumelles. Rachel got furious watching state-sponsored programming, where Minister Pomeroy purported to "go inside the jumelle bank" for "an inside look." He showed disembodied organs floating in goo, like a hydroponic flesh-garden, while he interviewed workers who stiffly recited Republic talking points totally detached from reality. No workers had the courage to say out loud what was whispered everywhere: Jumelles are complete clones of people. They

ARE people. Rachel was more eager than ever to get on with her work, to liberate the jumelles and expose the Minister's lies. But even as her bones knitted, the rift between her and *the Society* festered.

Then one night, the radio at her safehouse had crackled with a communication. Eden was on the other end. *Why had she come back? Why had her guardians let her?* Eden hadn't seen étienne's brains splattered all over the portal, but she knew the danger of returning to Tartairos. It didn't make sense, but one thing was certain: Rachel had to get Eden out of that hole as quickly as possible.

FLIPPER WAS IRKED, but not surprised, that neither his sneakers nor his socks had dried overnight. Still, his annoyance paled in comparison to his gratitude that he and Eden hadn't been discovered. About an hour after they had hunkered down, they had heard footsteps in the office above. In the pitch black of their hiding place, Flipper froze, and he assumed Eden did likewise. He pictured her pointing her pistol at the door above them and wondered how many rounds she had left. After what seemed like an eternity, but couldn't have been more than ninety seconds, the footsteps retreated, and they were able to breathe again.

But sleeping was another matter. Groping around in the darkness, Flipper had felt a slim chain hanging from the ceiling. He gave it a gentle tug, and a soft, red light came on. That revealed a couple of bedrolls, which smelled like a rainy day at the dog pound but were at least more comfortable than the dirt floor. The light also revealed a lattice of spider webs up in the rafters and along the walls, and Flipper couldn't help but worry if this planet was stocked with venomous arachnids. Eden had no trouble falling asleep, but the nervous, creep-crawly feeling on his skin had kept Flipper awake all night.

"You don't have to stay with me," Eden said, shortly after she woke up. "I doubt anyone got a good look at you. You can go."

"Where?" Flipper asked. "I have no idea where anything is."

"Sh!" Eden warned. A second later, Flipper heard the muffled sound of vehicle tires crushing gravel. Eden drew her pistol and angled herself towards the door.

"How many bullets do you have left?" he whispered.

"What's a bullet?" she asked.

"The thing that shoots out of the gun."

"I don't understand."

"You have to put bullets in to make them come out."

"You do?"

The floorboards above creaked, and there was a clump, like a two-by-four or a baseball bat landing on the boards. Flipper doused the red light. Creak, clump, creak, clump. The pull cord zipped upward; someone had tossed the rug aside. They'd seen the door. Flipper had no idea how Eden could have such mad skills with weapons, when she didn't even know a gun had to be loaded, but he said a quick prayer that her skills would hold up.

Then came three knocks in quick succession followed by two slow knocks.

"Friends," Eden sighed.

The door creaked open, and light flooded the hole. Eden scampered up the ladder and Flipper followed. Squinting slightly from the flashlight beam, he grasped a hand extended towards him, and let a young woman steady him as he took his final step. The woman was really a girl roughly his age. Her close-cropped, auburn hair was all wrong, but it framed a familiar face. Flipper's jaw dropped, as he grasped her by the shoulders. "Raquel?"

CHAPTER
SIXTEEN

"I ask not for any crown
But that which all may win;
Nor try to conquer any world
Except the one within."
— Louisa May Alcott

"I'M SORRY," Rachel said, "but it's impossible to save your friend. I wish it wasn't, but the hospital is like a fortress now. Even if we could break in, we'd never get out alive."

"We've got to do something!" Flipper demanded.

"There's nothing to do," Rachel said. "We can't even send you home."

"I wouldn't go without Tee!"

"Little man, you need to calm yo'self down."

Flipper turned toward that low, rumbling voice and saw a dark hulk clogging the doorway. The house seemed to tip as he stepped into the living room.

"Guillaume, you remember Eden," Rachel said. "This is Flutter."

"Flip-per," he objected. "It's not that hard."

"Only I don't care."

And for the moment, Flipper didn't care either; he couldn't believe what he was seeing. First a French-speaking girl who looks like a blue-eyed Raquel, and now a huge tub of apple butter carved in the likeness of Lima Autufuga. Also speaking French. Fortunately, Raq...*Rachel* had outfitted Flipper with a translation device he wore like a hearing aid to help him follow what they were saying. *Unfortu*nately, the gadget did not help him make sense of what he was seeing. "What is happening?" he gasped. He took a step back, half expecting to bump into himself.

"Guillaume is an orderly on the hospital ward, where your friend Tara is being held," Rachel said. "He helped us get Eden out."

"Yeah," Guillaume nodded, "but that was then; this is now. You'd need an army to get in."

"So, let's get an army!"

Guillaume gave him a look like, *Let the grownups handle it*, or something. Flipper could tell they were not going to get along, and if push came to shove, Flipper was liable to get shoved into a trash can. Or a shoe box.

"We cannot let Madame Charbonnier use Tara Hartzwell the way she wants to use me," Eden said. "That's what they are going to do, isn't it? If they don't find me?"

Guillaume nodded. "That's the word on the ward."

"We have to stop her!" Eden pleaded.

"We will!" Rachel said. "But you being here doesn't make it any easier. Now we've got to worry about you and her."

"Or forget about her," Flipper said. "What's she to you? She's not your friend."

The slap he got for that remark nearly sent his head into the kitchen. And it would have been worse if Guillaume hadn't stepped in. It was like Tee pulling Nolan off him at the *CD*. Except having another guy pull an angry girl off of him was even more humiliating. Rachel kept berating him, and Flipper slumped into a chair, rolling his head in frustration. *Get me outta here*, he thought. *What am I even trying to do?*

———

"INCOMPATIBLE!" Madame bellowed. "How can that be?"

Inspector Desjardin stifled an impulse to laugh, and the Director of Life Extension took a breath. "Well, the creature is an alien life form, Madame." S/he (the Director's personal pronoun, emblazoned on s/he's lapel as a warning to the unwary, complete with phonetic assistance, so all would know to say 'suh-hee' in s/he's presence) offered Madame the test results. "Tissue sample testing indicates that if you employ this creature's organs, you risk a forty percent chance of fatal failure."

"Alright," Madame sighed. "Then find compatible recipients. There must be someone waiting anxiously. A donation from the Head of State would play well in the media."

The Director's mouth hung open.

"What?" Madame demanded. "Is it incompatible with...our entire race? Come, tell us, can you use it or not?"

"M-madame," the Director stammered. "one might question your right to the specimen. I mean, surely if she, er, *it*, was complicit in stealing your jumelle, then taking her, *it*, as restitution would be warranted. But..."

Desjardin stifled another chuckle as the pronoun afficionado tripped over the pronouns.

"But?" Madame rose from her chair and strode out from behind her over-sized desk. "What would s/he suggest we do? Set it free? Can s/he imagine the propaganda *that* would generate? Senior officials of the People's Republic admit they could not tell the difference between an incubated jumelle and a sentient alien! Wouldn't the *'jumelles are people'* crowd love that! Life extension would be over, and s/he, my fine doctor, would find s/he-self hanged from a lamppost by a Restorationist mob. Is that what s/he wants?"

"Of course not, Madame."

"Then do something with it!" Madame bellowed. "Use it for mulch, for all I care, but get it out of my—*the people's*—hospital."

The Director bowed obsequiously and prepared to make s/he's exit. As s/he turned, Inspector Desjardin put a steadying hand on s/he's shoulder. He'd been biding his time, because his update on the hunt for Madame's missing jumelle was not going to please her. But the Director's presentation had given him an opportunity.

"There is another way, Madame," Desjardin said. "Implant a tracking device, then set it free, quietly. And let it lead us to the rebels."

"With Foundation Day less than a week away?" Madame demanded. "You want to just hand them ammunition against us?"

"They don't need any," Desjardin reminded her. "They already have your jumelle, securely tucked away. We've got to do something to bring them into the open."

Madame was skeptical, but not dismissive. "What makes you think the rebels would be interested in this creature?"

"What we can count on is that *it* will be interested in *them*."

——

FLIPPER SPENT the day at the safehouse doing nothing under Guillaume's watchful gaze. Rachel had called in the big boy for his truck but kept him around in case Flipper refused to follow orders. Rachel made a series of phone calls to people who didn't seem to want to talk to her, and as the day wore on, it became clear she wasn't getting any help as regards Flipper, Eden, or Tee.

"It's impossible," she told him for the elevendieth time.

"Everything's impossible until somebody does it!" Flipper shot back. He wasn't sure where he'd heard that before, but it sounded familiar.

"You know what's not impossible?" Rachel asked. "Getting shot in the head and having your brains splattered."

"Well, maybe that's a risk I'm willing to take!"

Her nostrils flared. "Have you ever seen it?" she asked.

Flipper squared his jaw. "Have you ever seen second degree burns from a deep fryer accident?"

Rachel flailed her hands open towards Guillaume, as if to ask, "Can't you stuff him somewhere?" Flipper took the hint. He retreated to a musty, overstuffed chair in the corner and stewed.

Hours passed. Nothing. Flipper was climbing the walls.

"What's up at the hospital?" he asked. "Is she still alive at least?"

"They'll call when they hear something," Guillaume drawled. "Little man, you…"

"Yeah, I know," Flipper said. "I need to calm myself down."

They had dinner with no news. Hours later they went to bed with no news. Then, in the middle of the night, someone shook Flipper awake. A hand covered his mouth.

"I want to help Tara Hartzwell," Eden whispered. Flipper nodded and she withdrew her hand. "You know how to drive an automobile?"

Flipper nodded, although he wasn't sure if the cars on this planet operated on the same principles. They'd ridden in a truck from the riding school to here, and it seemed pretty similar. He dressed quietly and followed Eden into the front room.

Guillaume was sleeping on the couch, snoring like a grizzly. That put Flipper further on edge. Chronic snorers, even though they set off a racket no one else could tolerate, were notoriously shallow sleepers, and any slight noise might awaken them. The last thing Flipper wanted was to poke that bear in the middle of the night. And it didn't help that the floorboards of the old house creaked like in a bad horror movie. Flipper followed Eden to the front door and watched her pick the keys to the truck off the hook. *Okay*, he thought. *Key operated, that's good*.

He closed the door as quietly as possible behind him and then tip-toed around the side of the house to the truck. This would be the test. The vehicle looked at least three decades old, and who knew how much it might backfire when Flipper turned the ignition. *Here goes*, he thought, drawing a deep breath. He braced himself and turned the key. The engine coughed, but quickly turned over. It was humming as he backed it out, but then the engine started knocking and *bang!* In the rearview mirror, Flipper saw a billow of black smoke. Two more bangs followed in quick succession before he had backed the truck onto the road. Then the door to the house burst open, and Guillaume hustled after them, just as Flipper hit the accelerator and sped down the roadway.

"You are going the wrong way," Eden said.

"Are you sure?" he asked.

"Positive."

Flipper spun the wheel and hung a U-turn. He really hoped Guillaume wouldn't come out into the middle of the street. He further hoped that Rachel wouldn't come running and shoot out the tires. As they whizzed past the house, Guillaume just flailed his arms, like a castaway trying to signal a passing motorboat.

"Where to now?" Flipper asked.

Eden puffed her cheeks. "The city. Then I don't know."

———

THE DIRECTOR RAISED eyebrows on the ward when s/he arrived so early in the morning after staying late the night before. S/he had lingered long enough to implant the tracking device without any of the staff seeing. Today s/he'd come early to prepare the jumelle, or whatever it was, to leave the ward. The sooner the creature would be out, the better. S/he didn't like Inspector Desjardin to begin with; he projected a clichéd machismo, outmoded and overbearing, which an enlightened individual such as s/he had long ago relegated to Tartairos' tragic history of unremitting warfare. S/he liked the Inspector even less when he was breathing down s/he's neck and making accusations about s/he's professional competency. S/he also didn't like Madame Charbonnier's policy of secrecy and denial. Why not tell the public the truth about jumelles? They are clones, but that doesn't make them people. People, after all, are creators, shaping themselves and the world around them. As creators, they controlled destiny. Jumelles, on the other hand, were creatures. Creations. Laboratory products. Property of their primes. "Stop acting like we have something to hide," s/he had told Madame time and again. "We should show pride in our advances!"

But Madame was obstinate. She insisted that jumelles in human form would naturally elicit sympathy from the ignorant masses. "They haven't been properly educated," she said. "They are shallow thinkers, seduced by superficialities. They see something that looks human, they conclude it must be human. We must present a comfortable fantasy they don't have to think about." In vain had Madame 'killed god,' s/he concluded, if she would merely replace one fantasy with another, equally divorced from reason and reality.

And speaking of divorce from reality—*this business about aliens!* The creature looked completely Tartarian but had peculiar anomalies on the cellular level. So, yes, she,—*it*, whatever—was an alien. So, what did that mean? Was Tartairos under imminent attack from extraterrestrial teenagers? It was all too much. And the Director feared s/he was getting an ulcer over it. The two pints of black coffee s/he had drunk to pry s/he's eyes open also weren't helping s/he's nerves.

S/he had removed s/he's coat and was hanging it on the hook behind s/he's office door when a nurse knocked on the door jamb.

"Yes, Beatrice?" s/he asked. She handed s/he a package. "What's this?"

"Items you sent to the laundry yesterday."

The Director broke the seal and saw a green dress and undergarments. "Thank you. Start to revive B9, please."

"Revive, sir?"

"Yes, someone from the Inspector's office will come by later." S/he handed the nurse the package of clothing.

"What time?" Beatrice asked.

"I don't know." S/he hadn't been told and hadn't asked. S/he imagined the ward would either have to babysit a flic or an alien until the other was ready. "Just get it cleaned up and dressed."

"Should I have food sent up?"

"Am I running a hotel?" s/he snapped. Stomach reflux burned s/he's throat. *When is this day going to end?*

It wasn't ten minutes later that Beatrice came running into s/he's office. "Doctor, come quick, something's wrong with B9!"

The creature was lying on a gurney, extubated, but not breathing. Its heart had stopped. A medic was performing cardiovascular resuscitation.

"What do you expect?" the medic asked no one in particular. "Sedate, revive, sedate, revive. No creature's heart can take that."

"Can she take a shock?"

"We'll find out."

"Charging."

The medic placed the paddles on the creature's chest and ordered everyone, "Clear!" There was a hum and the creature bounced. A pause, and the creature didn't move. The medic held the paddles aloft as he pressed his ear to its chest. Lifting his head again, he looked over to the Director, who nodded back.

"Charge again."

They repeated the process. Higher voltage, and the creature bounced higher.

"I've got a beat," the medic announced.

Beatrice spread a blanket over the creature. The Director watched the blanket rise and fall, then walked back to s/he's office.

The next knock at the Director's door came an hour later. A youngish, rather upright but scruffy man announced himself as Lt. Gagnon of the Citizens' Militia.

"Inspector Desjardin sent me. I'm to pick up...." He apparently didn't know how to finish the sentence.

The Director led him back to pod B9, where the creature was still lying on the gurney in a semi-stupor. The creature noticed them hovering and lolled its head to the side. "So, what's the plan? Am I getting chopped up?"

"To the contrary," the Director said. "You're being released."

The creature stared dumbly at them. "What?" it finally said. "To go where?"

"The Lieutenant will explain."

"You're going to be integrated into society."

Its green eyes squinted, and it rolled to a sitting position. The blanket fell away, revealing that Beatrice had dressed the creature. The nurse gathered the blanket and tossed it into a nearby linen basket. "I don't belong here," the creature objected. "You've got to send me back."

"Quite impossible," the Lieutenant said.

"Why?" the creature demanded. "You have the machine. You have no right to hold me."

"We're not holding you," the Lieutenant said. "I'm taking you to a safe place."

The creature covered its mouth to cough, then opened its fist, where it had caught a glob of bloody sputum. Beatrice was quick to offer a tissue.

"That's nothing," the nurse said. "We did a lung biopsy; that will clear up in a couple of days."

The creature winced and reached a hand to its ribcage.

"We took some marrow," Beatrice explained. "And a tissue sample from a kidney."

The creature found its shoes on the floor and started to put them on. It stood, wobbly, and stepped away from the gurney, then stared into an adjacent pod.

"What about him?" the creature asked.

"Property of the Inspector," the Director said. "He's scheduled life extension for next week."

The creature's eyebrows peaked, and its lower lip quivered, as if taken by pity. It placed a hand on the glass of the pod, muttering, "I'm not leaving without him."

"You have no choice," the Lieutenant said.

"He's a boy," the creature snapped. "Kind of a creep, but still a boy. You can't carve him like a turkey. Wake him up, you'll see, he's a person, he deserves to live!"

The Lieutenant took hold of the creature's arm and escorted it, yelling obnoxiously, out the door. "Get your hand off me, you can't —" *Blah, blah, blah.* Finally, a welcome silence fell over the ward, and all the Director could hear was the machines humming.

Beatrice lingered at the pod, where the Inspector's jumelle was flexing and releasing its muscles under electro-stimulus. "He deserves to live," she said wistfully. "Wouldn't the Inspector love to hear that."

Yes, the Director mused. *Wouldn't he?*

———

"YOU WERE SUPPOSED TO WATCH HIM!" Rachel yelled. "That's the whole reason you're here!"

"Person's gotta sleep," Guillaume grumbled. "And who'd of thought he'd be that crazy to go off when he don't even know where he's at?" He jammed his right foot into his shoe and tugged hard at the laces. "Eden, too. She don't know where she's at. Cray-fools gon' get 'emselfs killed."

"We need a car," Rachel said.

"Good luck with that."

The city was fifty miles away. Eden and Fluster would make it there in an hour. Then what? Stake out the hospital? Try to get inside the Life Extension Ward? It was suicide. Eden hadn't done anything to disguise herself; she was still the striking, younger version of the most famous face on the planet. The only question was which law enforcement agency would claim the prize.

The phone rang and Rachel let Guillaume answer. She immediately wished she had grabbed it and grew increasingly irritated as he nodded and *yupped* through the call, without telling her what was being said. Finally, he cupped the receiver with his other hand and said, "The hospital released Tara Hartzwell."

"What do you mean *released?*"

"A flic walked her out the building."

"Does that sound like a release?" Rachel asked. "Madame Charbonnier would never let her go."

Guillaume shrugged and put the receiver back to his ear. Three *yups* later he hung up.

"Good news is someone's sending a car."

"And the bad news?"

"It ain't coming soon."

———

THE COP INSISTED Tara call him "Lieutenant," because "it is fitting to observe all formalities." He took her downstairs to a bus stop, where they waited at the end of a long line. The air held a foul odor, and the sky was a sickly grey tinged with yellow. Whether it was the dull light or an actual absence of pigment, the scenery and people's clothing were uniformly drab. After about twenty minutes, a bus arrived, too crowded to take more than a handful of riders. They moved closer to the head of the line and waited for the next bus.

"Don't you have a squad car, Lieutenant?" Tara asked.

"Police are public servants," he said curtly. "We don't deserve luxuries the average citizen does without."

"How's that work out with the crime fighting?"

"Do you enjoy being impertinent?"

After another ten minutes, three buses arrived together. The first was packed and the last two were pretty much empty, so they got on the middle bus and found seats in the front. The ride was slow, as the bus stopped at every other corner and always seemed to hit the red light. Eventually they turned onto a broad boulevard that led uphill to a tower of dingey, mottled brass with opaque windows the shade of month-old asparagus.

They got off the bus in front of that building, evidently a landmark called Foundation Tower. Tara spotted what seemed to be a cornerstone, which read: Est. Year 0, Peoples' Era. They passed through security and took an elevator to the fortieth floor, where an armed escort accompanied them to a private elevator. That car ascended to a shadowy but ornate atrium. As their escort pulled back the retractable gate, grooved pilaster beckoned Tara's eyes upward, only to hit a low ceiling of coarse, worm-swirl stucco. A tall, young woman with a proud mane of dark, tight curls greeted them. As she spoke, Tara heard the mystic chords of a finely tuned harp, expertly played. The young woman turned, and they followed her into an expansive parlor that might have served as a museum. Artwork hung on every square inch of the walls and sculptures populated the space like guests at a mythological cocktail party. Accent tables were strategically placed, displaying here and there delicate animal figurines. Mostly horned beasts: a ram, an ibex, maybe a water buffalo, as well as satyrs and minotaurs. In the center of the room was the harp. Tara watched the lank fingers fan over the strings to produce a sound of unworldly beauty that chilled her bones. The player paused, tilted the harp off her shoulder and onto its base, and raised her platinum head.

"You've had time to think," Madame said.

"Actually," Tara said, "I've been unconscious."

"Sometimes it's best to let the subconscious do its work."

Madame rose from the stool and crossed to a sliding panel window, looking out onto a veranda and the cityscape beyond. "Come here, dear."

Dear? Tara stepped toward the window and squinted into the glare. It seemed as though the whole world lay below her. Beneath a greyish yellow haze, she saw tiny people walking, standing, waiting for a bus that was ten minutes late.

"You've been *down there*," Madame said derisively. "We've done our best, but it's a brutish world. Still far too many of those leaden-eyed masses. Rule is difficult, yet it's far better than to serve." She turned and gestured towards a small, parlor chair. "Sit, dear. We're going to have a chat."

The chair's wooden frame was ornately carved. Tara thought, *Is it Baroque?*

Teri's voice: "Then don't sit on it."

"Dad joke!"

"Jinx!"

Tara blinked to refocus her mind, and the chair creaked as she settled onto the hard, black velvet. Madame sat in a tall, Victorian, wing-backed chair of red leather. *The Red Queen*, Tara thought. *Off with her head*, Teri's voice answered.

"Tea, Chérie," Madame commanded.

Chérie, the young lady who'd greeted them, placed a wooden cutting board on the table between Madame and Tara. It was what Madame Vignon had called *charcuterie*: an assortment of cold meats, sausage, and paté, along with sliced bread and apple wedges, which were starting to turn brown. Chérie went to a demilune table by the window, where a tea set was arranged. Her tawny hands poured two cups.

"Do you take sugar?" she asked. "Of course, you do." She sweetened the tea and brought the cups forward, serving Madame, then

Tara. Beneath the sweeping raven eyebrows, Chérie's hazel-and-amber eyes smiled with mischief, accentuated by a light sprinkle of nutmeg flecks on the sweet caramel of her nose and cheeks.

"Tea, Officer?" Madame asked, as if daring the Lieutenant to say yes.

"No," he answered. "Thank you." He retreated a step abruptly, brushing a pie-crust table with his hip. The table tottered and a clay bison toppled, breaking a horn. Madame's eyes flared. "My apologies," he muttered. Chérie scampered to remove the broken object. Madame trained her eyes on Tara.

"There's been some thought that you could be useful to us," Madame said. "And usefulness can be rewarded." Madame stirred her tea, tapped the spoon musically on the rim of the cup and placed it on the saucer. She raised the cup to her lips, but stopped short of drinking to say, "Please, eat up. You must be starved after so much time."

Tara imagined Flipper chowing down, shoveling *foie gras* into his pie hole. She certainly had no reason to be shy; Madame owed her at least the courtesy of a meal, and her stomach was literally growling. But instead, she tasted the tea. It was green and much too sweet.

"Tartairos has you now," Madame said. "However you got here, there's no going back. Everyone who could have sent you back has fled. Disappeared. We have the machines, but no knowledge of how to use them. Since you must live here, it's time to start thinking of Tartairos as home. And how you might be made comfortable."

Tara found Madame hard to look at. Like Teri from a time machine. After forty years of...*what?* More than the simple passage of time; some exhaustive, corrosive fight. Survival-at-all-costs. At once depleting, yet eerily fortifying. But...*for what?* Tara wondered for a moment if this wasn't Teri, given the trajectory Teri'd been on—overly studious, uptight about popularity. Or, was this Tara herself? Her beast mode unbridled for decades, she'd have clearcut all human contact, ripening at long last into a twisted hermit in a gilded tower. Her mind recalled a faltering Ebenezer Scrooge, pathetically asking, "Are these shadows of what must be or what might be?"

"What do you want?" Tara asked.

"Only that you realize how lucky you are. We mustn't be immodest, but your appearance is an asset. It makes you special."

You've always been the Hartzwell twins. That was special.

Special by association. Never unique. Tara recalled her desire to separate from Teri. How that had grown throughout freshman year until, halfway through sophomore year, her heart was ready to burst. She just wanted to tell Teri to leave her alone, just not even talk to her at school, just go away.

And then she'd gotten sick.

Careful what you wish for.

I didn't wish for this.

Madame was standing behind her chair now, resting her elbows on its back and leaning in towards Tara. "You should embrace being special and claim the perquisites that come with it."

"I told you I don't know anything."

"You're no doubt resourceful."

Almost against her will, Tara took another sip of tea. The sugar was overwhelming.

"They will contact you. You will contact me. I will take care of you."

Security. Status. But.

"What will you do to them?"

"That's nothing to worry your pretty, *young* head about," Madame said. She crossed to a far wall of floor-to-ceiling bookshelves and extracted a volume. She brought it to Tara. "I want you to read this carefully. It will give you some background. We shall shortly be in touch."

Tara eyed the cover: Charbonnier: A Journey of Self-Creation. When Tara looked up again, Madame had left the room, Teri's faint presence also seemed to have fled, and Chérie stood over Tara, hands clasped solicitously at her waist. *Cheryl's been made a drone*, Tara thought. *My drone.*

"Madame appreciates loyalty," Chérie said. "She can make life very pleasant."

Against the wall, the Lieutenant was impatient to leave. He strummed the fingertips of his right hand on the crimped rim of the pie-crust table. Tara imagined him tossing it like a *Frisbee* across the room, but he just turned toward the atrium.

In the elevator, the Lieutenant was even more stiff and formal than before.

"Is Madame also a public servant?" Tara asked.

He stood silent. Answering would only get him in trouble. As they descended, Tara fanned through the pages of Madame's book, wondering if the secret was in there, the answer to how the very image of her sister and herself had become a monster.

CHAPTER
SEVENTEEN

"A time is coming when men will go mad,
and when they see someone who is not mad,
they will attack him, saying,
'You are mad; you are not like us.'"
— St. Anthony of the Desert

IT WAS cold now on the shadowy street and a vindictive wind, laying waste to the rush hour stragglers, cut through Tara's dress. Still no squad car, but this time the Lieutenant hailed a cab. Tara tried to read the dust jacket of Madame's memoir, but the back of the taxi was too dark. Closing the book, she asked the Lieutenant, "So, you like working for her?"

The bearded chin turned, as the Lieutenant looked absently out the window. After a moment, he said, "There was a bear in the woods. The smaller animals were frightened, because it was large and ferocious. The fox said, 'I can no longer skip along the path, for fear of running across him.' The badger agreed and said, 'I must stay in my lair to avoid him.' The rabbits said, 'We must stop having babies for he would surely devour them.' But the birds, who at that time made their nests on the ground and in the low bushes, said, 'Let us make our homes in the treetops, where he cannot reach us, and go on singing as always.' They invited the other animals, but only the squirrels joined them.

"After a time, the bear was hunting for honey on a hilltop and tore open a dead oak, angering the bees inside. Thousands of bees swarmed and stung the bear around the eyes. The bear staggered blindly, swatting at the bees with its paws, and fell off a high ledge onto the rocks below. The birds saw how the bear had died and flew throughout the forest announcing the news. But no animals heard them, because out of fear, they had given up living and were no more."

"What are you," Tara asked, "the Aesop of this place?"

"Something like that."

"Well, that's a cheery tale," Tara told him. "Got another?"

Apparently not. The cab pulled up in front of a three-story building set back from the street and surrounded by a wrought-iron fence. It gave off a vibe of an olde-timey mental institution. The small front yard was weedy, and as the gate creaked open, Tara thought she saw a rat scamper into the shadows.

"Coyotes aren't doing their job," the Lieutenant said.

"Maybe they're hiding from the bear."

The Lieutenant rang the front doorbell, setting off tubercular chimes, and they waited. Dry leaves rustled behind Tara, and she jumped. A buzzer sounded, the kind that rudely eliminated a contestant on a game show, and the Lieutenant pulled the door open. They entered a dark reception area, where a dull mosaic of forgotten tiles lay yearning for an archeologist's brush, and the Lieutenant led Tara to the desk.

"Is this Inspector Desjardin's charge?" a pigeon-shaped lady asked.

The Lieutenant nodded, and the lady rose from her perch.

"We have a room ready upstairs." She waddled a few steps toward the staircase at the rear, then stopped to ask, "How do you like to be called?"

"You mean my name?" Tara asked.

"Oh." She stared, like Tara was a talking dog offering an insight into Aristotle. "Alright," she said finally.

"It's..."

"Eden!" a voice called from the landing.

Tara looked up to see a pregnant woman leaning against the railing. She moved quickly to the staircase and stood waiting, as though she expected Tara to run to her.

"I'm not Eden," Tara said, as she followed the desk lady up the stairs.

"Oh, yes, I'm so sorry," the pregnant woman said, a little too earnestly. "My mistake."

"I'm Tara."

"Pleased to meet you," she said, with the stiff formality of a mobster who's been tipped that you're wearing a wire. "I've got pregnancy hormones; they make me a little..."

"This way please," the desk lady interrupted, gesturing down a dank hall.

Tara glanced at the lower level. The grimy mosaics witnessed to the Lieutenant being gone. Tara leaned toward the pregnant woman and whispered, "I need to find Eden, and the friends that helped her escape."

"Is this some trick?"

"Find Eden; she knows me."

"You, uh, Tara!" the desk lady called.

Tara looked deeply into the pregnant woman's opal eyes. She stared until she saw a faint promise, then headed down the hall.

———

RACHEL DIALED one supposed friend after another trying to get a place to stay in the city. No one picked up. She couldn't stay with Guillaume, because all ward workers were under suspicion, and they never knew when the flics would break down a door. Then she got an incoming call: Maggie.

"Rachel, I don't know if you remember me."

Rachel waved Guillaume to the window to check if anyone was

outside. The flics might have turned Maggie and gotten her to call, so they could trace the signal. Rachel should have burned this cell-phone long ago, but replacements were hard to come by. And, honestly, she'd held out hope of hearing from Maggie, especially if she was under pressure to abort her baby.

"Maggie, where are you?"

Maggie gave the name of a women's facility Rachel knew from her work with other expectant mothers.

"There's a girl here who looks exactly like Eden," Maggie whispered. "She wants to meet you."

"Yeah, we'd like to meet her, too," Rachel admitted. But it was too obvious a trap. The only reason Madame Charbonnier would release this Earth girl was to use her as bait. Still, Tara was the key to resolving the whole problem. If Rachel had her, she could reel in Eden and Flubber.

"We want to help," Rachel said. "But your phone could be tapped, and they could be watching the residence."

"True."

"We need you and the girl to go for a long walk. Then call again."

"Okay."

"We'll figure how to help without bringing the flics down on all of us."

"Okay."

Rachel hung up and stretched for the ceiling, as if she was lifting the world and shaking it.

"More trouble?" Guillaume asked.

"When do we get that freaking car?"

———

EDEN WOULDN'T TELL him where to go, other than "into the city." Flipper wanted to know what the plan was, but all she would say was, "Tell you later." As they got closer to town, Flipper got increasingly nervous. He'd just left the only people who could get him back home, and when they met up again, they wouldn't be inclined to help him. He'd only risked angering them to save Tee, but now he had strong doubts that anything Eden had in mind would do the trick. As they turned off the freeway, following a sign that said Hospital for Special Surgery, Flipper finally put his foot down.

"Eden. What is the plan?" he demanded.

"A trade," she said, as the hospital loomed like a fortress in front of them.

"What?"

"I trade myself for Tara."

"Are you crazy?" Flipper hit the gas and drove past the building. "How's that a plan?"

"How is it not a plan? I planned it."

Flipper reminded himself this girl had probably never seen a Tom Cruise movie. "First of all," he said calmly, "once they have you, who says they'll release Tee? Second, you know what they're going to do when they get a hold of you, right? Eden, they're going to kill you!"

"I thought you wanted your friend back?"

"I do," Flipper insisted. "But we need a plan to keep you both alive."

He felt like turning around and driving straight back to the safe house. He'd throw himself on Raq— *Rachel's* mercy. But then he saw…a vision. They'd hit an area of town that looked like a low-rent Times Square. It was an open plaza with several jumbo screens projecting video images. All around the periphery, workers were assembling bleachers, as if a major event was due to take place. Flipper slowed the truck and gawked.

The video screens showed public service announcements featuring hip, attractive, young people. The PSAs told how to "mask up" on bad air-quality days, how to behave if you were followed by a coyote, and how to anonymously report anyone who violated "the norms of society." But the message that really grabbed Flipper's attention encouraged citizens to claim their monthly ration of cannabis. A strangely familiar, bespectacled man with a droopy mustache explained that "stress kills," but "cannabis soothes and relaxes."

"Who's that guy?" he asked Eden.

"It says 'M. Pomeroy, Minister of Public Communications.'"

"Oh, yeah." Flipper chuckled to himself. "The government's giving away free pot. They actually want their people stoned."

Flipper pulled the truck over to the curb and parked. He watched the image on the screen dissolve to black. Then white letters faded in, as another PSA began. This one asked, "What is a jumelle?" Where had he heard that word before?

The same guy, Pomeroy, interviewed medical people, who all gave some version of the same answer. "A jumelle is genetic material that has been duplicated. For example, systems of organs. A spinal cord. Skin tissue." Some doctor explained that "Jumelles exist so if a person has an accident or illness, they can have a vital part replaced. Quickly, efficiently, and inexpensively."

Flipper turned to Eden. "Are they talking about you?"

She nodded.

Flipper turned back to the screen. Droopy mustache guy was standing in front of one of those tanks people float in to relax. "Let us see," he said, "what a jumelle looks like." He lifted the lid and the camera crept closer. There in some kind of gooey fluid, were... organs. There was no body, no skin, or bones. There wasn't even a brain.

"Is that what they say you are?" he asked Eden. Again, she nodded.

The scene cut to a home—pretty luxurious—where droopy mustache asked some rich lady, "Is there any truth to the rumors that jumelles are actual people?"

"That's absurd," the lady said. The screen cut to a closeup of her, and Flipper's eyes bugged out. He spun his head toward Eden.

"Is that...?"

"She is Madame Charbonnier," Eden said. "My prime. She lies to the world, and they believe her."

The video with the Madame continued. She had been some sort of leader of a rebellion that caught fire. The video showed the whole planet ablaze with a purifying flame. *The Revolution*, it proclaimed, had freed the people and the land. The people progressed because their dreams, their desires, and their spirit were embodied in one leader, sworn to do their will: Madame Aliénor Charbonnier. She was the rock selected to be the cornerstone of the new foundation. Foundation Day was coming, which Flipper took to be some kind of global commemoration. That's when the kernel of a plan formed in his mind. But how could he get it to pop?

"You've got to have other friends," Flipper said. "Weren't there other people who helped you escape?"

"I remember a building they took us to, when they woke us up."

"Do you know where it is?"

Eden nodded. "It's close to the hospital."

"Alright." Flipper spun the steering wheel left and pulled out from the curb. "Let's see if anyone's home."

———

TARA WAS SURPRISED to get a private bedroom. Not exactly private; there was another bed. But the desk lady told her the other woman had checked out that afternoon. So, once again, she had to deal with the specter of an empty bed. She also learned that dinner had already been served, but if she was hungry, she could go down to the kitchen and forage through the leftovers. Tara was pretty ravenous; she couldn't remember the last time she'd had solid food, so she went down to the kitchen, pulled some meat off a chicken carcass, and made a sandwich. She also managed to hide a paring knife in her bra and take it back to her room.

She sat now on the edge of her bed, her dress drawn up to her waist, the flesh of her upper thigh pinched, and that knife poised to make its mark.

"What are you doing?" a voice—not *Teri's*—asked. Tara wasn't sure the voice was real until she heard it again. "Are you okay?"

The pregnant lady with the opal eyes stood at the edge of the other bed. She was either a phantom, or the locks on the doors didn't work.

"The locks don't work," she said. "In case you were wondering."

Tara put the knife aside and stood, pulling her dress down.

"I made that phone call," she said. "It's going to be okay." She walked around the bed to the nightstand and picked up the knife. "Tomorrow, we'll go for a walk, and I'll explain."

So, Tara had gone to sleep without cutting and without opening Madame's book. In the morning, the desk lady brought breakfast to her room.

"I wasn't sure you'd be up to meeting the other borders," desk lady said. "We don't want you to be under any pressure."

Tara got the impression desk lady didn't want her mixing with anyone until she could be sure Tara wasn't a threat. Tara ate in private and showered in private, then dressed in some second-hand clothes from the bureau. They smelled of disinfectant, or maybe insecticide.

When Maggie knocked and suggested they go for a walk, Tara felt a wave of relief. She needed fresh air and open space. But that same stench from yesterday, subtle but pungent, put a damper on that. The sidewalks were crowded with people dashing where they had to go or standing idly because they had nowhere to go. The park they eventually entered was odd, too. The lawns had gone to weeds, and dandelions carpeted the open spaces. Their fluff floated freely — no children gave chase — and created a white haze below the omnipresent, brownish haze. Trees resembling cottonwoods were in bloom, too. Their threads formed webs in the upper branches, giving Tara an uneasy feeling that she might be walking into a trap.

As a coyote pup chased a rat, Tara coughed and tasted blood again. She thought about spitting, but didn't really want to see the red glob, so she swallowed.

"Does this park have a water fountain?" she asked Maggie.

"Yes, but you shouldn't drink from it," she said.

So, they just walked. Tara still didn't know if she could trust Maggie. She was attractive, not just the dark, unfathomable eyes and the delicately sculpted lips, but her smile pinched a cute, little dimple high on her left cheek, which Tara found childlike and endearing. She seemed sincere, but Tara forced herself to remember she could easily be a spy. Meeting her had been too convenient. At first, Tara had been so suspicious, she even doubted Maggie was pregnant. But she'd let her touch her belly and feel the baby kick. That was real enough.

"Is it safe to talk yet?" Tara whispered. Through the park, they'd walked at least a mile, all the time looking to see if they were being followed. No one seemed terribly interested.

"Alright," Maggie said. "I have a phone number for a girl named Rachel. She helped Eden escape. We need to find a toll phone."

Good luck, Tara thought. Maybe this planet was different, but Tara hadn't seen a pay phone anywhere, other than rural gas stations, for as long as she could remember. They walked through a maze of vines where wild grapes grew. Birds picked at the fruit and flew aggressively close to Tara and Maggie, as if to scare them away.

"This used to be a vineyard," Maggie said. "For centuries, it passed down through one family. The city grew up around it, and every year, the owner would invite the people onto the grounds to celebrate the harvest."

"What happened?" Tara asked.

"Madame decided it was too much land to be held in private hands. She wanted it for a public park. So, she brought charges against the owner. Nobody remembers what exactly, but he was convicted as an enemy of the state and his land was seized. Now his vineyard belongs to everyone."

They came out through the vines to a stone building, overgrown with tangled vegetation. Tara guessed it must house the wine press.

"What about the wine?" she asked.

"Oh, there's no wine anymore."

About a hundred yards farther on, they exited the park, and it was like stepping out of the jungle onto Broadway. Tara squinted as she viewed a plaza, lit by jumbotron screens on all sides, assaulting passersby with advertisements, not for glitzy products, but rather to warn them of public hazards. There seemed to be an endless number of crushing issues, from viruses passed through "the outmoded, male-centric tradition of handshaking" to "offending a member of an historically marginalized group through inadvertent assertion of privilege." Prominently featured in these PSAs was the lithe, smiling young woman from Madame Charbonnier's apartment.

The glitz was so stupefying that Tara failed at first to notice the centerpiece of the plaza. There were five huge, concrete pedestals arranged on a rectangular mosaic in a W pattern. But only one pedestal still had a statue on it. The bare pedestals bore graffiti and signs of breakage, hinting that the bronze figures had been violently uprooted. The surviving effigy was, of course, Aliénor Charbonnier.

Maggie tugged Tara's sleeve, urging her towards a row of pay phones, almost all in use, which at least indicated they worked. They walked to the last phone, and Maggie dug into her purse for some change.

"How did you meet Rachel?" Tara asked.

"I, um, it's complicated."

That non-answer raised Tara's suspicions again. As Maggie dropped a couple of coins into the slot, she must have read something on Tara's face. She seemed to brace herself before saying, "You might as well know. I used to live with Inspector Desjardin. He's the father of my baby."

Not good, not good, not good. Tara's eyes darted around the plaza, looking for anyone who might be a cop.

"It's okay," Maggie said, as she pressed the numbered buttons. "We're broken up. And, yes, I have considered he might be using me to get to Rachel."

Tara could hear the phone ring.

"Hello?" Maggie said. "We're at Bourgogne Place. Here, talk to her."

Maggie handed the receiver to Tara. "Hello?"

"Who is this?"

"My name is Tara Hartzwell. I was kidnapped and brought here, because I look like Eden Grant. I want to go home." *Too much information*, Tara knew. But words just started gushing when she opened her mouth. Tears, too.

"Have you seen Eden? Has she tried to contact you?"

"No."

"Well, she might."

"Then what?"

"Then the flics will probably grab her and your friend who's with her. They crush our movement further, and nobody goes home." After a pause, the voice said, "Get it?" rather harshly.

"I get it," Tara said. "What can I do?"

"Don't try to meet Eden. Come to Bourgogne Place every day at ten in the morning and again at three in the afternoon. Bring a book, sit, and read. Someone will approach you and say, 'I read that book in the summer when I was twelve.' Repeat that back to me."

"I…read that book. In the summer when I was twelve."

Tara heard a click, and the line went dead.

———

"WE MADE videos of all the jumelles," he explained. "We were going to broadcast them like we do all our messages, by cutting into the state's transmissions. But Rachel…. What can I say? She screwed up. She pushed to get one last jumelle through the portal. By that time, the flics had caught on to us. They killed two of our jumelles." Then with an apologetic glance toward Eden, he corrected himself. "Our people." He puffed his lips, and let out a slow stream of air, before saying, "Rachel's lucky she's alive."

Eden's friend Gilou was a wirehead, a bulky nerd, and most usefully, a hacker. He ran a computer repair shop that looked like an *AOL* rummage sale and fronted for a safehouse upstairs.

"So, anyway, nobody's really trusting Rachel's judgment right now." Gilou pushed back from his desk. He laced his fingers together, rotated his hands to thumbs down, and stretched his arms high over his head. He then relaxed his arms and folded his hands over the crown of his shaved head. "We're all for the cause, but nobody signed up to die."

"So, you never broadcasted the jumelle tapes?" Flipper asked.

"One line-up," he said. "After that, no. We've been too hot. And, um, Minister Pomeroy got out in front and produced all these phony 'documentaries' with ridiculous props and insider interviews. Nobody was going to believe us after that."

"You still have them?"

"Yeah," he sighed. "Even though they could send me to prison for an awfully long time. I couldn't bear to destroy them." Gilou queued up one of the videos. Flipper watched a redheaded kid talk about the thrill he got from playing the violin. "He's one who didn't get away. Him and, uh, one of the first ever. He was gone seven years. Safe. Had a life. Had to come back and help free 'his brothers.' They shot him. Carved him up." Gilou's nostrils flared, and his lower lip quivered.

"Sounds like you've got a score to settle," Flipper said.

"What do you suggest?"

"As long as it's a battle of videos, you can't win," Flipper conceded. "They've got the production values. The budget. And they can saturate the airways. You've got one chance to land a knockout punch." Flipper paused for effect. He waited until Gilou's and Eden's eyes begged him to speak. "We do it live."

———

"TWO DAYS, Inspector, and still, they are at large." Madame Charbonnier, as usual, was not happy with the progress of the investigation. "I permitted you to free this alien, because you said it would lead you to the rebels. Obviously, that has not happened."

"But, they have made contact," Desjardin insisted. "The subject goes to Bourgogne Place twice every day. Sits on a bench and reads a book for an hour, then goes back to the facility. The creature is waiting to be contacted."

"But no one comes!" Madame shrieked. "Because you've been clumsy, and they're on to you. They are using this creature as a distraction for you, while they plan some other abomination. While they help more traitors escape, perhaps to the far reaches of space, because you haven't gotten to the heart of their organization."

"It's only a matter of time."

"What made you think this creature mattered to these rebels? That they would take any risk for its safety?"

"Because I know how they think and what they believe," the Inspector said.

"And what is that exactly?" Madame demanded.

"That every life is precious."

———

FLIPPER WAS EXPOUNDING on his plans when the shop's entrance bell sounded.

"Stay here," Gilou whispered. He closed his laptop and called, "Coming!" As Gilou parted the curtain and stepped into the shop, Flipper crouched behind the worktable. Eden had gone upstairs to grab a sweater and might return at any second. Flipper strained to hear, but all he got was indecipherable mumbling. He crept from behind the table and tiptoed to the doorway. Through an opening in the curtains, he saw only Gilou's back. Then his wide body listed a bit to his left, and Flipper spotted Rachel.

"I get that you're mad at me," Rachel said. "Everybody is. But couldn't someone even send a car? How long is everyone going to freeze me out?"

"I don't know," Gilou said, "How long do you think Jules and Étienne will stay dead?"

"That's cold, Gilou."

"Well, Jules was my friend."

"He was mine, too," Rachel cried. "Look, I just need someone to deliver a message. Someone with a clean record the flics wouldn't suspect."

"You shouldn't be running operations," Gilou said. "You should be lying low, waiting for the heat to die down. Otherwise, you're going to get more people hurt."

"But this girl is in trouble."

"We're all in trouble!" Gilou shouted. "Which is why you're on ice. Deal with it."

"Y'know what? Fine," Rachel spat. She marched to the front door, pounding the floor with her cast, then spun back around. "But if you see a pair of oversized ears with a skinny kid between 'em, tell him I found his Earth chick. Tell him to come get me before they carve her up."

She jerked the door open and stormed out. Flipper held for a second, stunned, then lunged after her, but Gilou barred his way.

"She knows where Tee is!"

Gilou gripped Flipper tightly by the shoulders. "One thing at a time, boy. One thing at a time."

"She's the whole reason I'm here!"

Eden passed through the curtain. She crossed her arms and pulled the sweater tight against herself. "You want to get your friend and leave?" she asked.

Flipper stared at Eden, then back at back at Gilou, who raised an arched eyebrow.

"Or do you want to see your plan through?"

———

"WHAT CRIME HAVE WE COMMITTED?" the prisoner demanded.

"You violated our borders. So, let's start with illegal entry. Then espionage. There are several assault charges, which your friend will answer for. Two of my officers are having their jaws wired as we speak."

The young prisoner smirked, apparently pleased with his performance.

"We were attacked," the elder prisoner said. "The right to self-defense is universal."

"There is no right to resist arrest," the Inspector stated. "You refused the officer's commands."

"We didn't understand; we don't speak your language." The prisoner cupped the headset as evidence of his claim. Yet the girl had spoken fluent Tartarian. "An agent of yours mistakenly took the wrong girl."

"So you said."

"We came to get her back."

The young prisoner said something unintelligible. He gestured for the headset, and his older companion handed it to him. "You know where she is. You're holding her."

"She is at liberty."

"Then take us to her!"

"She is at liberty because it suits Madame. You are in jail for the same reason."

"Look," the elder said, reclaiming the headset, "you know we're telling the truth."

"What is truth?" the Inspector mused. "On Tartairos, truth is what Madame deems true. All else is fallacy, heresy, betrayal, and treason."

"How do you live like that?" the elder asked.

"Carefully."

———

AT FIRST IT was just blackness and pinpricks of light. But as Jean-Luc's eyes adjusted, contrasts began to show, and objects took shape. He was sitting in a pod, waist-deep in gel. The overhead lights in the ward were out, so the only illumination came from various monitors.

"Do you remember where the shower is?" a voice asked.

Jean-Luc's throat was raw, so he just shook his head. He pushed up with his arms and swung his left leg out of the pod onto a step box. He pivoted a quarter turn and lifted his other leg out. He held himself unsteadily as the gel slid from his trunk and legs onto the floor.

"Don't worry about the mess," the person said.

Jean-Luc swallowed, needing to speak. "Why?" was all he could muster.

"You're leaving," the person said. "Go, wherever you things go. Disappear."

Jean-Luc padded across the floor to the shower stalls along the far wall. They were designed to rinse off the reclining, unconscious bodies of jumelles prior to surgery. Jean-Luc turned on the water, crouched, and plunged his head under the stream. The water was cold and bracing, and he was soon wide awake. He soaped up and rinsed his whole body. The person held out a towel and pointed to a pile of new clothes on a nearby gurney.

"Hurry and get dressed. They'll be waking up soon."

Jean-Luc spotted a couple of ward workers, unconscious on gurneys.

"Yes," the person said, "I took a page from your book. Laced their coffee with sedatives. Then snuck up on them with a hypodermic."

"My book?" Jean-Luc asked. He pulled on a pair of trousers.

"Your friends, those radicals. How they broke the first group out."

Jean-Luc sat to put on a pair of shoes.

"What do you want me to do?"

"Just go!" the person said. "You know you belong to Desjardin, and you know what he intends. If you don't want to be sliced and diced and sewn inside him, go!"

"What about the rest?" Jean-Luc held an open palm out to the room where lights on maybe ninety or a hundred pods flickered.

"This is between me and Inspector Desjardin, if you don't mind. I could just as easily have sabotaged your pod, let you die in there, so your organs would be useless. Consider the great favor I'm doing you, and just vanish."

"Are you the one who trained me to kill?" Jean-Luc asked.

"What an absurd question!" the person laughed. "The primes choose the content of the cortex tapes. Desjardin wanted you to have certain skills. We designed the tapes to give you those skills. He also wanted you to have an appetite for the ladies. So, you're welcome."

Jean-Luc wondered at that. The jumelle he'd hunted: he'd wanted her. For some reason he didn't comprehend, he'd been willing to do violence to take her, yet the urge had somehow pained him, even as he was forcing himself on her. Images flooded his mind, not of her, but of other girls, women, memories of moments he hadn't lived, but had been fed. Sickening acts of domination, by men drawing pleasure from cruelty.

He looked at the person before him, this slack, flaccid excuse, this scheming, deceitful wretch, and another urge arose.

"You think you can make me a killer," he asked, "and then tell me what to do?"

———

THE CALL HAD AWAKENED Desjardin before dawn. He'd gotten to the hospital within half an hour to find the lower half of the Director's corpse dangling from an open pod and his head submerged in blue gel.

"Why is he still in there?" he demanded.

"We thought you'd want to see how we found him."

I'm surrounded by idiots, Desjardin thought. He was also surrounded by dozens of empty pods and three more corpses: the guard who had been stationed outside, along with two attendants. The Restorationists were growing more extreme, violating their supposed beliefs in the "sanctity of all life." Or were they? The pod in which the Director had been drowned just happened to belong to the Inspector's own jumelle, who just happened to have been trained as an assassin.

"How many were removed?" he asked.

"Ninety-six."

So, almost a hundred jumelles, perhaps led by his own, were loose in the capital on Foundation Day. Madame was not going to be pleased.

———

"SHE COULDN'T HAVE MEANT for you to go there today," Maggie said.

"She said every day. Twice a day."

"But this is Foundation Day," Maggie insisted. "The plaza will be jammed with people. Flics everywhere. Rachel wouldn't dare show her face."

"Then she'll send someone else," Tara said.

"I don't think so. I think we need to call her again."

Maggie pulled the cord, signaling the bus to stop. They got off and walked to a corner store, where the black outline of a cannabis leaf intermittently flashed in the center of a green, neon plus sign. "The apothecary will have a phone. And we can get some dope, too, if you want."

Tara looked at Maggie's extended belly and scowled.

"Oh, never mind, you're right."

They waited ten minutes on line for the pay phone. "Why don't you people have cellphones?" Tara grumbled.

"You need a special license," Maggie explained. "And you have to prove you need one. Or you can buy them on the black market. They're not cheap, and the fines are high if you get caught."

Finally, Maggie was able to place the call, but there was no answer.

"Let's just go there," Tara said.

"It's going to be a mob scene," Maggie warned. "But whatever."

———

THREE DAYS HAD PASSED. They'd gotten no food or water. A guard would periodically stroll down the corridor, raising their hopes of being freed or at least getting fed. He'd sweep the cell with his flashlight and move on. *What is the point*, Fr. Chandler wondered, *of letting us slowly waste away?* Was it simply the banality of evil? A callous, unthinking disregard rather than active malice? Or was the objective to crush their spirits? The priest gripped the cell bars and strained, but what was the point?

"No way out," he muttered.

"There's always a way," Nolan said. "The key is in the pattern."

"What?"

"The guard follows a pattern," the youth explained. "How he walks. Examines the cells. Where he stands and when he turns."

"When he turns?"

"It'll require violence, Father."

The priest bowed his head. "The Lord delivered Peter and John from the dungeon. If it's His will…."

"Doesn't God help those who help themselves?" the youth asked.

"That's not the Bible, it's Aesop."

"My bad. But our chaplain in Boy Scouts used to say, 'You can't lean on a shovel and pray for a hole.'"

Fr. Chandler nodded. "Sometimes, good men must do bad things," he conceded. "We'll pray on it."

———

RACHEL WAS SOAKING in the tub when the phone rang. She'd pressured an old school friend, who wanted nothing to do with The Movement but owed her a favor, to let her crash at her apartment for a couple of days. Now, with her friend at work, and fed up with the bulky cast that had been slowing her down as she traipsed all over town, she'd decided to dissolve the plaster, at least to the point where Guillaume could cut it off with a pair of hedge clippers. He was due in half an hour, and Rachel had no idea how long she'd have to soak. She was relaxing in the warm water when the phone rang, jolting her to attention. She reached awkwardly for the phone, perched on the edge of the sink, and didn't get a firm grip. The phone fell through her fingers, bounced off the side of the tub and into the water, sending a jolt of electrical current throughout her body. Her jaw clamped shut and her muscles went into spasm. Fortunately, the phone shorted out.

As Rachel lay in the bath panting, her first thought was gratitude that the device had not been plugged into the wall outlet. She most certainly would have been electrocuted. Her second thought was for the phone. It was fried, and now she was even more cut off from any possible help. *What else might go wrong today?*

"You hear about the ward?" Guillaume asked, as soon as Rachel opened the door. "Someone raided, I mean *raided* the place. Every jumelle is gone."

"That's not possible." Rachel clumped over to the sofa with her wet cast trailing puddles and white plaster flecks behind her.

"Possible or not, somebody did it," Guillaume said. He took a huge pair of hedge clippers from a drawstring sack.

"I guess the *Society* is still in business," Rachel moped. The biggest blow ever against Madame's murder racket, and she'd been frozen out!

"Wasn't us," Guillaume said. "I called around; nobody heard."

Guillaume eyed Rachel's cast, as if contemplating the best approach to avoid lopping off flesh. "You want me to start at the knee or the toes?"

"Knee," Rachel said. "They might have been lying."

"Don't think so. I even stopped by Gilou. He says they got something else cookin', but woul'n't tell me what. Plus, peeps got killed. That ain't our way."

"Well, Pascal's jumelle."

"Was gonna die anyway," Guillaume huffed. "We gave him a fighting chance. And he let us save a dozen."

"Plus, or minus," Rachel muttered. She couldn't gloss over casualties, especially when she'd caused them.

Guillaume crouched beside Rachel and slid one of the blades inside the cast. He forced the wooden handles together; the plaster buckled under the force of the blades then split. Rachel jumped.

"You okay?"

She nodded, and he pushed the blade deeper, cutting again. A few more slices and they were able to peel the cast off her shin. He cut down to the heel, and Rachel slid her foot out of its seven-week prison.

"So, somebody besides us has, *what?* Like eighty or a hundred naked jumelles hiding somewhere?"

"An' who knows what's in their minds? Might not even know they're naked. I mean, if nobody told 'em."

Rachel placed her foot flat on the floor and stood. The ankle was stiff and sore, but it took the weight.

"You ought to wrap that if you're gonna walk on it," Guillaume advised.

"Yeah," Rachel said. She had a lot of walking to do.

———

THE FAR END of the park was like a homeless encampment. People had gathered overnight to claim space on the expansive lawn that fronted Bourgogne Place. Tara quickly understood why. Workers had erected a stage adjacent to the pedestals and were now assembling the components of an even larger video screen behind it, rising high above the colonnade that separated park from plaza. Maggie explained that in a couple of hours, a series of concerts would take place. One band after another would perform as warmup acts for the big event: the annual public appearance of the Architect of the Revolution and Head of State, Madame Charbonnier.

"This is your big national holiday?" Tara asked.

"It's mostly an excuse to get high," Maggie replied.

It wasn't yet ten o'clock, but the air was already thick with marijuana smoke, which stung Tara's eyes. The aroma always reminded her of a dead skunk in the road.

"C'mon, before we get a contact high," Maggie said. Tara noticed that Maggie was visibly waddling. She had to be eight plus months along. She wondered if nine months was usual for babies on this planet. But she didn't even know what they considered to be a month.

At the plaza, Maggie sat on a bench reserved for the elderly, disabled, and pregnant. Tara tipped her head towards the right side of the stage.

"I'm going to find a spot there to read. Or pretend to read."

Technicians were on the stage now, setting up microphones and cameras. Maggie had said the event would be broadcast all over the globe. Tara circled the five pedestals and found a granite bench that wasn't occupied. She sat and opened Madame's book to where she'd left off. After two days of failed rendezvous, she was halfway through the memoir. It was a personal history of Tartairos since its last great war, concluded some eighty years ago, that had led to the "global unity" being celebrated today. National borders, along with their customs, languages, and religions had been eliminated, in favor of the one culture, one language, and no religion of the victors. Madame Charbonnier had been one of five "Architects of Renewal," serving on the "Global Planning Committee" that "breathed life back into a devastated planet." But she hadn't exactly breathed life into her associates. The other four architects, whose statues had once stood on those vacant pedestals, had been exposed for secretly holding "regressive ideas." Mobs of outraged citizens had toppled their statues and taken their lives, one by one, until Aliénor Charbonnier had seized absolute control.

The book was full of ruminations on democracy that weren't very democratic. Madame had the power to suspend elections whenever they appeared unfavorable to her, and to call for elections spontaneously when it suited her purposes. Asked about her immense power, she'd famously said, "The body has many parts but only one head. For democracy to work, the will of the people cannot be scattered, it must be centered in one person, one actor, one force." She'd held her position for roughly fifty years, and if Tara's last audience with her was any indication, she had no intention of retiring.

Time passed, and the sun baked the top of Tara's head. The book was boring her and making her sad. A band onstage was playing very loud, sing-song tunes about the glory of global unity. The show was so lame and so saccharine, Tara almost expected a chubby, purple dinosaur to come out and dance. Plus, the granite slab was so hard, her buttocks had fallen asleep, and she was starting to lose feeling in her legs. Craving a good stretch, Tara closed the book with a groan, as a low voice rumbled, "I read that book in the summer when I was twelve."

Tara lifted her eyes towards a huge, dark mound of a man obscuring the sun, and squinted into the round face of Lima Autufuga.

CHAPTER
EIGHTEEN

"I have been so long master that I would be master still,
or at least that none other should be master of me."
—— Bram Stoker, *Dracula*

"YOU DON'T KNOW ME," Lima's double said, crouching to sit beside her. Tara scooted over to give him room. He rested his elbows on his thighs and buried his mouth in his cupped hands. He was perspiring heavily.

"I'll make this quick," he said. "We think you been chipped, a'ight? Little flic trick so Desjardin knows 'xactly where you are. 'S why I shoul'n't be talking to you. But things 'bout to get *cray-cray*, so we coul'n't wait no more. So. One hour. Blue van's gon' be parked just 'round that corner. Inside, a doctor gon' remove your chip and take you to Rachel. Good luck."

With that, Lima's double hauled himself to his feet. He glanced about the crowd before turning back to Tara. His bronze skin glistened with an aura of refracted sunlight; his visage flattened and warmed, turned translucent as stained glass, and seemed to dissolve in front of her, as if he was passing from one realm to another. Tara blinked him back into focus. She didn't want him to fade away, any more than she wanted to believe that her Lima, her friend who'd stepped in to help her, had left her world, violently and pointlessly.

"Oh, an' if you see your friend," he said, "tell him I want my truck back." Then he ambled into the crowd, which could have been right in front of Tara or dimensions of space-time away. She scanned her surroundings to see if anyone had been watching, expecting to see a dozen or more undercover cops leap out and tackle him. The crowd moved in slow motion and the sound was muted, like an unseen hand had turned down the volume—so low that Tara could hear the pulse inside her ears. That's when Tara saw him, that Lieutenant, a stone's throw away. He didn't move, didn't signal anyone to advance. He just watched Tara watching him, until she blinked, and he was gone. *An hour*, Tara thought. Could she last that long in this brain-frying heat?

A military orchestra on risers began to play, and a team of young dancers trotted to the lip of the stage. As Tara stood to stretch, the volume of the sound around her came back, full force. Startled, and a little woozy from maybe standing up too fast, she recognized Chérie leading the dance. Tara hobbled over, stiff legged, to rejoin Maggie, who was still on the bench. As the music crescendoed, onlookers craned their necks toward the far end of the plaza. Tara realized the music now was a fanfare, hailing an entrance. That's when the jumbotron sprang to life with images of Aliénor Charbonnier, and the plaza took on the feel of a Super Bowl halftime show. Groupies went mad, crowding the stage, jumping up and down, while the rest of the crowd kind of yawned and talked, munched their snacks, and lit another joint.

"The ones cheering," Maggie said, "they're paid."

The jumbotron played a montage from Madame's long public life, as a narrator recited her accomplishments and quoted over-the-top praise of her leadership from various sources.

"Same script every year, basically," Maggie said.

"You shouldn't be here," someone said. Tara turned to see Chérie, glowing with perspiration from her workout. "You should be in Madame's box." Chérie pointed to bleachers off stage left, where well-dressed people sat comfortably, shaded by an awning. None seemed to be sweltering in the harsh sun. In fact, a row of misters was keeping them cool and relaxed. Chérie handed Tara a plastic card on a lanyard. "Madame is waiting to reward you."

Tara eyed the badge that displayed her picture with the letters V-I-P.

"You mustn't keep her waiting."

———

NOLAN HAD REMOVED his shoes so he could move silently across the floor. He rolled from his bunk and crept to the cell door. Before the guard turned back to face him, he'd reached through the bars and grabbed him by the collar. He'd yanked him up against the bars and, reaching his left arm around, had closed the choke hold. As Nolan applied pressure, Fr. Chandler groped to get the keys off the guard's belt. The man's life literally depended on Father getting the keys off quickly and opening the door, so Nolan could release him, but his fumbling seemed to go on forever. By the time the priest had unlatched the key ring, the guard had quit struggling.

Father opened the door inward, and Nolan let the body slip into the priest's arms. They paused for a terse prayer, then Nolan helped Father carry the body to a bunk.

"Father, would you...?" Nolan asked, and the priest closed the man's eyes.

"I'm sorry," the priest said. "My fault. Not yours."

"Forget it," Nolan whispered. "Next play. Clock's running."

They'd gotten free of the cell. The building would be another matter. Or so they thought, because as they approached the first secured door at the end of the corridor, they saw the command desk on the other side was deserted. Father found a key that fit, and they opened the door onto an empty hallway.

"Where is everyone?" Nolan asked.

Fr. Chandler was reluctant to attribute what was likely dumb luck to divine intervention, especially when they'd left a corpse in their wake. "Maybe it's a holiday."

"In that case," Nolan said, "let's find the party."

———

CHÉRIE SKIPPED AWAY and an entourage entered. A military escort swept Madame onto the stage to wild cheers from the groupies. The Cool Zone Kids stood and applauded. The jumbotron shimmered with iridescent colors in dancing, rapid-fire patterns, and there she was, center stage at the microphone, dressed in a military flight suit, hands clasped high above her head in the 'salute of our struggles' she'd popularized decades ago. Still holding her hands aloft, she opened them to the crowd, keeping them attached at the thumb and meeting at the tips of her forefingers to form an open triangle between her hands, the symbol of the missing capstone, the unfinished work of global society's master builder. Waves of people returned the signal.

Tara felt a surge of exhilarating energy course through her. Joy. Ecstasy. She could throw herself into the chanting crowd and lose herself. She'd be rid of the petty problems of the 'I' and finally be part of something greater and grander. Tears welled up, mimicking tears of joy.

But why? Tara wondered. There was no basis for her to feel this way. Something at the back of her head or the depths of her gut warned her not to be deceived by runaway emotion. Still, Tara placed the lanyard over her head.

"Are you going?" Maggie asked.

"I don't know," Tara said. "Maybe just a few minutes. To get out of the sun."

Madame spoke kindly, modestly. "This day is about you," she said. "The Revolution was for you. To build a new foundation, upon which you could prosper in peace."

Peace, Tara mused. Could Madame offer that, really? She could surely lift Tara above these rat-infested streets. Feed her well. She might even be kind, if only…. All Tara had to do was show she wasn't a threat. That she wasn't in league with whoever, whatever, was conspiring to overthrow her. She simply had to be useful. But could she put aside Madame's cruelty? That smiling face was a lie. *She means to destroy Eden*, Tara heard herself say. But what did that mean anyway? Who as Eden? And what had she ever done to command Tara's loyalty? This place, here and now, was where fate had brought Tara. Shouldn't she make the best of it?

"You are the Foundation!" Madame told the crowd. She had reached the climax of her speech; her volume built; each phrase punctuated with a thrust of her fist. "Your desires! Your freedom! To create yourself in the image you choose!"

Then suddenly, the video and sound cut out. The screens were pure white, and Tara could have heard a pin drop. At first, she wondered if something wasn't going wrong in her head. But, abruptly, an image filled the screen—the face of Madame from decades ago. Only not Madame.

"Hello, citizens of Tartairos," Eden said. "I'm sure you recognize my face."

Maggie gasped and drew both hands to her mouth.

"What is it?" Tara asked.

"I was there when she made this. In the factory. The night she passed through the portal."

Madame and her entourage stood dumbfounded. Madame sputtered into her dead microphone, as Eden's voice thundered.

"You've been told that jumelles aren't people. But that is a lie. Look at me. Am I not whole? Complete? Alive? But under Madame's law, I'm only property, fit only to be carved into parts to extend her life another forty years."

Madame gesticulated wildly; she wanted someone to cut the power. The jumbotron went black, but the other screens, the video billboards on the surrounding buildings, all carried Eden's image and her voice continued to boom across the plaza and into the park. Then Eden's image dissolved, and she reappeared against a different backdrop, her face flushed with passion.

"They'll tell you now this video is a fake," she cried. "An illusion."

"This is new," Maggie said.

"But what if I walked onto the stage right now? And stood beside Madame? If I held my hand out to her? Could they say that was fake, too?"

No, Tara thought. *Don't be a fool!* She scanned the plaza from one end to the other, and there Eden was, poised at the edge of the park, under the archway that opened onto the plaza. She wore a hooded jacket, covering her hair and pulled down over half her face, but it was unmistakably Eden, head bowed and marching for the stage. Tara ran to cut her off and was able to yank her sleeve, halting Eden for a second, so one set of green eyes pierced the other.

"I can do this," Eden said. "Let me."

And Tara lurched sideways. *"I can do this,"* and *Teri pushed her sister's hand away. She gathered the top sheet, clouded with blood, into her tight fists. "Let me."*

As Eden marched to the stage, Tara saw Teri, as never before, determined, settled, steeled to meet her fate. At the foot of the stage, Eden unzipped the hoodie and tossed it aside, unfurling her blond hair to catch the sun, and bounding up the steps as onlookers stood aghast. The feed to the video screens was live now, and Eden spoke into a microphone that wrapped from behind her ear to her mouth.

"You've been hunting me, Madame," Eden said. "Well, here I am."

Madame stood ossified. People flooded into the plaza from the park. Drivers abandoned cars in the streets and ran to see the spectacle. Security pressed the crowd back from the lip of the stage, as Eden crept closer to the monarch.

"Was there something you wanted to say to me?"

Now Madame's face was up on the screens, a closeup that must have come from a body camera on Eden. The hard lines stiffened as her jaw clamped. The veins in her neck stood out. That's when the real madness started.

A column of teenage protestors dressed in green hospital scrubs forced their way through the arch that divided the park from the plaza. Chanting "Freedom or death," and holding signs reading *Freedom for Jumelles!, Not My Prime's Body!*, and of course, *Jumelles Are People!* , the column pushed toward the stage. At the head of the column, his dark hair matted with sweat, his face flushed with anger, Jean-Luc exhorted his army to seize the stage.

The shoving got so violent the stage began to shake. A speaker toppled and crashed only a couple of feet from Madame, bringing focus back to her and the showdown with Eden. The plaza screens displayed a split image of their faces, until Madame drew the pistol from her shoulder holster and fired a shot that struck Eden above the left eye. Her head snapped back and to the side; her body listed, right shoulder forward, then fell like a tower of dog-eared books.

That shot unleashed the carnage. Guards on stage fired into the crowd, shredding bodies in torrents of red. Tara ducked and pulled Maggie onto the ground beside her. A stampede was on. Panicked masses ran, but the still-surging protestors dragged cops from the stage, disarmed them and returned fire. *Blue van*, Tara thought, and lifted her head to catch a glimpse of an escape route. A bullet splintered the bench above her head, and she ducked down again.

"We gotta go," she told Maggie, and urged her to half crawl, half run after her. They ducked behind one pedestal after another, slipping in the blood of some downed bodies, then scrambled to the granite bench. They climbed over the bench to the base of the colonnade when Maggie doubled over in pain.

"It can't come now!" Maggie cried. "It's too soon!" Tara helped her onto the ground, where the concrete column provided some cover. They were on the periphery of the plaza, a short dash to the street where the van was supposed to be, not that Tara expected that plan to hold. Police in riot gear closed ranks at the top of the plaza preparing to approach the stage, which was completely under siege. They beat at the crowd with metal batons, but they were too few to penetrate, and the stage fell to the crowd. Injured guards were thrown off the stage. Eden's lifeless body was trampled, and Chérie, her mop-top twitching spastically side to side, was tossed from the stage like a rag doll and lay splayed on the concrete, where rioters stomped her. Madame, surrounded, began climbing the scaffolding that held the overhead lights. Protestors shook the scaffold, as they chanted, "Tartairos has you now! Tartairos has you now!" And Tara felt that chant in her soul, as if it was directed as much at her as it was to Madame.

Lights dropped from their overhead fixtures, shattering on the stage. That's when Jean-Luc abandoned the stage; he fired a couple of shots at the riot squad, then dodged return fire by weaving through the statutory pedestals and bounding over the granite bench. He landed in a heap at Maggie's feet.

"Are you happy to see me?" he asked Tara, apparently unsurprised at their reunion.

"What have you done?"

"We're breaking the grip of Tartairos," he seethed. "You want your freedom, you'd better keep going."

"I can't leave her," Tara said.

"She'll be fine," Jean-Luc said, grabbing Tara by the wrist. "She's an actual person. She's got the law on her side."

"She's coming," Tara insisted, but Maggie twisted her arm out of Tara's grip.

"He's right," she said. "I'll be okay if I lie quiet. But I can't run. Go!"

A shot deflected off a column, and chipped concrete dusted Tara's hair. Jean-Luc fired two more rounds, as Tara crept around the colonnade, and together, they bolted toward the street. To Tara's surprise, a blue van was parked across the way just up the block. As they approached from behind, the rear doors burst open, and a vaguely familiar girl waved them in. As they tumbled across the bare floor of the van, the girl pulled the doors shut and yelled to the driver, "Go! Now!"

"Rachel?" Tara gasped, as the van lurched forward then stopped. Three quick, loud pops and shattering glass brought Tara's head low and her knees to her chest. Her hands covered her head, and she sensed slivers of glass had fallen into her hair. Jean-Luc was braced against the opposite side of the van, ready to fire through the narrow window into the front cabin. But he lowered his pistol in disgust. Tara raised her head slowly. She saw the windshield, pocked with gunshots and laced with cracks. In the driver's rearview mirror, she saw this world's Lima, slumped back, his head lolling to the side, rivulets of blood pouring down his shirt.

"We have tear gas," a voice called. "Grenades as well, if you insist. Toss your weapons through the window into the front seat." Reluctantly, Rachel drew a pistol from a shoulder holster beneath her jacket and handed it to Jean-Luc. He dropped her weapon and his onto the passenger seat.

"Now, come out slowly," the voice commanded. Rachel opened the doors, letting in wails of terror from the fleeing crowd. Tara slid on her tail to the bumper, where several cops with guns drawn flanked Inspector Desjardin, who shouted above the crowd noise, "Turn around and place your hands behind your back."

Tara complied. But hellion shrieks and a near swipe from panicked stoners gave Jean-Luc the distraction he needed. He swatted the hand of a Sergeant, throat punched him, and picked the sidearm from his hip holster. He pinned the Sergeant's back tight to his own chest, grabbed Desjardin by the shirt and tie, and pressed the barrel of the gun to his temple.

"Headshot, Inspector. No one comes back from that."

"No!" Tara cried. "Don't kill him!"

"He was going to kill me. Weren't you?"

"Don't do it," Tara said. "I'm begging you."

"It's what he programmed me for!"

"And that's why you shouldn't!" Tara crept slowly to her right so she could look Jean-Luc in the eyes. "You want to be a person? You've got to act like more than a program. You've got to listen to the voice inside that says the programming is wrong! Otherwise, you'll never be more than his creation!"

They stood frozen in a tortured tableau: Jean-Luc, Desjardin, and the Sergeant, crushed between them, still wheezing from the throat blow. A ring of officers struck A-frame poses, sidearms leveled at Jean-Luc.

"If you want to live," Desjardin said quietly, "this is not the way."

"What if I don't care?"

"Do as the girl said."

"Yes," Rachel whispered. "That voice? It's what Madame fears more than anything. It's the voice she thought she killed. But it's alive in the heart of every person ever created."

"You are a person," Tara asked, "aren't you, Jean-Luc?"

A walkie-talkie squawked. "All units proceed to Bourgogne Place. Code red. Repeat, code red." Over her shoulder, Tara saw the riot in the plaza playing out on the video screens. Madame clung to the light structure as it listed one way, then the other. She wrapped one arm around the rungs of the ladder and aimed her pistol down at the protestors shaking the scaffold.

"You want to answer that call?" Jean-Luc asked.

"Alright," Inspector said. "Lower your weapon."

Jean-Luc let go of the Inspector's shirt and handed him the Sergeant's pistol. The Sergeant cocked a fist to strike Jean-Luc, but the Inspector stepped between them.

"Turn around."

"Shouldn't you go save your monarch?" Jean-Luc asked, as the cuffs clicked onto his wrists.

"No," Tara said. "Go to Maggie."

The Inspector pursed his lips. "Hurry it up," he told his officers.

"She's trapped there," Tara said. "She's gone into labor. Your baby is coming."

The Inspector looked towards the plaza, muttering, "I have no baby."

Smoke, released to disperse the crowd, hung thick near the ground, obscuring the battle between police and protestors. But Madame loomed large above the mayhem. Her face—clenched like a fist in defiance, framed in Medusa tendrils of twisted vanity, wrath, and lust for power—that face mocked all impulse towards pity.

"Lieutenant," the Inspector said, "take charge of the prisoners. Sergeant, you men, come with me." As Desjardin trotted toward the plaza, Tara hoped it was for Maggie.

"Hold it," the Lieutenant told her, and he reached into Tara's hair and pulled out a long shard of glass. He placed that shard in his palm and his fingers searched her hair for another. Tara's eyes went back to the screens, to the agony of the tyrant self, her death grip on the scaffold, in defiance of all hope or reason. At last, the structure swung hard behind the stage and Madame lost her hold. She tumbled through the air to the flagstones of the plaza, and her body burst on impact. From behind a dumpster, a coyote crept forward and eagerly lapped up her blood. Tara couldn't watch; she twisted, and the Lieutenant grabbed her shoulder.

"Augh," he said quietly. He'd closed his hand on the shards. "Just a scratch," he said, reaching into his back pocket for a hand-kerchief.

The smoke was getting to Tara now. Streams of people, fleeing the riot, floated out of the grey clouds in slow motion. With her hands cuffed, Tara couldn't rub her eyes, but she tried to blink the sting away. Then the smoke took on a sweet, familiar odor, and two figures floated out of the mist. Tara melted forward against Nolan's chest. His heart was pounding, and he was out of breath.

"I knew you'd come," she whispered.

"Him?" someone shrieked. "Where's he even been?"

But Tara paid no mind to Flipper.

"Do you see the pattern?" Nolan asked. His voice, usually so mellow, had a sharp urgency to it. "How the pieces all fit together? The pattern is the key."

A hand squeezed her shoulder. Her eyes went to the black sleeve, then up the arm to Fr. Chandler. Her heart sank for a moment, as the pieces fell into place. "I'm dead, aren't I?" she asked.

Father didn't say anything. But Tara's wrists weren't cuffed anymore. Father took her right hand and traced a cross on her palm.

"The car killed me, didn't it?" she asked. He drew a cross on her other palm. "Please talk to me, Father. The way you talked to Teri."

A police van pulled to a stop beside them, and the doors opened. The Lieutenant ushered them all aboard: Flipper, Rachel, Jean-Luc, Nolan, Tara, and Father. Lights flashed red and blue, but there were no sirens. Fr. Chandler sat stone-faced across from her, his complexion a marble gray, but brightened here and there with flickers of golden light, as if votives burned on his lap.

"Where to?" Tara asked. "I'm going to my judgment, right?"

No answer. No one spoke for the longest time, until Flipper said, "I'm sorry we lost Eden."

Don't be.

The van hit a rough patch of road and Tara got bounced around on her seat. Her eyes caught Jean-Luc's and he turned away.

"At least they didn't harvest her," he said.

Tara almost laughed. Not that it was funny, just an odd take on the old story. She wondered, had *they* lost Eden even before the first harvest?

There was no harvest, everything there was ripe to pick.

You know what I mean. How long were they there before they lost everything?

It doesn't matter how long. And they didn't lose everything.

One lousy mistake and everything gone.

Not everything.

Everything but each other, but they probably blamed and hated each other. Hated themselves. Yeah, a lifetime of self-loathing; maybe that was the harvest of Eden.

That's not how the story ends.

Expelled. Exiled.

You're forgetting.

Tara thought hard. Tried to remember the lesson. She was blank and stared at the mute statue of Fr. Chandler.

Pray.

Oh yeah, here? In the world of no God? Still her mind nagged at her. What did the nuns used to say? *O happy fall, O necessary...necessary sin.* But wasn't all sin pain and waste and...vanity? *All is vanity.* How could sin be necessary?

They rode for maybe an hour before the van pulled off the highway into an industrial complex. They stopped outside the factory that held the portal, and the cops ordered them out of the van.

"You know how to operate the machine?" the Lieutenant asked Rachel. She nodded. "We're sending these troublemakers home."

Rachel booted the machine and started inputting data. *Why was this necessary?* Tara wondered. *If it's all been an illusion and the secret's been found out, why continue?* Tara looked at the Lieutenant. His eyes somehow seemed kinder than when he'd dropped her at the women's home. She asked, "What's your name?"

"Gagnon."

Tara knew that name had meaning; it lay somewhere in the back of her mind.

"Did the Inspector go to Maggie?" she asked.

"He didn't say."

The arch of the portal was illuminated now, and fog drifted in, chilling the room. Rachel stepped back from the controls and said, "We're ready."

"Okay," Gagnon said. "One at a time." He pointed at Nolan to go, but he hesitated like he didn't get the play call. A cop prodded him forward. Tara thought of the night they'd sat by the dancing fountain: Nolan pointing out the constellations and talking about forty billion baby bear planets. And she'd believed for a moment that somewhere happiness was possible. Nolan hunched his shoulders and disappeared into the mist.

Flipper was next.

"Tee," he said. "I kind of made a mess out of trying to rescue you."

"It's okay."

"Did you hear I stole a car? I'll probably get thrown in juvie."

"No," Tara assured him. "No one goes to jail for what they do in dreams."

"Oh. Good point. So where are you going? Not the bad place?"

Tara shrugged. The cops glowered at Flipper, and one pointed him toward the portal. *Poof.*

"Thanks,... Tommy."

Fr. Chandler queued up next. He was himself again, but solemn, and seemed at a loss for what to say. Silence hung in the chill air between them until Tara couldn't stand it.

"When will the terrors start?"

"What do you call what's been happening?"

"I mean for real."

"Meet whatever comes with humility and an open heart."

"Father, I hope..."

The priest gently rocked his head in an encouraging nod, as the corners of his mouth curled in a sly smile. "That's a good sign," he said. "There are only two places where there is no hope. Heaven, where they don't need it. And hell, where they've abandoned it. It's the same for faith."

"Where am I going, Father?"

"You misunderstood something important that brought you to the brink of despair. Do you remember what it was?"

"I just…"

With his thumb, he traced a cross on her forehead. Tara trembled.

"I didn't want to be one of those dim people who live in the past. Who rely on something old and gone."

"You see, that's an error. Christians don't live in the past. We're really the only folks who live in the future. That's when all things will be reconciled to Our Lord. And we're already there."

"But Father, I'm not there." And Tara wept.

Father took her right hand, turned it over, and traced a cross on her wrist. Then he did the other hand. He took a step back, then walked briskly through the portal and was gone.

"He's going, too," Gagnon told Rachel, pointing to Jean-Luc. "Inspector's orders." A cop removed his handcuffs. Jean-Luc massaged his wrists and flexed his hands. At the threshold of the portal, he turned and mouthed "thank you" to Tara, then stepped off.

It was Tara's turn to go. But where would the portal take her? In grammar school, the nuns had said when you die you stand before the throne of God. You see all your sins and good works, and Jesus judges you on your life. After that you enter heaven, are sent to purgatory, or get cast into hell. If you have a mortal sin on your soul, you go to hell and torment for all eternity. The horror of that reality hit Tara. She'd failed her sister and she'd failed herself.

She turned from the portal and buried her face. She felt hands on her arms and lifted her head. Gagnon's eyes seemed to beckon, to comfort. She gazed at the kindly face of the young, bearded man. She looked down into the hand that held hers, to the cut the shards had made in the center of his palm, and she felt less afraid.

In the mist of the portal, like static resolving or a pixilated image taking shape, the scene formed of Teri's hospital room. Mom and Dad outside talking hospice, Tara inside gripping Teri's withered hand. Tara, seeing the blood, calling the nurse. Teri gripping Tara's hand, "I can do this."

But Tara wouldn't let her. Deep in her soul, Tara knew what Teri had meant; she was leaving. Like a baby bird pecking the shell that held it captive, Teri's soul was battering the clay vessel that encased her, keeping her Earthbound. Teri had made up her mind. *But how dare she!*

Rather than help Teri leave, Tara had fought to keep her. *I will not let my sister die,* she'd said. *I will not let You take my sister!* She'd gone to the chapel, but hardly to pray; she'd gone to make demands. Kneeling in the flowery chamber, her garden of agony, she heard, "Your sister is going her own way."

It was gently spoken, and Tara might have accepted it, except for the mockery that followed. The diabolic screech. "Didn't you want separation?" it laughed. "You have it now. Isn't it precious?" Unable to discern one voice from the other, Tara could not pray, "Thy will be done." She railed, "My will be done." Of the opposite choices made in separate gardens millennia apart, Tara had rejected meek obedience and had chosen angry defiance. As a spoiled child in a tantrum, and in despair of not getting her way, she'd ratified the first sin of pride. She'd fallen. She'd missed her chance to say goodbye.

"Where were you?"

Frightened, confused, alone. Naked. Angry. Vengeful. Ashamed. Hating herself and hating her Creator; striking at herself to strike at her Creator. Destroying herself to—

O happy fall...o necessary sin...that gained for us...

Gained? Tara looked for him, but her Lieutenant was gone. Still, something remained, a faint reassurance that He'd been there all along.

Alone, but no longer crushed by loneliness, Tara looked back into the fog that was fog again. Somewhere in the deep, deep distance was light. The light was warm. And though it might have been ten thousand lightyears away and borne to her from a long-dead star, Tara believed. That light was where she belonged. And before her, in the abyss, glowed small orbs of light, steppingstones forming a trail that led to the greater light. She could go forward.

The harvest of Eden wasn't sin, death, or exile; it was mercy.

Tara stepped across the threshold and felt herself ascend.

EPILOGUE

"The pupil dilates in darkness and in the end finds light,
just as the soul dilates in misfortune and in the end finds God."
— Victor Hugo, *Les Misérables*

TARA EMERGED as from a deep sleep into a blazing light. She was sweaty and cold, tangled in coverings. Her head ached and, touching it, she felt grit on her scalp. Then she saw fine, white grains on her fingertips. Salt?

"You had an exorcism."

Tara batted her eyes and saw Jeremy at the foot of the hospital bed. "What?"

"And brain surgery."

"Jeremy!" Mom cautioned. She leaned in from a chair at Tara's side. "You did not have brain surgery. You had very minor skull surgery to relieve pressure on your brain."

"An exorcism?" Tara asked.

"Not *an* exorcism, just special prayers *of* exorcism."

That seemed like a distinction without a difference.

"Fr. Chandler sensed you were struggling… 'with things not of this world.' He scattered some blessed salt around the bed, and we prayed."

"I didn't levitate?" Tara asked. "Climb the walls?" She was half-teasing, but really needing some reassurance. That drew a weary smile from her Mom.

"No," she said, taking Tara's hand in hers. Tara felt the beads of a Rosary rest in her palm. Not the weighty, semi-precious stones, but the light plastic. In the dimness of the room, they gave out a faint glow, and Tara recalled a string of lighted steppingstones. "We thought we might lose you." Her mother's tears fell onto Tara's hand, which she squeezed and kissed.

"I was selfish," she said.

"We've all been."

"How long—?"

"A week."

It seemed like eternity. "So, it's…Sunday? Morning?"

"Dad's at Mass with Stacy. He'll be here soon."

Tara spent the night at the hospital and got her release the following afternoon with instructions to stay home for another week. She got a bunch of text messages asking how she was doing and when she'd be back, and if it was okay to come visit. Reading off the screen made her head hurt, but she was suddenly reminded she had to *Google* something. She tried every keyword she could think of: Lima-Autufuga-Fremont-High-School-Explorers-Varsity-football-shooting-homicide. All she found were short items about the team and how they expected to have a fine season. Then she switched from Web to News and an article popped up on the first line:

FREMONT BALLERS JOIN RIVAL WRENS ON THIRD NIGHT OF PRAYER VIGIL

Tara's friends had filled the school chapel every night following the accident to pray for her. On Wednesday, Lima had brought the Fremont football team to join them. She tried reading the story, but it blurred out behind her tears.

Tara secretly made a date with Raquel for Wednesday after school.

"Can we go for a drive?" she asked her Dad, who was working from home in the dining room to keep an eye on her. Tara was feeling pent up again. All she'd done in three days was walk Sammy around the block. She'd gotten so bored, she'd actually sat down with Jeremy and showed him what little she knew about playing clarinet. He decided that maybe it wasn't a girl's instrument after all. He'd also apologized for blabbing about her sleep-driving and offered an oath of secrecy about her exorcism. He might not be as big a little dork as she thought. Anyway, now she needed some space.

"Where to?" Dad wanted to know.

"Somewhere quiet. In the fresh air."

"Teri?"

"Yeah." But that was only part of it. For the rest, she needed some information. "And I'd like to see the owner of that car. To apologize."

He looked up from his computer screen. "Maybe you should wait 'til you feel better."

"I think it will *make me* feel better."

"Then maybe I should take you." He pushed back from the table and folded his hands in his lap. He was ready to drop everything to help.

But Tara insisted, "No, that would look like my parents are making me. I want to do it, 'cause it's the right thing to do."

Dad struck a few keys on his computer, and Tara heard the whir of the printer underneath the kitchen island. She trotted over and retrieved the newly printed sheet with the driver's name and address.

"Thanks, Dad."

TARA TOLD Raquel she wanted to make one stop on the way to the cemetery. "Great. You want me to roll up on the Fremont campus in my St. Stephen's outfit?"

"You can stay in the car. I'll be quick."

"I'm not letting you out of my sight!"

So, they parked in the school lot and walked down to the football field. The team was practicing in full pads. Tara could spot Lima from forty yards away.

"Okay, you see him. Can we go?"

"I gotta talk to him. If I can."

Tara got the chance when a scrum went bad, and Lima landed hard on his shoulder. He trotted off to the sidelines dragging his right arm low at his side. "Stinger," someone said. They helped him off with his helmet, jersey, and pads.

"Oh, this will *not* be pretty," Raquel said, meaning the rolls of corpulent flesh. But what caught Tara's eye were three large pock marks on his chest and abdomen. Quarter-sized craters.

"Lima!" she cried, and he tilted his head towards her.

"Tetara," he muttered, and left the group attending him. Catcalls filled the air as he trotted to the girls at the fence. "You better?" he asked.

"Yeah, I guess."

"We heard. My moms and me been prayin' for you."

"Yeah, and you turned your boys out."

"Ain't no thing," Lima said. "Ain't like they doin' homework."

"Anyway, thanks."

"You still with Seven?"

"Oh, that's not really a thing." Tara's eyes went to the scars. "If you don't mind me asking…?"

"*Nada*," he shrugged. "Wrong place; wrong time. Just lucky I'm so fat."

"Don't listen to him," the coach yelled. "He charged a playground shooter. Took the gun away. He's a hero."

Lima blushed and yelled back, "Maybe if you kep' your eyes on the field, we could win some games!" Lima cocked his head from one side to the other and rolled his shoulder. "I gotta get back. Glad you're better."

"Thanks."

. . .

THE TERRACE WASN'T QUITE the same. There were new graves all over. The girls sat in Raquel's car just looking at the rows of marble headstones.

"Do you want to go alone?" Raquel asked.

"No," Tara said, but once they were standing at Teri's grave, she kind of wished she'd said yes. She wanted to tell Teri about all the craziness she'd been through, the weird dream she'd had all week, and how her mind had made up this girl Eden. She fumbled in her thoughts, and tears gushed, and Raquel looped her arm around hers and squeezed. "I miss you so much," she blubbered.

After they both cried, Raquel offered her a tissue. "If she could, what do you think Teri would say to you?"

"Get over yourself." And as Tara said that, she heard Teri speak with her. A chorus in unison followed: "I'm not touching you! Stop hitting yourself! Hello, Ball! You get away with everything! You will *never* be the cool twin!" Tara laughed to herself as she heard "Don't you dare say, 'Look what you made me do!'"

As they walked back to the car, Tara felt like a dam had burst; she could speak again, and she needed to let everything flow. She hadn't told anyone yet about her flight to Tartairos. "I had some wild dreams. Must have been the drugs or, I don't know, angels and evil spirits? Anyway, you were there. And you were good."

"And?"

"You helped me. And Flipper."

"You dreamed about Flipper?"

"C'mon."

"Okay, sorry," Raquel grimaced; the corners of her mouth tugged on the veins in her neck. It wasn't a good look.

They trudged back to the car, neither knowing what to say. But, once they were buckled up, Raquel seemed like she had to get something off her chest. "I've been going through something, too. I don't know if I can talk to you about it."

"What?"

"I gotta talk to someone. And you're probably the wrongest person."

"What *is* it?"

"I didn't lose a sister. But I lost a chance to be a sister."

Raquel dug into her purse and pulled out a photograph. She admired it, wistfully, as she rattled on, keeping the image just out of Tara's view. "This lady's in college and she got pregnant, and the boyfriend, he wants nothing to do with the kid, so my parents, they arrange an open adoption. Five months they're doing this, dropping hints to me, but not coming right out. Then two months ago, it looks like it's going to happen, and they tell me, and I *Zoom* with the Mom and get to know her, and I'm so excited and she gives birth, and we're all excited, but still not telling anyone. And she was just born last week. And here she is."

Raquel—finally!—passed the photo to Tara of the newborn in a pink blanket, cradled in the arms of a young Latina in a yellow hospital gown. The mother was petite with large, opal eyes, a delicate mouth with finely curved lips, and a slight dimple high on her left cheek.

Tara gave a barely audible pant, "Maggie."

"You know Magdalena?" Raquel asked. "She lives in Arizona."

"Um, no," Tara said. "She just looks familiar."

"Anyway, she's keeping her baby. The boyfriend came back. Now he wants it."

Tara felt a pang for Raquel, but also a glow of relief she couldn't explain. Silly, because there had been no Maggie, no Desjardin.

"And I can't even be mad," Raquel cried, "because the right thing happened. Only my parents, this happened to them before, so I don't think they'll ever try again."

RAQUEL SAID she felt better after "crying it out," and she was okay making the final leg of their trip. But the drive there had Tara's gut fluttering. The car was registered to a Robert Kirkwood, one town over. It would be roughly 4:30 when they got there. Tara wondered if anyone would be home, and how they might react to her showing up on their doorstep. The house turned out to be modest, but nicely kept with a meticulously manicured lawn bordered by blue anemones, red echinacea, and yellow gloriosa daisies. A silver-haired woman was on her knees weeding the bed by the walk.

"Mrs. Kirkwood?" Tara asked.

The woman sat back on her heels and lifted her head. Her mouth dropped open, and she clutched the gardening claw to her breast. Tara's legs went rubbery, and she knelt in front of the lady, whose tears flowed freely down her sweet face.

"I guess you recognize me."

"I was praying you'd be alright. I was driving."

"I'm sorry for giving you such a scare."

"But you're alright?"

Tara's heart hurt for this lady. She couldn't believe no one had told her Tara had recovered. "Yes."

Tara helped Mrs. Kirkwood to her feet and the lady pulled her into a tight embrace. "Oh, I'm afraid I've soiled you," she said.

She invited the girls for iced tea. They sat on her back deck, looking at all the marvelous colors in her yard.

"I've always planted for four seasons," she said. "My mother loved her tulips and daffodils, but I always said, when I get my own garden, it's going to bloom year-round."

"It looks like a lot of work," Raquel said.

"Yes, but well worth it, even with my arthritis. Of course, some days, the spirit is willing, but the flesh is weak."

"I'd like to help you," Tara said. "If you think that would be alright."

ALL IN ALL, the week went quickly. A change had come over the shattered Hartzwell family; gone was the pressure to appear perfect, and everyone felt freer to spontaneously cry or laugh or hug. They talked more easily about Teri, and retold stories that brought back warm memories. By Friday, Tara was feeling so much better that she went ahead and got ready for school, and then had to beg her parents over breakfast to let her go in for half a day.

"I'll take you," her Dad groaned at last. "But I don't know how you're getting home."

"Trust me," Tara said. "Finding my way home will never be a problem again."

"And just what does that mean?"

They were fairly quiet in the car all the way to school, then a block away, Dad started sputtering about "not feeling the pressure," "staying within herself," "taking every moment as it comes," all his old coaching clichés. Finally, Tara just had to cut him off.

"Dad, I got this."

They turned into the drop-off lane and pulled up at the curb. Tara pulled her backpack from between her feet onto her lap, then hesitated.

"Dad, what would you say, if I went back to golf?"

He gave one of his slow, rubber-face reactions, mouth turned down like the Greek mask of tragedy. "I'd say, 'Give it a shot.'"

"Thanks, Dad." She kissed him lightly on the cheek and pushed out the door.

Tara joined the flow of students heading towards the quad. Junior Hall had already thinned out when she reached her locker. She spotted Flipper making another sales pitch, this time to Raquel.

"You want to get to Washington? One word—crowdfunding."

"I have a feeling that's two words."

"It's a compound," Flipper said. "But look, more than half of all crowdfunding campaigns fail. Why? Because they don't have a system. You work with me; you get my proven system."

"And how exactly did you prove your system?"

Flipper never got the chance to explain, as Tara dropped her backpack at his feet and grabbed him in a tight hug.

"Uh, Tee?" he said. "What, what…?"

"Nothing," she said, letting him loose. "Just, thanks."

"Y'know, I've got a girlfriend now."

"What??"

"Yeah," he explained, opening his phone's photo app and scrolling through. "This girl—might have been the one you saw that night—she comes into the *CD* and she's all, 'Is this a place of hamburgers?' in kind of a strange accent, and I'm like, 'We got the best!' and she's, 'Why do you call them *ham* when the meat is of *beef*?'

so, we get to talking, and...*boom-ba-bing!*" Either he couldn't find a suitable picture of the girl, or he was waiting for a crowd to form for the big reveal.

"And know what's funny?," he continued. "She's an alien. Yeah, just moved from Poland." He finally turned the screen to Tara, showing an image of Flipper in a *CD* booth with one arm around a petite, blonde girl with somewhat pointed features. Tara couldn't tell the color of her eyes.

"So, I'm like a goodwill ambassador. Soon to be ambassador of good lovin'."

"Well, that's...great."

"So, any chance of you and me, that's—"

Tara was halfway down the hall before he finished the sentence. She was moving so fast, she hardly noticed Nolan turn the corner.

"Hey, Tar—"

"Going with the flow!" she roared, in full beast mode.

Her next stop was Fr. Chandler's office. She wanted to know what was up with 'the exorcism,' if she had said anything in her sleep, and if he could help her makes sense of what she remembered of her dreams. And she needed to thank him. But those were the details. In the last week, she'd been thinking a great deal about life, and if her experience had taught her anything, it was how little she knew. *What was the point of everything?* How could she free herself from all the forces around her that seemed to be dragging her down? How could she be a better friend, a better sister, a better person? Suddenly, these basic questions had a special urgency, and she was determined to get answers.

Father was in, which was rare, and not besieged at all sides, which was even rarer. They sat and chatted in almost a relaxed manner. Tara learned a lot she hadn't known about Teri's final days.

"There used to be a lot more focus on the last things," Father said. "The Church emphasized the importance of being ready for death, and how that readiness, the consciousness, really helps us to live. Then people decided religion shouldn't be gloomy; it all had to be sunshine and rainbows. But that's not how life is."

"No, it's not," Tara agreed.

"People say, 'Live each day as though it's your last,' but they usually mean to satiate yourself with all the pleasure you can. They rarely say, 'Get your spiritual house in order.'"

"I guess Teri put hers in order?"

"Well, she was the orderly twin, right?"

No argument there. But after a brief, maybe uneasy pause, Tara had to ask, "Do you ever feel like, this isn't enough?"

"What isn't?"

"Y'know, running a pricey prep school, in the suburbs. Like it's not *missionary* enough?"

Tara thought she read "now that you mention it" in his eyes, but the young priest was not one to open his binder and share his flow charts. "Why do you ask?" he wondered.

She didn't really know, except, as she said, "I just hope you know it's important."

With that Father glanced at the wall clock. "I'm sorry I don't have more time," he said, pushing his chair back with finality, "but I've got to meet with a transfer student. It's always tough to come in after the semester has started. I'm going to walk him around and get him settled."

"Okay," Tara said. "You think maybe later…?"

"Oh, definitely," he said. "Come by anytime and pepper me with questions."

"And you can add the salt."

Father chuckled as he pulled the door open for her. Tara hiked her backpack onto her shoulder and spun, only to come to a dead halt. Standing in the entrance was a tallish, lean but muscular youth with jet-black, spiked hair.

"Oh, Jack, you're here!" Father said. But Jack wasn't looking anywhere near the priest; his cool gray eyes were fixed on Tara's, and her emerald eyes on his. After a beat, Father said, "I feel like I'm interrupting something."

"No," they both assured him.

"Nice to meet you," Tara said as she squeezed past.

"Wait, please," the boy said. "I feel like I should apologize. I kind of made a bad first impression. I've had a huge chip on my shoulder since my Dad forced us to move."

"No harm done," Tara said.

"But I still think I've seen you before," he said. He scratched the back of his head. "Do you… golf?"

"Ye-ah," Tara answered slowly, expecting him to recall her immediately as part of a blonde tandem. It would be absolutely impossible for him to know Tara golfed without pairing her with Teri.

"Did you play AJGA in Sacramento a year ago? In August?"

Oh. Wait. Teri didn't go. She'd sprained her wrist.

"You remember me?" Tara asked, meaning *me by myself*, alone, singular, solo? He couldn't, but….

He smiled as though the question was funny. "Yeah," he nodded.

Everything's impossible, until somebody does it.

ABOUT THE AUTHOR

Kevin Rush is a former Catholic parochial school and high school teacher. He is an award-winning playwright and screenwriter. His books include *Earthquake Weather, a novel for Catholic teens*, which Michael Pritchard called "an incredible, thoughtful and brilliant revelation of teenagers in the San Francisco Bay Area," and *The Lance and the Veil, an adventure in the time of Christ,* hailed as a "big, bold Biblical saga to fire the Christian imagination" (*Kirkus Reviews*) and a "very welcome and very gripping and very beautiful work of fiction." (Jack Fowler, *National Review*). *Online Book Club* called his third novel, *The Wedding Routine*, an "amazing book" with "a lot of dynamic characters" whose interactions "produce nothing but comic gold." Comedic actress Laura Orrico said *The Wedding Routine* is "real, raw and heartwarmingly funny. In the 'song and dance' of life, this lovely story teaches how to lead with your heart. It showcases how helping people not only benefits those receiving but is therapeutic for those who give." More of his writings can be found at *kevinrush.us* and his author page on *Amazon.com*.

www.ingramcontent.com/pod-product-compliance
Lightning Source LLC
Chambersburg PA
CBHW070534120726
47909CB00007B/2130